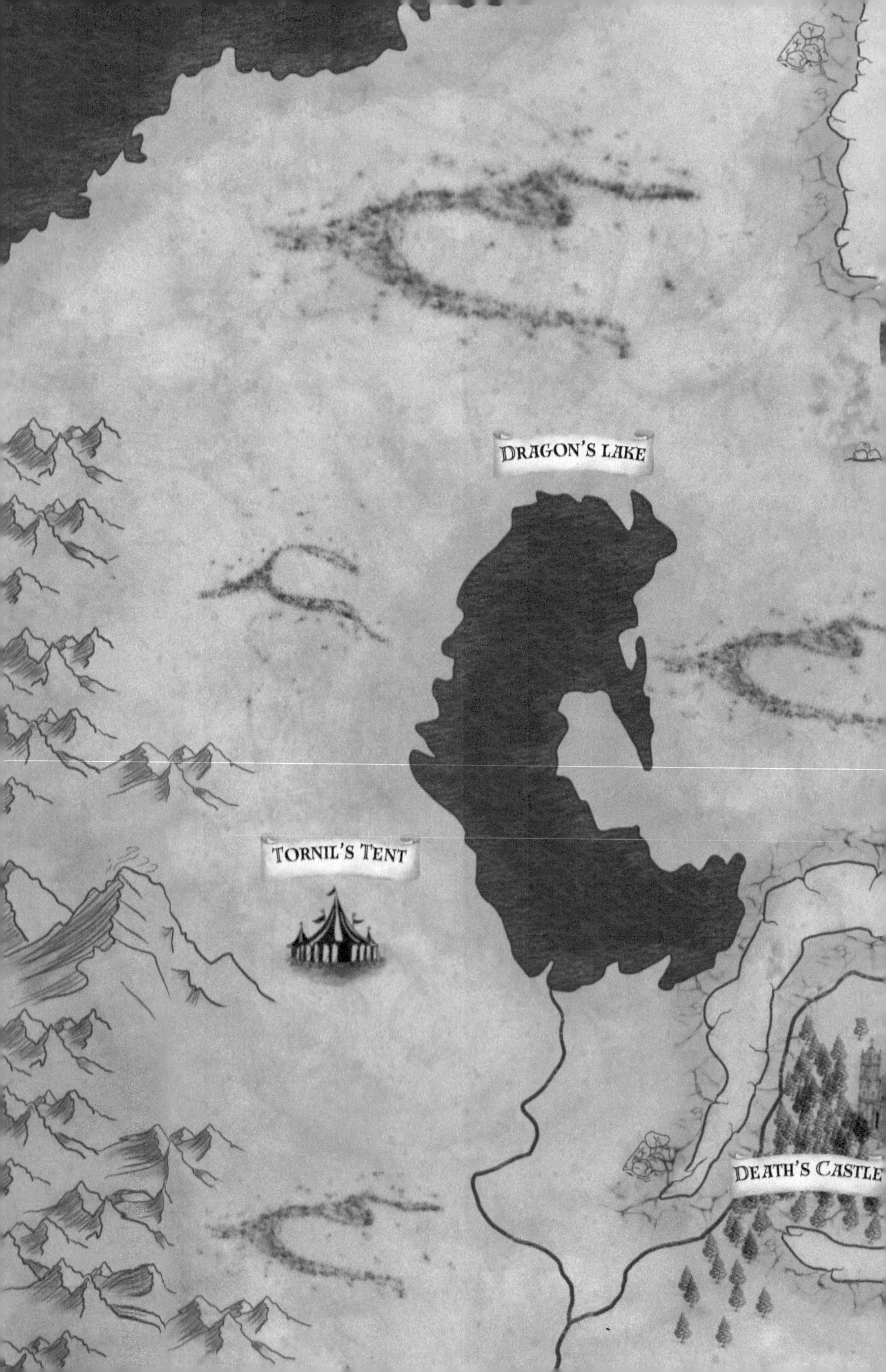

DRAGON'S LAKE
TORNIL'S TENT
DEATH'S CASTLE

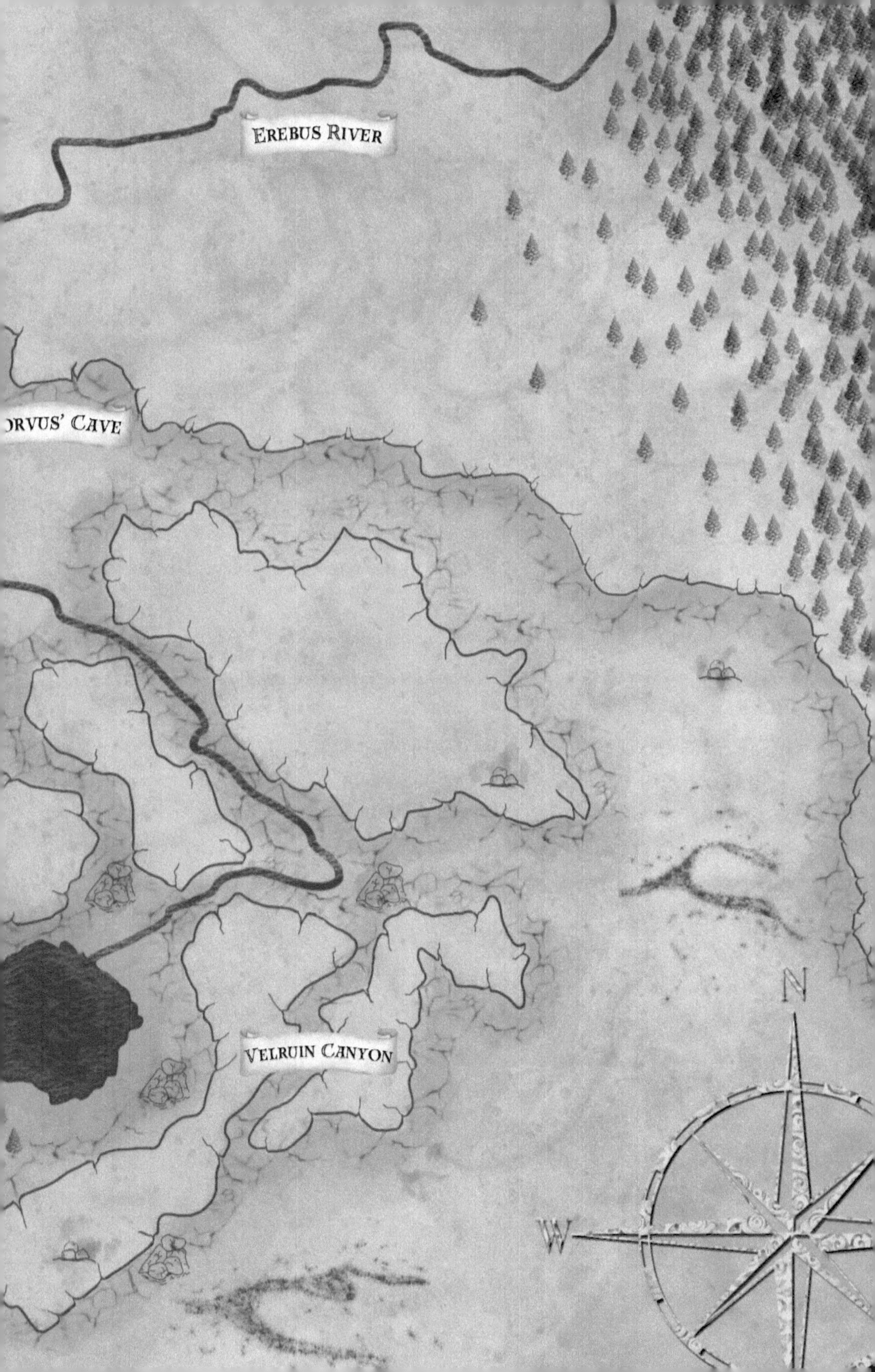

EREBUS RIVER
ORVUS' CAVE
VELRUIN CANYON
N
W

Author's Note

Family and friends, if you're reading this, thank you as always! But fair warning—if you thought reading *Kissing Fire* and then looking me in the eye was awkward, well, Cheating Death is soooooo much worse. The spice in book one? That was like mild taco sauce compared to the ghost pepper-level heat in this book.

Everyone else, Welcome! Supportive readers like you are what has made this dream of mine come true. I really enjoyed exploring writing fantasy in this book. In *KF* we see a lot happening on Earth but I am happy to tell you that you're going to get your own little trip to Hell ;) It's actually a lot more fun than you think.

But just remember, there are religious themes and characters in this book. The world and story I've created are products of my imagination, and while they may draw inspiration from various mythologies and religious concepts, they are not meant to imitate, represent, or comment on any specific religion. It is important to me that readers understand that this story is not intended to offend or challenge anyone's personal beliefs.

As it is my wish that all readers are able to experience CD in a safe and fun environment, here is a list of some of the major notes of advisement: Satan, Devil, demons, Gore, Family Death, Mention of Rape, Murder, Sexually Explicit Scenes. For those who like to be extra prepared, there's a full list available on my website.

Once you're ready, grab a snack, get comfy, and enjoy the chaos!

Cheating Death Playlist

Funeral by Teddy Swims
I Want To Live by Annapantsu, Borislav Slavov
She's My Collar (feat. Kali Uchis) by Gorillaz, Kali Uchis
Free Again – From Endless Dungeon by Lera Lynn, Arnaud Roy
Something To Hide by grandson'
Crazy in Love by Sofia karlberg
Evil People by Set It Off
Humankind by David Kushner
LET THE WORLD BURN by Chris Grey
THE DEATH OF PEACE OF MIND by Bad Omens
The Greatest Fear by Parkway Drive
RUNRUNRUN by Dutch Melrose
All the Saints of Notre Dame by Baby Jane
I Was Made For Lovin' You by YUNGBLUD
hell of a good time by Haiden Henderson

Chapter 1
Parker

I think I'm about to be arrested.

The cop berates me, crowding in my personal space. I'm pretty sure he just spit part of his lunch on me. Ruben sandwich, maybe. His breath smells atrocious, but I'm forced to stand here and take it. I try to glimpse his badge, but his arms are flailing so much that I'm not able to catch the name on his chest.

His really large, *rounded* chest. I mean, the man is as rotund as a ball. I bet if I pushed hard enough, he'd just roll away. Then, I wouldn't have to deal with the lunch currently being sprayed into my face or his stupid questions.

"Are you even fucking listening to me?" he snarls.

I'm not. I can't recall a single thing he's said in the last 15 minutes while he's stood, yelling a thousand questions at me that I can't answer.

No, I don't know how four people went missing.

Yes, I really was passed out the entire time.

No, I don't know where the fuck my best friend is.

Well—that last one is a lie, but he doesn't need to know that. It's not like I've known for very long, either. Val snuck into my room like a shadow in the night, scaring the absolute shit out of me. The minor heart attack I'd received after seeing her appear, as if from nowhere, didn't dampen the joy I'd felt at that moment. She'd hid in the darkness of my room like she hadn't been missing for almost a week.

I'm still exhausted from all the hours I've worked searching the entire Beaverhead National Forest for four bodies I know will never be found. The days before Val showed up had been full of struggle and exhaustion, but adrenaline had fueled me through the long hours. Pure terror was the only thing keeping me going through the long days and nights, searching for the last person I call family. I wouldn't lose her, too.

Now, pretending that I don't know what's going on is its own kind of torture. I have to lie to the people closest to me—pretend I didn't smuggle my best friend to the Heath Cabin last night.

I mean, there's still so much I don't know. I have no idea about the two members of the Polaris Fire Team who somehow managed to disappear. Nor do I have any idea what happened to Tucker.

My chest squeezes at the thought of the young firefighter—his tall, lanky awkwardness, willingness to learn, bright green eyes and messy brown hair that flash in my mind like a bright memory. He radiated happiness. People always considered me the happy-go-lucky one, but that's a learned skill. It's easy to bring joy into a room with a good joke. Tucker was truly happy, no front or jokes were needed.

It fucking *burns*, losing him. He had so much life left to live.

I grit my teeth against the thought, forcing my mind to focus on Officer Whatever. As I told Valencia last night, there's no reason to dwell on the unknown.

"I swear to God, if you don't fucking answer me," Officer Whatever spits, and a drop lands on my clenched cheek.

I force myself to relax, my jaw muscles slowly loosening enough so I can answer. "I'm sorry. Would you like me to listen or answer?"

"You little shit, I'll—"

"Do we have a problem here?" A voice barks from my left.

Saved by Chief Miller.

I look at the Chief, a pleading look in my eyes. He doesn't react in any way, simply looks between me and the officer before focusing on Officer Whatever. "Is there a reason you're interrogating one of my team members on our station lawn?" Chief Miller asks.

"This Mother—" the officer blurts, barely stopping himself before the curse leaves his lips. "He knows something." He points that big meaty finger my way again. "It's in your best interest that he confesses what he knows before the entire police force gets brought into *your* mess."

"Officer... Paral, this is a very emotional situation, and handling it with compassion and professionalism is the only way we can figure out how four firefighters are still missing. We have conducted searches nonstop over the last week. My team is distraught, exhausted, and beyond confused. I can assure you that no one here knows what's going on. Targeting Lieutenant Rand, just as he's coming in from an 18-hour search, is a little cruel considering finding missing persons is your problem, correct?"

I have to clamp my teeth together to keep from laughing. In a handful of seconds, the Chief delivered the politest burn I've heard in a long time.

Officer Paral's face has turned a shiny shade of red and I swear, a vein on his forehead dances with each beat of his overinflated heart. Chief Miller has him in a vise, and we all know it. The entire station has been running *ragged*, myself included, for the last week. Conducting searches over hundreds of miles in the park. If we were guilty, why would we all be working so hard?

That fun little team building exercise we went on seemed like a walk in the park compared to what we've been going through. If only they had left clues behind. It's getting harder to not spill that Valencia made it back. What could I even say, though? *Hey, Valencia made it! She came and saw me last night. Oh, where has she been? Well, she said she was stuck in Hell for a bit, but she swears she doesn't know what happened to the other guys.*

Yeah, that's not going to happen. The Polaris City Fire Department has been radio-silent over the last couple of days. The day after the fire, they sent a team to retrieve the ashes of their two fallen firefighters. We assisted in the retrieval—but they didn't mention their two missing team members. I thought it odd then, but now I know nothing in this situation is as it seems.

I can't wrap my brain around the fact that Heaven and Hell are not only real—they're battling in a celestial war. They've brought the fight to Earth, and my best friend has become involved in a very dangerous way. According to Val, it had been a literal angel who'd knocked my ass out before holding Tucker hostage. My chest clenches at the thought of what Tucker went through.

"Look at him! He's been staring at the wall for the last twenty minutes I've been talking to him. He knows something, and you are all hiding it. I'm coming back with a fucking warrant and you better pray your shit is squeaky clean, Chief

Miller," Officer Paral spits out. He stomps off back to his cruiser, slamming the door and peeling out with a squeal of his tires.

"If you hadn't just come in from a shift, I would seriously suspend you. Parker, what the hell? We are all trying to figure out what's going on. The last thing we need is to piss off the police department." Chief Miller tries to chastise me, but it's clear his heart isn't in it. I imagine he's only saying this because he feels obligated to say something after that shit show. Either way, I'm over it.

"None of you understand what this does to me. Valencia is the only family I have left. I have been searching nonstop, day after day, spending hours out in the field, hoping that I'll find her because I *refuse* to lose another family member. So, I'm sorry that Officer Dipshit is angry, but *so am I*." All of the fear and anger I've been holding in over the last week bleeds into the statement, and I ignore the ache in my chest that follows. My shoulders sag. "I'm really fucking tired."

Chief Miller just nods his head, patting me on the shoulder. "Get some rest, Parker; we'll find them... I just hope whatever we find doesn't tear this team apart."

My steps echo off the concrete floor as I trek into the station. Normally, a hundred different things create an ambient 'lived-in' sound that fills the area. Now, it's silent. Everyone has passed out, trying to catch a few hours of rest before we head back out for another round of searching. I would've been in here an hour ago, but it was my turn to check the equipment back in—and then Officer Paral caught me on the lawn. I would've loved to avoid him, but we've been instructed that doing so would reflect poorly on us. We're not guilty, but it's also important that we don't *look* guilty—Bill and I especially, given that we were the only two on the mountain when the rescue team returned to collect us.

We had both barely started to wake, but we were out enough that we'd had to be carried into the helicopter. After some testing, they determined we had passed out due to a lack of oxygen from having inhaled some of the smoke from the forest fire. Neither of us had our masks on, but there wasn't much smoke in that area by then. Either way, it gave us an alibi. A reason to be knocked on our asses with no answers as to what had happened to the rest of our team.

Still, Officer Paral has an issue with our story for some reason. He's been coming round since day one but hasn't caught Bill or me alone—until today.

I get to my room and undress, not bothering with a shower. The sheets are beyond disgusting anyway, and what's one more day of sleeping on ash and soot? I roll around in an attempt to get comfortable, but the blankets scratch against my skin and my stomach continues to roll uneasily even though I'm lying down. It's been doing this since the first night back. They wouldn't let us begin searching until we were cleared by the paramedics—which had taken almost twelve hours—but getting back onto the field and searching had given me purpose. It gave my mind something to focus on other than reality.

Trying to sleep offered no peace from my damaged thoughts. The panic I'd felt as I woke in the helicopter, drugged, woozy, and disoriented, still haunts me. There was nothing but terror left when I realized Valencia wasn't in the helicopter with me—it was simply as though she and Tucker had vanished, like ash in the wind—and there was nothing I could do but search every inch of Beaverhead National Forest until I found them.

When she showed up in my room, roughed up but alive, joy had washed away the fear. As she told her story, my heart broke, but nothing could overshadow the fact that she was back. After I dropped her off at the Heath cabin with Corvus—who apparently is a literal demon, but I have purposefully not given that much thought—I went directly to the park to help with search and rescue efforts. There were still missing people out there, if only technically.

A few small fires had sparked up over the week, but the other teams had been able to manage them. Thankfully, no one asked our team to do anything other than search for our colleagues. Chief Miller had even remained by our side the entire time, only taking a small break to clear us with the police department on that first day.

I have no idea what we're going to do about Officer Paral. He knows something, or at least thinks he does, and I have no idea how. I haven't told a single person about seeing Val or taking her to Heath Cabin. Sure, I took her there in my truck and made a few stops along the way, but she'd remained hidden the entire time.

Officer Paral just has a gut feeling; unfortunately for me, he's right. I just have to get Val out of Montana before he finally catches on.

***

My eyes flutter open as my racing heart beings to slow. Another nightmare. At this point, my sleep schedule is so off that I don't know when I last slept through the night. The bright light from my phone blinds me briefly and I squint to see the time. Nearly 9 PM. I only got a few hours of sleep.

Clangs and bangs echo down the hall through my open door, and the smell of coffee wafts into my room—the aroma helping wake my tired bones. I can't help but groan as I get up. My muscles scream in refusal, but I push on.

I throw on a pair of jeans, not bothering to check they're clean. I forgo a shirt and head to the kitchen, where Bill ambles around, pulling random things out of the cabinets as he gets stuff ready. It smells like cooked food, but I can't see any.

"Bill, you okay?" I ask, leaning against the counter. He simply huffs in response and continues working without a word. I get it. He's in the same position as I am, unsure of how we had been spared while two of our other teammates had disappeared. They cleared both of us eventually, but Bill had taken the events pretty hard. He's older—has no kids—and looks down on us younger members as family. He and Tucker have always been close. I wish I could tell him what I know, but I can't. I can't put everyone in danger like that, so the secrets sit on the tip of my tongue like acid.

A beep comes from the oven, breaking the silence. Bill turns sharply and yanks a pan out, setting it on the island counter. A steaming breakfast quiche fills the room with the delicious smell of sausage, eggs, and peppers. Silently, I grab a couple of plates and silverware, serving us each a portion, and sit on one of the bar stools.

We eat in silence, and though it burns me, I offer him the only thing I can: company.

Footsteps fill the room as more of the team walk in. The smell of fresh food and coffee must've woken them all. Jake loads two plates, and Jack fills two glasses with chocolate milk before they sit down. They're like clockwork, an extension of each other, and need no words to communicate their needs. I envy their closeness—how they always have someone by their side, no matter what.

Greg grabs a plate, sitting beside me. He told us during our first break from searching that he's put his notice in and won't be coming back next fire season. Sadly, I don't think any of us will be.

Bill can retire at any time, and I imagine he probably will after all of this. The twins have no connections here; they could go anywhere in the world, and they'd still have each other.

Chief Miller's family is here, so he's stuck, but a hundred of other fire teams would love to take him. He would have no issue finding a new team.

That just leaves me. The quiche turns to ash in my mouth as I realize that if I want to stay with Val, the only family I have left, it might just mean leaving Earth entirely. So many questions swirl in my brain, but I don't give them a second thought. I don't care what dangers I may face or what lies ahead in the parts of the universe that I know nothing about.

I won't hide from the potential dangers, not this time.

Chief Miller clears his throat, drawing everyone's attention. "So, I know everyone is exhausted. We'll head to the main camp and then drive along Elkhorn Creek to the old, abandoned lumber yard. It's a while from where they went missing but it would be a good place to get away from the elements. We can't go far; the police department will be here in the morning to question us, so we have to be back by sunrise."

"Why are they questioning us?" Jack asks, looking around the group before refocusing on Chief Miller.

"They just want to get everyone's stories and make sure every detail has been covered." I can tell by the look on the Chief's face that he's not happy about it.

"We've already been questioned twice—Bill and Parker three times! What do they want from us?" Jack seethes, his fist clenched around his fork. Jake looks equally angry but seems fine to let Jack ask the questions.

I guess no one knows that Officer Paral was here again earlier this evening. I've been asked to explain what happened *four* times now, and my story has not changed.

"Another officer was here this afternoon and cornered Parker when we got back. I called their Chief, and we worked it out. They'll come and ask their questions one more time in the morning, and then leave us alone. It's just a precaution. Everyone here has been cleared, and Parker and Bill will be fine. We just need to jump through their hoops one more time, and then we can move on with our lives."

No one comments on the fact that *moving on with our lives* might just mean having to move on from losing two team members in one night.

I don't have the heart to tell them it might be three. I refuse to be left behind, so if Val goes to Hell, I'm going with her. Considering I've now gotten my ass kicked by an angel twice, Heaven doesn't seem that much fun anyway.

CHAPTER 2
VALENCIA

I'VE BECOME ACCUSTOMED TO this heat—this burning that courses through my body, leaving trails of sweat at the back of my neck. The hair there is damp and sticky. My skin is scorched and aching. I can't escape the heat—it's wrapped around me like a cocoon of fire.

The air in the cabin is cool, bringing a chill to my exposed skin. I snuggle deeper into the source, feeling his hot breath sear the soft skin on my face. Large arms hold me close and his heart pounds in a steady rhythm. I indulge in each resounding,

Thump thump.

Thump thump.

Thump thump.

It echoes in my ears, filling empty holes in my once-shattered heart that has been so haphazardly repaired. Each breath he takes is like an inhale of my own.

I drag my fingers through the light dusting of hair on his chest, my fingers bumping over the valleys of muscle. Darkness looms behind my closed eyes—but there's comfort in it. I see the landscape of his body with my fingers, using touch alone to paint the picture of his delectable body in my mind, filling the blanks with my memories. His tan skin is covered in dark artwork. The sky is tattooed across his chest; whimsical clouds, endless stars, a patchwork galaxy that's all his own is written right into his skin. The sky bleeds into lines and shapes that travel down his arms to his fingers.

Corvus. A Lord of Hell. The King of Crows. A demon I've claimed as my own.

His large frame wraps around me, all long limbs and scorching skin. Our legs are tangled and our upper bodies are pressed tightly together. We're both naked, since we didn't bother to dress before we fell asleep last night, and his thick thigh is pressed tightly between my legs—which doesn't prevent me from feeling the dampness that's gathered there.

Heat radiates from his body in waves, seeping through my skin and making my clit pound in a steady rhythm alongside his heart.

There are so many questions that blur through my brain as I lay and explore his body. We've finally, fully opened up to each other—opened our hearts to the possibility of being together—but we won't be able to bask in this intimate space for long. There's so much to do.

According to the state of Montana, I'm a missing person. I'm struggling with the mystery of my lineage and the past that still haunts me. I gave up my soul to be a pawn in a celestial war I know so little about.

I have no idea where we'll go from here or what it will take to find the answers I so desperately seek—and don't get me started on the millions of problems those answers could present. All I know is that this man so intricately wrapped around me is pivotal to it all. I will fight to ensure he stays by my side until the end.

I just hope we can survive the answers we unearth, and that they don't tear us apart at the seams.

The first order of business is finding out what we're going to do about the little problem of my currently being considered a missing person. Thoughts of that night plague me instantly, so little time has passed and everything is still so fresh. The memories are too vivid to avoid. My heart breaks all over again as images of Tucker's lifeless body, lying in the ash, consume me and tears well in my eyes, but I fight them away, painfully trapping a sob in my throat.

No sound comes out, but the pain is ever there. Corvus is the only thing that holds me together. His limbs wrap around me tightly and constrict the pieces of my shattered heart, holding it in place. I choke down the pain and focus on the problem, using it as a way to push all the hurt aside. For now. It will come back, likely with a vengeance, but I'll shove it in the dark little box where I've stored all of the other memories that haunt me.

There will come a day when I unleash that box on the world, but today is not that day.

Today is for problem solving. World-ending can come tomorrow.

However, I'm unsure how to avoid the officials searching for me this very second. Parker may already be back out on the mountain range searching for bodies that will never be found. At least not in Montana.

I've disappeared through the cracks of this world into a realm of the unknown. I'm no longer a part of Earth and its humans. Hell has my claim now. There's also my angel lineage to consider. I'm trapped in a never-ending battle between realms most don't know are real. I've become a ghost to the friends I left behind. Parker is the only one who knows I'm still alive. He's easily the most important, but letting go of so many is not so easy. Do they think I've chosen this fate, disappeared into nothingness and accepted defeat at the top of that burning valley? Have I drifted away in their minds as nothing but a painful memory to suffer if their dreams?

I hope I find my way back to them; I don't want to be a haunted memory or another missing puzzle piece that settles at the edge of their consciousness and deepens their pain. They're in a blissful state of unknowing while I grapple with the savage truths.

I dance with the Devil as vultures circle above.

"Good morning," Corvus mumbles into my hair. Shivers race through me, my body begging for more of him. Unfortunately, we don't have time right now. I have no idea when the Devil expects me back in Hell, and the last thing I need is her showing up while we're in the middle of having sex.

"How'd you know I was awake?" I ask him quietly, not wanting to disturb the calm peace of the quiet room.

"Do you want the easy answer or the truth?"

"Uhm, the truth?"

"I can hear your heartbeat pick up," he draws my body tighter to his chest.

"Wow, that's impressive," I murmur back. "So you can hear really well?"

"Yes, though there are limitations. My senses are at their weakest in my crow form, but it means I can portal in and out of Hell whenever I want, so it seems like an even trade to me. In my demon form, my senses are unrivaled. There's not a being on Earth or in Hell that could hide from my true demon."

"Will I ever get to see your demon?" I ask, curious about this other side of him I've yet to meet.

"Pray you never have to," he responds sharply, tightening his arms around me as if to protect me from the darker side of himself.

I understand why he's apprehensive to show me the true demon. Even I struggle with sharing the dark sides of myself, afraid it will cause someone to think differently of me. All I can do is be patient and wait for when he's ready to share. I *will* see his demon one day, even if it scares the shit out of me when I do.

I decide to let the topic go to focus on more pressing matters. "So when does the Devil expect me back?"

"I'm... not sure. He didn't say," Corvus mumbles, his words vibrating through his chest to my back.

He. So I was right; Corvus is unaware of the Devil's true identity. My mind starts to spiral with questions about the Devil, the demons she created, and what my new life in Hell is actually going to look like. I can't get answers to most of those questions, unfortunately. Not that I owe any loyalty to her, but for some reason, a part of me wants to keep her secret. She never asked me to, but I do, nonetheless. A thought flashes through my mind—if she created Corvus, wouldn't that make her his mother?

Lifera. I remind myself. Lifera created the demons and is the true Devil. *Lilith* is made up, according to Lifera; a human name to help the men of that time feel good about what they were doing—but who knows what the truth is. I never spent much time learning about religion, and that lack of knowledge is really starting to get on my nerves. My only comfort is that, so far, everything I've learned seems to contradict the little I thought I knew. Apparently, humans are notorious for getting the facts wrong, so maybe not knowing all the lore isn't the worst thing. I have time to figure it all out. And who better to help me than a literal Lord of Hell?

Thinking of Corvus as my boyfriend seems immature somehow. It feels as if we're so far beyond such a menial term. What we have is something that has transcended time and space and crossed into the unknown. We've built something that ignores the rules of the natural world to create realities of its own. I wouldn't have it—I wouldn't have *him*—any other way. Maybe Parker's right, maybe he is my soulmate.

"What's life like back in Hell?" I ask to distract myself from topics that make me spiral rather than settle.

"Maybe we should stay here until the Devil demands you return. Life in Hell is a constant battle against Death. Everyone and everything is trying to kill you. With your new powers still emerging, they'll be after you even more." He toys with a strand of my hair that lays across my body. His calm tone betrays nothing of his feelings about returning to his home realm.

"I can't stay here. I'm a missing person, and it's a small town. One glimpse of me by a local, and we'll have the entire state of Montana bearing down on us."

"What about your friends at the station?"

I can hear the concern in his voice, but I don't focus on it.

"I'll see them again someday," I mumble, my voice catching as I force the words out. I don't know if it's true, but I have to try and believe it is, or else I'll crumble with the weight of what sacrificing them really means.

"It doesn't have to be this way. If you want to see your friends, we'll make it happen. Fuck the angels, fuck the state of Montana, and fuck the Devil. All that matters is us." As he speaks, one large hand presses softly against my shoulder, pushing me to my back so he can look into my eyes. He's leaning upright on one of his forearms as he looks down at me. He's so handsome, my heart catches. His heat burns my skin when we touch.

A fire lights in my soul when he stares at me with those chocolatey amber eyes. My chest aches like my ribs are being forced to expand around the pressure growing in my chest. As quick as a breath, that warm ache turns into an anxious inhale, and the pressure under my ribs is no longer pleasurable. I'm terrified that he'll be ripped away from me—like everyone else I've ever loved has. I simply can't afford to lose anyone else. I may be voluntarily leaving them behind, and I appreciate what he's trying to offer me, but I can't willingly put my team through any more risk than they've already faced.

As much as it breaks my heart, taking some time away from them is probably the best thing I can do for them. For now, I'll figure out what the Devil really wants from me, how to control this intense rage that tries to control me, and who was responsible for killing one of my friends.

"Thank you," I say softly, placing my hand on one of his scruffy cheeks. His hair and beard are longer and wilder than I've seen. It's a good look on him, this unruly image that so expertly matches the energy that rolls off him in waves. It draws me in like a shadow to a darkened forest. I crave to reach out with my claw-tipped hands and drag that darkness out of him to feast on its decadence.

My heart rate spikes at the thought, and Corvus inhales sharply, his nostrils flaring as he catches the scent of my arousal. His eyes darken, no longer amber, just pools of black, full of desire. It's like a monster—this *need* we share custody of, consuming and drawing us into each other. It bounces between us, causing a constant volley of lust to flow from one end of our tethered soul to the other.

Though now that we're *both* damned, who knows where the tether actually goes.

With a growl, he leans down and captures my mouth. His skin burns with a vengeance, searing me everywhere we touch. The thigh that's pressed tightly between my legs shifts suddenly, causing a moan to escape me as it forces pressure against my already swollen clit. It's torture, this all-consuming need to ravage and be ravaged.

A husky purr rolls out of his throat as he devours my mouth, making love with his tongue and teeth. I lean into the sensation, allowing the desire to flow through me as it washes away my doubts. Time stands still as we connect in such a primal way. He steals the air from my lungs with his savage devotion to utterly destroy the distance between us.

Shivers shoot down my spine as his warm hand tracks a path across my feverish skin. I want his touch everywhere. Everything else fades away as I float suspended in the anticipation of his hand tracking lower, lower, *lowe—*

RING! RING! RING!

We both jump, pulling apart as obnoxious Christmas carols blare into the peaceful silence.

"What the fuck is that?" Corvus grumbles into my neck, causing tiny shocks to ricochet down my neck from the erotic sensation.

RING.

RING.

RING.

More Christmas music echoes through the room, creating an annoying multitude of *fa la la la la's* that bounce off the walls.

"It's my phone," I grumble, trying to reach the nightstand. Parker gave it to me when we met at the station, though he mentioned he'd had to hide it because it was almost confiscated as possible evidence by the police. There isn't anything incriminating on it—but still, not needing to worry about getting a new one was helpful.

"Obviously, but what is that awful singing?" Corvus questions with a deep scowl, reaching over me to grab the phone. It's Parker who is calling, so there's no time to explain the intricacies of why I choose to have Christmas music as my year-round ringtone.

"Hello?"

"Val! *Ugh,* thank God. Y'all need to get out of the cabin *right now.* Police are on their way to search it for evidence!" Parker rambles. There's a static edge to the sound, but I still hear what he says.

"Oh fuck!" I snap, trying to scramble out from under Corvus' heavy body. He moves swiftly, but instead of exiting the bed from his side, he swoops me into his arms and drags us both off the bed together. My naked body sticks to his, the evidence of our shared night still on my skin. I ignore my wild hair and burning skin as I rush to put on fresh clothes. The dampness between my legs immediately dirties the clean underwear. As Corvus finishes getting dressed, I start shoving my clothes back into the small bag I brought with me.

Muffled sounds come from near the bed, and I scramble to pick up my phone. The call with Parker is still active, his frantic voice trickling from the small speaker.

"Parker, calm down. We're up! We'll be out of here soon," I say, pulling the phone back to my ear.

"Good, because they'll be there in 15 minutes, according to dispatch! I won't make it there to pick you guys up before they arrive, so we'll have to meet somewhere else," he urges, a few words cutting out. The sounds of gravel and rock crunching under tires blares through the tiny speaker.

"Pick a spot to meet, and I'll get us there," Corvus suggests as he moves about the room, already putting stuff back in order.

I don't question how he plans to get us there, I just relay a location to Parker. He repeats it back to me to confirm right before the call cuts out. I don't try to call him back. We're about to leave, I'll see him shortly. Thankfully, he's only 10 minutes away from our meeting spot, too, so we'll arrive around the same time. I don't give myself time to consider that we're going to have to travel in his unearthly way. Neither of us have a vehicle here, nor can Corvus carry me as a crow. The last time I blipped in and out of existence to meet the Devil, my stomach revolted. When faced with a sick stomach or jail time—nausea here I come.

Corvus has the cabin put back together, but the familiar quilt on the cabin's only bed mocks me. I cringe, thinking about the freaking bodily fluids that are sure to be all over it. As my eyes track around the room, I see a thousand other areas that could carry hair or fingerprints. How are we going to clean this place in time?

"What's that look for?" Corvus asks as he ambles up to me, his dark clothes once again covering his muscular body. I don't have time to pout, but it's a shame for him to be covered up already.

"We can clean this place up all we want, but we're going to have to burn it down if we don't want our fingerprints or DNA to be found," I grumble, rubbing my hand across my forehead, trying to force a solution into my brain. I guess, technically, we were scheduled to be here before everything happened—but I doubt they'll care about technicalities.

Corvus looks between me and the bed before focusing solely on it. He's managed to rearrange the covers back into a perfect state and, as he stares hard at the bed, I see small puffs of smoke slowly beginning to rise from the quilted covers. I whip around, noticing more and more puffs popping up all around the room.

"Don't *actually* burn it!" I chide, grabbing his arm to draw his attention back to me.

"I'm not. I'm just burning away our *DNA*, as you put it." He ignores my hand on his arm and continues staring at the bed. As the final puffs of smoke float away, I walk to the still-pristine quilt and gently glide my hand over the top. It's not even hot to the touch. Without a blacklight, I won't be able to prove that the evidence is, in fact, gone, but with one last look around the room, I know I won't need to. Everything has been put back in its place, hiding any notes of our presence.

"You're definitely explaining how you did that later," I demand as we make our way outside into the October air. Halloween is just a couple of days away, so the air is crisp and cold now. There are no more sunny days with teases of summer. There's sure to be plenty of snow at the higher elevations, and it won't be long before the entire state is covered in it.

The fire team will be gearing up for the winter season. Some of the members will most likely take the season off to do other jobs, travel, or simply take the time to relax with family and friends. I imagine when they decide to stop the search for Tucker and me, the Ruby Valley Wildland Fire Crew will be no more. Too much trauma and mystery surrounds the team now. If the board doesn't tear them apart, the grief surely will. I hope they stay together if only to lean on each other.

"Valencia, we need to leave soon," Corvus says softly. My gaze shifts back to him, drawing me away from dangerous thoughts. "I can hear the vehicles; we only have a couple of minutes."

He doesn't pressure me though, and lets me bask in the moment. I take one last glance around the cabin, burning all the tiny details into my mind in case I never make it back here.

It's wild how, in four years, I never once found the time to visit this cabin. Now, some of my most cherished memories are here. It's where I learned that the world is more than I ever thought it could be, that my place in it matters, and that I'm worth something to someone—that I'm worth saving.

That I'm worth loving.

CHAPTER 3
VALENCIA

MY STOMACH ROLLS AS we portal through the endless darkness. It's expansive and confining at the same time, and I clamp my teeth against the nausea as we break through the invisible veil of Earth's reality. I still haven't had a chance to wrap my brain around the fact that I've been teleporting through time and space as if I'm just hopping around these unseen realms on a rideshare.

Corvus stands firm beside me, unaffected by the bizarre travel. My stomach is still churning, but it's thankfully already calming down. I guess it just takes time to get used to realm travel, which is not something I thought I would ever need to worry about.

Rocks crunch under tires as Parker's Tahoe pulls into the parking lot. We're back where it all started; the Lake Agnes trailhead parking lot is empty, besides us and a few birds who chirp through the morning air. It's peaceful to experience, but even the calm dawn ambiance isn't enough to touch the churning emotions that consume me.

It was the easiest meeting place we could come up with on such short notice. The mountain trails aren't busy this time of year, as the cold creeps its way in, so we shouldn't have to worry about any unsuspecting hikers. It was also easy for Corvus to visualize, which somehow matters. *The more you know, I guess.*

Tires skid as Parker slams on his brakes, and he hops out before rushing over and throwing his long arms around Corvus and me, squeezing us tightly.

"I was sure you guys would leave me," he explains as he holds us a little longer. His words are lightly muffled against the fabric of our clothes.

"Leave you?" Corvus questions. I can see his head turn in my direction, but I can't see his face over the top of Parker's unruly auburn hair.

Oops.

"Is now a bad time to tell you Parker is coming with us to Hell?" I state as quietly, as if speaking in a gentle tone will soften the blow of Corvus not only having to protect me from the deviants in Hell but my best friend, too. Parker leans back, releasing us from his tight hold.

"There is no coming with. *We* are not going to Hell, and we are *definitely* not bringing a human with us." Corvus reprimands, looking between the two of us like he's scolding two small children. He places his big hands on his hips and looks down at us in that dark and commanding way of his. Parker seems oddly quiet, obviously leaving it to me console the intimidating demon in front of us. It's out of character for him, but I let it slide as he's had an equally traumatizing week while I've been gone.

"We are," I say plainly, my stance matching his. "Hell and I have some unfinished business."

"You do not need to do this, Valencia. We can go to a beach somewhere and just *live*." His eyes plead with me to understand.

"I will not run from my problems, Corvus," I snap, an edge to my voice as emotions start bubbling at the surface.

"I'm not asking you to run; I'm asking you to be safe!" he shouts. A vein starts to rise on his forehead. I can see stress bleeding into every inch of his body. His hands clench into fists and his shoulders shake with each tense inhale. It's not anger that consumes him; it's fear. He fears all the ways our going to Hell could end badly. Only death and destruction await us there—but Earth hasn't been much safer, and I'm tired of waiting for something to happen. I've waited my entire life to understand why I lost my family. I was too young then to do anything, and I was alone. I'm tired of feeling like I'm not in control. That ends now.

"I understand that going to Hell won't be easy, but it's our only option. I can't sit back and let things go." I take a deep breath, forcing the tumultuous emotions back down before continuing. "I'm grateful you're here, but you died. Tu-Tucker died." My voice cracks, but I suck in air and force the rest out, "I want justice for Tucker, but I *need* to know why all this is happening to me—the meaning behind everything I've been put through. I'm haunted by the questions, by the losses. The things I've never gotten answers to and others that continue to pop up. Fate is trying to rip a pieces out of me, like they know something about me that I don't. I don't know why this is happening. I don't even know *what* I am or who my family were." The words somehow don't crack, but my chest caves in on a painful breath.

"I can't do that without you *and* Parker. He has to come with us, Corvus. I can't leave him behind. I know it's dangerous, but we're going to have to jump into the fire, even if it burns." I plead.

Corvus just stares at me in silence, neither arguing nor pushing the issue anymore. His arms hang loosely at his sides. A gush of air escapes his lungs, his chest deflating as the anger and fear take a back seat to something else. He draws me into his chest, whispering in my ear. "Whatever you need," he concedes.

I feel his warm lips brush against my temple, and it helps to burn away the remainder of my own fear and anger. Though it goes against his better judgment, he's willing to help me do whatever I need to heal—which means we're all going to Hell to hunt down a demon that doesn't know he's already dead, all in the hopes that he has the answers we're willing to risk our lives for.

"As cute as this is, it's cold as fuck out here, and I left my coat back at the station. So are we ready to go to the fiery pits of Hell? My toes are frozen," Parker says behind me.

I smile into Corvus' chest as it rattles against my forehead. Parker isn't lying though, it is cold out here. My body only warmed from being in Corvus' embrace. I know he's against taking Parker with us, but it's non-negotiable.

"I know. But fuck, it's going to be hard to keep him alive. Hell is no place for a human, especially one who still has his soul. He'll drive the damned crazy with his shiny goodness," he grumbles in return, brushing a hand down my back as I step away.

"We will protect him together. And we will listen to everything you say about our safety," I encourage, though I mostly direct my words at Parker, imploring him with my eyes to agree. He shakes his head rapidly but thankfully withholds any snarky commentary.

"And he'll have to learn how to fight," Corvus stresses. "You both will."

"Whatever we have to do, man. I just refuse to be left behind," Parker states confidently. I'm grateful that, for once, he seems to be taking this seriously.

Corvus just nods his head, looking between us. I can see the doubt flashing in his eyes, but he doesn't voice his concerns out loud. We'll cross any bridge we have to. Or we'll set them on fire to light the way.

Without preamble, Corvus wraps me in one long arm, holding me tightly to his side while reaching out to grip Parker with his other. After a quick glance between us, the veil parts and the world as we know it blurs, blackness descends, and we're off to Hell.

***

The sound of retching is the first thing to hit my ears as the ground hardens beneath my feet, and my vision clears to something more legible. My own stomach rolls, though now it's just an uneasy sensation and not actual nausea.

The world around me clears, and I get my first glimpse of Hell.

It's brighter than I thought it would be. Where I'd envisioned a realm full of darkness and shadows, the view before me showcases the exact opposite. Light blares down on us, causing the rust-colored rock of the cliff we face to shine radiantly. It's nearly blinding in its glare, and I'm forced to squint as my eyes adjust from the darkness of the in-between.

The cliff in front of us climbs high into the sky, the rock jagged in spots and flat in others. Randomly colored plants jut out at certain points—at least, I *think* they're plants. They resemble the leafy vegetation we have on Earth, but the colors vary greatly. Against the red rocks and colorful plants, the sky is as gray as a smoky haze. It's as if the sky is caught in a perpetual ash storm, though no ash falls. There's no sun from what I can see, but with how bright it is, I imagine there has to be something similar.

A large river flows somewhere over to our right, winding through a wide valley. Black waters roll softly, sputtering along. It's beautiful. The light shines on its surface, causing crystal-like glares to glow with every wave. I'm almost tempted to touch it and swim in its depths but it's thankfully far enough away that I can't give in to the temptation.

Looking around some more, I find that we're surrounded by dark mountains off in the distance. A valley of red sand stretches far and wide, extending between where we stand and the mountains. Smoke billows in plumes over one of the mountain peaks from what must be a large fire, but Corvus seems unconcerned as he watches me take in his home realm.

Parker remains bent over, hands on his knees as he continues to purge his stomach. He hasn't even had a chance to take in this new world around him, his eyes still firmly pressed closed in pain. A dark shadow slides across the ground, circling around us a few times. Corvus curses, looking up at the sky. I try to look up as well, but I have to squint against the brightness and can't see much beyond a dark blob that soars above in the sky. I can't tell its size or shape, but based on Corvus' reaction, whatever it is can't be good.

With a screech, the creature plummets down, heading straight for Parker, who is unaware of the danger above. Before I can yell out a warning, Corvus runs and leaps into the air, grabbing the blob as it nearly reaches Parker.

Landing with a thud, he holds the creature by its translucent wings. It thrashes in his grip but is no match for his strength. My face scrunches at its ugliness. It looks as if a dragonfly and an alien had a baby, but a grotesque and deformed one. Its body is made of bone and a sickly-looking green skin, covered in spores and leaking black sludge. Its face is angular and full of a thousand tiny teeth. There are no eyes or nose, just skin, bone, and a razor-sharp mouth made for devouring prey. It struggles in Corvus' tight grip, but he handles it with ease.

Right before my eyes, he grips the creature by its wings and neck, then proceeds to rip it in half. More black sludge spurts from the torn body, pooling on the ground where he tosses the creature's lifeless halves. Its spindly legs jerk a few times before settling into the stillness of final death.

"God, that sucked. Not doin—" Parker starts, wiping his mouth just as he catches sight of the... bug on the ground. He proceeds to turn and retch again. It *is* a gross sight—but seeing it dead is much better than seeing what it looked like alive, so at least he's able to ease into it this way.

"Not even five minutes in Hell," Corvus grumbles, shooting a pointed look at me, the bug, and Parker. It's too late to bother arguing more about why we brought him with us. Since he expertly handled the bug extermination, I'm sure we'll all be fine.

"What is that thing?" Parker asks, finally joining us. He walks in a wide circle to avoid stepping close to the dead creature, and the only evidence he was recently ill is the slightly pale tinge to his normally tan complexion.

"It's a Psocidfly. An insect species that typically prey on the smaller, defenseless creatures that roam Hell. It is usually harmless," Corvus grunts, passively insulting Parker. I really hope this isn't a precursor of what's to come. I knew we were bound to face danger along the way, but it would be nice for Parker to not be at risk of dying every five minutes.

Corvus is right. We need to learn how to defend ourselves—though, I'll give Parker a pass this one time, as I know the pain of teleporting for the first time.

"Where are we, Corvus?" I ask, trying to steer us away from Parker's human attributes.

"My home," Corvus replies as he walks to the rocky cliff in front of us.

Corvus uses one thick finger to draw an invisible symbol onto a flat part of rock, his hand moving with fluid motion. In the blink of an eye, the cliff face is no longer rock and plants but, instead, a deep red door covered in darker red symbols waits before us. It reminds me of the intricately detailed door of Heath Cabin back on Earth.

"This way," Corvus opens the door and beckons us inside. The entrance leads into an endless darkness that reminds me of the in-between, and my knees wobble in slight hesitation. At my pause, Parker halts his advance, waiting to see what I do before he continues. It's not like I think Corvus would lead us into a dangerous situation; I've just been so unsure of everything these days, and I know monsters hide in the shadows in Hell.

Corvus pauses just at the edges of the darkness to look back at us, and an eyebrow arches as he takes in my frozen form. Instead of making fun of my doubt, he simply waits for me to acclimate. His dark stare is as endless as the room behind him, and I remind myself that I've befriended one of the most dangerous creatures in Hell and that the monsters that hide in the shadows should stay hidden.

Befriended. I scoff internally as I resume heading inside Corvus' home. More like seduced and fallen for.

As we make our way inside, we're met with further darkness. Corvus shuts the door behind us and mutters a few sentences I can't understand. The room is sightless, thanks to the light from outside being shut out. I can just barely make out the edges of furniture around the room and various walls, though they have a weird texture to them, so I'm not really sure they're even walls.

"Fuck, it's dark," Parker mumbles beside me, and a loud rattling sound comes from my side. I look toward the noise, finding Parker stumbling around with his arms outstretched like he's blind. He's already run into a small table, and he fumbles around with one hand, trying to right it. I can see the edges of the room, but he's acting like he's be dropped into a void.

I didn't notice how much my vision has changed, but I can't deny it any longer. The more I learn of the world, the better I see it. It's a poetic balance when I think about it.

"Sorry, I forgot you can't see," Corvus quips from behind me, and a snapping sound echoes quietly. In a flare of bright light, a fire blares to life in a fireplace to our right, casting an amber glow around the room. Sparks flit angrily, hovering around the logs rather than floating to the chimney above. My brows furrow as I focus on the sparks some more, stepping closer as a memory tickles the front of my mind. Corvus' sharp words stop me.

"Give them time to settle before approaching."

"Them?" Parker asks worriedly, looking around the room. He's straightened what I now see is some makeshift lamp that he must've run into. I, too, look around the room, taking in the details—but I also don't see any creatures. Before I can ask, Corvus explains as he walks around, lighting several oil lamps.

"The fire sprites. They're what you're seeing in the fire, though from that distance, they probably just look like unruly sparks. They're typically harmless, but I've let the fire be cold for too long, and they're most likely in a volatile mood. Best to let them warm back up before approaching. They're small but vicious." He indicates, tracking a particular ember with his finger as it flares around the flames wildly.

I slowly step closer to the fire and watch—it's like a choreographed dance as the fire sprites flit about. There are five or six of them, I think, but it's so hard to track their movements that I can't be sure. They mesmerize me with their chaotic beauty. From this distance, they're just little blobs, as Corvus said, but I long to get a closer look. Before the urge can take hold, Corvus approaches, quickly taking my attention off of the lively fire.

"Welcome home." He's looking down at me with such warmth in his eyes, that I don't need the fire to feel the heat. A smile lifts my lips as I take in his handsome face. It's strange to think this could very well be my home for the remaining future I have.

The room is large and open. What I thought were textured walls are actually bookshelves standing next to each other. They're not overly full, but there are books and trinkets on almost every shelf. There's a sitting area with a couch and chair by the fireplace with a woven rug beneath. In the back corner, there's a kitchen, though with the lack of modern appliances, it's hard to tell if that's its actual purpose. A hewn rock ledge juts out from one wall by the kitchen, two wooden chairs next to it. The kitchen leads into a dark corridor that I can't see beyond, though I imagine it's as much of a surprise as this room has been.

The floor, walls, and ceiling are all made of the same red rock of the cliff, though it's a shade darker in here and the warm-toned rock provides a comforting depth to the room. Most of the space lacks decoration beyond furniture and bookshelves, but somehow it's more of a home than any I've had since my childhood home.

My shoulders bunch with tension as grief flares through my senses. The thought of the house that was once so full of love only to be burned to ashes is a living nightmare, and I'm taken aback by how easily it sneaks into my thoughts when my guard is down. The walls I built around my emotions are the only defense I have against my tragic memories. When they start to crumble, those emotions float to the surface, usually at the most inopportune times.

A large hand slaps down on my shoulder, drawing me back to the present.

"Nice digs, man," Parker drawls as he takes in the room. His eyes sparkle from the fire, and a smile covers his face. No longer is he plagued by the uneasiness of his stomach nor is he concerned that he's in Hell—he's just taking in his surroundings. Goodness, how I wish I could be more like him at times.

"It's simple, but it's one of the safest in Hell, at least." Corvus fiddles with something in his hand before setting it on a bookshelf. "I can show you around now if you'd like, or we can wait till later if you're tired from the travel. There are plenty of rooms if you wish to rest."

Thankfully, realm travel has gotten easier, but something about the stress of everything piling up has my eyes fluttering with fatigue. Parker still looks slightly pale, so even though he's full of boundless energy most times, I'm sure he could benefit from some rest as well.

"A nap would be nice," I state, walking up to Corvus. "Want to show us the rooms, and we can get that tour later?"

He nods. "Follow me."

We move deeper into the cave, through the dark hole in the wall by the kitchen. As we move back into the darkness, Parker grabs the back of my jacket to use as a guide. I can see Corvus' silhouette in front of me but nothing beyond him, so I grab onto his shirt as well.

"I'm sorry about the lighting. I'm not used to it being an issue, and it will take me a while to add lighting throughout the whole cave. For now, we'll have to use lanterns." He explains as he turns into another tunnel.

As a low light flares to life, I realize we've moved into a new room. The walls are made of the same rock as the rest of the house, though this room is rounded in shape. The circular room boasts a large bed—a small table beside it—and a nearly empty bookshelf. It's darker here, though he sets the lamp on the desk, which casts more light around the room. The bed is covered in dark blankets and pillows and could easily fit three or four people if they snuggled closely. There's a dark sheet of some sort hanging to our right that Corvus pulls to the side.

"It's a small bathroom," he says, leaning in to light a few candles that sit on a small rock ledge. "All the water here is fed from hot and cold springs that run below the cliff."

I take a minute to explore the room and bathroom—which is like one of those open shower rooms with everything inside. It makes sense for such a small space, and I commend Corvus for thinking of it.

"This is amazing. Did you do all of this yourself?" I ask him, lightly touching random surfaces around the room. It's not as warm in here as the main room, but it's still comfortable.

"Yes. A friend of mine helped at times, but it was mainly me." He leans against the rounded wall and watches me explore. Parker is already flopped on the bed, eyes closed and hands clasped across his stomach—but he's not snoring, so I know he's awake and listening.

"How did you do this? I mean, this must've taken forever to dig out—it's solid rock." I marvel at the feat and slide my hand across the semi-smooth wall.

"I wouldn't say I dug it out—at least not in such a rudimentary method. There were methods involved that are beyond the human understanding of construction."

"If so, then why use lanterns for lighting? Why not, I don't know, use fire?" Parker questions from the bed. He's leaning on one elbow, though his eyes blink slowly as he tries to stay awake.

"Fire is unpredictable and not an element many can control, especially not for long periods. Technology is risky to use—even dangerous at times. Though we have a lot of modern advancements here in Hell, some things are better left to the 'old ways,' as humans would put it," Corvus explains, nodding towards the tiny, wild flame that moves around in the glass lantern.

Parker just nods in agreement before laying back down on the bed and closing his eyes once more. I smile as he flops back. The man can sleep anywhere, and it doesn't matter that he's entered a dangerous realm full of beings begging to devour him whole—he heads into a peaceful nap with ease.

CHAPTER 4

CORVUS

IT'S STRANGE; THIS SENSE of doubt fills me as I lead Valencia through my home. She marveled at the details of the guest room we put Parker in, and I hope she feels the same sense of wonder when I show her my room. I could show her another guest room to stay in, but there aren't really made up that are ready for a guest. Plus, I'm a selfish demon, and I refuse to put her in any bed other than my own.

She follows as we snake back through the dark hallways. I'd have to add more lights throughout the halls to ensure she and Parker can make it safely through the passageways. There are many, and it's easy to get lost if you're unsure of all the twists and turns. One hall in particular leads directly to the two springs that rush through the mountain—without proper care, it would be easy to fall in.

Two more turns, and I'm leading Valencia into my most sacred space—the one room no one else has ever stepped into besides me. I don't trust easily, so the last thing I want is to close my eyes at night, afraid of a knife headed for my back.

She steps into the room, and I take in the look of wonder on her face. She stares at the tiny lights that are scattered across the ceiling by the thousands. I imagine it's the same look I had when I found this place. Her smile widens. Her eyesight has grown far better than the average human's if Parker's earlier stumbles are any indication. There's a slight glow in her eyes as she looks around.

"What are they?" she asks without looking away from the ceiling

"I'm not sure. Some form of glow stone, I think. The things you find in Hell rarely ever make sense. You just have to enjoy the nice ones when you can."

"It's beautiful." Her eyes track around the room, following the glowing dots as they taper off toward the walls. It's not as round in here as the room we put Parker in, but there's also no sharp corners. You don't want to know what hides in the corners of Hell.

Valencia starts exploring the rest of the room. I remain silent, letting her become accustomed to the space. It's not very tidy; clothes are scattered around, and I left a dresser drawer sticking out that she barely misses. Her eyesight must not be as good as mine just yet, then, but she navigates the dark well, so I don't bother her. She spends a couple of minutes in the bathroom, and I listen as cabinet doors open and shut here and there. I gently tidy as she snoops in the bathroom. It doesn't make a huge difference, as there wasn't that much mess in the first place, but it gives me something to do other than nervously wait for her to tell me what she thinks.

As I close the dresser door, I feel her approach. She glides a hand down my back before stepping to the side, leaning a hip against the dresser. I turn to face her, taking in her striking beauty. She truly is a work of art, and if the Devil knew all her secrets, he would've never let her out of his sight. He covets beautiful and vicious things—and she happens to be both.

"What's got you so buried in your thoughts?" she asks, looking up at me with those ocean-blue eyes.

"Just getting used to having someone in my space," I respond, not mentioning my other line of thought. It was only yesterday that we professed our feelings and explored each other's bodies. I don't want to make her uncomfortable by throwing around the idea of love—it's too soon. I will keep reminding myself until I believe it. What happened in the cabin was more than I could've ever asked for, so I won't push her. She offered her body to me—and the Devil didn't send me to the Death Pits—so I'll consider it a win. My cock starts to harden at the thought of her naked beneath me, and my mouth waters at memories of her taste on my tongue.

She steps closer, our bodies now touching at nearly every point. My hands hang loosely by my sides, but it's taking everything in me not to reach out and grab her. I want to bend her over every surface in this room and paint it with the evidence that she is mine. There is no escaping me for Valencia. I am a life sentence, and I plan for our lives to be *very* long.

"Careful," I warn. She's started tracing small circles on my side, and it's driving me crazy. With each small touch, a thrum of energy paces through my blood.

"Now, what would be the fun in that?" she says with a little more than extra spark as she slips her fingers under the hem of my shirt.

"If you don't stop, the last thing you're going to be doing is resting." The words leave my mouth in a rough growl. I'm more on edge than I have been in a while. No matter that I just had her last night, my body begs for more. The *demon* demands more. It's an urgent need to claim her—remind her who she belongs to. On Earth, no other could compare to me. Now that we're in Hell, a thousand different beings would be willing to kill me just to be with her. And kill me they must, because over my dead body will I allow another to have her.

Just the thought sends anger coursing through me. A growl rumbles in my chest as I bend down and pick her up. Her legs instantly wrap around my waist. She leans in to kiss me, but I don't let her lips connect with mine. She growls in response before pushing her lips against my neck and sucking hard. I relish the pain as I walk a couple of steps to the edge of my bed. I toss her down onto her back, atop a pile of dark blankets. A small *humph* escapes her lips as she lands. She looks up at me angrily, but her chest rises sharply with each exaggerated breath.

"Shoes. Off," I snap, grabbing her left ankle to take off her boots. She doesn't stop me, but she also doesn't move to help.

"Fuck you," she snaps back.

"Oh, you're going to." An evil smile takes over my face as she growls at me in response. She really is a vicious little thing when she wants to be. Her left foot yanks out of my hand, but I don't bother chasing it; the boot is gone—I got what I wanted. Grabbing her right leg to take off her other boot, she starts to fight against me. Her eyebrows are tipped down in frustration, and her top lip is lifted up in a small snarl, but her arousal coats every inch of this room, and it's driving me insane. I think I'll combust if I don't get inside of her soon and, instead of helping, she's jerking around like a little hellcat.

With her other boot off and tossed away, I reach for the waist of her pants. She scrambles away, scooting farther back on the bed, but she's not fast enough. I grip her thighs and drag her back down to the edge, catching the tiny moan that escapes her when I do. She's just as hot for me as I am for her. She thinks edging me is fun.

I get the button of her jeans undone, and the zipper opens before her wiggling becomes too much. I'm forced to grab her jeans just to hold her still. She's got a smirk on her face as she watches me struggle to get her jeans off. She's sorely mistaken if she thinks I want to play games, and I'm about to prove that point.

I grip the sides of her jeans next to each zipper and begin to pull them apart. The seam rips at the slightest pressure, instantly tearing across her center. The loud sound of tearing fabric fills the room, each pop of the threads echoing off the walls.

"Hey, wha—" she complains, looking down at her shredded jeans.

"Hush," I interrupt, dropping the denim shreds to the side before placing a palm directly between her legs, the slick center of her panties damp against my heated skin. A happy rumble escapes my chest. "You can't hide this from me, Valencia. I can *smell* how wet you are." I press the heel of my hand against her clit, dragging a moan out of her.

I slowly rub my fingertips across her lips through the fabric of her panties, teasing her and myself as I pull the rest of the tattered jeans off her legs.

"Those were my only pair," she murmurs, her voice softer now. It has a slight hum as if she's holding back a moan.

I lightly smack my fingers against her cloth-covered clit, making her back arch and heels dig into the side of the bed. Her moan is loud, the purred sound bouncing off the rock walls. My cock hardens, pressing tightly against the fabric of my pants. I hum out a pleased response before saying, "Let me hear every little sound you make."

Another low moan crawls out of her. She's already so wet, her underwear and the inside of her thighs are soaked. I push them to the side, getting my first view of her pink slit. It's glistening, covered in moisture, and just waiting to be wrecked. How badly I want to flip her over and destroy her. *Own her.* I can't, though; she's not used to my size yet, and the last thing I want to do is ruin her for myself—only everyone else.

I settle for sliding my fingers through her wetness before slowly working one finger inside of her. She jerks at first before settling into it with a deep moan. One of her hands starts to tug at her bra, but she's unable to get it off while lying on her back. I kneel at the edge of the bed, bringing myself closer to her delectable body. It's such a pretty view, seeing her lying almost naked before me. I start to slip another finger inside her, slowly opening her up and preparing her for me. I can't wait any longer, I want her too bad, and with my face now right next to her pussy, my resolve has crumbled completely.

Frustrated that she's still got clothes on, I focus intently on the fabric of her bra. Small puffs of smoke start to rise from the edge. She doesn't notice right away, her head tipped back against the mattress as she rocks against my fingers. It doesn't take much thought on my part, and I know the exact moment she feels what I'm doing.

I watch her reaction as I burn her bra away. Fear sparks in her eyes as a small flame bursts out of the smoke, burning her bra to ash. It travels slowly, following each line of thread as it reveals her breasts, one nipple at a time.

"It's not burning me, but it's warm," she says, confused—unsure of the flames despite how they do not actually burn her skin.

"I would never," I say back, focusing harder to quicken the flames. It's a fun trick, and I'm happy to show it to her, but playtime is nearly over.

Valencia mumbles out a sigh as I slide one finger across a taut nipple. I draw a sharp hiss from her when I pinch it tightly between my fingers.

"Fuck," she groans, laying her head back on the bed.

"That's for not trusting me. For thinking *I* would burn you," I snap, switching to her other nipple and squeezing it between my fingers. She rocks harder against my fingers—at this point, I'm no longer moving them as she uses me to fuck herself—though, based on the frustrated moans coming out of her mouth, it's not enough. I quickly burn her underwear away, not wasting time on the trick of it.

"I do trust you," Valencia snaps, looking me in the eyes. She doesn't look away as our eyes connect. I'd say our souls connect, but I know better. The Devil owns our souls now. We're just two beings floating in the universe; our only tether is to each other. There's no doubt in her eyes, no hesitation or worry.

I grip her hips tightly and push her up the bed as I burn my own clothes away. She sucks in a gasp as my cock bobs free from the flames. Her eyes track along my body, taking in all the tattoo-darkened skin, scars, and muscles. I used larger flames on myself to burn the fabric away as quickly as possible. The amber light glows in her eyes briefly before settling back to her normally bright blue. They look bioluminescent now with the reflection of the glow stones shining back.

I laugh softly to myself. Going to need to kill and destroy something soon before I turn into a pussy-whipped puddle.

"You trust me? Fully?" I ask her as I grip her hips and pull her body to me. Her thighs spread wide against my hips, opening her up fully. Wetness shines between her folds, sparkling nearly as much as her eyes do.

"Yes," she says slowly, as though unsure.

"It's okay to be nervous," I respond, dragging the tip of my cock through her wetness, spreading it around her clit and then teasing from front to back all over again.

"I'm not."

"How brave," I purr with an evil smile.

Her legs tighten against my hips as if to pull me closer. I fucking love how eager she is, and edging her has become one of my greatest obsessions. One of these days, I'm going to tie her up and edge her until she comes so hard she passes out. Not this time; no, I have something special in mind.

I concentrate a small portion of my power on her nipples as I slowly push inside her. She's so warm I feel like she's set my dick on fire, and a low groan rushes between my gritted teeth as I work my way into her tight channel. Devil, take me; she's so fucking *wet*.

She moans loudly as I pick up my pace, quickly sliding in and out. A wet slapping sound echoes off the rock walls each time our bodies meet. Between her moans and the sound of our bodies colliding, it sounds like a sex symphony in here.

"Corvus, good *Go*—go-goodnight, what is happening to me?" She asks with a moan. Her hands are gripping her breasts tightly, holding them high up on her chest. I don't stop fucking her. Each thrust slams my body against her, causing shutters to rake through her. I won't punish her for almost slipping this time. What I'm already doing is torture enough.

"How's that feel, baby?" I ask with a growl as I watch the two tiny flames dance around her taut nipples.

"It-it's hot," she moans, tipping her head back as I ramp up the heat. The small flames prettily dance across her delicious body. Her tan skin is flushed, and the pink ring around her nipples now resembles the dark red of wine, stained from the heat. A new gush of wetness floods her insides, slipping out around my cock as I slam into her, continuing the brutal pace.

The smell of her floods my senses as I continue to drive forward. Sharp notes of her scent flow through my body, making me wild.

With one hand on her hip, I drive into her, holding her tightly against my body. I reach the other hand forward and grab a fistful of her hair, pulling her head up. She sucks in a gasp before meeting my eyes. "You thought I would burn you, my little fiery tigress? How sorely you're mistaken."

I release her hair and return my grip to her hips. She moans loudly. At this point, between me fucking her and the flames, I'm not sure she can take much else. I've always loved testing the limits.

I slow my thrusts slightly, giving myself more time to concentrate. I watch the tiny flames on her nipples dance before sending a thought to the left flame. It responds instantly, moving away from her nipple and heading south.

"No... Please..." Valencia moans, writhing on the mattress. Her left hand has now replaced the flame, pinching her nipple tightly.

Sending the flame straight to her clit, I groan, "Beg. Fucking beg for it."

I thrust hard twice, causing the flame on her clit to bounce. Her eyes roll back into her head as she comes. I don't think the sound that comes from her can be considered a moan. It's so loud that I swear I hear rocks cracking further into the cave. Parker definitely heard her that time. No matter that I have noise-dampening sigils on every doorway—a woman with that level of pleasure could break through any sound barrier.

Her pussy clamps down so tightly that I can barely move. No longer able to thrust inside her anymore, my cock just pulses against her inner muscles. It drags a groan out of me, my back shuttering as I try to hold off coming a little longer. I can feel the burn starting in my lower back. I'm right on the edge, and if she squeezes me any tighter, I'm going to blow.

"*Ugh*, Corvus, I can't take anymore." A sharp jerk runs through her muscles as she tries to pull away from me. I growl, holding her hips a little tighter. She'll probably bruise from my tight grip, but I don't care; I'm too on edge to stop. The true demon is too close to the surface.

"You can take it all," I snap, a graveled edge to my tone.

She looks at me closely, examining my face, and I bare my teeth at her as I thrust in and out, only moving the slightest bit even though she's still soaked. A small smile takes over her face before she shifts to the side.

Distracted, I watch as she leans around, her hand sliding down the bed toward our joined bodies. The flame on her nipple burns out, leaving behind a rosy hue to her normally pink skin. The flame on her clit is barely visible anymore, almost completely burned out after my attention was pulled elsewhere. She shifts her hips to the side a bit, rising to nearly rest on top of my thighs before her hand slips underneath her body.

I don't catch on fast enough, so I can't stop her once I realize her goal.

"*Mmm,*" I moan as she presses her fingers up behind my balls while gripping them in a soft, cupped hand. She rolls them in her hand slowly as she pulls my hips in tighter with her thighs. I shudder at the feeling, my back burning as I tensely hold off for a little longer. Between the pressure, her soft touch on my balls, and the tight wetness around my cock, I'm no longer able to hold back.

"Fuck, fuck, fuck, *fu—*" I can't stop the moan as she forces me to come inside of her. My legs shake, and my back curls against the force of it. What a little *minx*, forcing me to come before I was ready.

"You're sexy when you come, Corvus. Don't hold it back." Her soft fingers slide away from my skin, now covered in our combined arousal. The flame on her clit has completely sputtered out, leaving just her beautiful body in view. I slowly pull out, watching dazedly as cum slips from inside her. I shake my head against the thoughts that flood my mind. Now is not a good time to acquire a new breeding kink.

Valencia squeals lightly as I lift her into my arms and carry her to the shower. We don't take long—just long enough to wash away the sticky aftermath. The warm water fills the room with steam, blanketing us in a humid cocoon. After washing, I shut off the warm water before wrapping her in a clean towel. I enjoy taking care of her in these small moments.

"Goodness, that shower felt amazing." Valencia absently states as she slowly dries her body. I take a second to enjoy the view before responding.

"This cliff has cold and hot springs running through it," I remind her. "It's why I chose it for my home, most of the others only have hot water. The shower is pretty rudimentary, but it beats having to swim in the Erebus River."

"What's the Erebus River?"

"You saw the black river just outside my cave door?"

"Yes. It was beautiful—I've never seen water so dark. It looked like it was full of tiny black diamonds," she murmurs, her brows tipped down in thought.

"It is beautiful, but whatever you do, *never* go into the Erebus River. It's smart practice to not go into any body of water in Hell, but *especially* not that river."

"Why?"

"Erebus River is home to darkness and shadow. From its depths, evil is born. Whether it be a vicious creature or a particularly damaged soul, nothing that comes out of that river is good. No one who has fallen in has ever come back out. Or if they did, they wish they never had."

"Okay," her voice stutters a bit as she takes in the warning.

I approach her slowly, pulling away the towel before wrapping her in my arms. She leans into my body heavily, resting most of her weight against me as she snuggles into the embrace. "No matter what happens, I will do whatever I can to ensure you and Parker are safe here. It won't be easy, and there's a lot you both need to learn, but it's not impossible. We'll get through this," I mumble as I hold her closely, my hand resting on the back of her head, holding her against my chest.

"I know, it's just all been so fucking much. A month ago, I didn't know any of this shit existed and now I'm literally living in *Hell*. I feel like a toddler, having to learn how everything works all over again," she grumbles in response, her hot breath warming my chest.

"I'll be your Daddy."

She pulls a face. "Gross! Never say that word again. Like ever." She slaps my arm and pushes from my grip. I let her go, a smile on my face. I have no interest in her calling me daddy, but I knew she'd hate it—and that it would take her mind off the shit-pile of problems we're currently facing.

"So," she faces me as she steps away, placing her fists onto her hips, "what the fuck am I supposed to wear?"

I laugh as she stands there, completely naked, as beautiful as a mountain sunset—with a stern look on her face. "Clothes are in my dresser."

She rolls her eyes and heads back to my room, leaving me alone in the bathroom. I toss the towels in the basket on the floor and follow her.

She's opening drawer after drawer, her scowl growing deeper with each one she opens. She slams the last one shut before angrily turning to me.

"What bitch's clothes do you have in your house, Corvus?" she snarls with a scowl.

I suppress a laugh, though it comes out as a snort. "No one's, kitten. The dresser is enchanted; it knows what the person opening the drawer needs. Every piece of clothing is perfectly suited to the opener's taste and preferences, as well as size. Watch." I open the top right drawer, pulling it as wide as it will go. Inside, every piece of fabric black as night. Pants and a shirt sit on the right, and black boxer briefs and socks sit on the left. I pull the boxer briefs out and put them on. They're tight against my thighs but not too tight—the perfect fit. Her eyes widen; there was likely something different in the drawer when she'd opened it.

"Why the fuck were the drawers full of lingerie when I opened it?" She points an angry finger while opening the drawer beside mine again, where an outfit similar to my own now waits.

"It knows your *every* need." I try to wiggle my eyebrows up and down.

"That sounds a lot more like it's fulfilling *your* needs," Valencia murmurs, seemingly again shocked that the outfit is different than what was there before. The pants she pulls on fit her perfectly, showcasing her sculpted ass and toned legs, and the dark maroon shirt contrasts nicely with her dark hair and tan skin.

I grab her around the back of the neck and draw her to me before leaning down and dragging my lips against hers. The kiss is soft and sensual. An appreciation for the connection we just had and a promise for later. I lean back, looking into eyes bluer than any ocean in Hell. I lean in for another kiss, possessed by a need only she can fulfill.

"*Val!*" Parker's terrified scream echoes throughout the entire cave.

CHAPTER 5
VAN

HUMAN.

The word is a growl in my mind—a loud sound that reverberates through my entire body, consuming my every thought.

I knew the female was here. I could hear them. I could *smell* them. I couldn't escape what they were doing. Luckily, my needs had already been met, thanks to a vicious little demoness from Tornil's circus—otherwise, I'd be battling the primal need to join them.

It is to be expected. Corvus' needs have not been met. He has not taken a lover in many years. He was once ravenous, flitting through the entire population of Hell as he were sampling a buffet, though none ever captivated him as thoroughly as this one has. I haven't met her yet, but she must be something special to capture and hold the King of Crows' eye.

The noises they make together echo throughout the cave, but even without my heightened senses, there would be no masking the stench the *human* emits.

I track the source of the awful smell, poison flooding my veins the closer I get. The darkness of the cave passageway doesn't hinder me in the slightest. I have the best eyesight in the entire realm, thanks to my Fae heritage.

I round the last corner silently. It's not necessary to sneak up on the human, I could hear its slumbering snores as soon as I walked through the door. What a pathetic creature, sleeping in the face of danger.

I'll show it. I'll introduce it to the severity of Hell. It will be a swift and sharp lesson. I don't know how it snuck into Corvus' home. Plenty of humans roam

Hell, even if they never last long. Somehow, this one has survived Hell long enough to find a place to hide in this cave.

While Corvus is preoccupied in his bedroom, I'll remedy him of this parasite.

The orange glow of a lantern flickers across the rock walls as I sneak into the room. It's a spare room—one of many Corvus has—only, this is one of few that are actually furnished. A hushed snarl escapes my clenched teeth as a strange wave of jealousy flares through my blood. I do not have a place to call my own in this realm or any other, and the *one spot* in this entire universe that I thought would always be mine is currently being desecrated by a *man*.

He's average height, only taking up part of the bed. My tall frame nearly hangs off the ends when I sleep here. He's fully dressed and lying atop the covers—*my covers*—but he's dead to this world while he floats around in the dreamscape.

Anger boils hot in my blood as I play through endless scenarios of how I should exterminate this little vermin.

Memories of other humans briefly flash through my mind, until this man's face bleeds in with the rest of them. My thoughts to take an even darker turn.

I left the Fae realm—the only home I've ever known—to escape the atrocities the humans there had enacted on my life. Now, I find myself in a realm full of dark and depraved species that would love nothing more than to either stab me in the back or derive a way to use me. For many years, I escaped the horrors of what I faced there, but the walls I built against them crumble as I realize no realm in this universe will offer me peace from their torment.

The man stirs in the bed, jerking my attention out of my past and into the present. He's clearly dreaming, and if the scrunched look on his face is any indication of what it's about, I'd imagine it's not a pleasant dream.

I allow him to suffer a little while longer in Nightmare's domain. I'd let the demon lord have him if I felt he'd actually punish the human, but Nightmare is as soft as the sweet dreams he secretly creates—even if I'm the only one who knows it.

Not even Nightmare's terrors would be enough punishment to appease me of the human's presence. He *must* pay. All humans are vile and greedy creatures, thinking they're the smartest, most cunning beings alive.

They may be cunning and creative—but they're also weak. Oh, so weak compared to a being like me.

I plan to prove that very point, starting with this human right here.

I grab an exposed ankle—just above a pair of boots—and tightly wrap my fist around it, squeezing. His leg jerks against the sting, and his eyes begin to flutter open. I don't give him time to fully wake; I don't want to bother defending against an attack, no matter how useless it would be. I pull him off the bed by his leg, smiling viciously at the pained grunt that whooshes from his chest when his back slams against the ground.

He starts to struggle, kicking the backs of my legs and clawing at the fingers I've coiled around his ankle, but it's futile. I am infinitely stronger, and no amount of fighting would ever allow him to best me—without even considering the many powers I have at my disposal.

I don't use a single one, though, choosing to insult him with my strength alone. In the Fae realm, it is considered a great grievance to lose a battle against another without the interference of their power. This human is far too bland and unintelligent to get the slight, but *I'll* know, and that's enough. For now.

"Let me go!" he snaps, his anger a sharp blade in his tone. I chuckle instead of answering and don't release my hold.

Dirt scrapes against the ground as I drag his flailing body through the cave system. I could've ended him where he lay on the bed, but I felt it was proper to take him out into the sandy valley. Clearly, his first death that landed him in Hell wasn't punishment enough. The Devil has clearly lost one of his souls.

Thinking of the Devil makes me even angrier. My shoulders tense, and my teeth clamp painfully together. Quickening my steps, I rush through the cave with the human in tow.

As I breach the doorway to the living room, I'm jerked backwards. My shoulder pulls against the strain, and I snarl at the pain, turning to look down at the man. He's stretched from fingertip to ankle as he grips a bit of rock at the edge of the doorway.

"Let go," I snap, squeezing my hand even tighter. I wonder briefly how much more it would take to break the weak little bones in his ankle, crippling him even more than his human nature already does.

"Fuck you," he throws back, focus intently latched to his hold on the rock. It's not near enough, but he doesn't know that. I could easily pull him away from the wall. It would most likely break all of his fingers and quite possibly the ankle, too. On second thought, that doesn't seem like such a bad idea.

As I am gearing up to yank him away from the rock, his loud scream echoes through the entire cave.

"*Val!*" There's terror and fear in his voice but also anger and defiance in his eyes.

What a little rat. Putting on a show.

The realization that this is not some random lost soul who's snuck into Corvus' home comes to me suddenly. Now that blind rage isn't clouding my senses, I can almost see the brightness his intact soul emits.

I throw his ankle away as if it were poison and he grunts in pain as his body hits the ground.

What has Corvus done?

No longer will I be the most coveted creature in Hell. Demons and dark beings alike cause mayhem and commit murder to get to me. Whether their goals are to kill me, take me, or something else even worse. And I'll no longer be alone in that turmoil.

Once the damned learn of this man, nothing will be able to save him.

CHAPTER 6
VALENCIA

I BREAK FROM CORVUS' passionate kiss and tear through the passageways. I can see a little bit of the walls around me, but swiftly realize I have no idea where I'm going. I stop abruptly, turning around to find Corvus, but his large body slams into mine, nearly toppling us both to the ground.

"Sorry," he says and steadies us both. He grabs one of my hands and, this time, leads me through the halls. "They're this way."

"*They're*?" I snap, mostly concerned with who the other person might be.

"It seems Van and Parker have finally met," Corvus responds. His voice is as calm as ever, but I can tell by the quickness in his step that he isn't entirely comfortable with the situation, either.

I vaguely remember that Van is the friend Corvus mentioned that night at the bar, and I try to recall what he had said about him then—but so much has happened since that all I can remember is Corvus mentioning they're a lot alike.

Maybe this won't be so bad after all. Maybe Van just scared Parker.

As we finally reach the light, confusion mars my features. I find Parker sprawled on the ground, gripping his shin while staring at the person currently standing over him with the most menacing aura I've ever felt.

And that's including the demon Lord of Hell I just slept with.

If there were ever a person to embody the full force of nature, in both body and soul, it would be Van. His dark, coppery skin glows in the firelight, and his sharp features cast deep shadows across his face. Long, dark hair lays against his chest, and small braids and beads break up the otherwise straight strands. His face is angular and fierce, and there's so much tension in his body that he seems as sharp as a knife.

Not to mention the fact that he towers over all of us by inches—Corvus included.

"Van, what's going on?" Corvus demands, not so subtly stepping between Van and Parker.

Van snarls as if the motion re-ignites his anger. "What am *I* doing," he hisses—the sound nearly animalistic. I turn, ignoring what he says next—tone hushed—and check on Parker.

"Are you okay?" I ask, frantically checking him for injuries. He jerks as I accidently bump one of his legs.

"Captain Crazy dragged me from my bed. Like a *doll*. What are these people eating? They're so strong," he whisper-yells, sneaking a glance at the two males standing behind me. I shoot a quick glance over my shoulder and suck in a silent gasp. From the floor, they look like giants, towering over us with their impressive bodies and oppressive auras.

"I don't think we want to know," I quietly say back, rolling up his pant leg to get a closer look at the leg he'd been holding. "There's some bruising, but I don't think it's broken. Do you think you can stand on it?"

"Yeah," Parker grunts and I help him to his feet. He stumbles for a second, unused to balancing most of his weight on one leg. "Will be good as new in no time."

"That is no reason to attack him, Van! He is a *guest*. You know the rules," Corvus stands with his hands on his hips and stares Van down—even though the other man is taller than him. Van doesn't appear as angry as he was, but there's still a viciously dangerous edge to his demeanor.

"I know the rules, and still it does not change the fact that *he* does not belong here," Van snaps back, not even sparring us a glance.

"What rules?" Parker and I ask at the same time.

"There's ru—" Corvus starts but is cut off by Van.

"Shut up, Rat," Van snarls, finally looking our way. Though we stand side by side, and I'm only a few inches shorter than Parker, there is no mistaking the fact Van's venomous glare is trained right on my best friend.

Oh. Hell. No.

I had so many hopes for this meeting—for Van and Parker to get along, so I knew there was *someone* else watching out for my best friend. Now I worry I may have to watch Parker's back from an enemy far too close to home.

My blood boils at the thought. I don't know who this motherfucker is, but he will *not* threaten my friend. My fingertips burn with a familiar sensation as my claws beg for release, and the bloodlust haze slowly clouds my vision. I try to suck down the harsh emotions, but I'm nearly already boiling over.

"Nope," Corvus mutters before stepping close to me. He grabs my shoulders, digging his fingers into my arms to break my thoughts away from the situation, and I'm able to focus on the pain enough to bring myself back. Mostly, at least. There's still an edge of feral hunger, but I try my best to ignore it.

"He cannot talk to Parker that way," I snarl at Corvus. My body still faces Van but I've broke through the haze enough to flit my eyes to Corvus.

"Give him time, he has his own issues," Corvus pleads softly. We're all too close for the others to not have heard, but he still comforts me, ignoring the other two.

"Oh, it's fine Val. Degradation is one of my favorite kinks," Parker snarks, brushing his hands off on his jeans. They didn't seem hurt, but now that I'm looking closer, they do appear slightly red.

A growl echoes through the space—so loud, it's like a giant grizzly stands in place of Corvus' friend. He huffs a few more growls before snarling. "Silence."

"Listen buddy, I'm a talker, so you're just going to have to get used to it," Parker snaps right back. *Really taking the bull by the fucking horns, Parks.*

A rough laugh escapes me, though I try to keep it in. Thankfully, due to Parker, I'm no longer worried about my claws unexpectedly ripping through my fingertips. The rage is already gone, my heart rate and blood flow already back to normal.

First on the agenda: learning to control these claws.

Corvus focuses his attention back on the others.

"Van, you've got to calm down. He is Valencia's best friend and a guest. You know what that means. Do not try to attack him again, or I will be forced to fight you—and we both know that will not be good for anyone."

"You would protect this vile creature? Choose him over *me*? I have been your friend for years—*hundreds* of their worthless years, Corvus. Is that how far your loyalty goes? All that time washed away at the first cunt that gives you the time of day?" His shoulders are tense, fists clenched tightly by his sides. His dark black hair shines in the firelight, and his green eyes glow with suppressed rage. He's barely holding himself together, but I can see the cracks; I've felt the same ones. The despair that tries to rip you from the inside out. It's nearly unbearable to witness, knowing that this isn't selfish anger but something far more broken.

If it wasn't for the clear devastation of betrayal in Van's voice, I'd probably far more angry at his statement. He's clearly hurting, so I remain quiet to not throw salt in the wound.

Corvus is not as unaffected by Van's words, and rushes his friend with that smooth grace that makes him both beautiful and deadly. Faster than my eyes can track, Corvus has Van by the throat. He kicks Van's legs out from under him, forcing the large man to his knees. A darkness consumes Corvus, and it's as if he draws the shadows from the room into himself. I guess this is what it feels like to be on the outside of the fight.

"It is all those years of friendship that is keeping me from ripping your tongue out of your fucking mouth. Do *not* speak of her that way." Corvus towers over Van's kneeling form as he spits the words through clenched teeth.

"I do not mean to offend your mate, friend, but I cannot take losing you to a human. Haven't they taken enough from me?" Van pleads, air wheezing from his constricted throat.

Something is seriously wrong with him. The raw emotion in his voice sends a punch of pain to my chest. I know that feeling well—that horrible, sickening feeling you get when you have to beg for the one good thing you have left. As angry as I am that Van hurt Parker, he's clearly got a lot going on and it feels wrong to force him to suffer further.

I'm about to speak when I hear Parker clear his throat beside me. "If the issue is me, just tell me what I need to do to help him be more comfortable."

Van's eyes instantly zero in on Parker, just as a predator would its prey. Another growl starts rumbling through his large chest, but it's suddenly cut into more of a gurgling sound as Corvus once again squeezes Van's throat. Corvus holds Van's neck so tightly the tattoos on his knuckles turn gray from tension, and the skin under his fingers becomes a vicious red.

"I appreciate the offer, Parker, but you cannot change being human any more than he can change how affected he is by your presence. It is his responsibility to work on it; you've done nothing wrong," Corvus calmly appeases Parker while maintaining firm control on the wild creature Van has become.

"Still, if I'm able to do something to help, I should. I don't want to trigger him if I don't have to," Parker rebuts, showing once again that he truly is the sun that we all just orbit. He was literally attacked by Van moments ago, and is still trying to put Van's needs first. If it were me, I'd have used claws first and asked questions second.

"Just make sure you are never alone with him. I can control his outbursts until he is able to control himself," Corvus responds, still staring Van down to clearly convey his point.

"I understand," Van says quietly. There's a new rasp to his voice that wasn't there before—which is probably just windpipe damage—but, based on the bruises around Parker's ankle, I guess it makes them even.

Corvus slowly releases Van, who stands with a fluid grace. He doesn't touch his throat or even flinch in pain, but instead turns towards me, bowing his head slightly. "I have wronged you and your... *guest*. I will leave and give you time to settle and me time to think. Until then." Without another word, Van stands and disappears through Corvus' front door, quietly shutting it behind him. My mind races at his departure.

I can't wrap my brain around what just happened. Only a couple of hours in, and our stay in Hell has already turned into a shit show.

"Well, that went well," Parker deadpans from beside me.

I can't help but laugh. What have we gotten ourselves into? "What the fuck happened?" I turn to look at my best friend, who is still mostly balanced on one leg.

"I don't know! One minute, I'm starring in a weirdly erotic nightmare, and then *boom*, my back hits the ground and Captain Crazy is dragging me through the cave. I think we're gonna need some weapons if we're to have any more visitors stopping by, Corvus." Parker looks at my demon, pointing down at his bad ankle.

"Van is the only being in the entire realm that can get into this cave without my help. There will be no other visitors, I promise. Now, sit on the couch and let me get some ice for your ankle." Corvus points Parker in the direction of a dark-brown leather couch. The fire in the hearth still burns, and the quiet snaps and pops fill the space in our silence.

Parker hobbles to the couch and promptly flops down, setting his ankle gingerly on a small trunk that has been turned into a coffee table. I stare into the fire for a moment. How I am going to manage to keep us alive in this place? Have I set us up for failure, bringing us to this place where even friendship can mean death?

A large hand grips the back of my neck, warm fingers nearly wrapping around to the front. "Don't think so hard, tigress, it will all work out," Corvus softly murmurs into my ear, his warm cheek pressed against the back of my head while his thumb lightly rubs the side of my neck. I lean into his body for a second, taking advantage of the comfort he offers.

"So, can I still have a weapon in case your friend comes back?" Parker asks from the couch behind us. I expect Corvus to argue, but he instead agrees.

"I will get you a dagger to keep with you at all times. It won't kill, but it will really fucking hurt and offer you time to escape. But, whatever you do, do not use it on Van."

"Well, that defeats the fucking purpose then. He's the one who's trying to drag me out of bed to kill me," Parker snorts, adjusting himself a little to get comfortable.

"Why shouldn't he use it on Van? He needs to be able to protect himself," I argue and step away from Corvus to join Parker on the couch. I need to sit for a minute to gather my thoughts. The leather is warm and comfortable beneath me, and in another life, I could see myself curled up right here, with a good book in hand, getting a nice cuddle from my favorite demon.

"It will only make Van angry—and not even I would be able to control him then." Corvus looks between us slowly.

"You mean that *wasn't* angry? Why else was the dude dragging me out of here like he was possessed or something?"

"Van is one of the most powerful beings in this realm. He has more powers than I even know of, and nearly every single one of them is honed to kill. He is the perfect predator—you'll know when he's angry."

"If you're trying to make me feel better about being here, you fucking suck at it," Parker responds dryly.

"I never said coming to Hell would be easy. We've just got to deal with what gets thrown at us." Corvus stands, hands on his hips, and looks down at us.

"Well, I really expected it to be at least a little more fun."

I can't contain my laugh. "Fun? Parker, it's Hell. It's literally supposed to be the opposite of fun."

"Not true. For some, sure. But there's a whole lot of sins that are really fun, and demons don't strike me as the rule-following type, so you can't tell me there isn't at least something fun going on around here." The look Parker gives me is so genuine, I almost believe him. I turn to Corvus for backup, but based on the evil smirk on his face, I don't think I'm going to like what he's about to say.

"Oh, demons are the best at having fun," he purrs in that sexy voice of his that I know means nothing but trouble.

Fucking Hell.

Chapter 7
Valencia

"Before we get to the good stuff, we have some things that we need to take care of first," Corvus says, fumbling around with one of the bookshelves.

"Like what?" I tip my head back onto the couch to stare at the rock ceiling above. It's not as pretty as the one in Corvus' bedroom, but there is a strange comfort to the room nonetheless. It's a weird feeling, knowing that an entire cliff sits right above our heads, yet I appreciate its protection more than I feel its weight sitting on top of me.

"First, healing Parker's ankle. There can be no weaknesses. For either of you, but especially for Parker." Corvus finds what he's looking for and slams a little box closed. He strides over to where we sit on the couch and plops himself down on the trunk next to Parker's raised ankle. "May I?"

"It's fine, man, probably just sprained," Parker tries to argue but I can see the tension in his leg as he tries to pull it away from Corvus' hand.

"It's not broken, but it is injured—and that is a death sentence if you ever leave this cave. If you cannot leave, then we must leave you here alone. Why come—"

Parker promptly lifts his injured leg and plops it down on the demon's thick thigh with nothing but a quiet hiss of pain, convinced as soon as Corvus mentions that being injured means Parker would have to be alone. Corvus readjusts Parker's leg without comment, slowly sliding his pants up until his slightly tan and very bruised ankle is displayed. It's swollen, covered in patches of red and purple, and I wince as memories of my own ankle injury play across my mind. What is it with us and injured ankles?

Corvus uncaps a small jar that's filled with a nearly opaque cream, which he slowly starts to rub into Parker's skin. Parker's leg jerks a couple of times before I see him relax almost entirely. "It's warm," he murmurs, his eyes drifting closed.

Before I can ask what it is, Corvus explains. "This is called Taraxa Balm, taken from the Taraxa plant. It is a vine-like plant species that feeds off the smoke and ash in the air. A weed, a nuisance to most as once rooted, and is an invasive plant that will vine around anything. Story goes that a demon was once napping against a tree, only to wake ensnared in a prison made of Taraxa vines."

Parker hums in contentment, seemingly free of pain now that Corvus is treating his ankle with this balm. He takes a deep breath before asking, "How come it's so warm?"

"I'm doing that. Without heat, Taraxa balm is simply a lotion. When heat is applied, the plant's healing properties are released into the skin. It's not as effective as healing powers are, but it is better than just leaving you to heal on your own."

"How are you producing the heat?" Parker asks. He's so much better at this—asking the right questions even when he's distracted. I always seem to forget to ask.

"All beings in Hell have the ability to withstand any fire besides angelic fire. The stronger the demon, the more it can withstand. With time and practice, the ability to withstand fire eventually transforms into the ability to control it. There is a saying in Hell, *beware the demon with hot skin, for he can burn you from within*. It's why my skin feels hot to touch for most, because of that ability to control and manipulate fire. Over time, my control has grown so much, I can control it with just a thought."

A flare of heat rushes to my cheeks and I know my face is tomato red but, thankfully, Parker's eyes are still closed, so he doesn't see it. I've become quite acquainted with that particular ability.

"Back to this balm you're using," I say, trying to steer the conversation away from where it's currently going. "How does it heal?"

Corvus gives me a knowing smirk but doesn't comment on my change of topic. "Unfortunately, I am not well versed in the intricacies of plant life here in Hell. Think of this as something that has been passed down through generations, per se. The knowledge of *how* it works hasn't really been shared; we just know it does.

Van would know more; he likes plants and nature, though we have very little of it here."

"Is Hell all rocky mountains and sandy valleys, then?" I ask, curious whether the small glimpse I caught of Hell outside of Corvus' cave was really all there was to see in this unknown realm.

"Not in the slightest. Much like Earth, there are many terrains to Hell. It is truly vast, but something to remember: if it's beautiful, it's likely ten times more deadly. That's why everyone in Hell usually keeps away from those areas, no matter how badly we wish we could enjoy them."

I feel like I can hear a slight tinge of longing in his tone, but I don't push the topic further.

"Okay, give it a while, and you should be good to go. It's not completely fixed, and you may feel random twinges of pain here and there, but you'll be able to run from danger if you need to." Corvus lays the now-healed ankle back onto the trunk. All that remains is a normal-looking, slightly tan, hairy ankle.

"Wow, that stuff is amazing," Parker exclaims, slowly twisting his ankle one way and then the other. "And who says I run from danger?" Parker says with a mocking look, his smile no longer strained.

"I do," Corvus plainly states. "You see danger, and you run like your life depends on it, because it does."

"I thought we would be getting weapons and fighting lessons?" I ask Corvus as he puts his magic healing cream away.

"I will work with Parker, and you will work with Van. I just have to convince him to come back and not lose his shit again." The last part is mumbled, but we both hear it.

"What was his problem with Parker?" I ask, feeling once again like I'm always full of a thousand questions yet never getting enough answers.

"It isn't my story to tell. But I can share that it's not Parker's fault; its Van's responsibility to manage his reactions. He's not had to before as there aren't many humans here."

"There's not many humans in Hell? Now I know you're lying." I could almost laugh. There's absolutely no way at least some of the human population didn't end up here.

"You misunderstand, there are plenty of humans in Hell, but they're not free roaming as we are. They go straight to the Seven Rings to receive their punishments. Very few make it out of there, and those that do don't last long roaming Hell." Corvus makes his way back over to us, slowly settling into a large brown leather chair that matches the couch Parker and I still sit on.

"So, the Seven Rings is like a punishment deal?" Parker asks him, finally joining the conversation.

"Exactly that. It is a prison of sorts, and not somewhere you'd ever want to go."

I take a deep breath, cataloging that information for later. "So now that we've taken care of Parker's ankle, what's next? You said we had a few things to do?"

"Yes, two more. One, I need to give you all an official tour of the cave. It's important you know how to get around here without me in case of an emergency."

"I thought you said no one else could get inside?" Parker sits up straighter, finally pulling his leg off the trunk and setting it on the floor. He lifts his body, adjusts his clothes, and settles back into the couch—slightly more alert than he was when we got here.

"Nothing is ever absolutely guaranteed," Corvus says softly.

Parker and I don't bother to respond and nod our heads in agreement. We've both been on the shit end of that truth too many times to count.

"And the last thing?" Though I have a suspicion on what it might be, I need to hear it from him.

"Lastly, we need to speak to the Devil."

"I was hoping that wasn't going to be what you were going to say," I mumble, looking back up at the ceiling and getting lost in the memory of my first encounter with the Devil.

"But we all expected it, right? I mean, it's why we're all here—to talk to the Devil and figure out what's going on." Parker brings up a very good point. The Devil knows things, and though I didn't have enough time to ask her before, maybe I'll be able to now. Questions swirl before my eyes like tiny concussion stars. Or maybe I just have a headache.

"The Devil will have known that we've been in Hell this entire time. No one leaves or enters this realm without his knowledge. He'll be expecting us soon, but I want to show you around first, just in case we're too tired when we get back."

He. Again, I am reminded that Corvus doesn't know the whole truth about the Devil—and, for some reason, I still haven't told him.

We get up, Parker and I stretching briefly while Corvus grabs a lantern from a side table. A flame spontaneously flickers to life, filling the room with far more light than I would've thought it capable of.

"Wow, that's bright," Parker exclaims, briefly squinting his eyes.

"Glass from the sands of Hell shines as brightly as the souls that are lost here," Corvus responds, leading us back into the hall that delves deeper into the cave.

"At what point do we assume he's making this shit up?" Parker asks as Corvus leads us into a now-brightly-lit walkway.

"Can't anything be real, so long as we believe it is? Even if it's so wonderful, it can't possibly be true?" I ask Parker in return.

"Okay, Valencia Prime, preach."

I can't help but laugh, and for the first time in a long time, I feel it might be real.

Corvus leads us through the cave, pointing out more rooms like the one Parker stayed in earlier. He admits that he made a mistake by putting Parker in the room that Van normally stays in, and that it may have played a part in Van's severe reaction. The more I learn about Van, the more I begrudgingly understand him.

Corvus explains that he'd given Parker that room as it's the only one that's both free from dirt and has working bathroom. He also says he will warn Van upon his return and have him prepare another room for himself, dismissing Parker when he offers to stay somewhere else. He says Van must give Parker his room, to make up for the rules he broke.

It was another caveat of Hell that surprised Parker and me. As Corvus' guest, Parker now has some protections in place from Corvus and anyone else who enters the cave. Corvus isn't sure who created the rule, but it's one of the only assurances beings in Hell have of safety. Find yourself invited into someone's home as a guest, and you're suddenly safe from any and all ill-will that comes your way from the host or any other in that space.

Politically charged '*guest-friendship*', Corvus explained—a relationship built on a foundation of respect from host to guest, and vice-versa. The rule requires that the host provides any guest with food, adequate accommodation, and—most importantly—safety. Of course, all for a price; guests are expected to bring with them stories and offer to open their home in return. He assures us Hell wasn't always this respectable—that the Devil got the idea from the ancient Greeks.

Either way, the origin of the rules of hospitality don't matter—so long as we understand we're required to abide by them. *Everyone* in Hell. Pretty damn good safety policy if you ask me, though I'm not sure it's such a good thing for Van to owe Parker now. I hope it doesn't create even more resentment between the two. From all I've heard, Van would be the best ally we could have, and I'd rather one of the most powerful beings in Hell have my back instead of feeling worried he's going to stab it.

My favorite thing we encounter during our tour of the cave is the river room, as Corvus calls it. The room consists of large open space that reminds me of my old high school gym but is still rocky, as all areas in the cave are. Filtering out of the far walls, two rivers run through the room, flowing in opposite directions. Above the river on the right, large plumes of steam drift into the air and billow throughout the cavernous space, giving it an almost humid atmosphere. From where we stand, the river looks multicolored—red tinted like the rocks that surround it with bursts of other colors, that flow along the rapids. Pops of vibrant purples and teals swim through the fast-moving current as tiny bubbles of pearlescent white boil along the surface. There's the slightest smell, tainting the air with a tinge of sulfur and something bitter. Minerals breaking down as the hot water rushes past the rocks.

The river on the left flows in a stark contrast to the raging red of the first. Small pops of crystals burst from the river's surface, like snow rising from the surface. The water is clear as ice, transparent like glass. I can see the dark rocks along the bottom, but they don't detract from the sheer frenzy of the waves. Streaks of blue rush through the water, reflecting the light like a cut diamond.

The sound of the rushing water is loud, filling the cave with its tumultuous noise. The place where both rivers meet crackles like an explosion of atoms every second. I watch, transfixed, as snowflakes burst from the waves only to be melted by the humid steam above in a continuous dichotomy of ice and fire.

It's a magical view and in the center of the room, a large crystal-clear pool surrounded by rocks stretches out. And, on either side of the pool, small waterfalls cascade into the water where the rivers meet.

"The two rivers keep the pool at the perfect temperature at all times. And if you wish for the water to be hotter or cooler, you simply drift to one side or the other," Corvus explains as he walks us along the sandy outskirts of the pool. It's surrounded by rocks and boulders of all sizes to prevent anyone from walking too close to the rivers while allowing access to the clear, calm water. "Van and I spent a long time turning this room into the oasis it is, but as I said before, all beautiful things here are dangerous. Whatever you do, *never* get in the rivers, themselves."

With that warning, he leads us from the room and into the rest of the cave. There are a few large storage sections, two rooms for 'containment' as Corvus puts it, and another larger room meant for training. This one is the size of a football field, filled with all kinds of wooden structures. I recognize some of the training equipment, like the weapons and some weights, that look oddly alike what we used at the station, however, much of the other equipment is wildly outside what even my imagination can conjure.

Parker, giddy from the river room, seems to release his inner child in the training room, nearly running off to explore before I'm able to grab the back of his shirt and keep him with us. His excitement is palpable, bursting out of him in uncontained energy, and I'd be lying if I said I wasn't at least a little intrigued as well.

The whole way through our tour of the cave, Corvus' bright lantern showcases everything in clear view. He mentions taking the time to add a lighting system throughout the cave. The prospect of living in Hell becomes less scary by the minute. Corvus has built a home that can ensure our comfort and safety, giving us a place to relax and settle. Sure, there's work to be done—lighting on the top of the list—but I can't help the ideas of decorating that flash through my mind. I couldn't see any personal objects in the cave like Corvus keeps on his bookshelves in the living room, and visions of making this cave a real home for all of us fill my mind.

We have one last thing to deal with before we can settle into our new home.

Our conversation with the Devil, herself.

Chapter 8
Valencia

The trip to what Corvus calls the Devil's palace is like all the other trips he's taken me on before. There's a brief flash of cold nothingness before the world comes back into focus, and the change in scenery is like a shot to the system as light momentarily blinds us. My stomach turns, but, for once, I don't feel nauseated from the trip.

Parker, on the other hand, is again positioned with his hands over knees, losing his stomach off to the side of where we stand. He leans over a bush that I think is supposed to be some kind of animal, but there are too many appendages near its face to tell for sure. Looking around so I'm not watching Parker throw up, I see we're surrounded by a whole garden of trimmed, animal-shaped bushes of all different colors. A few that are green—like what we would see on Earth—but the majority come in a variety of shades. Much like the plants lining the cliff atop Corvus' cave, most of these don't look like anything I've seen before.

The rest of the garden is comprised of rocky walkways and large patches of purple grass-like plants. I'm guessing purple isn't right...it's what my brain can recognize but it's more of a brown, that somehow shines with a violet depth.

Corvus watches Parker for a few beats before heading in the direction of the large house. I guess, given its size, calling it a palace is a decent description. There are multiple wings, each more than one story tall, with more windows than I can count. From our position, I can also see a large staircase leading up to a set of tall double doors made of rock and stone—though, these seem to be manufactured, as opposed to the rough, natural look Corvus' home has. There's a square-like structure to the palaces overall shape, but between intricate wrought-iron balconies and wooden window overhangs, covered in brightly-colored plants, there's an elegance and beauty to it. All the windows are dark, and no light shines from within, but the glass seems to sparkle in the oddly gray light.

That's where Corvus now heads, the red gravel path quietly crunching beneath his black boots. I pat Parker on the back before pulling his shoulders up and dragging him along beside me.

"How are you not sick," he asks while wiping his face with the back of his flannel sleeve.

"You get used to traveling that way. It only took me a few times before I was no longer throwing up."

"Well, that can't come soon enough," he mutters, a slightly green pallor remaining on his face.

We both turn quiet as we meet Corvus at the top of the steps where he waits, facing the garden instead of at the doors.

"Just know, everything you say from here on out will spread like wild-fire—and there won't be a creature or demon in Hell that doesn't hear about our conversation. If you wish to lie, make sure it's a damn good one. You don't want to find out what happens if someone catches you telling it," Corvus tells us in a hushed tone. If it's true that our conversations will be heard, surely someone has already heard us? I can't see anyone else in the garden with us or in the windows that look out of the hidden rooms inside the palace, but I'm starting to think that seeing isn't all that's required for believing.

With everything that's happened and everything that I've learned, invisibility doesn't seem all that farfetched.

Parker nods his head, once again choosing to remain quiet. I mimic him, nodding as well. Satisfied with our acknowledgement, Corvus finally turns and heads into the palace.

Inside is nothing like I expected. Considering the opulence of the gardens, I'd expected a more luxurious atmosphere to the interiors, but it's decorated no differently than a modern hotel. One of the medium-range ones, even. Not too high class, a little bland, and mostly white overall.

I don't know why, but I expected to see more of the homeliness like there'd been in the room when I'd first met the Devil. Now *that* room had personality. It was lived in. *Loved.*

This space feels like whoever lives here hasn't cared to add their personal touch to the space. And all *white*? I can't help but feel like it's the strangest color option imaginable. It's not that I thought there would be blood coating the walls, but I guess I expected a darker, more... spooky look.

There's so much to the Devil to be learned, yet how can anyone decipher her behavior if she hides her true self from everyone?

These thoughts continue to swirl around my head as Corvus leads us through one bland hallway after another. It feels like entire minutes tick by, but logically, I know it has to have been much shorter. The whole time we walk, we don't see another soul. No service staff, no guests—no one but the three of us.

I'm not sure if this is comforting or adds to my apprehension.

We take a sharp turn around a corner and suddenly, the bland white hallway opens up to a large ballroom. Green and beige mosaic tiles stretch across the floor in front of us. Long sheer curtains hang from the tall ceilings, and the windows on our left are full of beautiful glass artwork. The light from outside shines through the colored glass, staining the room in a rainbow of color.

There are paintings covering nearly every wall, barely leaving an inch of white between them, and the bright light illuminates the different sizes and styles of all the artwork. There are large Renaissance portraits, abstracts full of color and movement, realism showcasing dramatic scenes, and even full-bodied sculptures that sit on shelves hanging from the walls. Some paintings have large ornate frames and some paintings are without. There's even a small sticky note tacked to the wall in the space between two abstracts. I can't see what's on the note from here, but I can tell a scrawling script covers the bright pink surface.

My eyes quickly track the wonders on the walls before settling on the most magnificent piece in the room. In the center is a large marble sculpture of two men battling. I have to tip my head back to see it in its entirety. Stone seems to barely brush the dark ceiling above, where a ring of modern lights shine down.

Both creatures have wings, and their naked, masculine bodies are on full display—large and commanding, despite being in a room full of amazing art. One creature has wings made of feathers that look soft to the touch despite being made of stone. His head is adorned with a haloed crown. Long hair seems to flow in a nonexistent wind and a wavy sword is clutched in his fist, raised high in the air. His face is stoic as he looms over the other creature—as if this battle means nothing to him.

The second creature's wings are leatherier in appearance, and it's impressive that the artist was able to show the difference between the two textures. His face is full of emotion, brows tipped down in frustration, mouth gaped in a wail. Horns burst from a head of wavy hair, and a spiked tail wraps around his muscular thigh. He's falling backwards as if having tipped over an unseen edge.

Stepping around Corvus, I approach the sculpture to get a closer look, drawn to its beauty and quietly subversive qualities. They have their battle on top of a rock, much like what I've now seen showcased all over Hell. The creature with the horns has a set of chains wrapped around his torso and one of his arms—and though some links appear to be broken, they clearly prevent him from defending himself from what appears to be a deadly blow dealt by the other. His free hand is outstretched, fingers spread wide as if in a plea for mercy.

Neither wears clothes, their bodies covered in muscle, practically rippling with it. The strength they possess is visible even in this still form. Striations of muscle strain in all directions. They have muscle groups I didn't even know existed. They're both uncovered, however, and there are no stone penises to distract from the story they're trying to tell, which slightly surprises me. I feel like nakedness is probably celebrated in Hell.

As I breathe in the scene, I note that there is a clear winner—though I wonder more and more if I like or hate the answer.

"This is the very history of this realm, trapped in stone. It is my favorite piece I own." A silky smooth voice says from the other side of the sculpture.

I hear one of the guys hiss a breath between their teeth as the person walks around the statue to stand beside me. Neither of them comments, filling the silence with their heavy breaths. I turn to look at the newcomer but quickly look away. It's the same as before—just like the first time I met the Devil. Whenever I try to focus on her, the image of a man and then a woman flash so fast they blur together. I'm unable to concentrate on any of the details without a sharp ache beginning to pound in my head. Slowly, I learn that if I look away from her, just off to the side, the pain dissipates and I'm able to see a somewhat clearer-but-still-blurry image.

In this form, he's the Devil I expected. A tall man, still in what I assume is a suit, with a lazy and calm demeanor. He holds his hands in his pocket, as if this were any old art room, and we're visiting on some random day. This version of the Devil is as seductive as he is allusive; however, the female version of the Devil is no less dangerous despite the secrets she's allowed me to learn. I struggle to connect the two in my head, yet they still don't seem like the same person.

It throws me for a second, and I find myself at a loss for words. No one else speaks, so we all wait in silence. My eyes are continually drawn back to the statue, trapped by the story it tells, until my brain finally catches up to what the Devil said when she first showed up.

"It's beautiful," I finally return, though I don't look in her direction. Looking at the statue again, I'm able to notice even smaller details like how the horned figure also has a spiked bracelet around his ankle that seems to dig painfully into his skin. There's a scaled snake that wraps around the base, hiding within the holes of the rock. It takes me a second to find its head, latched into the back of the one with the horn's knee.

"I'm sure at some point I thought it was beautiful. Now all I feel is anger," the Devil responds, the sound of his voice so masculine and confusing. I remember thinking the female Devil's voice was pure lust, yet it now seems no different to a normal man's I may cross on the street. It must be a part of the glamor, yet I'm still confused why she chose to reveal her true self to me. Sure, looking at her causes me discomfort when she's glamoured like she is now, but I'm sure she could've explained that away. The moment I first laid eyes on her, and that headache blasted through my brain, she gave herself away without a second thought. Even Greta was surprised. *Worried*. I'm not sure I'll ever know why she did it or why I've kept her secret.

"If it's your history, then I can see why you'd be angry." I look at the chains again, noticing that even though links are broken, there is no doubt that they keep their captive trapped.

"My history," the Devil hums, voice full of some dark emotion I can't decipher. "What part do you think causes that anger?" The Devil asks, stepping a little closer until we're nearly shoulder-to-shoulder. A deep growl rumbles through the room, but we both ignore it. Corvus is clearly unhappy with the proximity, but I trust him. He wouldn't let anything harm me—not even the Devil.

"At first, I thought the chains were the worst part. To be trapped and helpless, unable to fight or defend yourself to the best of your ability," I respond quietly, feeling the chains wrapping around me even as I look at them. The Devil hums in response but waits for me to continue. "But, now that I've looked longer, I realize the real bitch of it is the snake, striking from beneath. An unseen adversary whom you would have never thought to defend against in the first place." I talk to the Devil as if she is one of the men in the sculpture, but I know that neither is the right gender to accurately portray the Devil, herself, so it must be a representation.

"Very astute." A light pitch to the otherwise masculine voice. It's like, for a second, her true self shined through. "And do you know why I showcase this piece?"

I feel like I know, but I don't want to get the wrong answer, so I shake my head.

"Because it is a reminder that no matter what I do to prevent the angels from coming to Hell and wreaking havoc across my realm, it has always been one of my own to betray me." The words are cutting, edged in emotion so that I can hear pain in them—the pain endured at each betrayal.

"If you're in need of some allies, I know a few loyal people who you could ask." Parker's voice shocks me so much I jump slightly before turning and giving him a wide-eyed glance.

He and Corvus have been silent through this whole conversation, observing more than participating, but I can't know how the Devil will react to a human interrupting our conversation. Fear starts to build in my chest, causing an uncomfortable stitch in my side with each breath.

Before I can panic for too long, the Devil responds, "Loyal allies? Coming from a human?"

It's not like the Devil laughs directly in Parker's face, but I think the sarcasm in the masculine tone is a dead giveaway of their doubt.

"You think because I'm human, I'm incapable of being loyal?" he asks, voice not showing one ounce of fear—which would surprise me less if it was the Devil's female version he was talking to, but as far as I am aware, he's seeing a man. A well-dressed man, and *attractive* if I had to guess. But Parker doesn't back down from his question, looking into the Devil's eyes with a surety I didn't know he possessed.

The Devil briefly looks at me before settling back on Parker. I can't see the expression on his face with how blurry he is when disguised as a man, but he hasn't killed Parker outright yet, so I just have to hope that means he's not going to.

"I guess you're right. I should not judge you based on the millions of humans who have come before you. I should let you prove yourself!" The Devil declares with a gleeful tone. I know whatever comes next is unlikely to be good. Corvus quietly groans behind me, which just proves my thought even more.

"Devious allies *is* something I am having a problem with right now. There seems to be a very naughty demon out there, taking orders from someone other than me—which just won't do. So, since you're so eager to be trusted, I will let you find this demon and bring him to me for questioning. How does that sound?" The Devil raises a brow at Parker, and though it sounds easy enough—especially with it being three against one—I open my mouth to disagree on his behalf.

"What is the demon's name?" Corvus responds, forcing me to snap my mouth shut and withhold my refusal.

I can hear the taunting laugh in the Devil's voice. "Davgus."

The name means nothing to me, but when I look at Corvus to gauge his reaction, his eyes are wide. However, he doesn't refuse right away. Whoever this demon is, it must be someone Corvus thinks we're capable of handling, and if this little mission gets Parker on the Devil's good side, then I guess it's not entirely a bad thing.

"Perfect, it's settled," Parker confidently states. "We find this demon for you, and you..."

"I what?" The Devil asks him, clearly confused.

"You will accept our loyalty and then..."

Each time Parker pauses, a sentence bleeding off into a questioning silence, I realize he's waiting for the Devil to admit what he will do in return for us. It's a bold tactic, though not unexpected from him.

"Oh, I see. Yes, you will bring me this demon to prove your loyalty and in return, I won't kill you the next time you step foot in my palace." With a flourished movement that looks something akin a mock curtsey, the Devil turns and promptly disappears.

I stand frozen until we're once more in silence, then turn to Parker to reprimand him—but Corvus catches my shoulders, shakes his head and points to his ears to remind me that anything we say can and will be spread throughout Hell. So, I grit my teeth and give Parker a pointed look before following Corvus. It takes much less time than before, and when we get to the gardens, my mind is so full of toxic possibilities that I remain silent until we're once again back in Corvus' home.

CHAPTER 9

VALENCIA

"WHAT THE FUCK WERE you thinking!" I holler at Parker as soon as we make through the door. The fire is still going in the hearth and the room is comfortable—but nothing seems to ease the fear still churning inside me.

"I was thinking that he was clearly leading the conversation to that exact outcome, and I just moved it along faster," he grumbles, arms and hands held out to the side.

I pinch the bridge of my nose. "Parker, the Devil wasn't giving out death threats until after you chimed in," I remind him.

"Yeah, but we expected that anyway. He's the Devil, so, like, we're not all that surprised about that, right?" he exclaims as if his logic makes all the sense in the world. And, I guess in a way, it does.

Clearly, Parker needs a lesson in self-preservation but I won't worry about that now. The mission has already started, and it's too late to turn back.

"Okay, who is this demon, Davgus, and why does the Devil want him?" I ask Corvus.

He's sitting quietly on one of the couches, watching Parker and I argue. Somehow, he's managed to dress down in the little time we've been back. No longer is he wearing dark jeans and a black, long-sleeve top; now he wears dark lounge pants, no shoes, and a comfy-looking tank top that hangs loosely from his large body. I have to remind myself that it would be most inappropriate if I jumped onto his lap right now and devoured him, but it takes some strength to hold myself back.

There's a look on his face—a knowing look—as if he knows what I'm thinking and feels the same way. There's also something else, a look that's more guarded—and I'm not entirely sure what it means, but it fills my gut with a sour feeling.

"Davgus is... a demon who is mostly known for being a conniving asshole, who will do anything to anyone to gain power."

"Oh, big surprise," Parker murmurs, throwing himself onto the large leather chair, a petulant look on his face.

"And why is the Devil sending us to capture a demon who is known for being a backstabber?" Corvus flinches slightly, which only racks up my suspicions even more. "What do you know?" I demand, watching as his body relaxes while his eyes still hold onto something. Something he isn't telling me.

"The sooner we get this demon to the Devil, the sooner we can distance ourselves from any more of the Devil's attention. First priority, I need to get Van here so he can start training you. I will also need his help preparing to hunt Davgus." Corvus blatantly ignores my last question. Unease starts to unfurl within me but I can't afford to live in doubt, so for now, I have to trust his judgment.

"How do you plan to get Van here *and* convince him to not try and kill Parker again?" I rest my hands on my hips, still too wired to sit.

"The first part will be easy. I imagine he is already on his way back. The second part, while not so easy, will be taken care of," Corvus replies.

"So, how many times will I have to worry about him trying to kill Parker?"

Corvus looks at me quietly for a beat before stating, "Near zero."

"*Near* zero? As in, there *will* be a few times? Goodness gracious, I'm fucked," Parker laughs with true humor, but I can see the warning hints of stress as he rubs his hand through his hair.

"Like I said, so long as you're never alone with him, you won't have to worry about it," Corvus urges, but for the first time, I see a desperation in him that I haven't before. I'm reminded that Van is Corvus' best friend, and they've spent many more years together than we have. Though how Van reacted irritates me, I understand. And, with that understanding comes the conclusion that I need to try and make this work for everyone, because I have a feeling—sooner than later—we're all going to need each other. Van included.

"We will make it work, Corvus. I know you will keep Parker safe, and Van is your friend, so we will do what we can to keep him safe, too," I interject, walking around to the back of the couch he sits on. He watches my every move until he no longer can.

In the kitchen, I search around before finding the small pocket in the wall I saw him use earlier in the night and pull out a couple of cold beers from a small flow of freezing cold water. They're domestic, a brand I'm used to—the same tan can and red lettering I've seen all over Montana. I bring the cans, handing one to each of them, before settling into the couch beside Parker. They both nod their heads in thanks, quietly enjoying the first cold sips.

"Van is important to you, so he's important to us. We will do what we can to make his stay here as painless as possible. But we need to know what will trigger him, or at least some sense of his reason for hating Parker as much as he does." I'm so out of my depth in this realm that it's a waste of energy to try and decipher the actions of a species I know nothing about, but I try, nonetheless. "If you can't tell us his story, that's okay, but at least tell us *something* about him so we're not going into this blind."

Corvus sighs, taking a long drink. "Van is from a completely different realm to Hell. It's called Sycoraxia. In his realm lives all kinds of species, but the primary two are the Fae—like Van—and humans. Before you freak out, these humans are not like the humans on Earth, not anymore at least. They're a dark and corrupted version of your species. Long ago, when your ancestors first found that realm, they indulged in its grandeur but became greedy when the Fae demanded they conserve their consumption of the realm's limited resources. Deadly battles broke out, and for many years, the two species were caught in a very perilous war. Van was a part of that war, suffered because of it, and following this, decided that Hell is the better place to be and refuses to ever go back."

"Wow, humans ruining it for the rest of us, big surprise," Parker says. He's not wrong, we've both seen what can happen when humans embrace their darker sides. Now knowing more of the story, I don't blame Van for leaving.

"It must've been bad if Hell is the better option," I murmur. I've not been here long, but I already can see how his choice must mean Van's home *really* sucked.

"For him, the worst," Corvus states quietly.

There's such a profound note to that statement. That, for at least one person, Hell may be a place of solace—a refuge from the travesties they've already been through. As impossible as it seems, it reminds us that every situation is different, and we can never judge someone based on purely our own experiences. So, this is more than a simple hatred of humans that Van's dealing with; there's a lot of history there. I rub a hand across my forehead. How can we make all of this easy for everyone involved?

"This doesn't make things any easier." I hate to complain, but things are more complicated than ever.

Corvus opens his mouth to respond, but a crash draws our attention to the front door, and we turn as Van's tall body stumbles through the door before he turns and promptly slams it behind him. He puts one hand against the patterned wood and breathes deeply for a few seconds. His clothes are tattered, he's covered in blood, and I can see a few deep cuts running along his legs and arms.

"What the fuck, Van?" Corvus snaps, hopping up from his spot and rushing towards him.

Van stands abruptly, and side steps Corvus before heading straight for Parker and me. I jump up as well, taking a small step in front of Parker. It's a pointless move, I already know I'm no match for him, but it's instinctual.

Van stops directly in front of me. I shudder against the urge to cower, his frame tall and imposing, but also much less menacing than before, despite all the blood. His expression is more serene this time, as if he's no longer consumed by the wild rage he felt earlier.

"My lady, the tongues of all who despise you so far. They will not be able to talk badly about you again. I cannot give you my own tongue, so I gave you three others. I should not have said those things." Van responds in a respectful tone.

Before I can react to that statement, Van reaches out, holding a small leather bag up to me, a beseeching look in his eyes.

A dark liquid drips from the bottom of the bag, a morbidly silent gesture. I want to refuse, because its *tongues*, but this is a creature unlike myself—from a place I've never been to—and maybe, in his culture, this gesture would be received with the utmost regard. So, despite the curling in my stomach, I lightly grab the bag from his grasp.

"Thank—"

He brings up a tanned hand and swipes in a cutting motion. "Do not thank me. To offer your gratitude would put you in my debt, and we will be better suited on even ground. In my culture, gratitude is implied."

I nod, a smile on my face. Not that I know what the fuck to do with a bag of tongues or how he even found those who were talking badly about me. Regardless, though gruesome, it's a kind gesture.

Van nods in return before stepping to the side and casting a dark look at Parker, who stands behind me. His eyes are clouded, as if shadows bleed from his soul. A vein starts to bulge in his forehead. I pray he doesn't freak out because I don't want to have to use my new gift as a weapon.

"For you, *Rat,*" Van snarls, the words more a growl than speech. He slowly raises a bloodied object and offers it to Parker. Unlike what he gave to me, this is not covered in a nice leather bag and it still has fur on it, though most of it is just chunks of meat and cartilage. Blood drains from my face and I grow hot. What the fuck is it with this guy and body parts?

Parker, bless him, grabs the dangling body part without hesitation, nodding his head with a smile. I can't imagine how gross the chunky bits of bloody meat must feel in his hand. Van cants his head to the side as if surprised by Parker's reaction.

"It is the windpipe of a bone rat that annoyed me. To remind you of what you are and how I chose to not rip your throat out when I had the chance." By this point, Van is little more than a snarling beast, and I'm starting to wonder if Parker's lack of reaction is throwing the Fae off, so he's trying to get a reaction with his words.

Parker just laughs, as if it's truly funny that he was just given a gift of some poor creature's *windpipe,* and that he should be thankful that windpipe isn't his.

Van jerks at the sound, taken aback. With one last growl, he storms off into the deeper parts of the cave.

Chapter 10

Corvus

"Well, considering the options, I feel like that went fairly well," I scoff, stepping to Valencia's side and taking the bag of tongues out of her hand. I lightly kiss the side of her head, taking a second to breathe her in. Like this, I can smell her smoky, citrusy scent but as soon as I step away, the smell of demons assaults my senses once more. Whoever Van silenced must've been terrified, because I can still smell their fear permeating from the little leather bag.

I'm not sure what I'm going to do with them. Throwing them away would be an insult to Van, but it's not like I want them stinking up my cave. Maybe I can hang them on a string outside the door or something. For now, I'll toss them in one of the cold stores and deal with them later.

"So, what should I do with mine?" Parker asks, lifting the still-bloody windpipe Van gave him. He's grimacing now in place of the smile he wore earlier. I've got to give it to him, to accept such a gift with gratitude, even when Van was trying to instigate a fight, was impressive.

"We can't throw them away, so I will have to put them in cold storage until we can find a home for them." I reach out to take the windpipe from him, but he pulls it away at the last second.

"In that case, I think I will keep it in my room as a reminder. Thankfully, it doesn't smell bad," he responds, though still makes a face. I can see that some chunks of meat have slipped between his fingers, and though the blood doesn't drip from it anymore, his hand is still covered in gore. "Though, maybe I could get a nice leather bag for it like Val's has?"

I laugh. "Yeah, I think I can do that at least."

I head to the kitchen and grab a leather bag out of a large cabinet that's built into the rock wall. Handing it to Parker, I watch as he stuffs the offending body part into the bag and seals it tight with the leather straps attached at the top.

Van's behavior must seem strange to them. Van is a creature of nature, and where he's from, such gifts would show his prowess and capabilities to defeat enemies and provide meat. In his culture, they would be coveted gifts—yet Val and Parker likely see them as dismemberment, items taken from some poor unfortunate soul.

Van is most likely in my training room, destroying all of my innocent training dummies right now.

"You guys stay here for a bit and let me go talk to him, then we will all start tomorrow fresh. Training starts in the morning, so you'll want to be rested," I advise, knowing there's no way they're truly ready for what Van and I are going to put them through.

"Parker will be fine while we sleep?" Valencia asks, clearly wondering if Van will be able to control himself while everyone is asleep.

"Parker will be fine, but that's why I need to talk to Van," I encourage, wanting to get to Van sooner rather than later to get ahead of his anger.

"Not to be that guy, but what do we do about food? I mean, I'm oddly not very hungry, but I feel like it's been a long time since I last ate and I don't want to wake up and train on an empty stomach." Parker snoops through my open cabinet, thumbing through the various bags and jars, but his focus is on me.

"Yeah, it's weird, I'm not really that hungry either, but I literally haven't eaten in, like, 24 hours," Valencia responds, her eyebrows dipped down in confusion.

Shit, what a crap host I am. I've been so concerned with everything going on that I hadn't thought to feed them. "Time moves differently in Hell. Even though it seems like a lot of time has passed, maybe it actually hasn't. When it comes to stuff like this, just listen to your body. If you're hungry, I have some cold meats and cheese that should be pretty similar to what you're used to on Earth. Tomorrow, after we train, we will think of some better food options for you guys."

I lead them to the other side of the kitchen and show them where the food is kept. The cold stuff, like meats and cheeses, sit on shelves in the same pocket I store beer. The ice-cold water from the river flows through the pocket, making the stone cold enough to keep the whole pocket cool. It's not cool enough to freeze without being directly in the water, but it works just as well as a refrigerator would on Earth. It's easier to give them this now, knowing they'll most likely enjoy it, than try and decipher which of the other foods they'll prefer.

I grab the meat and cheese and set it on the counter. "The meat is from an animal here in Hell that is similar to a cow. The cheese is from the same animal, but I can't promise it will taste like the cheese you're used to. You guys snack, and I'll go deal with Van."

I provide them with a small board to eat off of and a couple strips of fabric for napkins before leaving them to it. Now I can deal with the much bigger problem of figuring out how to manage Van's outrage.

***

As expected, I find Van in the training room, in the middle of destroying one of the training dummies. He hits it repeatedly with two wooden batons and both straw and feathers fly with each hit. A loud *thwack* echoes throughout the room.

I approach him slowly, taking a deep breath. I know what's coming.

With a growl, he turns my way, one wooden baton up in the air, poised for attack. He pauses, ready for a fight, and I walk over to one of the weapons racks, grabbing my own pair of batons.

"Five minutes, that's all you get, and then we need to talk." I turn to him and settle into my own fighting stance. He doesn't give me a second to rest before he charges, deadly intention in his eyes.

We battle for dominance every second of the five-minute fight. He's scrupulous in all his tactics, yet his face is contorted in anger. The vein on the side of his neck pulses wildly. There isn't a drop of sweat on his body from exertion, yet his heart is racing and he grunts with each impact, teeth gritted so tightly, I fear his jaw might break. There is no calm in his flashing green eyes, just anxiety and fear.

My side aches from the heavy blow to my ribs he landed early into the fight. He limps slightly on his left leg, clearly no better off than I am after I slammed my foot into his knee. It's like a twirling dance, and from the outside, maybe that's exactly how it looks. Choreographed. Neither of us truly intends to hurt the other—just to expel some energy. And, in Van's case, perhaps to release some emotional tension. This is also retribution for having put him in this position in the first place. So, I fight without complaint, suffering through each shot he gives. Once this fight is over, we will be even, and I will be much more likely to successfully convince him to leave Parker alone.

We both breathe heavily, fighting this intensely is not easy, and he's not been holding back. The five minutes are coming to an end soon; only seconds remain, so he doubles his efforts. The wooden batons fly through the air so fast that I can hear them whistle as they fly by my head, and I jump to the side to avoid a vicious strike to the temple that would've definitely knocked me out.

Irritated that he's taking this so seriously, I kick out at his injured knee. He expects it, jumping back slightly, but his left arm becomes unguarded from the move. Lightning fast, I swing my baton, smacking it into his wrist and forcing him to drop it to the ground. Our rules when we fight are always the same: never try to *actually* kill each other, if you get knocked out, you lose. If your weapon hits the floor, you can't pick it back up.

That's all we really care about, so with a growl, he steps over the lost baton and charges one last time. Because he's fighting with pure emotion, he's sloppy, and I'm able to crouch down and flip him over top of me. He lands on the ground with a loud *thud,* and the air wheezes out of his lungs.

He lies still and quiet as his breathing slowly returns to normal. When he opens his eyes to look at me the vicious animal is no longer present; only my best friend remains.

"I am doomed to never escape these vile creatures," he murmurs, staring at the ceiling above us. He looks an absolute mess. His clothes are still all torn, the cuts on his arms and legs are red and, though they're now healing, look like they must've hurt.

"Parker is not like the Sycoraxian humans, Van. You've got to give him a chance." I slowly sit on the hard ground beside him. We've been through so much over the years that it truly pains me to be the cause of his anguish, but I'm stuck, and the only way I can see us getting out of this is if Van learns that Parker isn't his enemy.

"I know this, yet I find it extremely difficult to look at his face and not see theirs looking back at me." He lies so still, his arms down by his sides as he focuses on the ceiling. His breathing is now soft and even, no sign of the fight we just had left.

"Then close your eyes."

"It is not that easy, and you know it. I can *smell* him. It is like every movement he makes assaults my senses, and I am unable to escape it."

"I will get him to shower in some scent blocker," I offer. It honestly isn't a bad idea anyway, and I might have some stored in the cave.

"That would... help," he hesitates.

Part of me wonders if he even *wants* to get over his hatred for humans, or if it's been so long, it's easier to stay this way than it is to change.

"We need to train them, starting as soon as they wake up. You can train Valencia. She needs help with controlling her powers. I will train Parker." It's a solid plan, and ultimately what we would be doing even if Van didn't have an issue with Parker. He is far more knowledgeable about combat training using powers. Though I am considered a highly powerful demon, most of my power relates to realm travel and the ability to use my familiar form. I can use fire in combat, but it's taxing. Overall, I'm better with my fists and weapons. Van, on the other hand, has a plethora of combat-ready powers he's able to use at will, which makes him the perfect trainer to help Valencia learn about her own abilities.

"I will train your mate," he agrees and finally sits up, his dark hair hanging down his back, nearly touching the ground.

I stand and reach out a hand to him to help him up as well. He takes it and unfolds his tall body from the floor. His movements, even when he is still, are lethal.

"I'm not going to have to worry about you while we're sleeping am I?" I question, wanting to ensure he's not thinking irrationally before I take off to send Parker to bed and get Valencia into mine. My body begins to buzz with heat at the thought.

Van curls his top lip in anger but says, "I will go wash in the pool and prepare myself a room while you all *rest*. The human is not in danger from me while we are here in this cave." With a soft pat on my shoulder, he calmly walks out of the training room and heads towards the river room.

Van is incapable of lying, so if he says Parker is not in danger here, then he's telling the truth. It didn't escape me his assurance of safety seemed to only extend to inside these rocky walls. Who knows what will happen once we leave?

Whatever happens, we will deal with it as it comes.

***

I find Valencia and Parker talking animatedly about some firefight they must've done. Both use their hands and arms to tell their versions, each growing excited. They laugh simultaneously; the combined sound is something to cherish. I know having Parker here in Hell isn't going to be easy, but the happiness that he brings her makes it worth it.

I silently walk towards them but it's no use, she senses my presence when I'm a couple feet away and turns her bright blue eyes on me, a smile still on her face.

"Goodness, you trying to scare me to death?" she asks with a laugh, a hand on her chest in mock fear.

"If I wanted you dead, you would've already been *devoured*, Kitten," I purr at her, my intense lust bleeding into my tone.

"*Annnd* that's my cue!" Parker exclaims as he gets up off the couch, picking up one of the Hell-sands lanterns from the side table. "Now, just light this baby, and I'll be on my way."

"You remember how to get back to your room?" I ask incredulously. I've only shown him the way twice—and once was in the pitch black, so there's no way he was able to see where he was going that first round.

"Oh yeah, for sure. I have a knack for navigation. If I've seen it once, I can usually get there again."

"Interesting. Well, just don't wonder, Van is in the rivers room, so go straight to your room. And don't wonder throughout the night, I'll be—"

"Oh you don't have to explain to me, I really *don't* need to know what you'll be doing. So, just light my little thingy, and we're good," Parker laughs, giving a red-faced Valencia a teasing look.

I send a flicker of a flame to his lantern, casting bright light into the cozy living room. He nods his thanks and heads off into the cave without another word.

"Are we going to bed, too?" Valencia asks.

"I'm tempted to bend you over this couch and see how far this cute little blush goes," I breathe in her scent and drag a fingertip down the side of her neck to the collar of her shirt, tipping it slightly under the edge.

She sucks in a gasp but pulls away. "That will not be happening. Let's go to your room if you're going to be a needy animal." With that, she starts to walk in the direction Parker went but she can't hide her arousal from me, I can smell it on her—how wet she's getting at just the thought of me taking her right here in the living room, where anyone could see.

With a growl and a stiff cock, I follow her like a love-sick dog.

CHAPTER II
VALENCIA

A WARM BODY IS tucked into the bed beside me, and though I wish to cuddle into him deeper, nature calls. He stirs as I get up, but I rush to the bathroom before he can stop me, wanting to take a second for myself. There's no door, just a flap of fabric, but despite expectations, it blocks out all of the sound from the other room.

After going to the bathroom, I quietly undress and flip the switch on the wall that Corvus said controls the water.

Water so cold you would think it was ice shot out of the showerhead so fast, I didn't have time to get out of the way. "Ah!" I quietly screech in surprise as I flip the switch back off. The left side of my body feels frozen.

"You have to turn them both on for warm water," Corvus laughs from the doorway.

I just groan in response and switch both nozzles this time before stepping into the water. It's blissfully warm, but I'm looking for scorching hot, so I slowly turn the cold side off until I'm satisfied with the temperature. A content sigh escapes me as I let the hot water wash over my head and down the rest of my body.

Corvus makes more noise as he ambles around the bathroom, doing whatever he does for a morning routine. Since there's no shower curtain for privacy, I just close my eyes to give him some space and settle into the hot water. I just need a second to wrap my brain around everything that's happened so far.

There are no clocks here, so I have no idea what time of day it is. It's nice though, getting away from the oppression that is constantly checking a clock. There's a freedom to it. It's not that we don't have a ton to do—because I can feel the never-ending to-do list already starting to weigh on my shoulders—but we at least don't have a time-schedule we have to follow.

My stomach growls, reminding me that the snacks we had last night, though surprisingly good, won't be enough to sustain me for a long time. Breakfast is definitely top of the list. Though, I imagine the cinnamon rolls I'm craving are probably unlikely.

Cold fingers wrap around my biceps and draw me into a chilly chest. I squirm against the hold. "Let me go! You're a damn ice cube!"

He chuckles before switching our places, taking my spot in the hot water.

"Corvus, I wasn't done!" I pout, already feeling a chill from being outside of the water.

"Don't be a water hog," he smirks before ducking his head back under the water. I roll my eyes, but he misses it.

His dark hair flattens against his head while big rivulets roll down his body. His arm stretches high, causing his abs and biceps to bulge. I quickly grab a bar of soap out of one of the wall pockets and start actively showering. Ogling him is fun, but there's no time for what would come next.

A low growl rumbles from him, drawing my eyes away from my legs and back up to his face. The heat in the look does plenty to warm me right back up, and I set the bar of soap back down, bringing my sudsy hands up to my body.

I've changed my mind. With a demon this hot, there's *always* time.

I slowly drag my fingers through the suds on my stomach, inching towards my breasts. My nipples peak with desire as I get closer.

He stands, staring at me with liquid brown eyes that have darkened with each movement. His body visibly strains as he holds himself back, muscles rippled with veins, heaving under the hot water stream. Droplets glide down his chest and thighs, catching in the valleys of his abs and Adonis belt. I bite my lip to keep my own moan in as his body captivates me.

"I said I wanted to hear every single one, and I meant. If you're moaning for me, you're going to let me hear it," Corvus states as he reaches forward and releases my lip from my teeth with his thumb. Our eyes meet once again as he pulls me closer by my chin. "The only moans I shouldn't hear are the ones you make when you're choking on a mouth full of my cock."

I moan out loud at his words as the implications of them send fire into my belly. My clit slowly starts to throb, and I know if he pulls away now, I'll be taking matters into my own hands.

"You think you can make me choke?" I ask with an arched brow. Funny thing is, we *both* know he can. I think he's got enough going on down there, my *vagina* choked on him.

"You little brat." His other hand snaps out and grips the hair at the back of my neck while simultaneously tapping my ankle with one of his feet. "Get on your knees then, if you're so eager."

"The rocks are cold," I pout. It wouldn't matter if this room was made of ice, I'd still be burning with desire for him, but I don't want to give that away.

"You should've thought of that before you decided to taunt me." He takes a deep breath, leaning in so close our lips almost touch. "You can either get on your knees, or I can bend you over and force it down your throat."

He stands tall and looks down at me expectantly.

"Guess you'll have to make me, then," I tease, pulling against the grip he has on my hair until I feel it sting, sending liquid fire through my body.

Without comment, he pushes my head down and presses against the back where he still has a firm grip on my hair. I catch myself on his thighs, my hands slipping down them a bit, and grip him tighter. My fingertips dig into the thick muscle to hold myself up.

He grips the shaft of his cock and directs it toward my face, the soft, velvety tip brushing against my cheek. I open my mouth but he doesn't move and continues to brush it softly against my lips. I nearly groan in pleasure at the connection.

"Stick out your tongue."

I listen, instantly sticking out my tongue as far as it will go. When he brushes his tip against it, I can taste the slightly salty precum that has gathered at the tip, and his taste makes me ravenous. I press forward to take more of him into my mouth.

"Not yet, baby. You gotta warm up to it," he slowly drives forward, the tip just barely passing my lips, and I don't have enough time to savor it before he's pulling back out. Too eager to wait for when he thinks I'm ready, I shift my body at the same time he slowly thrusts forward, forcing him into my mouth nearly to the back of my throat.

"Holy shit, woman," he curses as he forces his hips back a bit so I can breathe.

I squeeze his legs even tighter, following him and forcing more into my mouth. It's tough since he's not only long but thick. I can feel the skin on my cheeks stretching almost painfully but I ignore it and press for even more. I don't want more air; I want more of his cock, my mind now completely taken over by the need to please him.

Finally overwhelmed by his own desire, he surges forward far enough that he's caught in the back of my throat and can go no further. I hum in pleasure at finally getting what I want, but it's short-lived when he starts pulling back again. Before I can demand more, he thrusts forward, finally choking me just like he promised.

"You. Don't. Listen," he hisses under his breath, each word exaggerated by a harsh thrust of his hips. I try to keep up with his thrusts, but he's definitely in control now, and I am merely here to give him a hole to fuck.

And he *fucks*. It's dirty and sexy in the best ways. The water from the shower, now blisteringly hot against my feverish skin, washes over my hands on his thighs and brushes my face each time I'm pressed against him. His hand still holds my hair in place, and I'm not able to move very far unless I'm willing to rip some of it out—and part of me is afraid I'm consumed with so much pleasure, I wouldn't mind if he accidentally pulled too tight.

Corvus' hips stutter, a low growl echoing around the rocky room, but he doesn't stop and keeps thrusting hard and deep as if to prove a point with each one. Drool drips from my mouth, making a mess of my face, but it makes it easier for him to slide all the way back. An especially deep thrust slides down my throat, forcing it open and allowing him to reach parts of me no one has ever touched.

I've always enjoyed this part of foreplay—how his hot skin glides across my wet tongue, and pressure builds in my throat as I contract around him. I can't help but moan at the intense sensations, mouth full of his salty taste. He's in control, owning my mouth with his whole body, yet we both know I'm the one who's really in control of this pleasure. Not even being a powerful demon could save him from my teeth if I wished.

I opened my mouth willingly because I love the feeling of his thick veins rubbing inside my sensitive mouth. I love the intensity—the danger as he takes away my air.

The distorted sounds of a gurgled choke replaces his moans, and my body tenses from the lack of air. My eyes roll into the back of my head, and he pauses for a second before pulling back enough to let me suck a gasp of air in through my nose.

"Finally," he groans. "You did so good, choking for me," he praises, a smile in his voice. I can't see his face from this angle, but it makes me hotter to know he's enjoying this as much as I am.

He wraps his other hand around my throat, tilting to the side a bit so he can wrap all four fingers around it. I think he's going to squeeze and choke me more, but he just keeps his hand there. A few moans later, I realize he can feel himself deep in my throat, and I nearly come from the thought alone. I swallow as best I can despite him still thrusting into my mouth, wanting to moan but not being able to.

His skin is hot against my lips making it easier for him to slide in and out despite the mess. My jaw is starting to ache, but the throb in my clit is driving me crazy enough I don't care. I'm ready to come—to get us both over the edge—but in this position, I don't have a choice but to take what he gives and nothing else.

"Take a deep breath, this is going to be intense, but you can handle it," he tells me in a strained voice, slowly pulling out as he does. I'm not sure where the intensity is going to come from when he's already been esophagus deep. I pray his cock can't magically get bigger—there's only so much a gal can take. But, despite my apprehension, my muscles tense in anticipation, earning me another small thrust and a soft groan.

Heat bursts along my clit, making me jump as the sensation scorches my senses. Before I can pull away and investigate, Corvus thrusts all the way back in, and I gag. His hand that's been buried in my hair slides down my back, slipping past my ass and burying into me. The angle doesn't offer much room, so his fingers don't go very deep, but between that, the heat at my clit, and him still fucking my mouth, I'm ready to come in seconds.

I moan around his cock as he pulls away, the vibrations rattling in my throat.

He comes with a cursed, "Fuck, fuck, fuck."

I swallow as much as I can, but he pulls out, dragging some of his cum from my mouth. It's salty on my tongue, but my mind is mush from what he's still doing to me. My cheek rests against his still-hard cock as he leans farther over my body. A wave of ecstasy builds as his fingers dive deeper inside me, and the heat at my clit rages into an inferno a second before his fingertips press harshly onto the swollen nub. My legs shake as I try to remain standing through the intense pleasure.

"I want your cum, baby," he pleads, and I come on demand for the first ever time.

My body is awkwardly slumped over, my weight balanced on one shoulder that's pressed against his thigh. I lean there for a second, panting to catch my breath as the hot water washes over my back, and Corvus brushes his fingers lightly up and down my spine.

What a way to start the day.

Chapter 12

Valencia

After finishing our shower, we dress in a rush and head to the main living area. The dresser of magical fashion was being an asshole this morning and kept offering frilly dresses until finally I got a more suitable outfit—but it's still over the top. Corvus just laughed at the drawers and drawers of lacy fabric, but now his eyes won't leave my body. The black long-sleeve shirt is tight, like a second skin, and the tactical cargo pants look better suited to a modern military movie than a training session in Hell.

I expected a lot more leather and straps, but maybe I'm confusing Hell with cosplay.

Parker is somehow awake and in the kitchen, snooping around even though we looked through everything already last night.

"Please, for the sake of my sanity, tell me you have coffee or something like it," Parker pleads, not bothering to look up from his search.

I perk up at the chance of coffee and look at Corvus, but his frown tells me I'm about to be disappointed.

"No coffee. If you guys want some, we'll have to buy it from someone, and it's a pretty hot commodity. I'd go to Earth and get some myself, but I don't want to risk the time jumping drastically before I get back."

"What if you order it to go?" Parker asks sarcastically.

Corvus just rolls his eyes, walking into the kitchen. I can't help but check him out in his tactical gear as well.

Parker finally notices what we're wearing and frowns, crossing his arms as his eyes widen. "Wait a second. What's this?" Parker points to my black shirt.

"How come you guys got cute matching outfits, but I'm still wearing yesterday's clothes?"

"How do you know this isn't mine?" I gripe, shooting him a scowl.

"Because you do not have this good a sense of style." Parker tilts his head to the side as if waiting for me to argue.

"Well, look at you!" I snap, gesturing to his lumberjack outfit.

"We're not talking about my style!" Parker argues. I ignore his statement, knowing he's right.

"So I'm guessing he doesn't have a sadistic magic fashionista dresser in his room, then?" I ask Corvus, taking a seat at the kitchen table to watch him work around the kitchen. I'd like to help, but considering I know nothing, I don't want to get in the way.

"What? I want one!" he exclaims, giving Corvus a pleading look.

"We'll get you one, they're just hard to find, so you'll have to use ours for now," Corvus responds as he throws a cast iron pan onto a fire grate. After throwing in some meat, a fire roars underneath the grate and the smell of cooking meat starts to fill the room. For the first time in a while, my mouth waters as the smoky aromas fill the air.

A few minutes later, two plates are set on the table, filled to the brim with different looking meats on them. The smell is delicious, but the appearance is slightly off-putting. One of them looks nearly identical to a sausage link but smells more akin to a roast, while the steak-looking *blob* definitely smells like bacon. And, my personal favorite, there's also a red circle of charred meat with snakeskin on the outside. The first two have me nearly diving in, but the obvious bit of snake is giving me pause to doubt.

"What in the fuck is this?" Parker exclaims, poking his knife at the snake steak. The tip doesn't penetrate its skin.

"Snake," Corvus deadpans, eating from his own full plate. It's sitting on the counter next to him, and instead of using a fork, he simply stabs into the already cut pieces with his knife and brings them to his mouth.

"Isn't that sacrilegious?" Parker picks up his fork and starts to cut a circle around the snakeskin, separating it from the meat. Since his knife won't penetrate the skin, itself, it takes him a while.

"We don't worship snakes; the Devil is our leader," Corvus responds, but it is one of those nonanswers, in my opinion.

Considering Parker's response, he must agree. "To-*mato*, Ta-*mato*."

I leave them to their conversation and start to eat my own food. Picking up my fork, I dig into the other two options—instantly loving both. The bacon-smelling steak tastes like a prime rib that's been wrapped in bacon, and even has a wonderfully crispy outside, while the roast sausage tastes like it's been marinated in *au jus* sauce for days.

I leave the snake alone, too afraid to try it. Though the portions seem large for what I would normally eat in the morning, I don't feel overfull. Oddly enough, I appreciate the high-protein meal over the normal sugar overload I eat for breakfast on Earth. This meal feels like the kind of meal you eat for fuel, not enjoyment. Though I wouldn't mind an icing-covered cinnamon roll one of these days.

Corvus leaves the counter and steps beside me. With a flick of his knife, the snakeskin falls away, and all that remains is a normal-looking steak.

"Is that better?" he asks, smirking down at me.

"You mean to tell me, you watched me struggle with mine for *five minutes*, and you could've shown me that!" Parker huffs before stuffing another bite into his mouth. He's not only devoured both steaks but has nearly finished the sausage as well.

Corvus ignores him, cutting my remaining steak into small pieces and holding one up for me to try. Now that it's not covered in multicolored scales, it's less scary, so I lean forward and take the small bite. Flavors burst on my tongue, and for a second, I feel like I'm going to choke. It's almost like someone dumped a whole bottle of seasoning into my mouth, and the abundance of flavor burns my throat, making it hard to breathe. I quickly finish chewing and swallow it down, grabbing the glass of water Corvus is already holding out for me and slamming that down, too.

"That one is always hit or miss—you either love it or you hate it," he laughs, watching me down the full glass of water.

"Hate," I cough some of the water out. "Definitely hate."

After clearing our plates, Corvus tells me to head to the training room to meet Van while he gets Parker some new clothes. At first, I'm worried about getting lost in the dark passageways, but he assures that me Van worked throughout the night to get some more lighting put up and that they lead to the training room.

We all walk through the halls briefly, Parker chatting away with Corvus about the types of meat, but I'm so nervous about training with Van that I miss the conversation entirely. When we make it to Corvus' room, he pulls me in for a quick kiss before patting my ass and pushing me along. So, with a deep breath, I make my way there, following the string of lights.

I hear Van before I see him. The loud *thwacking* noise echoes along the passageway before I even round the corner. The room is brightly lit, and even though it's wide open, with training equipment spread throughout, he's easy to spot.

Van stands tall directly in the middle of the training room, hitting a wooden post repetitively with a pair of dark batons. As I step closer, I can see how beaten both the post and the batons are, having suffered much damage. I don't want to interrupt his flow, so I stand quietly and watch.

His moves are so fluid that they look like a dance. Each hit starts before the previous one even lands, creating this flow of destruction I imagine would be deadly. He has the same style of beige pants on—only, his feet and chest are bare. A long string of beads hang from his neck and rattle softly with every move. His dark hair is pulled back into a long, black braid that lays against his back and his copper-toned skin shins with sweat, yet he doesn't stop or slow down.

Eventually, he stills, taking a deep breath before finally turning to face me. A tingle of fear builds in my chest, my lower back muscles tense, as if to prepare for an attack, but he just smiles at me. It's nearly blinding, the subtle beauty that streams from his face. Dark green eyes and sharp features, yet they're softened by his kind expression.

This is not the same person who dragged Parker from his bed.

We stare at each other for a few seconds, neither feeling the need to fill the silence as we analyze not only our new training partner but the realization this is the person we now share Corvus with.

He must like what he sees, because he finally breaks eye contact to set his batons down and gracefully folds himself into a seated position on the floor, his legs crossed.

"Join me, Lady," he urges, gesturing to the open floor in front of him.

"You can call me Val; I'm not really a lady," I say as I settle into the same position, though much less gracefully than he did.

He nods his head, tilting it slightly as if thinking. "This is a nickname?"

"Yeah, my real name is—"

"Don't tell me," he interrupts me, cutting my sentence short. "There is power in a name, and I have not earned it yet."

Unsure of what he means by power in a name, I simply nod and accept that it must be something normal in his culture.

"Ignore what rules of politeness you think you know. Similar to how I said to not thank me verbally. In my culture—to the Fae—an offer of gratitude can be used as a debt. The same goes for the fact that there is power, or *ownership*, in knowing one's name. I would not do this to you, but many others would, so it is good to start practicing now." He starts stretching, his long limbs nearly reaching me, though I sit quite a few feet away.

"Okay, what else should I know?" I ask, following along with his stretches, no longer feeling the strain in my body from the fight on the mountain. Whatever the Devil did to heal me, she did it well.

"The Fae are also unable to lie, though that does not stop us from being deceptive. I think it actually makes us more likely to deceive, when we can hide behind it being the truth."

I nod my head but don't respond, knowing that can't be all there is to know about his kind. I've heard something about Fae once, how cunning they were. But that was also from an old woman who worked in a crystal shop that and was also trying to sell me a vial of skunk spray to 'attract a lover'. I'm not sure whether anything she said was true, so I erase all knowledge I think I have of mystical creatures.

"Most Fae are not violent creatures and prefer battles of magic, wills, and the mind over fists and weapons, but do not let that fool you. They can be just as dangerous and sometimes more vicious. They are often extremely powerful as well. Where I'm from, the powers tend to correlate with animals and nature, though others sprinkle in through the generations. Thankfully, I am usually the only Fae in Hell, so you shouldn't have to worry about meeting another of my kind anytime soon."

He slowly stands up and begins another round of stretching, now focusing on his hips and knees.

"What about the other creatures in Hell? What should I know about them?" It's not that I feel like Corvus has kept that information from me on purpose; we just haven't had time to talk about it.

"There are too many to list, with too many dangers and powers combined, that we could be here for a whole century just talking about that. Best you learn about them along the way." He finally stands tall, his hands on his hips as he watches me finish the last stretch of his routine.

"The hard way, you mean? Like that bug that almost killed Parker in the first five minutes of being here?" I realize my mistake a second too late. Anger flashes in Van's eyes, and suddenly, the calm exterior bleeds into something scarier. Something far deadlier.

In a flash, he regains control of himself, his normal calm expression back on his face.

Note to self, don't mention the crazy redhead to the deadly seven-foot warrior.

"You are wildly out of shape and have no control over your body, much less your powers," he notes, analyzing me harshly. I imagine his comment is based more on the anger he just felt. It's true, I'd been slacking over the last few weeks, even before everything happened on Earth. Now I'm going to pay for it; I have no doubt Van will make sure of it.

"You couldn't even lie a little bit to spare my feelings?" I mutter, though I'm mostly joking.

"If I could, I still wouldn't have," he responds sharply, but I see a glimmer of that smile return to his eyes.

To start the training session, Van leads me through a few different cardio-based exercises, and though I hate them, I do them without complaint. If he thinks I need more cardio, then I'm gonna do more cardio. I promised Corvus I would do what it takes to stay here without question.

At first, it's honestly not that bad—all the years of training for long hikes with large packs has definitely helped. It's when he starts the 'power' part of our training that it all goes to Hell. Again.

"What do you mean, draw the power from my ass?" I curse incredulously. We've been at this for hours, and not so much as a single claw has appeared. And everyone keeps saying powers with an 's'—as in plural, but I'm starting to feel as if they're all full of shit.

"Don't be difficult for no reason. You know I didn't say it comes from your ass," Van snaps.

"You said, 'imagine it's coming from the best part of me,' and buddy, that's it." I'm frustrated, sweaty, and—overall—*over this*. Corvus and Parker never even showed up. I bet they stayed away to protect Parker from Van's wrath, I just wish they would've taken me with them. He's a hard teacher, giving no concessions. Each time my claws failed to come out, we ran laps.

So many fucking laps.

I take it back. I hate cardio and never want to do it again, fuck my promises.

"Val, pay attention," he urges, drawing my focus back to him. "It's likely one of your parents was an angel, which means your power is stored in a place of goodness. Good feelings, good emotions, good intentions—anything like that can draw your power out. Focus on something good, and then channel that to your hands."

I close my eyes once again, drawing back into myself. When we started this earlier, I almost went into what felt like a trance, searching inside myself for something I couldn't find. Now that he's brought up my parents, the only thing I can feel is despair and grief. It consumes every part of me, like a black ink that flows into each corner. No spot inside of me is safe from the feeling.

"You're doing it again; just focus on something good." His tone reaches a harsh point, causing the darkness that's growing inside me to snap.

"There's nothing!" I yell, throwing my hands out wide. "There is nothing good left. It's all grief and despair on constant rotation. I lose everyone I'm close to, and it has eaten me from the inside out. Find another way because there's nothing good left."

The words tumble out, emotion nearly choking the words before they escape. I can't believe I snapped like that when he's just trying to help. I drop my head in shame and draw my hands up to rest against my forehead but two large hands grip my wrists tightly, pulling my hands away.

"Hey," I snap, instantly yanking my hands away in reflex. I freeze when I get a good look at them. There's the little bastards.

My claws have finally made an appearance. I missed the burning sensation this time. I also notice this skin isn't as torn as before, more-so tightly stretched across my knuckles. Small red cracks have popped up around my fingertips but they don't bleed down my hands like they have before. It's uncomfortable, but not as painful as it has been—not like when they first ripped through my skin from pure desperation.

"Interesting," he murmurs, looking between my hands and eyes before slowly letting go of my wrists and leaning back once again. "Okay, withdraw them, and then release them again."

I splutter, stressed that they even popped out in the first place. "I don't know how I did it."

"Whatever you were thinking of, go back to that memory, and then focus that feeling into your hands." He directs me with such confidence that I decide to at least try. After a couple of minutes, the memory of a random shopping trip to Target is what gets them to go away. The pain is much less evident, but watching talon-like claws slowly slide back into my fingernail sends an uncomfortable shiver running down my spine.

"Again," is all he says, looking at my hands without blinking.

I close my eyes once again and pull on the memories of my family. Despite my intention, memories of my little brother and I playing with some baby goats stream through my mind. It was my favorite time of year. We had goats and sheep on our small farm, and each season, we'd have more babies than we could handle. When I turned 9, my parents taught me how to bottle feed them. Elijah and I would spend each evening caring for and playing with them. Sitting there, it's like I can faintly hear his laughter as a particularly sparky baby goat jumped off his back, knocking him to the ground. They then surrounded him, and it was like a burial of tiny hooves and soft ears. I pulled him up in a panic, but his infectious giggles echoed until we were both laughing.

A tear falls down my cheek as the memory slowly fades away, and instead of a happy evening with cute baby goats, all that remains is a house full of fire.

That burning desire to figure out what happened to my family rears its ugly head. It wasn't gone, and I doubt this need to understand will ever be completely gone until I have answers, but I had at least put it in a small corner of my mind. Now, it's a dark and ugly monster that wishes to rip through my skin and hunt those answers down. Even if I have to rip them from the throats of the guilty.

"Wherever your thoughts just went, stop them," Van demands, his tone sharp and pleading.

I open my eyes to find him leaning towards me, eyes fixated on my hands. "You parent's weren't just angels, were they?"

"No," I sniffle, wiping the tear off my cheek with the back of my clawless hand. "One of them was a human; I just don't know which."

"That's not true."

"I'm not lying," I tense, my shoulders drawing up as the conversation continues. Even though I can lie, I hate being called a liar.

"I'm not calling you a liar, I'm saying that's not the truth. Whoever told you one of your parents was human was wrong." Van abruptly stands, the movement shocking me enough to make me jump.

"Then what in the Hell were they?" I demand, more agitated now than comforted.

"A demon."

Chapter 13

Valencia

I feel a pit open up in my chest. Because that can't be true.

Can it?

Sure, it was nearly unbelievable that one of my parents was supernatural. An angel. Now Van's trying to convince me that one of my parents was a demon. Truly unbelievable. There's no way I can wrap my brain around it. Neither of my parents seemed to be anything other than ordinary; we were an average rural family. Small town farmers with little to our name but rich in what we had with one other.

Secret powers and mystical creatures? That wasn't even bedtime story material; Elijah and I always got too scared. Our parents stuck strictly to princess and superhero stories.

I try to think back to their individual personalities, but all I can really remember is that they each had dark hair and blue eyes, like mine. We all looked so much alike, there was no mistaking we were a family. Yet, I can't quite picture their faces anymore—can't work out their distinguishing features, no matter how hard I try. Elijah is easier to see, but maybe that's because we spent more time together.

I spent so long erasing them from my mind that I'm realizing I may have done too good a job. Now, even though I want to focus on the good memories, all that remains are blurry figures of people who I know in the depths of my soul but can't see. I've fought so hard to understand what happened in a memory I can barely recall. Still, I'm driven by this urgency to *know*. If I can just figure it out, maybe I can prevent it from happening to the people I care about now.

Van ran off minutes ago, leaving me sitting in the large training room, alone on the floor with my sour thoughts. He'd surely gone straight to tattle to Corvus about this newest life-altering news.

What do we even do with this kind of information? It doesn't seem plausible, a demon and an angel falling in love, much less starting a family. It's not like it was an accident—they'd had *two* kids. Sure, I could see myself potentially being the result of a crazy hookup. But Elijah, too? No way. I may not remember their faces but I do remember they loved each other just as much as they loved us.

Something isn't right here. Someone out there knows what really happened to my parents, and I have the feeling it's going to cost me more than I'm willing to pay to figure it out.

I hear footsteps approaching but I don't look up, almost afraid of what I might see, but he sits beside me without a word.

"This changes nothing," Corvus declares after a moment, his voice that calm baritone I love.

"I think it changes everything," I mutter, finally looking into his dark eyes. They're focused on me, taking in every feature on my face as if painting the picture into his mind.

"It does... and it doesn't," he murmurs, breaking eye contact to look across the training room. "It actually answers some questions I've had."

"How does it answer anything? How did he even know that one of my parents was a demon?"

"Power comes from our emotions. For demons, they usually come from more explosive feelings, like anger or fear. For angels, the opposite is true. We all assumed that one of your parents was an angel because of your ability to withstand holy fire. The claws did throw me off at first, as shapeshifting is usually a hellish power, but there have been a few rare cases of angels being able to manage a partial shift. I should've thought of it sooner, honestly, but the possibility was so unlikely, it didn't feel worth looking into."

Corvus looks around, seemingly still deep in thought.

"If I'm part angel and part demon, what does that mean?" I ask, starting to feel the worry at what's to come creeping up my spine.

"It means your power is in constant balance. Light and dark, good and evil, all rolled into one. It will be even more important that Van teaches you to control your power because one day, you could be more powerful than all of us, and that's a dangerous thing to be."

"If that makes me so powerful, why haven't more tried it? Shouldn't there be a whole population of hybrids?" I think of the differences between the angels and demons I've already met and sort of answer that question for myself, but since Corvus can't read my mind, he gives me his own answer.

"Typically, we can't stand each other long enough to start families, much less even hookup." His words confirm my theories. "The few who have tried, typically resulted in unsuccessful pregnancies. If the child of a match isn't perfectly balanced between their angelic and demonic sides, they're born with only one. I can only speak of the rare few I've heard about in Hell, and they usually never mature beyond a lesser demon."

He looks to me, pausing his thought. His eyes rove over my body, as if checking for something. When I arch my eyebrows in question, he doesn't comment on the look, choosing to continue his explanation of the hybrids. "To have their being ripped in half like that drives them crazy, but I'm sure some of them are out there, roaming Hell."

"That's sad," I murmur, thinking of the demons who were born with half a soul; destined to become crazy. It's not a fate I'd wish on anyone. "So if being part angel and part demon makes someone go crazy, why didn't I?"

"I have a few speculations," he starts, shifting around to get into a more comfortable position. He opens his mouth but Van rushes into the room and cuts him off.

"We must go now. The demon you're after is at Tornil's Tent," he urges, rushing over to the weapons rack to grab his discarded shirt and a knife that he tucks into his waistband.

"What's Tornil's Tent?" I ask Corvus, following him as he gets up and rushes over to Van.

"You're sure?" Corvus demands, our conversation having died a quick death with the announcement.

"You seriously question me now? You know Danti likes me more than you; she told me," Van counters, the same edge to his voice.

There's a short battle of wills before Corvus turns to me with a vicious smile on his face.

"We're going to a party," he purrs.

***

It takes us a while to get everyone together and ready for the party at Tornil's Tent. Corvus demands I change, so I shower off my day of training and get dressed. At first, the stupid dresser only offers one option, consisting of a red lacy dress, until I threaten to set it on fire if it doesn't give me something else. I don't necessarily know how to do that, but the dresser must take me seriously because, after that, I don't see a stitch of red lace.

I was given a few options, all dressier than I would've picked for myself if I had full control, but the black jeans fit great, and the top isn't all bad either. There's still too much lace—each sleeve is made of it, baring my arms to the elements—but it's been nothing but warm in Hell, so I don't worry about getting cold. The frills along the deep V-shaped collar are a bit irritating, and the pointy, studded cuffs seem a little unnecessary—but who am I to question the fashion in Hell?

Maybe spikes are all the rage.

My black Doc Martens were an added bonus, and something I will definitely be keeping an eye on. There's nothing worse than losing a good pair of shoes.

As I'm about to leave the room, ready to go, when Corvus enters and blocks the way.

"What's wrong?" I ask, worried about the nervous look on his face.

"Nothing's wrong, I just wanted to give you something." He looks down at me with a gleam in his eyes, but doesn't move.

"Do I have to guess what it is?"

"No," Corvus puts a hand on my face, his large palm warm and comforting. "Where we're going tonight is a dangerous place, full of demons of all kinds, and some of them are not fans of mine." He takes a deep breath before continuing.

"It will be no secret what you mean to me, therefore, you will have a very large target on your back. If you're not able to stick by me, stay with Van. No matter what, do not be caught without one of us tonight, okay?"

I nod in agreement, already on board with not being alone. I don't mind being social, but a room full of demons I don't know seems a step beyond 'social anxiety'.

I grab his hand, kiss the inside of his palm, and then move to step around him.

"One more thing," he says, making me pause. Corvus reaches into his pocket and pulls out a small, red velvet box.

I suck in a gasp, my heart skyrocketing. Is he about to *propose*?

"Tonight is sure to get wild, and even being by my side might not be enough to deter some of the more curious demons. You're going to need something to show that *you're mine.*"

He slowly tips the velvet box open to reveal the two most stunning earrings I've ever seen.

Tears well in my eyes even though I try to force them down. He tilts the box toward me, placing it in one of my hands. The small, dark red stones are rough, as if they've been taken directly from the ground, wrapped in beautiful gold wire, and given to me. They catch the flashing starlight from the glow stone on the ceiling and flare. It's like the stars have been trapped inside, and he's given it to me for safe-keeping.

My mouth gapes like a fish out of water as I try to figure out what to say. The 'L' word almost comes out, but I hold it in, not wanting to ruin the moment with word vomit.

"The stones are called ember garnet, and they can be found at the bottom of burnt-out lava pits—hard to find and even harder to obtain. They're nearly impossible to cut, which is why the stones are still rough and unpolished. I didn't think you'd want polished stones, anyway."

My chest fills with so many emotions that I can barely keep from blurting out a thousand different things at once. They're perfect—so perfect I can't find words to describe how much it means to me.

"They're beautiful, Corvus," I finally reply.

"They're a mere accessory to the true beauty," he responds quietly.

Can someone say, *swoon-worthy?*

As I study the gems, the lights around us are reflected off the rough surface, and a dark pit seems to glow at their center.

"How will people know they have such meaning?" I ask, curious of the mystery behind the pretty stones.

I swear, I see a light blush tint Corvus' tan cheeks, but it's hard to tell in the low light.

"In this realm, natural resources tend to have a mind of their own, like the taraxa plant I told you about. Because this realm is populated by so many powerful demons, the bleed-off of that extra power has seeped into the very makeup of the realm. It's believed ember garnet is the stone of fate, itself. That mining the stone is tied to your very fate and will only come to you when you really need it. Lava is rarely found in a cooled state in Hell, so it's not easy to find. That makes ember garnet a coveted commodity, not only as a jewel but as a weapon. It's the strongest material in Hell and can't be manipulated by magical powers, it can't be broken once forged, and can cut through anything in Hell and many of the other realms. To obtain such a stone and give that to another is seen as a *very* meaningful gift."

He pulls his red stone knife out of a hip holster and holds it up. The blade glints just as the earrings do.

"When I got the stone for this knife, I needed something to protect myself. But, more than that, I needed to remind myself that everything I'd done, that had led me to that point, was worth it. I told myself that if I couldn't mine the stone for the blade, then I wasn't on the right path." His voice trails off, lost in the memory that the blade inspired. "This time, I wasn't even looking for the stone. I was trying to figure out why Dumah was after you, and then—there in front of me—appeared a cooled lava pit. Like it knew my path before I did. As soon as I saw the charred ground, I got on my knees and dug."

He holsters his blade and grabs one of my hands, squeezing lightly. "I didn't even know how I felt about us, then—just that I *had* to get the stone—because one day, I'd see you wearing them and you'd be a queen in your own right, and I'd die before I let anyone else give them to you. It had to be me. Seeing you wearing them helps me know that everything I've done, all the bad shit and the shadows in my past, were simply stepping stones to get to you."

Tears sting my eyes at his heartfelt expression and the softness of his voice. Clearly, we've both been on the same journey, worlds apart. Thousands of tiny moments in our lives that have come together to put us on the same path—to this moment where a pair of earrings show that even the fates approve of our union. That the shadows in our past were a part of our journey to each other. Fate hasn't made it easy, but is *anything* that's worth having?

I silently put them in my ears, loving the look Corvus gives me as he watches.

Without another word, he grabs my hand and leads us through the cave to meet the others.

As we all make it to the living room, I realize we're all in all black.

"What's wrong with a bit of color?" Parker groans, looking down at the black, long-sleeve shirt he's wearing. He pulls it away from his chest, looking down at the color as if offended.

"Doesn't hide the blood," Corvus' deadpans, looking as devilishly handsome in black as he always does. He has a set of black leather straps wrapped around his shoulders that clasp in the front, just under his chest. The tight straps pull his shirt tight into his body, accentuating the lines of muscle. He has a vicious-looking red blade strapped under each arm, but I can't seem to take my eyes away from his large frame.

A warm feeling in my chest starts to grow, and I look away from them so it doesn't show on my face. The last thing I need is Parker to call me out for looking at Corvus with 'goo-goo' eyes, as he likes to call it. I'm supposed to be some overpowered hybrid, but becoming teary-eyed at every turn isn't a good look.

"Parker, you should stay—"

"Don't even think about leaving me behind," Parker snaps.

"It's dangerous, Parker, we have no idea what we're walking into, and you're *human*," Corvus explains, emphasis on the 'human' part, as if that explains all.

"Guess what? That's never going to change, and I can't stay in this cave forever, never seeing anything outside of these rock walls. If you trap me here, I *will* go insane." Parker's stance is confident despite the tension in his muscles.

My chest burns at the sincerity in his voice. I don't want to put him in harm's way, but I also fear for his mental health. I couldn't imagine never being able to leave, either, but I have advantages that Parker doesn't.

"Parks."

"Don't start with me, Val. If you can honestly say you'd stay back if you were in my shoes, without a fight, then I'll stay. But if you can't—if neither of you can say you'd do the same—then I don't want to hear any more about me staying back when everyone else is leaving. I am not a pet to be contained because you're worried. I may be human, but I know how to defend myself."

His shoulders are tense, red hair dark in the dim light. His bright blue eyes burn with resolution. There's no keeping him here if he doesn't want to be. I'd never force him to do anything, and unfortunately, that includes keeping him in the cave. It may be safer, but a crazy-from-isolation Parker wouldn't be my best friend anymore.

"We'll all go," I confirm. Corvus watches me quietly for a second before nodding.

"We're going to portal there. It's going to be unpleasant again but try to stay alert if you're able. We can't portal straight inside the tent; Tornil forbids it. So, we'll be just outside the main doors. Unfortunately, it's the most dangerous spot. Just stick close and stay between Van and me at all times."

We both nod, trusting him completely. If he says it's dangerous, you bet your ass I'm gonna believe him. Who am I to doubt a lord of Hell about the ongoings in Hell?

Before I have a chance to ask where Van is, the lethal man strolls in, head slightly hunched as he comes out of the passageways and into the living room.

What's it like being that tall? I feel like it must be annoying since he's probably always ducking or without pants that are long enough to fit. The black pair of pants he's wearing now are long enough, but he walks stiffly as though uncomfortable. Sure, being able to reach things would be nice, but I'd take climbing on a chair to get stuff over constant high waters any day.

Van doesn't so much as look in Parker's direction, and for once, the wily redhead doesn't make an asinine comment. Corvus looks around the group as we all settle close to him before nodding, and then we're off.

Chapter 14

Valencia

This is not a party, it's a damn Circus! Crowds of people mill around, surrounding campfires, dancing to silent music, or even passed out in the dirt... at least, I hope that guy was just passed out. Because if he wasn't, then he was definitely plain ole' dead.

I hear gagging, but it thankfully ends quickly. I turn to look at a green-faced Parker, the color of his skin clashing with the dark red of his hair. Portal travel really does not sit well with him, it seems.

I feel fine. No stomach-turning or nausea. I was so distracted by our surroundings that I didn't even notice that the normally sick feeling I always get is simply gone.

"Pathetic," Van growls in Parker's direction.

"Hey!" I snap at him.

"Van," Corvus' sharp tone elicits a sheepish look on Van's face—not something I ever thought I'd see. It makes his normally angular face look almost boyish. I feel for Van, knowing that his reactions are somewhat out of his control, born purely of desperation and trauma from whatever he's experienced in his past. I let it slide, not wanting to reprimand him any more than our short comments already have.

Corvus didn't have to tell me, but I imagine it's more important than ever to show a unified front, and that even the slightest crack in our group could get one or all of us killed. It doesn't take a battle strategist to know you're better off in a group when surrounded by the enemy on all sides.

As Parker gathers himself, I look around us. Dark red dirt spans as far as the eye can see, interspersed with patches of deep maroon, like something has seeped into the grains over time. The air is thick and humid, a stench of wrongness that's stale and presses against my senses.

I want to avoid looking at the body that lays face down. Facing the reality that it actually is a dead person feels like more than I can take, but my eyes betray me and I glance towards the body. Muscle memory kicks in, and I find myself checking for signs of life almost instantly. He's still, frozen in time. One arm is bent at an awkward angle and his legs are crossed at the ankle while his chest is as stagnant as death. I can't see his features because his head faces the wrong direction. Purposefully.

I rip my eyes away, not wanting to focus on the body for a second longer, but it does nothing to ease my worries. Creeping sensations of terror crawl up my spine like spiders, their tiny legs stabbing into my senses. They alert me to the realization that there are many more bodies lying around in a similar state of stillness—too still. Lumps of shadows in the dim light, hidden in between the signs of debauchery—and there is plenty of that around. No one pays us any mind, nor the bodies that line the ground.

It seems to me that they're *all* drunk.

Everyone's stumbling about or falling over, clearly well past tipsy and on their way to blacking out.

I see a couple making out, the woman perched on a man's lap, devouring his face as they kiss. I guess the proper terms would be female and male, or maybe they go by something else entirely. Whoever they are, they're going at it. When he slumps backwards, falling off the log he was sitting on into an awkward heap on the ground, I realize that maybe she *was* devouring him.

No kissing strangers on the dance floor tonight, that's for sure.

Not that the burly demon beside me would allow that to happen. I imagine the pretty, red ember garnet earrings he gave me are enough of a sign to keep everyone else the fuck away.

Corvus mentioned this would be the most dangerous part of the trip, but everyone seems so drunk that I wonder if they even know we're here.

"Tornil must've known we were coming; he gave the miscreants the Devil's Cider," Van says quietly as he brushes against my arm with his elbow. We're standing so close that everyone is still basically touching.

"I'm sure Danti warned him," Corvus responds, resting his hand on my lower back to lightly urge me forward.

Parker steps beside me, finally no longer green around the edges, and we start making our way to the main doors of the circus tent. This brings him closer to Van, who growls under his breath but ultimately keeps his nasty comments to himself for once.

We make it to the tent doors with no issue; everyone is truly too drunk off their asses to even notice we're here. Corvus holds the entrance open for us, and as we step inside. It feels like I've been transported to a whole other world all over again.

The tent walls are still the typical red and white striped canvas that we saw on the exterior, but inside, they soar higher than ever. The tent maybe looked to stand at 30 or 40 feet from the outside, but now the ceilings are so high, there's enough space for multiple walkways that span the open air above in addition to a balcony that shines with brightly flashing lights of all color. The place has to be at least six or seven stories in height. And, as I look, I notice there are people on the balcony at the very top. They're dancing, but they're so small that I can barely make anything out other than a mesh of color and movement.

There's also no support system holding the balcony up—just a free-floating plank that juts out from the edge. I have no idea how the people even got up there. Long strings of lights hang from the balconies, giving the space above us a warm glow where the floor is dark besides the various lanterns that have been lit along the edges.

A huge dance floor, filled to the brim with thumping bodies, takes up most of the space. A mix of red and purple light flashes over our heads, giving off a luxuriously passionate vibe. The opposite side of the room features the longest bar I've ever seen in my life, and though there are probably a hundred bodies pressed against its edge waiting for a drink, only two people are working to fill orders.

One of the bartenders is a tall, lanky man with bright blue hair and pale skin. He's wearing a mesh top that shows off his lean body and blue swirling tattoos that match his hair. He's got a young-looking face, boyish almost, with soft edges where there are usually hard lines. Dark eyebrows set off his otherwise muted features. I almost wonder if he's even old enough to drink, but then internally laugh at myself for such a thought.

Hell does not seem like the sort of place that has strict age limitations on drinking.

He flips bottles around like they're rockets, sending them soaring into the air before catching them easily with one hand. It's like magic, watching him. It isn't until the other man catches my focus that I'm able to look away from the show.

This other guy definitely looks like he's a bartender with dark, shaggy hair that falls in front of his eyes and patchwork of small tattoos. His features are much more angular, but I wouldn't guess his age to be that old, either. Instead of putting on a show, he keeps his head down, filling orders promptly before moving on to the next customer. He doesn't chat, nor does he stick around for long enough to hear what anyone is saying to him.

They're not as drunk in here as they were outside, but the crowd is definitely rowdy.

"C'mon, Tornil will know more," Corvus announces, and though his voice is loud, it's almost drowned out by the beating bass of the music.

We push our way through the crowd at first—the crowd forcing us to walk in a single-file line—and Corvus lets go of my hand to take the lead, positioning Parker and me between him and Van.

Even when he's on high alert, he still thinks of my best friend's wellbeing. *Thank Go—goodness—for small blessings.*

However, our single-file method swiftly becomes unnecessary once everyone around us gets a chance to see who we are. Or, more importantly, who *Corvus* is, and it's like a slow tidal wave seeps throughout the crowd. The more to notice, the more space they give us, until there's a clear path to the bar. I notice some strange features on some of the demons standing close as they watch us walk by, but the rest of the crowd is hidden from my view behind their backs.

A large enough spot opens for us to all stand shoulder to shoulder at the bar's edge, and Corvus walks right up to it before leaning on his forearms in an extremely relaxed position. It's definitely *not* the posture of someone who was telling me, not five minutes ago, that this place is highly dangerous.

Parker and I assume somewhat similar positions, except neither of us are nearly as relaxed, keeping an eye at everything that goes on around us, as if waiting for the knife that's sure to come for our back. There's no need, considering Van leans against the bar, his low back pressed against the top edge as he scans the crowd behind us. It seems he's on *watching for the back-bound knife'* duty.

The blue-haired showman slides over to us instantly, passing at least eight people who have been waiting longer but are apparently much farther down the totem pole. None of them comment on us skipping the line.

"You're favorite," cheers the bartender, as he passes a blank, brown glass bottle across the bar. I can't tell what's inside but I can smell the spices from here and can imagine it's strong. "Two lords in one night, what a treat! And for your guests?"

Two Lords? Corvus is obviously one, but who is the other?

Light blue eyes briefly focus on me, scanning me from head to waist before skipping along to stare at Parker. His hair is styled perfectly, the blue strands picking up the flashing lights to give him an array of multi-colored highlights. When Parker finally turns to see the man staring at him, his cheeks start to pink. His light freckles darken, and his eyebrows tip down in focus.

I watch as Parker starts to lean forward, pressing his body as close as he can to the bar before his upper half starts to tip over. The blue-haired bartender remains still, his focus on Parker unwavering, and I feel a strange sensation of heat start to build in my chest as I glance into his bright blue eyes. What I'd thought was just a light shade of blue seems almost illuminated now, and I swear the small horns on the top of his head have gotten larger.

A hand slams onto the bar top before us, causing both Parker and me to jump and breaking the strange spell. Parker looks away, his pupils blown and chest heaving. I look at the tattoo-covered hand on the bar. Lean fingers lead to an exposed forearm that's full of ink, muscle, and panty-melting veins. The black shirt he's wearing is folded just below his elbow, and despite the loose fit, the muscles in his arms and shoulders manage to peek out. After a slow perusal of his lean neck and strong jaw, I meet the eye of the black-haired bartender. He's giving the other a death glare, his eyes the color of the late evening sun. I never knew irises could be that shade of yellow.

"Tone it down, Baz, you know the consequences," his voice is as dark and mysterious as the rest of him.

So intrigued with what just happened, I almost ask what the consequences are—because, to me, it seems like they might've been Parker getting stripped down and fucked right on top of this bar, in front of a circus of demons. Not that Parker has ever shown a preference for gender when it comes to his lovers, but the last thing I want is to witness my best friend's death by public orgasm.

I can't handle the second-hand embarrassment, and I definitely don't want to see his bare, pale white ass.

Corvus and Van remain silent as they let the newcomer handle it.

Baz, blue hair with a staring problem, promptly nods his head and scurries away from us with one last look over his shoulder at our group.

"You'll need to keep your friend away from Baz, he's a menace when it comes to the pure." Dark eyes skirt over Parker, once again focusing closely on him more than any other in the group.

I feel hot air brush my mesh-covered shoulder as Corvus' deep voice whispers quietly in my ear. "This is what I was talking about; they can sense his soul like it's a beacon. Do not take your eyes off him once." I nod, not responding out loud. "Tornil, this is Valencia and Parker. Please consider them an extension of myself and should be protected at all costs."

Ah, the infamous Tornil, owner of this establishment. I want to congratulate him on such a successful venue, but I'm not sure what the etiquette is in such a situation and the last thing I want to do is cause an issue by being nosy. So, though it pains me, I remain quiet.

"Love what you've done with the place," Parker states to Tornil, gesturing around the room. "Is there a chance I could get a really strong drink?"

So much for staying quiet to not cause offense.

Luckily for all, Tornil chuckles and starts working on a drink. In a flash, we are both given two very different-looking drinks. Mine is a plain glass with ice and a whiskey-colored liquid that smells like apples and cinnamon. The other looks like s'mores has thrown up in it. Parker grabs his marshmallow-covered drink and moans at the flavor before I take the other, enjoying the burn on my tongue before setting it back down.

Everyone has been oddly quiet since we got here, and the anticipation is starting to kill me. Van speaks up for the first time since arriving, and I'm shocked to hear the cordial and polite tone from him. "Tornil, thank you for the drinks. We are here to see the event, is there ample security, or are we on our own?"

Tornil nods as if he'd been expecting that. "There was already another lord here tonight, so there is security in there already."

"Who?" Corvus asks.

Yeah, who? When Corvus told me he was the Third Lord of Hell, I just assumed he meant the third chronologically. It seems my assumption was wrong, and that he's actually the third *in line*. Which means there are potentially two more assholes we have to worry about alongside all the Devil's other bullshit.

Tornil just shakes his head.

"It's important." Corvus' voice morphs into something dangerous and demanding, clearly irritated that Tornil didn't answer right away.

"And so is keeping my head on my shoulders. I'm sorry, but he asked me not to mention he was here and I am inclined to obey." Tornil shrugs his shoulders, as if going against Corvus is easy-peasy compared to whoever else he's dealt with tonight.

CHAPTER 15

CORVUS

TORNIL ACTS LIKE HE didn't just refuse to answer a direct question from a lord of Hell. Not that I am trying to intimidate him, or have ever been known to use my title to get what I want. Whoever was here earlier tonight, is above me. That only leaves three options. Nightmare, the First lord, and the Devil himself.

Nightmare never goes out, so he's the least likely option. That leaves the First Lord and the Devil, and I'm not inclined to trust either. I'm also not willing to break the small comradery that Tornil and I have built over the years, so I don't press for more information. I could force it out of him, but that would be a severe violation of the trust we've built; trust and loyalty are the most expensive and most rare commodities in Hell.

It doesn't help much to know who it was, anyway. We were always going to be on high alert tonight, and thanks to whoever was here earlier, the security has been ramped up—so I won't have to worry as much. It's a small win I'm happy to take advantage of.

When Van told me that he suspected one of Valencia's parents was a demon, and not a human like we'd thought, I'd nearly hit myself in frustration. If it's true, it makes so much sense. It would answer a lot of the questions I've had about her abilities. I've been too worried about her mental health to press about her family and their lineage, but it seems the issue has already been pressed.

I'd found her sitting in the training room and had expected another tear-filled panic attack, but instead, she was calm and quiet, staring off into space. That had almost worried me more until she'd started talking, and although there was sadness in her eyes and her voice, it seemed curiosity had finally overpowered the other emotions.

Van had also mentioned that the shady demon, Davgus, who'd tried to kill me, would be here tonight. It's crowded here, more than usual, so I can only imagine the event that's taking place tonight is a big one. That's something I was afraid to admit that to Valencia. Her emotions are too volatile to play with without knowing for certain the warning would be useful, but the lie by omission feels like hot oil in my chest. I suppose sacrifices must be made somewhere.

"The booth is available for you, if you wish to watch the show from there," Tornil mentions, his eyes not leaving mine. He got a quick glimpse of Valencia and Parker but hasn't looked back since. I imagine it's a respect thing, which I appreciate. I'd rather not have to kill him for accidentally using his powers on Valencia.

I nod my head in thanks and steer our group towards the open passageway that leads to the big tent. Whatever the show is tonight, I hope it's not something gruesome.

***

I'm going to kill him.

Of all the shows I would've loved to bring Valencia to see, this is the absolute last option I would've picked.

Hundreds of demons stand shoulder to shoulder, drinking, yelling, and just having an overall rowdy time. It's much darker in here than it usually is, and instead of a large arena, there's a smaller circular stage in the center of the tent. A dome of wire arches over top, enclosing it. While it's empty right now, the dirt floor settled, the few, large dark spots serve as the only evidence that someone has been in there at all tonight.

Fucking Fight Night.

When I said I was hoping we wouldn't be watching something gruesome, this is literally what I was hoping *wasn't* happening tonight.

Fight nights in Hell are a notorious event, well-known throughout the entire realm. It's always random, never announced in advance, and no one knows who runs it. Tornil hates fighting, it's why he's banned it in the tent except when it takes place in the ring on Fight Night. However, he's also a capitalist, and I imagine that hosting this event makes him a lot of money. He would've told me if he ran it, of that I'm sure.

It's unknown who actually runs the fight nights, but if it were my guess, I'd imagine one of the shifter packs was in charge. Every fight night, there's always a group of young shifters who fight in an attempt to earn higher-ranking positions in the pack. I've never spent much time with the packs, as they usually despise the presence of other, non-shifting demons, but fight nights are their exceptions.

There are a few Red Guardian shifters around, working as a secondary form of security for the many shifters in attendance. Some are easy to spot, thanks to the large red emblem tattooed on their necks. It's a sigil of some sort, but it's a well-kept secret that only those in the pack know of. I spot some of Tornil's house security posted around the room, as well as a few familiar faces I've met over the years, mingling with the crowd. I imagine they're meant to be a sort of undercover security to ensure all patrons act accordingly.

It's Hell, so death and mayhem are typically a socially acceptable activity, but at Tornil's, fighting and killing is strictly forbidden unless it's in the ring.

Parker and Valencia stand to my side, quietly taking in the scene around them. I imagine they've not been around this level of chaos before, so I'll have to be sure to keep a bucket close for when the fighting resumes.

Van helps me to usher them to the one booth that's designated for any higher officials who attend. Thankfully, there's a roped-off path to get there, so we don't have to push through the crowd. Unfortunately, as we make our way, the demons closest to us take note of our presence, and many eyes skate over Van and me to look at the two others in our group. A particularly ugly-looking lesser demon reaches out his nasty arm, skin falling away as he brushes against one of the ropes, but instead of grabbing onto Parker as intended, his arm is cut off just below the elbow by a slick blade I had no idea Van was even carrying.

I roll my eyes, sure I'm going to get an earful from Tornil about Van breaking the rules *again*. If it weren't for Van's friendship with Danti, I doubt Tornil would put up with so much from him.

Parker groans in disgust and scurries closer to Valencia and me. No one else tries to reach for them, but more hungry eyes now look our way, drawn in by the pain and fear. I shove them toward the booth a little too hard, Valencia cursing me under her breath. The thin, invisible film of the sound enchantment brushes against my skin as we finally pass the barrier. The last thing I want is a room full of power-hungry demons overhearing any more of our conversations.

A few of the closer demons gasp, their fear permeating the air. They can't hear us, but *we* can hear everything. It causes the true demon in me to wake and scratch at my skin from the inside, begging to be let out and cause more destruction. I look around at the cowering demons that side-eyes us, apparently waiting for the fallout of me killing Valencia after the show of disrespect.

They don't know her, though, and that curse is the least bad thing she's probably going to say tonight, so instead of killing her as they expect, I smack her ass and pull a seat out for her to take.

It's a clear power play. I just showed everyone in this room that I place her above myself, now making her the third-most powerful person in Hell. She might not realize it, but she just made her first move for the proverbial crown.

Eyes widen in surprise, and those who stared with lecherous intent now look on with confusion and distrust.

Hell is not a place to not know about those in charge. '*Is this the leader who lets stuff go or is this the leader who will cut off heads at the slightest inconvenience,*' isn't a question you ever want to find yourself needing to ask. They know nothing about her, and that makes her ten times more dangerous.

Van eyes me warily, uncertain. Neither of us can be sure this is the right choice to make, but it's been made and all we can do now is hope that it doesn't bite us in the ass later down the line.

We settle in as the lights dim; the show is finally starting again. We're in the same booth I sat in when speaking with Danti not too long ago, yet the room around us has completely changed. Whatever Tornil spends on alcohol surely can't touch how much he must pay to keep this tent enchanted.

Turning in her seat, Valencia leans over towards me. "What's going on?"

For a second, I contemplate how I'm going to break it to her that she's about to see more people die than she likely ever has. Had I known this was tonight's event, I would've warned her and Parker—but it seems there's no time like the present.

"It's Fight Night. Every person who enters the ring must fight, often to the death, so prepare yourself for that. It's gruesome, but it helps to keep the mayhem to a controlled environment. Most of the fighters are shifters from the various shifter packs. They fight as a rite of passage—a way for them to gain a better standing in their pack. It doesn't always end up how they hope."

"Did you say shifter? As in *werewolves*?" She sounds shocked, which is slightly funny considering all the new species' she's already met. I relish her surprised expression, though. There will come the day when nothing about Hell is new to her, and it's just the same old dark world she's always been trapped in—*I trapped her in*—so, for now, I will appreciate that it still excites her.

"Yes. Technically not werewolves, though. Shifters. Wolves, panthers, bears, lions. Really, think of any kind of animal, and there's probably someone who can shift into it," I answer, smirking at her wonder.

"What's the damn difference? And, most importantly, *bear shifter*? As if god-damned werewolves weren't scary enough, we've now gotta worry about fucking grizzlies?" Her gaze is facing the front, watching as bodies shift around in antici-pation of what's to come, but I can see her eyebrows scrunch in confusion. Maybe there is a little bit of fear mixed in as well.

"Werewolves, as you know it, are controlled by the moon in an enchantment that has trapped them. They're usually humans but are also sometimes demons. They're cursed to lose themselves every lunar cycle. There are a few here, but most of them are extinct or have cured the curse. Shifters are demons with the power to transform their bodies into the animal their soul is connected to."

"So you're a shifter? With your crow?" she asks, wide eyes tracking my body as if she can see some secret buried beneath my skin.

"You could technically say that, but the shifters here don't recognize my ability as true shifting. My crow form is just an extension of myself and doesn't have a soul outside of my own. I'm just transforming the physical makeup of my body as opposed to shifters, who are more akin to a set of twins—the shifter and their animal counterpart, one soul that shares a home. They're able to connect with their animal on a spiritual level, but the animal has its own thoughts and feelings.

I control the crow. A shifter's animal controls itself and allows for partnership with the demon."

I can see more questions bouncing in her eyes, sparks of wonder and curiosity that dance in the bright blue orbs, but noise ahead of us breaks the connection and forces our attention away from the conversation and back to the night's events.

Demons shuffle around, mostly paying attention to the ring and eagerly awaiting the next fight, but I imagine there's someone out there watching us instead.

"What the fuck is on that guy's face?" Parker blurts.

It makes me once again happy that Tornil had the forethought to enchant this booth against eavesdropping.

"No one is near as disgusting as *you*, Rat," Van snaps from beside Parker. Though, his chair has been dragged to the edge of the booth, as far away from us as he can manage. It's the first insult he's thrown all night—out loud, at least. There were probably many more spoken in his head, but he at least kept them to himself up till now.

"Does anyone know why the Great Tree calls me Rat? I mean, it's not the worst nickname I've had, but I don't think I particularly look like a rat," Parker asks Valencia, eyes meet mine as if I should know the inner workings of Van's mind.

Van doesn't respond with anything more than a menacing growl.

"He said you reminded him of a rat-like creature, I think," Valencia responds with a mean look aimed at Van. "But I mean, you do have lanky limbs, eat too much, and secretly enjoy a cuddle. So, maybe he's actually spot on."

"You little witch! Well, you look like the Grudge." Parker crosses his arms in a pout.

I can't help but laugh at the incredulous look on Valencia's face. I'm about to ask her how her looking like a feeling can be an insult, but the rattle of chains cuts me off.

It seems Fight Night has begun.

Chapter 16

Corvus

There's no host to announce the night's events. Instead, a large man stumbles into the ring from one of the connected tunnels. He's clearly a shifter, if the large frame and bulging muscles is anything to go by. I'd guess a bear of some form, but it's impossible to tell while he's in his human form.

He turns to the dark spot in the cage behind him and flips it off, clearly pissed at the rough treatment.

From the outside of the ring, the dark space doesn't look like anything, but from inside, you can see it's a passageway to the inner workings of Fight Night. This particular enchantment ensures no one in the crowd is able to sneak into the ring and sway the fight. It doesn't stop someone from manipulating things from inside the ring, though. I know from my few experiences fighting.

Those were rage-fueled nights I try my hardest to not think about. The time shortly after becoming the Third Lord was filled with many emotions, and most of them weren't pleasant. I fought and killed nearly everyone I faced. A few of them deserved what they got, but some didn't. The young face of a newly-shifted wolf still haunts me from time to time. I hadn't meant to kill him, but unfortunately *someone* had wanted him dead, and they simply used me as the weapon. I still get dirty looks from those in the Hounds pack.

How was I to know their enemy set the young shifter up? Or that he was some special heir, the alpha's first son? I was hyped up on rage, and *no one* survived that night. I do feel guilty, though, so I give them more leniency than I do others.

A crash of metal on metal jerks me from the past. Lost in guilt, I missed bear shifter's opponent making his appearance.

"Oh shit," I hear Parker murmur right before a large arc of crimson blood sails through the air, covering the first few rows of demons. They're crowded around the edge of the ring, some banging against the metal. A body lies lifeless in the center, and the bear shifter pants heavily as he stands over the body. There's a darkness in his eyes, a type of blank void I know well.

He's facing his own demons tonight.

The next three fights end in a similar fashion. The shifter finishes them unnaturally fast, giving each of his opponents a quick, almost merciful death.

"How long does this go on for?" Valencia leans over to ask, a slight shakiness to her voice as she side-eyes the few peepers who still seem to enjoy watching us more than the fight.

"Until he wins 10 rounds or dies. Then, the next is thrown in, and the cycle starts all over again." I take in her slightly pale face and her low-tipped brows.

"That seems like it could take a long time?"

"It depends on how many signed up to fight. Or have been forced." It is a long time. But time doesn't really matter here so, in a way, it also isn't. The only way to determine the end is when the last body falls. Everyone here will wait until the last breath of the last fighter has been taken, and then they disperse to their next scheduled bullshit. The room is crowded, as fight nights always are. I scan the crowd for a second, searching for a face I recognize, but in a sea of angry demons, they start to all look the same.

"*Forced*?" Valencia gasps, drawing my attention back to her. She's now looking back at the new fight taking place in the ring. The shifter hasn't killed this new one yet, but considering the lesser demon was given a weapon, I imagine the ring leaders in the back just wanted to prolong it for show.

"Yes. Some of those who are here to fight are here against their will," I say slowly, wishing the calm in my voice will help prevent her from freaking out.

Wish not granted.

She jerks to her feet, her chair sliding back a few inches from the force. Despite the sound barrier surrounding us, many demons in the crowd turn our way. They may not be able to hear us, but they can damn sure see us.

"Valencia, sit down. I'll explain," I urge, pointing to the chair.

"No! How can I? You expect me to sit when there are literally people being forced to fight to their death?" She starts to pace, the small booth only allowing her to go a few feet each way, but the agitation is clear.

"Yes. Sit down," I growl. I don't take my eyes off of her, but I can feel the prickly sense of being watched.

"Don't you growl your little commands at me," she snaps, pointing a finger at my face. With her back to the crowd, she can't see the extreme reaction she's created with that little move. I smile viciously.

"What the fuck are you smiling about? This isn't funny!" she snaps.

I jump up to my feet, crowding her space. There's not enough room for both of us to stand, so she's forced to lean back against the wooden railing. I wrap my hand around her throat, squeezing slightly. Her eyes bulge in surprise, but she remains quiet. Her nostrils flare as I step closer, pressing our bodies tightly against each other.

Her pupils dilate as she feels the impression of my stiff cock pressing against her front. I hate that her snarky attitude turns me on, but it's a reality I will now live with every day.

I push our bodies flush and lean forward some more, pushing her upper body well past the edge of the booth railing. It forces us past the invisible sound barrier, giving every ear the opportunity to hear what I'm about to say.

"Tell me you think the shifter is sexy one more time, and I will fuck you in front of every single pair of eyes in here. And I will keep fucking you until everyone knows you're mine."

Her eyes widen in shock, and her mouth opens—surely to discredit everything I just said—but I don't give her the opportunity to retort in a way that messes up the ploy.

I drag us both back into the booth, but instead of allowing her to take her own seat, I force her onto my lap and groan quietly as her ass presses down on my stiff cock. She squirms as if to move off of me, which makes it worse, so I wrap my arms around her and hold tight.

"Sit still, or the lie will turn into a threat," I warn, whispering the words against her ear.

She shudders violently. Smoky citrus starts to permeate the air, and as badly as I wish the sound barrier blocked the smell, it does not. Everyone now knows that my woman is a brat, and she's also very turned on.

"Why did you lie?" She says it with much less venom, the sound breathier than before.

"Because it's better they think you're being a brat that's about to get fucked than a mysterious superpower who is going to wreck this entire place with all of us in it for something you don't understand."

She's quiet for a long time. Long enough for those still curious, possibly hoping for the show I so expertly lied about, to turn around. When every eye is back on the fight and no longer focused on us, she finally responds.

"Regardless of whether I understand the custom or not, I don't like that there are people here against their will," she says it with such force, that air rushes from her chest.

"Val, its Hell. We're all here against our will," Parker responds before I get the chance.

I catch Van's eye as he turns to look at Parker with something other than complete disdain. It's almost shocking, and I hope that—maybe one day—they'll be able to be near each other without me having to worry that Van is going to kill him every time he opens his mouth.

"Corvus, when we first met, you mentioned having to fight if we…" she pauses, the air quiet for a second before she can think of what to say. "Were *intimate*. Is this what you meant? You would've been forced to do this?"

My heart pangs at the reminder, and I try hard not to think about what could've happened had we not fulfilled the bargain.

"No," I murmur. "If I broke that bargain with the Devil I made before I met you, I would've been sent to the Death Pits."

"What's that?" she asks, a note of apprehension in her voice. I don't respond, trying to think of a way to ease her understanding that Fight Nights are tame compared to what happens in the Death Pits.

"It is a market for demons to punish their underlings. Mostly tied to bargains, but some enter gladiators for wealth or simply entertainment." Van supplies, not giving me a chance to answer.

"Van," I snap, urging him to shut up. Bright green eyes meet mine.

"The Death Pits," he continues, ignoring my warning, "are like what your human culture had in ancient times. Slaves were forced to fight in battle royals. Some for their freedom, some for their own wealth, but almost all for some form of punishment. Had you been intimate before Corvus fulfilled his bargain with the Devil, he would have served 100 years in the pits. A stupid bargain, if you ask me."

"Well, we didn't," I snap, angry at his meddling.

"You didn't tell me it was that serious," she scoffs, turning to face me. Fear is evident in her blue eyes.

"I didn't want to worry you. And I didn't feel worthy of you, so it didn't really seem like an issue. I resisted as long as I could, but I would risk it all over again if I had to do a do-over." I smile softly, her compassion bringing a softness out of me I don't normally show.

She quietly settles further into my chest and watches the fight again. I'm sure there are tons of questions whirling in her brain, but we all know this isn't the place.

The shifter goes through three more unfortunate opponents before things really start to get wild. All thoughts of our conversation abruptly go quiet as the savagery persists.

I lose track throughout the night, but it's got to be one of the shifter's last fights before he is officially done and let out of the ring. Considering the last few opponents have all had weapons while he's had none, I imagine he's one of the ones forced to be here. Either a rival shifter threw him in, and his pack was unable to get him out before he was put in the ring. Or, he's a rogue with no pack to protect him.

The cage still rattles with the voracity of the crowd. He ignores them expertly, putting down each opponent with ease. That is, until he's faced with two of the largest opponents he's fought tonight. Covered in armor and holding long, staff-like batons that spark at one end, they make a dangerous pair. With all the armor, I can't tell what kind of demons the opponents are, but whatever the shifter did to deserve this punishment, they want it to hurt.

Oh, someone *really* doesn't like him.

I sit up a little straighter, drawn into the main event. If he wins, against all the odds stacked against him, it will be a grand show of his prowess, and it's never a bad idea to have someone like that on your side. Better your ally than your enemy.

The fight starts as all the others did; the shifter waits patiently on his side of the ring as his two opponents communicate without words before simultaneously attacking from both sides. They reach him at the same time, but their strategy is off. Instead of swinging their staffs at opposite ends of his body, they both go for his ribs. With large paw-like hands, he grabs the ends of both weapons and yanks one closer while shoving the other away.

Both opponents fall gracelessly. Where one dances away from the danger, the other falls right into it. He grabs the one falling into him by the throat before slamming the sparking end of the second staff into the side of their head. Sparks fly, and the body flails and jerks before going completely limp. He drops the body and steps unceremoniously over it. It's the cruelest he's acted all night, usually going for a more merciful death than something as painful as 1000 volts to the brain.

The remaining opponent scrambles to his feet before reaching for something in a hidden pocket of his armor. I expect another weapon to be drawn, but instead, there is a quick flash of metal before he jams something into his own neck.

The reaction is instantaneous. Limbs distort and its spine curls. The armor rattles as the body inside transforms. As pieces of metal fall to the sand, a gasp echoes through the crowd. Where a normal-sized demon once stood is a grotesque giant of disproportionate limbs and red eyes. Who knew who this faceless demon was before the injection? Their dark, masked armor covers everything underneath but the red eyes are a notorious indicator that a demon that has chosen a dark path and is nothing but one of the feared creatures of Hell now.

I've heard about the transformative drugs in Hell. We've got everything here, so an injection that turns a demon into a monster isn't outside the realm of possibilities. I've never seen the effects in person—the drugs were thought to be a myth, a way to explain away the worst of the demonic creatures that roam Hell in their monstrous forms—but the reality is so much worse. The transformation can be voluntary—or not, depending on who wields the dangerous drug.

If the shifter walks out alive, it'll be a miracle.

The giant creature charges, its gait uneven as it thunders across the ring. The metal cage rattles as the thunderous pounding of its feet echoes in the large room. The crowd has gone wild, the scene worse than usual, even for Fight Night. But I guess this isn't a normal fight; this is clearly a set-up.

I growl under my breath, irritated that, once again, I'm stuck watching as someone loses their life simply for the drama of it all. I can't know if the shifter deserved it, but guessing by the grim faces scattered in the crowd, there's at least a few who think he doesn't. Fate says to listen to your instincts, and mine are screaming that, whoever this shifter is, he's important.

One clubbed fist is swung, but it's so large that it sails through the air and is easily avoided. The shifter pants wildly as he jumps out of the way of a kick that barely misses his leg. The creature has no skill to its movements, making them hard to predict. As the shifter is gearing up to knock the giant's legs from beneath them, he misses the backhand headed for him. Not even the gasp of the crowd could drown out the sound of the giant's hand swiping the shifter off his feet. His back hits the ground with a thump, and a pained groan escapes his chest. His boot-clad legs jerk as he presses a hang to the side of his head.

The creature charges, drawn in like a predator to injured prey.

Valencia gasps as the creature grabs the shifter by the ankle and throws him across the cage. The wired wall squeals as the shifter's body slams into it and lands back on the blood-covered floor face-first. The crowd goes silent. Only the sounds of shuffling feet on a sandy floor can be heard. Dust puffs into the air around his body as he lies still in the blood of those he's already killed tonight.

What a shame. To be taken out in the last fight. Irritation boils in my chest, causing my hands to heat. I itch to set the creature on fire but I'd only be asking for trouble for myself and my group. It's not just disrespectful to intervene, it's dangerous. Though everyone does it from the shadows, a blatant show of favoritism for one opponent or another is asking for a crowd full of demons to come after you with death on their minds.

We're all frozen in anticipation. He's still breathing, the rattling of each breath loud enough to hear, but he's motionless otherwise.

"Is he paralyzed?" Parker asks quietly.

I want to say no, but I'm not sure he isn't with how still he's being. His breaths start coming faster, and his body jerks a few times before a groan escapes him. He doesn't try to get up, just lies still in the sand as if he's given up.

The creature zeros in on his body before charging one last time, surely about to end his suffering, if nothing else.

Valencia rushes to the edge of the booth before I'm able to stop her. She leans over the railing, her upper body shifting just past the edge of the sound barrier. I'm not fast enough to stop her.

"Fight!" she screams.

Just as the giant leans over the shifter, one fist raised to the air, the shifter rolls away and kicks the wires to force his body away from the edge of the cage and back to the middle of the ring. He rolls to his feet, grabbing one of the long staffs from the sand before swinging around and jamming the sparking end into the back of the giant's knee.

The monster roars as it drops to a kneeled position. The shifter wastes no time and jumps onto the giant's back, using the staff to choke it. The monster thrashes, but its gangly, misshaped limbs are unable to reach the shifter as he pulls the staff against its neck as hard as he can. There's thrashing—and pure will from the shifter—before the monster falls to the sands.

The shifter jumps off and tosses the staff to the ground. His body is covered in cuts, bruises, blood, and probably a few broken bones. He wastes no time and grabs a large knife off the ground before hacking away at the back of its neck.

Blood spatters into the air, covering him as he severs the monsters head.

"He won; why is he doing that?" Valencia asks with a shudder. She sits back down on my lap, her body shaking, repulsed by the sight.

"Severing the head is the only way to ensure the creature is truly dead. And that he wins the round. It was his last, so he's free to stop fighting."

"Ugh, I hate this place," Valencia groans.

"I mean, the beginning wasn't too bad," Parker responds, but his face is paler than normal.

"Why are we here watching the fights, anyways? Aren't we supposed to be looking for the demon the Devil wants?" She shifts in my lap as if to get comfortable, but I'm sure it's from unease.

I curse myself silently; I got so caught up in the fights that I forgot we're here for Davgus, the demon who tried to kill me.

I feel a little better knowing that he's not in this room, at least. I hadn't seen him all night, and in attempts to eye every demon looking our way, I checked nearly every face in here. I still see Davgus' face in my mind, as clear as if I'm back in that moment. No, he's not here. Whatever tip Van got was a lie... or a ploy. There's no true way to tell.

Thanks to the shifter, it wasn't a complete waste. Now I just have to convince him that fighting for me is better than fighting for himself. And, if he's here unwillingly, I guess I'll just have to become his new master.

Valencia may hate me for using him against his will, but I will commit any number of crimes to ensure her safety. And I'll ruin us all in the process if I must.

CHAPTER 17
VALENCIA

"Let's go," Corvus urges, lifting me from his lap and onto my feet. I shiver against the chill, though it's more so due to the violent ending of the fight we just witnessed.

"Is it over?" I ask him, watching the crowd that still pushes against the cage, as if eager for more.

"For us it is," he answers ominously but I don't argue, happy to get out of here.

My stomach still aches from all the turning it did tonight. I expected Hell to be vicious and gruesome, but I wasn't expecting to witness sixteen murders in one night. Oddly, despite having watched him kill every opponent he faced, I'm drawn to the winner, almost... happy he didn't lose.

We stand as a group and leave the booth. Corvus holds onto my hand tightly, our fingers intertwined. It's a comforting connection, and something I hadn't realized I needed. Hearing that he could've faced 100 years of a night like this has had my body breaking out in sweats.

We walk through the room, dodging demons both standing and on the floor. Parker crowds against my back. The way my shirt collar pulls tight against my neck, he must have a hold of it. His own version of staying connected. I want to turn and see if Van is following as well, but I'm afraid to turn my back to what's in front of me.

Ever since the fights started, an uneasy feeling has filled me from head to toe. Something's off about this place. At first, I thought it was just the needless killing, but when Corvus told me there were people here against their will, a spark was lit within me.

I can feel the now-familiar heat in my hands, and for the first time, my claws are at the edge of my consciousness. I could release them with a simple thought. Who knew all those hours spent teaching me to call on them were wasted? All I really needed was to witness some gruesome displays of exploitation.

Corvus leads us through the crowd of demons, ignoring the jeering looks and snide remarks. His outwardly calm demeanor doesn't fool me, because the tension in his shoulders increases with every look or comment.

We finally break through the large group of bodies to pass through a literal wall. I jerk as Corvus heads right for it, but I'm not strong enough to pull him to a stop as he walks right through. My brain goes haywire as we walk into another open room. I didn't feel a thing, not a feather's touch of sensation as we walked through the wall. I turn to make sure Parker and Van are still behind us, and sure enough, my best friend stands, shaking his shoulders slightly as if just as grossed out about the weird wall as I am.

Van, on the other hand, looks everywhere but at us. His angular face is cast in shadow, the hollows of his cheeks more prominent in this darker setting. He scans the room, as if taking in every detail. I mimic him, noting all the people running around, in a rush for some reason, but there's nothing in here that gives me even the slightest hint of where we are.

Something is definitely up with this tent because it should've ended forever ago, and yet we keep going deeper and deeper into the impossible the longer we're here.

There are some large crates to my right, wooden and sturdy, but one of them rattles as if whatever is inside is not happy to be there. No sound comes from the crate, no animalistic growls or predator calls. Just silent movement that makes it all the more unsettling.

Corvus squeezes my hand twice before letting go to lightly grab the back of my head. He pulls me towards him, leaning down to speak quietly in my ear.

"That wall we walked through leads to the back of the fighting ring. It's not actually in Tornil's tent, so we've lost what little protection we had from him. Don't react to anything you may see or hear." He kisses the side of my head, briefly tucking a piece of hair behind my ear before standing and stepping slightly in front of me.

A male, as tall as Corvus but leaner, approaches our group. He's got shaggy brown hair, hazel eyes that shine in the low light, and a soft smattering of hair on his face. There's a grace to his movements—an ease to the way he crosses the floor. His tan pants and white shirt look entirely too human. He's barefoot, feet covered in dust from the dirt floor like he hasn't had shoes on in a while, and though his toes just being out in the open kind of creeps me out, at least they're not deformed or weirdly shaped.

"King Crow. A pleasure as always," the male bows low, a fist placed in the center of his chest. When he stands, those predatory eyes glance at me. He locks on, scanning me from head to toe, and his eyes widen when he sees the dark red-jewelry in my ears.

"I wouldn't if I were you," Parker pipes up behind me. "He's already given warnings about fucking her in public to claim her, but I imagine he's more likely to just rip your head off first."

The man promptly shifts his focus from me, though those hazel eyes now zero in on Parker.

"And who are *you?*" He asks with a purr.

The Devil damn Parker and his big fat mouth.

"Jamison—the shifter who fought tonight; give me his story," Corvus demands, not giving the male a chance to respond to Parker.

Jamison eyes Parker a little longer before focusing his attention on Corvus. "That's Orson. Bear shifter. Nomad, though it's suspected he'll join the Shaded after tonight. Or maybe even the Red Guardians. I saw a few of the RG's with their eyes on him. Sad story, truly. Supposedly, he was sold to the Market by his parents when he was young. This is his first appearance since he was in his early teens. Maybe we have a real-life Ghost pack member in our midst."

Jamison gives his story lightheartedly, as if he didn't just tell us that the man who went ten rounds to the death tonight is actually here because he was sold as a child. He also said a lot of other things I didn't understand, some of Hell's culture that must be common to them but just seems like random words strung together to me.

What is the Market? and *who is the Ghost pack?* There are so many questions I'd love to have answered, but one statement sticks with me above the others. '*Sold by his parents'*. If his parents aren't dead yet, I want to kill them for what they've done to this Orson.

The fire in my hands burns with a vengeance, and I really suspect they're about to come out to play until a sharp sting of pain radiates from one hand. I growl at the pain of my knuckles crushing together, giving Corvus a harsh look for his tight grip, but he ignores me, still focused on Jamison.

"Who owns him?" Corvus asks nonchalantly. The burning persists despite the pain.

"The First Lord," Jamison responds, the sneer evident in his voice. Whoever this *'First Lord'* is, I immediately hate him.

Corvus nods stiffly, as if he instantly understands. Unfortunately, he doesn't share with the class, so I'm left in the dark.

"If he's freed, tell him to contact me," Corvus tells Jamison before side-stepping him.

"I think not. No offense, King Crow, but Orson has been in captivity since he was a teenager. If he's freed from one master, I won't be the one who sends him to be caged by another. If you want him so badly, you'll have to get him yourself." Jamison stands stiffly as if a rod has been welded to his back, but there's determination in his eyes. His harsh tone stops Corvus in his tracks.

He slowly turns to the leaner man, a deadly gleam to his dark eyes, and a sick feeling of fear builds within me. It's the same feeling I had in Parker's Tahoe when I told him about how Dumah had left me to die on the mountain.

Corvus steps towards Jamison, who shivers but remains firm in his stance.

"I agree with him," I say, returning the favor by crushing Corvus' hand in my fist.

He doesn't flinch or react in any way, just shifts those scary eyes to me.

He's silent, not showing any sign of how he's feeling under his that dark exterior, and I stare him down in return, refusing to give in. He can brood and act as intimidating as he wants, but I know what he looks like when he comes and I've heard him confess his feelings for me. All of that has now steeled my spine to his darkness.

"As you wish, kitten," Corvus finally growls, the sound low in his chest. Some may think the nickname is demeaning, but the way he says it sounds as if he just confessed his undying loyalty to me—his one true queen.

I release a silent breath and nod to Jamison before pulling Corvus away so he can't change his mind, winking at Jamison behind Corvus' back. His eyes are wide with shock, and his mouth hangs open wide enough to catch a bird, let alone flies.

I see Parker tap his chin out of the corner of my eye and laugh beneath my breath before turning forward once again. Corvus is leading us further into the room. I have no idea what we're going to find, but every encounter has been eventful to say the least.

We're walking through the various groups of people who all seem to act like stagehands at a play; they scramble around, seemingly all running to complete some task, but there are no visible signs that anything is getting done. I freeze in my tracks, forcing Corvus to stop as well. Parker bumps into my back but quickly steps away.

"Jeez, what's with the brakes?" Parker asks.

My blood runs cold, the chill flowing throughout my entire body. I focus on a dark hallway to our right. I swear I saw a face I know—a face I now see in my nightmares alongside flames, his gruesome smile laughs and laughs and laughs as he kills my friend over and over again.

I didn't need a new nightmare to obsess over, yet the image replays in my sleep. I don't move. I barely breathe as I stare at the spot where I just saw him. It's empty now, just a blank dark, space—but something inside me tells that if I wait just a little longer, he'll be there again.

"Valencia," Corvus says to me, trying to get my attention, but I ignore him.

"What is it Val? Another hot shifter? Point him out," Parker pats my shoulder, looking around the room. There's warmth from the touch of his palm, but I don't feel it through the ice inside me.

"I would never allow you to disgrace *any* shifter with your vile touch, Rat," Van tells Parker, death in his voice.

"Can someone tell the Great Tree to stop being mean to me? It turns me on," Parker responds jokingly, earning a growl from Van. "Corvus, get your dog, I think it bites," Parker urges, stepping closer to me. The growl coming from Van is so loud, people scurry away from us.

Corvus and Van start quietly arguing, their voices not carrying any farther than our small group.

I ignore it all, focusing on the dark spot. I know he was there. I can feel it in my bones. If I'm patient enough, he'll come back. He has to. I didn't come all this way, to Hell itself, to let my friend's killer get away.

I may have come here to understand what happened to my family, to Tucker, but revenge sounds nice, too.

CHAPTER 18
VALENICA

MY PATIENCE PAYS OFF tenfold when the demon, himself, leaves the dark and steps into the room. He's drunk, or high, or some hellish version of the two because he stumbles in with a group of other demons surrounding him. There are probably six of them in total, but my brain could care less.

6 v 1 when I barely managed 1 v 1? Sounds like a great idea.

Logic takes a back seat, drowned beneath a primal roar of rage. The pain of my claws rapidly ripping through my fingers does nothing to dampen the viscous feelings that course through my blood. My pulse races, but not with fear. Fear is no longer my concern. This is a liquid heat that spreads like fire. Nothing else registers besides the intoxicating darkness.

I charge, my heart pounding with painful emotions, and I smile savagely as the demon turns his back on me in order to throttle one of his friends. A part of me—something buried deep in shadows—claws its way to the surface. I should be fearful of the foreign feelings it brings with it, but I'm not.

An *'oh shit'* comes from somewhere behind me, but that rage inside could care less. Everything is tinted with red as the demon settles in my sights.

Prey, with his neck exposed to a predator he doesn't see coming.

I run faster than my feet have ever carried me, forcing demons to scramble out of my way. A few of the demons in the group notice my approach, and they're quick to get out of the way—leaving their supposed 'friend' on his own. An island of his own making.

The sound of pounding feet follows, but they're not fast enough. I reach the demon with a flying jump and dig my claws into the sides of his neck. Blood spurts, covering my hands, arms, and face, but it doesn't deter me. I'm on a one-track mission.

Mission: kill this motherfucker.

The demon immediately thrashes, his large hands reaching up to grab at me with a howl of pain, but I've wrapped my legs around his waist and he isn't able to throw me off despite the way he wildly thrashes. A few of the demons in the group step towards, us but a blur of black flashes past, and Corvus tackles them to the ground, pummeling one in the face with his fist shortly after snapping the neck of another.

The others promptly step back, giving us a wide berth around. Some part of me wants to be shocked at the lifeless body lying on the ground—but that's a human feeling—and, when the rage is in control, feelings are nothing but nuisances.

My body jerks to the side as the demon I'm still attached to tries to dislodge me. A large fist is finally able to grab me by the hair, which is extremely unfortunate for me because he immediately yanks it, causing me to yell out a howl of pain. I ignore it as best I can though, and power through.

"Hey, backoff, asshole!"

"You stupid Rat!"

I hear yelling, and that familiar nickname catches my attention. I don't let go of the demon with my claws, but it costs me, nonetheless.

The demon manages to grab me by the arm and yanks me forward. He nearly rips his own throat out, my talon-like claws ripping through his skin as if it were thin fabric. Blood pours down the front of his body in a gruesome sight, but he stands over me unwaveringly.

I wish I could forget this demon's face, but it is engraved into my mind. Burned into my psyche so deeply that I don't know if I'll ever get it out. He's not tall or muscular and doesn't have any crazy, distinguishing features other than his ugly smile. Gangly teeth hang rotted and crooked, most of them black or downright gone. They're so much worse than the first time I saw his face. Which is maybe partially my fault, since the last time I saw him, I ripped his jaw clean off.

There's a wild edge to his eyes as he focuses on me.

"Who knew you'd come back for more? I do love it when they fight back," his gravelly voice sounds rougher than before, which I imagine has to do with the damage I've done to his neck. I kick my leg out, catching him in the ankle, but he does nothing besides jerk slightly.

I scramble to my feet, fighting to catch my breath. Now that we face one another, I'm much less confident than I was at first. The rage hasn't completely dissipated, but it's taken a back seat to the pain of having the air knocked from my lungs. I can tell the claws are still out, but considering that's the only thing I know how to do, he's going to wipe the floor with me if I don't get help soon.

I want to look around and see what's going on with Van and Parker, but I've learned my lesson with that already. I'd also like to call out to Corvus, but I don't do that, either. Fighting still goes on around me, but I'm not able to take my eyes off the demon in front of me.

Human instinct tells me to call for help. To run from danger.

But human instinct isn't in control. I can recognize the need to retreat, but something inside me has taken the wheel, and it refuses to do anything but fight.

With an evil smirk, he steps towards me.

I tense up to prepare myself for an attack, but it never comes.

The demon freezes, his eyes bulging from his head. He looks down at his hands, which now shake violently, but there's nothing there. His mostly pale skin starts to turn a light red, and beads of sweat gather on his forehead.

I'm frozen as well, unsure if his pause is a ploy to draw me in or if something is really going on.

"It's his blood. It's boiling from the inside," Corvus says, right behind me.

I jump at the sound, shocked and ashamed that I let him sneak up on me. I look him over, noting only a small cut on his knuckles. Just behind him, two bodies lie still on the ground. Big, dark rings of blood slowly seep from them, slightly turning my stomach. No matter how many times I see it, it still gives me the creeps to see a dead body.

"They're not dead, just taking a nap," Corvus says to me, clearly noting the way I look, sickened, at their still forms.

I want to ask what he means, but Van snapping at me draws my attention.

"You did good, my Lady, but *Rat* nearly got itself killed, and I was forced to save it. If you'd like, I will kill him now and eliminate the issue for all of us." The words shoot out as if they taste like acid on his tongue.

"Van, Parker is my friend," I snap, glancing over at said friend. He's smiling, bright white teeth shining in the dim light. Van may have hated it, but he protected Parker well because there isn't a single scratch on him.

"They're the same thing," Van responds, walking up to the frozen demon with a rope in his hand. I have no idea where he got it, but he starts to wrap it around the demon's body, strapping his arms tight to his torso and further immobilizing his legs. The demon grimaces as if in immense pain from every touch of Van's hand. He hisses each time Van pulls the cord tight.

People mill around as if nothing unusual is happening, and I watch for a second, worried someone will come to these demons' aid, but they all ignore us and move hurriedly in all different directions.

The demon draws my attention with a particularly pain-filled groan. I can't imagine that having your blood boiled from the inside feels very good.

"Davgus, it seems you've bit off more than you can chew this time around," Corvus says to the demon. I notice Van is standing just behind him, and judging by the hand placement, he must be holding the demon up on his feet. Corvus speaks with a familiarity that starts to make me uncomfortable.

"You're supposssssed to be dead," Davgus hisses in response. The 's' elongated and raspy. A pit grows firm and heavy in my stomach. I don't think this is just any random demon that the Devil wants.

Which means Corvus *knew*. He knew the whole time we were coming after the demon who killed Tucker.

Now I'm the one with boiling blood.

"You can thank your poor aim for that," Corvus steps up close. Regardless of my lingering anger, fear rushes through me as he gets closer.

"Impossible, my aim wasss true," Davgus argues, his red-shot eyes bouncing all over Corvus' chest as if looking for an explanation.

"Like I said, you've got yourself to thank for that. Now, how about you tell me who sent you?" A dark red blade flashes up to Davgus' neck, held steady in Corvus' hand.

Davgus seizes in pain upon contact with the knife.

"I think it's something elsssse," Davgus hisses, his body jerking to a stop before his eyes focus back on me. "I think you died, and someone saved you. What a debt to acquire, Crow." Davgus spits blood out of his nasty mouth, but it evaporates in a burst of fire before it reaches anyone.

"You know, my debts don't really matter. But yours? Yours are coming due. We'll see if the Devil has better luck questioning you," Corvus smirks, an evil look covering his face.

Those who still linger around us stop and gasp, equal looks of horror and pity among them. They must think speaking to the Devil is a fate worse than death.

Maybe for creatures that can't really die, it is.

"It doesn't really matter what you do to me; he still hunts," Davgus snaps.

"Who? Who hunts?" Corvus demands, his hands balling into fists

Instead of responding to Corvus, the demon looks at me.

"How pathetic, you gave everything for him, and yet he keeps things from you," Davgus hisses, blood dripping down the side of his mouth. Corvus turns, as if to stop him, but he continues to ramble more of the gory mess of words. "You might as well kill me now, or I'm going to kill your lover, *again*, just like I killed your little friend."

Pain sears through me, burning me from the inside out. I'm unable to stop myself from reacting. Even though I know he said it to antagonize me, deep emotional pain scorches the nerves that run to my brain and stop all logical thinking. Warnings flare in my mind, but they go ignored.

Control snaps like a frayed thread, and with it comes a twisted reshaping of something fundamental inside of me.

Warmth surrounds my hand as I bury my fingers in his chest. Sharp claws rip through fabric, skin, and muscle with ease. It takes a couple of jerks, but I wrap my fingers around the warm, beating heart, and feel the soft *thump thumps* against the smooth skin on my fingertips.

Davgus' body jerks a few more times. A slow trail of blood falls from one eye; his lower face and neck are completely covered. His eyes start to roll back in his head, but I squeeze my fingers tightly until his eyes flash back open, though somewhat unfocused.

"I promised you'd know what it felt like to take an angel feather to art. I'm sad, ripping your heart out is the only option I have." I start to pull, my fingers tightening around the hot organ. Red liquid floods from the holes around my fingers, brightened by the red tint of the rage. I'm so focused on my task that I don't notice the strange shifting of his body that happens around me.

"Holy fucking Christ," I hear from Parker behind me before the sound of his retching echoes around the walls.

I look up, expecting to see an exploded head or something equally gross, but instead am met with a face I never thought I'd see again.

"Thank you," he whispers to me in a soft tone. Too entranced with the heart in my hands, I didn't witness the transformation—the change between the demon I despise and one of my old teammates. Landon Michaelson was supposed to be on Earth, living out his life, being an asshole. He's not supposed to be here, in Hell.

Nothing changed. The clothes are the same, the body is the same, and yet Davgus' ugly face has been replaced with Landon's. He smiles softly, as if consumed with peace, before his eyes roll back into his head and his lifeless body slumps against Van's hold.

The drop in his weight forces my hand from his chest. A gaping hole remains where my fist once was, dark red and stringy from the torn muscles.

The small organ beats a few more times in my hand before going still, cooling almost instantly. The heat of the blood drops instantly when met with air.

I stare at the heart held in my hand, sickened.

I start to waver on my feet, overwhelmed entirely by what just happened. The presence inside of me that craves the control of my anger instantly retreats. It's a violent recoiling of every bit of strength that's keeping me standing. The absence is as sudden as the appearance, and yet this all the more staggering. I have to puppet my own movements, but every thought is consumed with guilt.

I'm in a familiar room, but everything around me has changed. Echoes remain of the primal instincts, but it's quiet in the cavernous space of what remains.

Strong arms wrap around and hold me. "Don't react, drop the heart and walk out of here with your head held high."

I'm frozen, unable to react even if I wanted to, so Corvus grabs the heart for me, tossing it on the lifeless body of my former teammate. The teammate I just killed. With my bare hands. The teammate who left us all on the mountain in anger because he lashed out. He attacked us, said awful things to me, but I never would've wish this upon him. I never thought I'd see him again. I wish it could've stayed that way.

Corvus wraps an arm around my shoulders, pulling me to his side before slowly moving us out of the room the same way we entered. I follow his direction, my head held high. I'm covered in blood and who knows what else, but I can't focus on anything other than the fact that Landon was here in Hell, and I just killed him.

It's a short trip out of the circus tent, much less crowded than before. They watch us as we navigate through the bodies that are still present. I notice that a few take a small step away from Van, but they otherwise they mind their space. They don't act like I they know I just killed someone. We aren't chased out of the tent, guards don't holler or demand we stop. We're not even sneaking out. I keep my eyes firmly on the back of Corvus' head, afraid to look at the demons around his. Will they be able to see the guilt in my face?

We make it outside with no issues, and it's a blessing because the shock really starts to set in. My hands shake uncontrollably, and the back of my neck grows clammy. My heart stutters in my chest to an uneven beat, racing one second and nearly stopping the next.

I'm so unfocused as to what's going on around me, that it's another stark shock to my system as the world around me whisks away into the nothingness of the in-between that Corvus travels through. It zaps me, leeching my dark emotions and sickened feelings. When we pop back into Corvus' home, my knees give out, and I land painfully on the rock floor. I have seconds to prepare before I'm leaning forward on all four and emptying my stomach.

Someone softly removes my hair from my shoulders, pulling it away from my face. I don't move. My stomach is settled now that I've gotten the sickness out, but my mind is on a riot path of guilt and shame.

"Please explain to me what the fuck happened back there," Parker demands around his own gagging. Van, thankfully, doesn't respond with his usual venom.

"Possession. It seems Landon was possessed by Davgus at some point." Corvus' deep voice curls over me, a soft safety blanket, yet his words induce dread.

"Then why did he look different? He didn't look like Landon until after." Parker pauses his rant. We all know what he's not saying. The demon, Davgus, was the same demon from the mountain, who killed Tucker and almost killed Corvus. That is until I started crushing his heart in my hand. Once Landon's familiar face was looking down at me, it was already too late.

"It's my fault, I didn't realize Davgus was a Parasite. It's a type of demon that's able to take on hosts through possession. They meld their features together so that when they take on a new host, the features change, yet the body is still the same. I'm so sorry, Valencia, I should've considered it," Corvus murmurs to me, gently brushing back my hair.

"He thanked me. Why would he thank me?" I choke the words out, guilt nearly breaking me. Pushing away from the pile of vomit, I lean up on my knees. My hands slip on my thighs, blood making the fabric slick. I whimper, bringing my shaky hands up to my face.

In the hustle of getting out of Tornil's without making a further scene, I didn't notice the carnage. There's blood everywhere. It's soaked into my clothes, the damp fabric pressing against my skin. I can feel the itchiness of dried specks scattered across my body. I gingerly touch my hair, but it's matted in wet strings. My right hand is the worst. The one I shoved in Davgus' chest.

Corvus takes the rag that Van hands him and wipes my face. It's cool and blissful against my fevered skin. Heat follows the chill, and within seconds, every speck of gore is burned from my body without leaving a single burn mark behind. He's so careful with the power, able to sear the blood from single strands of hair, but it doesn't wash away the stain on the inside.

"Landon was possessed by a demon that was willing to commit a number of atrocious things. Despite having no control over his body, he would be forced to witness everything first-hand. A Parasite demon takes control of the body and the features, but the host is still there, and lives through everything. He may not have been a good guy, but I don't think he deserved the things Davgus must've put his psyche through. I'm sure he was grateful for his suffering to come to an end. You offered him mercy, even if it doesn't feel that way."

"I could've saved him instead of killing him!" I argue, hot tears spill down my cheeks.

"You couldn't have. There is no happy ending for a host who has been possessed by a Parasite Demon. Unfortunately, death is the happy ending," Corvus urges me to my feet and pulls me to the couch, where he forces me down next to him. He holds on tight but doesn't crowd me.

"I just don't understand," I murmur, watching as Van cleans up after me. I use the hand gesture he showed me that is used as a sign of thanks, but he doesn't notice it.

"Baby, its Hell. It's not to be understood. It's to be endured," Corvus offers comfort with a slight squeeze.

It makes me sad for him, knowing he's lived here most of his entire existence, and yet all he can say about this place he calls home is that it's to be endured. Ruby Valley may have held some dark secrets for me, but it was still home. It still had Ole Joe's, it had my favorite hikes, the mountains I love, and the band of misfits who ended up becoming family. Regardless of the dark history, I loved Ruby Valley.

"Why Landon," I ask, not really wanting to know. "He was normal the last time I saw him."

"I suspect he was already possessed while on your hiking exercise. Didn't you say he was behaving strangely all of a sudden?" Corvus wipes the cloth under my hair, cleaning away the sticky sweat.

"Yeah, he was," I contemplate, remembering Landon's sudden change in behavior on the second day of the hike.

"He was fine the first day, acting like his normal asshole self, and then he acted completely deranged the second day," Parker confirms out loud.

Corvus nods. "Most likely, Davgus needed a reason to get close, and with Landon's typically aversive personality, he was probably the best option for a host. Parasite demons can only possess hosts who already lean towards darker emotions. It's a part of the general protection against them. But all they need is an open door, and they can sneak their way in."

I tip my head back against the couch and stare at the rock ceiling.

"If Davgus possessed Landon on the hike, then why did he show up on the mountain as someone else?" I ask no one in particular.

"Because we know," Parker pauses, pain in his voice, "knew Landon. We wouldn't have trusted him at that point on the mountain."

Pain sears in my ribs like hot fire. Each breath feels like a gigantic effort. It feels like we didn't stand a chance, all things considered. Not to mention, I haven't had a second of time to consider the impaction that Corvus knew exactly who we were heading out to find tonight. My heart is already too raw to think about it—but it adds to the pain nonetheless and makes my burning desire to understand everything, so I can prevent it from happening again, even more relevant. I can't keep fighting a losing battle.

I don't know whether we will ever make it back to Ruby Valley, or what it would even look like, considering the time differences between the two realms. What I do know, if I am going to be stuck here in Hell for the rest of my life, is that I am going to work damn hard for it to be something to treasure. No more of this *endure* shit. I am going to make this place my home, even if I have to start razing Hell to do it.

Chapter 19
Corvus

I'M AT A LOSS for words as we sit on the couch in my living room. Van has stalked off into the cave, doing his own thing. Parker is perched on the edge of the chair next to us, his head in his hands, fingers speared through messy locks of red hair.

Valencia is in my arms, but her skin feels as cool as the leather beneath us.

Thoughts flash through my mind, all begging for dominance. I'm concerned she hasn't said anything about how I knew who Davgus was, or more specifically, that he's who the Devil sent us after. But, since she hasn't brought it up, I hope that she hasn't caught on. It's a delusional hope; her sharp mind is one of my favorite things about her, and it's only a matter of time before she pressures me about that.

Valencia cares, even when she doesn't want to, which means that killing Davgus will haunt her. I refuse to think of him as Landon. It's better if we all just mourn his death as if he died back on Earth—because he did. As soon as Davgus possessed his body, his death sentence started. But I'm unsure if she will be able to feel the same way.

There's also the issue of moving forward. Killing Davgus definitely made me happy, but it only opens more problems. More thoughts to stew over and over and over.

The loudest yells, in my own irritated voice, are about how stupid I've been.

It's not a gigantic surprise that Valencia's old coworker was possessed. I probably should've seen it sooner, given all the details, but my mind has been overrun by thoughts of her and everything else pales in comparison.

She's not shaking as badly anymore, but I can still see a tremble in her fingers.

"Shit," I huff, once again frustrated with myself.

I lift Valencia onto my lap and then stand, carrying her through the cave. She squirms against the hold, complaining that she can walk, but I know that if she really wanted to get down, she would force me to put her down. I walk us both into my bathroom and turn on the water. It's blissfully warm as we step inside and the steam provides a warm blanket while we undress. She starts to take off her own clothes, but I don't let her, wanting to take care of her in this small way.

Giving up, she just stands and allows me to strip her before placing her in the stream of water. I rip my clothes from my body and throw them all in a pile in the corner. Instantly, the clothes burst into flames with the slightest thought, and I erase what little evidence I can of the night. Not for forensics but for the hope that it's one less thing to remind her of what happened. She's holding it together for the most part, but I'll shoulder as many of these moments as I can, if only to offer her a small bit of peace.

"I can't wrap my brain around what happened tonight," she murmurs, her eyes closed, head tipped back in the water.

"Don't. This place will make you go absolutely bat shit if you try to find a reason for anything that happens," I encourage. It's an unfortunate truth that she'll be better off learning now than later.

"What gets me, is that I didn't think *twice* about him after he left on that mountain. He just disappeared, and I was *happy* about that. I knew he was acting differently, yet I was so caught up in my own world that I didn't take the time to wonder about what was going on with him." Her voice shakes as she speaks, with a soft hiccup as she's overcome with emotion.

We're both on the same page. As soon as a parasite takes control of the body, they can alter it to appear like many different hosts they've already possessed. Giving them the ability to transform between many different looks. A truly hidden predator. There's a limit to their camouflaging abilities, but they're so secretive that it's not well known.

It seems the demon was closer than ever, yet I was too wrapped up in her to notice it. My normal ability to sense other supernatural beings around me is nearly nonexistent when she's near. There's something about her that steals my focus. And for us, for this one reason, it's a bad thing. So much could have been avoided had I known sooner.

My death. Her giving up her soul for my resurrection. Tucker's death.

Her face shifts into one of pain as she quietly struggles with the events of the night.

"I feel like," a sob escapes her, "I feel like no matter how many people I try to save, it just kills someone in the end. I'm a killer. Something came over me, and I just reacted. I didn't even mean it. God save the world if I start meaning it."

My skin burns lightly at the curse of the heavenly maker's name. She doesn't react in any way, so it must not affect her to say such things, but I feel it like a light yet irritating sting on my skin. It's there and gone in a flash, but noticeable.

"We're all killers. We just need to help you with your aim." I start to lather her body, cleaning away the evidence that the water didn't do by itself.

"Very funny," she says with a bite of sarcasm. "I killed Davgus, or Landon, or both—and we're no closer to finding out why this is all happening or where Tucker's body is."

Another choked sob escapes her, and it's like watching a wall crumble before me. Her lips press tightly together, and I know she's trying her hardest not to lose it completely.

"We didn't walk away with nothing. You killed a powerful demon tonight—one who has tormented not only us but most likely many others. You took away someone's abuser tonight. You *saved* someone. I know you don't see Landon's death as a mercy, but it truly was. And not only that, but we found out something very important."

I watch as the soap suds against her tan skin. Thoughts building in my mind to form a picture. There's definitely *someone* after us. And though we may have killed our only link to whoever it is, we didn't leave with no clues.

"Davgus said, '*he still hunts.*' That means whoever is after us is male, and I'd bet is someone extremely powerful if they are able to get a parasite demon to do their dirty work." Her eyes narrow in confusion. I explain before she can ask. "A parasite demon is considered to be one of the more powerful species of demon. This makes them much harder to control, as you never know when or if they'll turn on you and possess you in return. They're the only species of demon that can possess other demons. No one knows how they're created, but it's typically a death sentence to have that kind of power. For Davgus to be alive and free means he was almost certainly working under someone who offered him protection. And that someone has to be very powerful, because Davgus was exactly the type of demon to possess those above him."

Valencia nods, her bright blue eyes opening for the first time. Shame and regret shine brightly, but there's also the tiniest bit of hope mixed in.

"How long is the list of demons who he could've been working for?" she asks, turning to take control and wash her own hair. I work on washing my body, slow and methodical as I think through the list.

"Not long. Maybe five or six demons—and I'm one of them. That leaves the First, the Second, the Devil, and probably one or maybe two other high-level demons in Hell. All of which happen to be male."

"Or at least look like men," Valencia ponders. I watch as she studies the puzzle in her mind, shifting around pieces that I can't see. The sadness that clung to her like a shadow shifts—not going away, but moving, molding into her. She drops her shoulders slightly, like the weight of the grief loosens. I don't comment on the change, not wanting to break the spell of peace she's found.

She steps out from the water and grabs a bar of soap and a razor from the pocket in the wall. It's a small blue one I stocked from my last trip to Earth. I don't care what anyone says but shaving with a giant razor blade just doesn't make any sense when you can just use a disposable one. Modern luxuries at its finest.

"What do you mean," I ask, washing myself in the hot stream. Valencia's eyes track the streams of soap that run down my body, and heat gathers in her cheeks as her scent thickens when she catches sight of my semi-hard cock. I grab it, slowly rinsing the soap away and enjoying the way her eyes track my every movement. "Valencia?"

"You're distracting me," she mumbles, not taking her eyes away from my body. I let my cock go, but it's hard enough now that it stands on its own. A pearly white bead of precum rests at the tip. I'm nearly driven to my knees when she licks her lips at the sight of it.

"Talk first, fuck second," I say, a smirk on my face.

"Whatever," she snarks, going back to shaving. "I just mean, isn't there the possibility that they're only appearing as a male? Maybe one of these powerful demons is actually a female."

"That's not really possible as far as I know. The only shapeshifting I know of besides parasites is the shifter demons, and that's always to an animal of some sort."

"*Hmm*, interesting," she hums, but doesn't say anything further.

"We need to go tell the Devil that Davgus is dead; he asked us to bring him in for questioning, so we may face some consequences for having killed him. I just want you to know, I won't let anything happen to you. Whatever the punishment is, I'll take it." We switch places again, rinsing her body one last time before we both step out. The towels are soft and fluffy, thanks to the enchanted dresser.

"I'm not worried about the Devil." She says it like it's a matter of fact—as if he isn't the most dangerous being in this entire realm, and a few others.

"We disobeyed an order, and he's known for his lack of patience for such things. Remember, this is the same person who made me run through Hell for 6 years straight, while being chased by Hellhounds."

"You are also the idiot who fucked a nun after you were told not to." The look she gives me is vicious, as if pissed about to think about the fact I've had sex in the past.

"It was Halloween," I grumble, knowing it's not a good enough excuse, but I've unfortunately decided that it's my hill to die on.

"I have a feeling the Devil will be okay with it," Valencia says, ignoring my comment—but she does roll her eyes, so I know she heard me.

"Don't forget, he's on the list of people who is potentially after us," I remind her—and myself.

"That doesn't make any sense, though. Why save you if he's the one who killed you?"

"Your soul." It seems like a simple enough reason to me. He wanted her soul—he knew we were becoming closer, that feelings were becoming involved, and he figured that killing me was the quickest way to get to her.

"I'm just not convinced it's the Devil. What about the others?"

We make our way into the bedroom and I try to think about the others. The First is believable, but he hasn't been seen in years. He's basically in Hell's version of retirement, so I don't think he's our guy. The Second—Nightmare—is a very likely candidate, but he also snuck into the cabin while I was dreaming to send me a warning when we were still on Earth, which makes me believe it isn't him, either.

That leaves a couple other demons who could be responsible, but despite having the power to accomplish most of what's happened, they lack the structure and support of the other demons.

This wasn't a small thing or a petty squabble for power. This was a huge move—someone secretly working in the background to pull the strings of forces that have been set in stone for hundreds of years. Someone's lying. Someone is out there, working to unravel everything I've built in Hell.

I need to find them before they take away everything good I've fought for. Before they take *her* away.

Chapter 20

Valencia

Corvus is quiet as we settle into his big bed. The sheets are soft and it's instantly warm when I cuddle up to his naked skin.

Flashes of his soap-covered body flare in my mind, and I have to force myself to not jump him all over again. I swear I can barely get anything done when he's naked—it's like I'm in this constant state of trying not to land on his hard cock at every turn.

Ever since we've gotten to Hell, there's been a frenzy in my blood, a demand that screams I take him and make him mine. That I lick, bite, suck, and scratch him. That I mark him as mine, so everyone knows he's taken. This urge to *claim* him that I can't escape.

I've been able to ignore it for the most part, but it gets harder by the day. Then, add in the sight of his naked body, and I'm almost unable to control myself.

"Why are you so convinced that the Devil isn't the one that's behind everything?" Corvus quietly asks, the dark of the room only broken up by the soft green glow of the stones on the ceiling high above.

I'm not sure why, but I don't confess the Devil's secret. She never said I had to keep it, but there is a part of me that wants to—that's proud to keep it, knowing she trusted me when she's not trusted any others. Maybe it's a delusion, this thought that the Devil won't punish me for killing Davgus, but there's a feeling in my gut that tells me that she won't.

I'm not able to give Corvus an honest answer, and the thought of lying to him feels like intentionally taking poison, so instead, I remain quiet.

He doesn't push the question, but I can practically hear the wheels in his head spinning. I know there will be a day that I tell him. That I tell him everything. Which is exactly why I can't be mad at him for keeping the information about Davgus from me. He had his reasons. I know they weren't malicious, and considering I'm keeping things from him, too, I can't be mad about it.

I snuggle in closer to his warm body, enjoying the heat. I do notice he doesn't run as hot as he used to, not nearly as feverish as he'd felt the other few times we lay completely naked like this on Earth in the small cabin that seems like a long gone memory now.

Sleep takes me fast, the dark of the room and the exhaustion of the day drawing me under.

***

It's the same heat that helped me fall asleep that wakes me again. I feel it in my bones, burning me. Panic overcomes me, and I fear we're under attack and someone has set my blood on fire like Corvus did to Davgus.

It's the purred, "Don't move," that has desire replacing the panic. His voice comes from too far away, and when I stretch my arms out, I realize he's no longer beside me in the bed.

My blood burns for a new reason. The large room is covered in his scent, a strong smell of forest and rum. It's crisp and smoky—and drives me insane.

His large hands grip me by the hips, softly pulling me down the mattress to where he kneels at the end of the bed. My legs instantly wrap around his body, and he squeezes me tighter.

"I said, don't move." His growl is deep, filling the room with its menacing tone.

My ass sits atop his thighs, the soft hair tickling the backs of my legs. His hands rub up and down my legs, warming them as he positions me exactly where he wants me.

His cock is already hard and bobbing in between our bodies. My mouth waters at the sight of it, and I consider being a brat just for a repeat of the blowjob I gave him in the shower days ago.

Though, calling it a blowjob seems almost juvenile. That wasn't some frat boy, under-aged party blowjob. That was getting your face fucked by a demon who knows *exactly* what to do with his body.

Corvus grips my hips once again, his large hands dwarfing my body, before pulling us even closer. He lifts me a little higher, one large hand wrapped around my torso, holding our chests tightly together. With the other hand, he notches himself at my entrance and slowly lowers my body down, one glorious inch at a time.

It's like puzzle pieces fitting together, how perfectly we match. My back arches as I desire courses through me. I never really considered what a relationship with Corvus would look like, but being woken to midnight sex is absolutely an added bonus.

I moan as he thrusts softly a few more times, his hard cock spearing me to the point of a nearly painful stretch. It's the first time we've fucked without copious amounts of foreplay, and my body is definitely noticing the difference. Regardless, I'm eager for him. The wet sound of our bodies coming together fills the room.

"What a little slut your pussy is, greedy for cock," he mutters with a stutter in his thrusts. His thrusts are hard but not forceful, as if he understands my body can't quite take it yet.

I don't know if it's the shame from what happened earlier in the night or something else, but I crave the pain. I want him to be rough. I want his punishment. I know he'll put the pieces back together after he breaks me.

Against anyone's better judgment, I do exactly what he told me not to do.

I squeeze my thighs around his body, forcing us together in a rough thrust. The pain is low, but there as he fills me completely.

"Devil take me; you don't fucking listen, do you?" he asks, but considering the edge in his tone, I think it's more of a statement.

"What makes you think you're worth listening to, asshole?" I ask back, matching the edge but adding just enough sass to piss him off.

An evil smile takes over his face while his eyes darken. His scent grows even stronger, his eyes darker, and his grip on my hips more forceful. I gasp at the pain, knowing there will be bruises where his fingers are.

"This is going to be so fun," he responds, a dark edge to his voice. There's a flash of silver in his eyes, but it's gone so fast I almost wonder if I even saw it. He holds himself a little taller, and his features seem to become a little rougher, as if taken over by a darker side of himself.

He thrusts a few more times before pulling out, causing me to whine at the loss. He steps off the edge of the bed to his full height, and I lean up on my elbows, about to complain at the distance, but he grabs me by my ankles and drags me down the bed towards him. The squeak that escapes me is girlish, and I try to keep it from escaping, but he laughs at the sound.

I wanted to struggle against his grip out of principle—but he pulled me closer, so I got what I wanted. Picking me up, he carries me the short distance across the room. Once standing I hiss as the cold stone touches my bare feet.

"Oh, just you wait," he says as he holds me tight. He pushes my upper body down to rest on top of a large stone table that juts out from the wall. I huff at the feel of cold against my nipples. It feels good against my heated skin, but the chill quickly sets in. I'm warmed when he leans his body against mine, pressing his front to my back to speak softly into my ear.

"When you think about this later," he says, hands sliding down my arms to twine his fingers with mine before pushing them out wide, stretching my arms as far as they'll go. "And your ass and pussy are sore from how hard I fucked you. Just know, you did it to yourself."

I jerk, my body tensing with fear and excitement. Pain sears the skin around my wrists. I jerk again, attempting to pull my hands towards me, but the more I pull them, the worse the pain gets.

"Leave them," Corvus demands, placing my hands back to how he positioned them.

A soft glow catches my eye and a small rope of flame wraps around my wrist. I test it again, attempting to pull my arms towards me, but each time I do, the rope burns. The heat heightens the harder I pull, but so as long as I remain exactly as he put me, I'm completely free of the pain.

"Is this another one of your tricks?" I gripe, moving my ankles to ensure they're not secured, breathing a sigh of relief when there's no pain from pulling them together. There's something extremely vulnerable about this position. My body is completely open to him, and with the fire wrapped around my wrists, I'm forced to stay here, allowing him absolute control.

With anyone else, I think I'd be having a panic attack, but with him, it's almost a relief to give up my control. And he's right, I got myself here. I knew that being a brat would push him, I just didn't know he had this in him. Not that I expected Corvus to be a *sex equals missionary* kind of guy, but still, I'm a little shocked.

It's then that the rest of his statement catches up with me. "You're not fucking my ass, Corvus."

"No, I'm not," he agrees. I can hear him moving around, opening a drawer to shuffle stuff around, but I can't tell what he's actually doing since I'm forced to face away from him. He taps my ankles, with a gentle, "Open."

I listen instantly, spreading my stance as wide as I can comfortably stand. The table holds most of my weight, but I don't want to spread my legs too far and lose balance. Cool air touches the exposed lips of my sex, causing me to shiver.

He steps away again, making more noise behind me. My body still begs for attention, though the edge of desire has dimmed somewhat during the transition. If I'm left with my own thoughts for long enough, I'm not sure I'll be up for what he's planning anymore.

Corvus' heat returns, his legs brushing against the back of my own. He drags a hand down my spine, slowly teasing me with the lightest touch, and I groan at the sensation.

"I might not be fucking your ass, but this will be," he states, pressing something soft and cool to the dip in my low back.

"What?" I squeak, moving to turn back towards him. The pain in my wrists from the flames is nothing in comparison to the sting against my ass cheek as he spanks me.

"No moving, kitten, or I'll do it without lube," he warns sharply before spearing two fingers into my pussy.

I groan, my body pressing into the stone below me as pleasure overwhelms my body. The stone is now warm, like a comfortable embrace instead of a chilled punishment.

Corvus pulls his fingers out and drags them over the seam of my ass, pressing lightly into the tight ring.

I jerk involuntarily. I'm ashamed to admit that it was towards the pressure, not away.

"Greedy. So fucking greedy," he mumbles to himself, slowly rimming my ass with his wet fingers. I can't help the moan that rumbles out from my chest. No one has ever touched me there, not like that, and I'm shocked at how much I enjoy it.

His fingers are replaced by a cold liquid that he drips all over my lower back. It slips down the seam of my ass, covering me entirely from my back to the front of my thighs. He rubs part of it in, soothing the ache in the cheek he smacked earlier.

He still hasn't shown me or told me what he's planning on using on me, and the anticipation is starting to make my legs shake.

Finally, his fingers return, soothing the tight muscles and drawing unholy moans from me. The tip of his cock presses at my entrance, and like the greedy whore he says I am, I lean into it and force more in. Pain flares in my wrists, but the pleasure of him inside of me makes it worth it. It's like a wave that keeps building but never tips over. I ride the pleasure, constantly waiting for an orgasm that never comes.

He's slow and methodical, never giving me more than a little beyond the tip and never pressing his fingers actually inside my ass. After a couple of minutes of this torture, I'm nearly ready to beg for him to fuck me, any hole at this point, but to just give me something to get me off.

"We didn't discuss this, and I'd love nothing more than to fuck your ass for being a brat, but you couldn't take me there yet," he pushes his finger in slightly for emphasis, and the burn is hot and instant. "But you could take me, one day, if you trust me to get you there."

His voice is soft, deep and soothing. The demanding tone he used earlier now nowhere to be found. I realize he's trying to sound neutral, allowing me to decide without my being swayed by his feelings or control. I appreciate him for it, but he's driven me crazy to the point I'm not able to thank him for his thoughtfulness.

Instead of the sweet response I'd like to give, the idiot side of me responds, "I don't care what you fucking do, just make me come!"

"If you don't give me a straight answer, I'll leave you here on this rock without another touch," he warns, his fingers now pressing in and out of my ass slightly.

His thrusts never stopped, but they become more forceful with his words. I moan at the added pressure, loving the feeling.

"Yes, please, fuck me," I beg.

"Where? Where do you want me?" he questions, not giving in to the sounds of my moans.

"You know where!" I snap, unable to say what I want from the shame of wanting it in the first place.

His first response is a slap to my already raw ass cheek, causing the skin to heat intensely. His second response is a growled, "Tell me where."

Corvus thrusts are now nearly full, his length gliding in and out of me in steady jerks.

"My ass, please, Corvus—in my ass. In any hole, just pick one and make me come!" My voice is shrill and pleading as he drives me to a whole new edge.

"I thought you'd never ask," he purrs.

Chapter 21
Corvus

My balls fucking ache, and my cock is so hard I think it's turned to cement, but I'm not letting her come until I've fucked the brat right out of her.

Which will probably be impossible, but Devil take me, I'm going to try.

The flames I've wrapped around her wrist take some concentration to make sure I don't accidentally burn her, but it's nothing but a drop in the well of what I could do, given the right motivation. For now, the control over her body is intoxicating, and I plan to take advantage of it for as long as I can. She's not the type to easily relinquish control, so I know it's special how willing she is to follow my lead.

I pick the plug up off the stone and hold it in my fist for a couple of seconds while I slowly thrust in and out of her. I'm nearly shaking from holding myself back; it's my own punishment as much as it is hers. Once I feel like it's heated enough, I remove my fingers from around her ass and drag the soft silicone plug through her juices.

She's been obscenely wet all night. From the moment I woke her till now, her body has begged for what I'm giving. I rub her skin, massaging the stiff muscles in her lower back. She shuffles her hips as I press the tip of the silicone plug against the tight ring of her ass.

"Relax baby, it's going to feel good," I purr, ticking up the softness in my tone to soothe her. Earlier, the true demon was so close to the surface that I was sure she could hear him in the tone of my voice. I guess he's technically still me, but I'm so different in that version of myself that it almost feels like it's someone else.

Her body relaxes, but her ass is still too tight for the lubed plug to fit inside. I continue my thrusts, driving us both crazy with the steady rhythm. She relaxes a bit, but still not enough, seemingly too much in her head about what we're doing to just *feel*.

"You're doing so good, baby," I praise, slipping the tip of the plug inside before pulling it back out. I try to mimic my thrusts with the plug, but she's tense all over again.

She's too in her head, and clearly praise isn't working like it normally does, so I try a different tactic. "You're a greedy slut for my dick, but you won't take this little plug?" The degradation tastes odd on my tongue—not my usual style—but I know it's important to listen to your partner's needs, and I don't think she needs it's praise that she needs right now. I will sing her the mountains and moons any time, but sometimes you want a demon to talk dirty to you. And a demon I'm happy to give.

Her moan is loud as she arches further into me, the harsh words working to loosen her up. She pushes back against the fiery cords, hissing with pain but preening at the inches of my cock it forces in her. I shudder, heat gathering in my balls, beginning for release. I hold it back with a gritted smirk.

The plug nearly slides halfway inside this time, and I'm forced to retract it despite how it was almost there. The last thing I want to do is reward her with more pain.

I match the thrusts of the plug and my hips, pulling sounds out of her I've never heard. Her inner walls tighten around my cock, and I quickly realize that if I let her come while I'm inside her, I'll come, too, and our night will be over sooner than I want.

I drive my hips in as far as they'll go, pressing her front against the now-warmed stone, driving her sensitive clit against the rock. It's a softer texture than most of the other stone structures in the cave, but it still drives her crazy as I push her into it harder.

"Oh fuck, Corvus, I'm going to—" she doesn't get to finish her sentence before the orgasm is ripping through her. I force my hips to retract, pulling out of her before she clamps down and traps me inside. She groans in frustration as her pussy flexes in pleasure, not near as blissful as it could be, considering she's now empty and just squeezing air.

"You bastard," she growls at me, clearly unhappy.

I don't respond and just push all the way back in, resuming my thrusts with a vengeance. Now that she's come, the ring of muscles around her ass are loose and the plug slips all the way inside with only a few thrusts. It's a smaller one, good to start her on, and I know I've picked the right size when she beings moaning as it settles into place.

I can feel the tip of the plug rubbing against the top of my cock through the thin layer of skin. The muscles clench around me even tighter, and I know I've only got a few more minutes like this before I'm emptying inside her.

"That feels so good," she moans, pressing her forehead against the stone. Her fingers curl, as if searching for something to grab onto.

I grab the remote off the stone and press the first button.

We moan in unison, a song of our pleasure echoing in the cavernous room. The vibrating plug is on the lowest setting, but it instantly puts us both on the edge. I start thrusting faster, harder, trying everything to prolong the orgasm that is fast coming for us both.

"Corvus, I'm close!" she screams.

I dip down lower, my quads burning, but it forces my tip to press higher inside of her, where I hope her g-spot is—because if she doesn't come soon, then I'm coming without her. I can't hold it back. Between the foreplay of the anticipation, the rhythmic thrusting, the vibrating, and the vision of her spread before me, I've lost control.

My cock pulses with each thrust and my back bows over her as I come. "Now you're my little cum slut, aren't you?" The words are raspy and hoarse as I fill her up with so much cum it drips out of her.

She detonates beautifully, calling out my name as her legs shake from the force of it.

I move a few inches back and forth, forcing the cum out of her. I watch as it covers both of us, creating a mess. A part of me thrives at the view; it appeases the part of me that wants to claim her. A flash of her full of me, my child growing until she's round and glowing.

I shake the thought away, not willing to give it any more power by considering it.

I pull her from the stone and take us both to the bed. The flames blink away in an instant. Not a scorch mark or puff of smoke remains, and even I'm amazed at the level of control I have at times.

"I'm messy," she complains as I lay us down and cover us with the blankets.

"Like I give a fuck, you took all the energy right out of me through my balls. We'll clean up tomorrow," I throw an arm over her, effectively holding her against me. She snuggles into the warmth of my body.

"Corvus, that was... I've never... just, wow." Her voice is soft and filled with sleep, but I can feel the smile against the skin on my chest.

"You did so good, baby. I'm so proud of you." I bury my fingers in her hair, and press her tighter into me.

I don't know what life has in store for us, but nights like this might just make it all worth it.

Valencia buries into my chest deeper, her body entangled with my own. Her fingers play with the hair on my chest.

"How did you get the sex toys?" she asks softly.

I can't contain the small laugh at her shy tone.

"The dresser typically provides clothing and shoes, as it was enchanted for things you wear, specifically. But I had a witch include a spell in the enchantment for intimate items, as well. It's probably why it keeps showing you lingerie. I'd really love to see you in them."

"I thought you didn't let anyone in here? Why would your personal dresser need an intimacy spell?" She pulls against my chest hair, the sting sharp across my sensitive skin.

I really laugh this time, clamping a hand down on hers to release some pressure. "Because I hoped one day I'd have a reason to use it. But I assure you, anything that comes out of that dresser has never seen another second outside of its confines until you."

"Okay," she says, the word trailing off. I can hear the sleepiness returning to her voice, but she fights it. "Tell me something I don't know about you."

I contemplate the loaded question. There's a lot of years I've lived that I wish to forget. For many other years, I've lived simply for nothing but entertainment. Neither of which I wish to share with her.

"I was the general of a legion in Hell; a part of the Devil's army of demons. A legion's main purpose is to ensure the safety of demons, particularly from beings not of this realm—the angels, in particular—but there are a few others that have tenuous relationships with Hell. I decided to become a Lord of Hell because I had just lost my entire legion to an ambush. I was lost. Alone. Betrayed. I had nothing at that point besides my friendship with Van and a whole lot of anger. As fate would have it, not long after that, the Devil announced there would be a trial for another Lord Games Tournament. It seemed like the best option to move on from my past, and those I lost."

She cuddles in closer. "Why would becoming a lord help you to move on?"

I'm glad she didn't ask about the demons who fell that day. It's dangerously close to the dark years I don't want to burden her with, but it is a main factor that shaped me into the demon she knows today.

"Because if I ever allowed another to grow close to me, I would be more capable of protecting them as a lord." I can't contain the pain that seeps out alongside the words.

"Where was Van?"

"He was there." I remember that day as clearly as if I were looking through a memory glass. "He's the only reason I survived. Van was also a general, though he didn't have a fighting legion but instead led spies. When they showed up, nearly all were already gone. I was ready to give in, and then this 7 foot avenging Fae came to my rescue. I hated him for years for being too late. It was a dark time."

"That's why you guys are so close—trauma bonding. Parker and I are like that, too," she muses, her own memories rising to the forefront. "What about this cave—when did that happen?"

"I've been here since completing the Games. When I found it, I knew it was the only place I could trust living, after all the betrayal. I didn't want to live anywhere near the others. Or even have a home that was easily found."

"But you said Van is able to find it?" Her words are slowly beginning to slur, and I can tell she's close to sleep.

"Yeah, it was many years later, but we eventually rebuilt that trust. I can't repay him for all he's done to help me over the years." I think about everything that's happened recently. "But he sure is pissing me off lately."

She laughs like her best friend isn't in constant danger. "I think they'll figure it out. Parker is resourceful, and he has good survival instincts."

I hope so; it'll rip us apart if they don't.

CHAPTER 22
CORVUS

I CRINGE AT THE view of the Devil's palace. Its opulent garden and castle-like stone don't offer a single inch of comfort, given what's about to come. Valencia is convinced that the Devil isn't the one who's been after us, but I've known him for far longer than she has, and he's never been one to let go of such a fuck up.

I wanted to stop Valencia from killing Davgus but by the time I had the chance to stop her, the host was already dead and Davgus was no more. A fatal flaw for a parasite demon—to only exist as long as they are able to keep their host alive. It's a flaw I appreciate, considering he's no longer on the list of demons I have to worry about. Unless someone summons his soul back into another body, I can wipe my hands of the nuisance he's been.

Van decided to skip off on his own mission, and didn't let us know where he was going—just that he wouldn't be dealing with the Devil today. He hates him almost as much as he hates being around Parker. I can't blame him, and I certainly can't force him.

I noticed Valencia and Parker don't need as much food as they would have eaten on Earth. Whether that's due to the time differences in Hell, or if being in this realm affects their biology, I'm not sure.

"Remind me again why we're here?" Parker asks with a yawn. I have no idea what happened to him after we got back to the cave last night, but considering he's alive, he must've found his way around without antagonizing Van. I definitely appreciate his self-sufficiency.

"I killed... the demon we were supposed to bring in for questioning, so we're here to tell the Devil about it," Valencia answers, her shoulders relaxed and head held high. I don't see any nervousness in her stance and I wish I could say the same about myself. If I can, I'm going to ask the Devil to send her away when he punishes me. It's not something I wish for her to witness in the slightest.

"Odds are the Devil has coffee in here?" Parker follows closely to Valencia's other side, boxing her between us. He might not notice the significance, but considering all of Hell now thinks of her as one of the highest-ranking people stuck down here, it's a prestigious position to be in.

Many will have gossiped about the show we put on at Tornil's. If anyone doesn't already know what happened, they soon will. I wouldn't be surprised if the Devil himself has heard of it. We're more here for formality, anyway.

"I swear, I'd kiss him for some coffee," Valencia responds as we make it to the door.

I growl a low *no,* but she just laughs.

The walk through the white-washed palace is as uneventful as usual. No one stops us and nor do we see anyone else as we make our way to the great room's main doors. I breathe a sigh of relief when we walk into the Devil's personal favorite room. It's an ode to old Viking history, resembling a social hall that Vikings would have gathered in. The fire pit in the center of the room roars with a large blaze, effortlessly heating the space.

I was shocked when we walked into the mural room last time we were here. It's not a room I've ever had the chance to see. The statue in the center was stunning, and the story to go alongside it still rests in the back of my mind, but I don't understand why he brought us to that room that day.

The Devil lounges in his large chair, one leg over top of its arm while he reads.

Valencia softly groans beside me, and I catch sight of her rubbing her forehead out of the corner of my eye. My brows tip in concern, and I'm just about to ask her whether she's okay when the Devil interrupts me.

"I'd say I was disappointed, but I am ecstatic that the demon is dead. Did you happen to find anything out before you killed him, or were you completely useless with that, too?" the Devil asks in that even tone of his, never looking away from his book.

My spine stiffens, and I prepare for the punishment that's sure to come.

"I'm—" I start, but Valencia interrupts me.

"We found out that whoever is after us is male and he's strong enough to have a parasite demon under his control. I'm told there are only a few strong enough to do that, and two of them are in this room. So, you tell me—how close are we?" Her voice is strong and sure, as though she is completely unafraid of who she just demanded answers from.

The Devil slowly lowers his book to look at her, but I step in front of Valencia and cover her entire body with my own. "Excuse her, Sire, she is still coping with the knowledge that the parasite demon had possessed one of her friends. It's my fault Davgus is dead. Punish me." I can't help the pleading note that enters my voice, panic slowly crawling up my throat from the unhinged look that enters the Devil's eyes.

"I commend you for wanting to protect her, King Crow, but I think she's capable of standing up for herself." The Devil finally sets the book onto a table beside his chair and walks over to a larger table. One second, the table lays bare, and the next, it is covered in an entire breakfast feast. "Sit."

It's an order none of us disobey.

"*Ohmigod*, coffee," Parker moans, the cup already up to his lips before he even takes a seat. I catch the soft smirk that lines the Devil's face as he watches Parker take a seat and nearly down the entire cup—but he wipes the expression away when he notices my attention is on him.

Valencia has also taken up a cup of coffee, and begins to fill the plate in front of her with small portions of fruit and a piece of toast. Parker grabs a piece of every type of meat lining the table, as well as his own buttered slice of toast. Knowing they're her favorites, I grab a large cinnamon roll and place it next to her.

I leave my plate in front of me, not as eager to fill my stomach. It's all food taken from Earth, brands they'll likely recognize. We have similar items here, but the flavors won't be exact—and nothing beats a full English breakfast. Which saddens me, because it smells absolutely delicious—but I'm not sure what the punishment is going to be, and I'd rather not eat to just throw it up from the pain.

"So," the Devil starts from his seat at the head of the table. "You've come here to accuse me of being the culprit in your lover's death when I am, in fact, the one that brought him back to life. What's my motive?"

I try to respond, but Valencia once again beats me to it.

"I don't think it's you, actually. I was just testing you to see your reaction," Valencia replies, taking a sip of her coffee, not meeting the Devil's eyes. I notice he doesn't seem to care, happy to simply smirk at her while she blatantly disrespects him. The last demon who didn't meet his eyes doesn't have eyes to worry about *seeing* anymore.

"Well, my dear, I do hope I passed," the Devil laughs, but then directs his attention to me. He's seated at the head of the table, Parker beside him opposite where we are on his other. I placed myself between the Devil and Valencia intentionally, but now, with his attention directly trained on me, I regret my decision to sit so close.

"Sire, I would like to request that you let them leave before you punish me. It is not their fault, and I would like them to be free of the burden of witnessing it," I ask, with a respectful nod of my head. I cringe inside at the thought of what's to come but steel my spine against the fear.

"King Crow, I will consider your request if you answer me something first." His piercing eyes bore straight to my soulless center. "When have I ever punished you unjustly?"

It's a tough question. How can I truly answer that, if he's the one deciding what is and isn't proper justice. If you asked me, the punishment he gave me after the nun ordeal was a little over the top. And I've heard many rumors of his other vicious punishments. But, considering I don't really know the reasons behind any of those instances, I guess there's a small chance that he isn't as bad as everyone has made him out.

I try to think of an answer, a time where I felt he enacted a harsher sentence than was due. Even though I'd like to voice my opinion on what he put me through for those six years I was chased by his Hellhounds, I disobeyed a direct order—and with one of God's devoted followers, nonetheless.

He nods at my silence, taking that as an answer.

"If you had gained no knowledge before the pathetic demon's death, then maybe I would see the need to punish you. But your Queen has provided plenty of information on your behalf."

My eyes bug out of my head like small, inflated balloons. There's no way I heard him right. Not only did he just say that he's not going to punish me for a clear mess up, but he also called Valencia a Queen. He calls me King Crow as a sarcastic joke, not as a title of prestige—but his calling her a Queen without a note of mockery is like a direct endorsement.

He laughs at the look on my face.

The clinking sound of Valencia's porcelain cup setting on the wooden table catches my attention. I look at her, noting the calm on her face and the smile on her lips. Heat builds in my chest as rapidly as gratitude, and her smile grows as she catches my eyes. Her small hand lands on top of my thigh, and she squeezes lightly.

She's offering me comfort. I'm not sure what's happened but I think she's effectively wearing the pants in this conversation. I'm happy to give her the lead considering she's handled it so well so far. Maybe the Devil's right; a Queen doesn't need someone to jump in front of her when she's capable of winning battles all on her own.

Valencia finally breaks contact and looks the Devil's way. "If we've determined that you aren't who is coming after us, and we know Corvus isn't doing it, who do you suspect is left?"

We had this conversation last night, but it doesn't hurt to ask the leader of the realm his opinion.

"King Crow was right, there are not many who could control a parasite demon; each of the other lords are the most obvious candidates. The three lords were chosen for their ability to lead, but also their heightened levels of power. But each lord holds a different set of skills. Corvus here is most notorious for his ability to travel outside of Hell of his own volition. A coveted power many have tried to steal from him—for the opportunity to escape Hell without my permission. The Second controls the dreamscape, the land of nightmares. Also a very coveted power as this, too, allows him to travel to Earth, but only in his shadow form. The First is a difficult case," The Devil explains while slowly peeling a grapefruit from the table.

"Both the Second and Third lords were chosen greatly on their power levels alone. Each had to learn battle strategy—through the Games as well as through experience leading in Hell. The First was not nearly as powerful when he came into leadership as the others were, but he was an exceptional battle strategist, and easily secured his position as the First. He has gained power over the years as a lord, and is now considered the second most powerful player, after me."

"What can he do?" Parker asks, his plate nearly wiped clean. He sips on his coffee, looking at the Devil curiously.

"Necromancy. The First can raise the dead," The Devil responds, an edge to his tone.

Chapter 23

Corvus

"Damn, zombies in Hell. I did not have that on my Bingo card," Parker shudders in revulsion. It's so much worse than he can imagine. I have never seen the First Lord raise the dead firsthand, but I've heard the stories.

He's known for having lost all his troops in a particularly vicious battle with the angels—but, instead of cutting his losses and running, he brought them all back to life. While they did defeat the angels, they were also mindless beasts; demons with unimaginable powers but no mind or consciousness to control themselves. They not only took out the entire battalion of Angels, but also demolished the two groups of demons who showed up to help them. It wasn't until the third legion showed up and killed them for all a second time that the fighting finally came to an end. So many needless deaths in pursuit of domination.

It's rumored that the First was punished for the act, but no one has ever confirmed it to be true. He was gone for years, hidden away somewhere, but some speculated he was in a hibernated stasis to recover from the use of so much power.

The Devil says he didn't start out as powerful as he now is, which only means one thing. He stole his power. Likely from other demons or angels he's captured, but either way, it feels a grimy. I never liked the First, something about him always set me on edge, but I've never voiced my complaints.

It's customary for the lords to attend the ceremony after a new lord is chosen, but the First was evidently too busy to show for mine. Nightmare says he was there for his, but only briefly, and they didn't speak. There was another Second before Nightmare took the mantle, but no one has ever heard about what happened to him. It was so long ago that many don't even know his name.

"Who is left after the two lords?" Valencia asks, leaning forward on the table, and I'm snapped out of my thoughts and back into the present.

"There is Thalor and Tornil. Both are fairly equal in their power levels, but differ vastly in what they do. I would not suspect its Thalor, simply due to his position."

Valencia nods as the Devil explains, but the two names he mentioned are a shock to me.

"Thalor? He's that powerful? I know he's one of the Red Guardian's leaders, but I didn't think he'd be able to control a parasite demon," I question.

"Thalor's ability is what you would call a unique case born of unfortunate circumstance. He was captured and was subject to tests in a secret lab for many years where they attempted to separate him from his wolf. He was tortured beyond recognition but never gave up. In that pain, something new was born. They tried to take something from him but only succeeded in making him stronger."

This is all news to me. I knew there were many issues in the shifter communities, but I didn't know they were being experimented on. It sounds like something the humans would do.

"If you knew this was happening, why didn't you stop it?" Valencia asks, her brows tipped low on her face. She's struggling with this as much as she struggled with learning that Orson, another unfortunate shifter, had been sold by his family and forced to fight.

"I did not learn of his story until many years later," the Devil responds with an edge to his voice.

She's basically questioning his ability to lead, and she's walking on thin ice doing it. Before she can earn herself that punishment, I interject.

"Tornil makes sense, I know he's powerful, but he is too busy with his tent to be our culprit, and Thalor's position in the Red Guardian basically rules him out, too. So all that leaves is the First and Second lords—but I'm having a hard time believing it's either of them. What would they gain by killing me?"

"Exactly what I gained by your death: her soul." The room goes quiet as the Devil points to Valencia.

It's a bold statement to make, but not untrue. Had she not killed Davgus on that mountain, he would've taken her to whoever his master was, and they would've ripped her soul from her body. Or, Dumah would've fought for her. She says he left shortly after everything happened, so he had the chance but didn't take it. There are so many variables—still too many to paint a clear enough picture.

"Whoever it is, they're willing to go to great lengths to get to me. I have a feeling that this isn't over, so what's stopping them from sending another demon thug after me?" Valencia plays with a butter knife that's sitting next to her plate. She scratched the tip into the wood surface of the table, deep in thought. The Devil eyeballs the blemish but says nothing.

"I'd say you're right; whoever is after you is still working from the shadows, and it's only a matter of time before they show their hand again. I suggest you speed the process up and start hunting for them in the realm yourselves," the Devil offers, an evil smirk on his face. I have no idea why Valencia trusts the Devil, is so adamant it isn't him, but I'm certainly not convinced. When she looks at him, she almost looks *over* him—or she looks to the side, never directly meeting his eyes. It's odd, even for her, and I plan to question her about it later.

"You're suggesting we use her as bait," I growl, an uneasy pit forming in my stomach.

"I'm suggesting you start looking for who's after you before they find you." He says it like it's a suggestion, but his word is law—or, as close to it as Hell gets.

"I'm happy to do it Corvus, you know I didn't want to hide from this." She places her hand back on my thigh, but it doesn't calm me like it did before.

Parker sits quietly, his head volleying between us all.

"I'm not okay with that," I argue, my attention on the Devil. He's the one pushing it.

"Corvus, I can handle it." She pats my leg in an attempt to get my attention, but I can't take my eyes off the Devil.

What's his game? If I can just figure out why he's encouraging her to do this, I can stop it from happening. I'm not comfortable with the prospect of exposing her like that. How will I protect her if she's out on her own?

"No, I won't allow it." I push back from the table, the chair legs scratching against the floor, then turn and pace towards the fire and watch as a couple of sprites play in the embers.

She follows me up, her chair forcefully pushed back as she follows me.

"Corvus, we agreed—you *promised*—that we would do whatever it takes to figure out what's going on. We never expected it to be safe. How will we ever feel truly safe here if we don't start acting like we want to make a difference instead of hiding away from anything that could hurt us?" She comes to stand beside me and also stares into the flames, but doesn't offer her touch. I crave that connection right now—crave how just a single touch from her can calm me. The panic I'm feeling is new and dangerous, but I can't seem to let it go.

"I can't stand the thought of something happening to you," I admit, forcing the words out. It's a risk to admit this weakness in front of the Devil, but I've always tried my hardest to be honest with her and I don't plan on changing that now.

"Don't let your feelings for me cloud the path to our end goal. If we want there to ever be a time in our lives where we aren't constantly looking over our shoulder, then we need to put in the work now. It's scary, and dangerous, and there's a huge chance that one or all of us are going to get hurt at some point, but it's worth it. Our happiness is worth it. Can't you see that?"

I press the heel of my palm to my forehead to force away the ache that's started to gather there.

She's right. I hate that she's right, but that's *exactly* what will happen if we don't figure out what's going on and deal with it. However, knowing that and being content with it are two very different things.

"Spoken like a true leader," the Devil says from behind me, having joined our semi-private moment.

"I'm no leader; I'm just trying to survive," Valencia argues.

"I'd disagree, you just handled this situation perfectly. I'd almost wonder if you've studied strategy in your life before. You should consider becoming a lord, I'd trust you a lot more than some of these other degenerates." His voice is teasing, and it's not something I've ever heard from him before.

"Yeah, sign me up," she says with a roll of her eyes.

I turn to her, needing to see her face, and she smiles softly at me, lightly rubbing one of her wrists before reaching out to take my hand. I nod silently, giving in no matter how much my instincts warn me against this path we're going down.

"Very well! Now, I have another important meeting to get to, why don't you all leave and get started on your fun little journey!" He starts to leave, his steps light as he makes his way to the door.

"Wait!" Parker exclaims, standing from his chair.

The Devil pauses but doesn't acknowledge Parker in any other way.

I can practically hear Parker's gulp from where I stand.

"Do you have any extra coffee we could buy?"

Of all the things I expected him to ask, that wasn't on the list. Even the Devil seems shocked.

"*Buy*? You have the only demon in the realm who can go to Earth and get coffee for you, yet you want to buy it from me instead? Buy it with what money?" the Devil asks with a laugh.

"Well, I honestly hadn't really thought that far," Parker admits sheepishly.

"There are two things you have in currency, your body and your soul. Are you willing to sell either of those?" The Devil stalks closer to Parker, rounding the couch to step into Parker's personal space. Valencia moves as if to step forward but I stop her with a hand on her wrist and a shake of my head. The Devil won't gain anything from getting Parker's soul, and if he's willing to sell his body for some coffee, that's on him.

"What kind of coffee are we talking about? Because for the red can, I'd maybe offer some feet pic's but for a bag of authentic Chicago French Press I'd explore more... exposing options."

The severity of Parker's expression worries me, and I wonder if I'm about to interject and stop him from making a really poor decision.

The Devil is quiet for a moment before bursting out into boisterous laughter. His smile is manic, and the gleam in his eyes is predatory, yet he looks so young when he laughs like that. He shakes his head a few times before patting Parker on the back and turning once again to leave.

"Keep this one if only to have something to laugh at every once in a while," is the Devil's final word before leaving us all alone.

The door shuts with a soft *click*, and then Valencia is stomping over to Parker.

"What the fuck, Parks, *feet pic's*?" she snaps.

"What?" He says with a shrug of his shoulders. "You were thinking it, too."

"I was not!" She shakes her head, talking with her hands. "I'm not the one who just offered *the Devil* nudes in exchange for coffee."

"C'mon, I really don't see the big deal. It's my body, not my soul. And I *really* want some coffee."

"Parker, he could've taken that as a sign of disrespect, we've got to be careful."

"Honey, if the Devil cared about respect, he would've off'd your ass in the beginning of the meeting. It was a calculated risk. Corvus, back me up." Parker looks to me, standing just behind Valencia, but I'm once again shocked by this man's audacity. I'm at a loss for words, though he's ultimately not entirely wrong.

"It's his body, if he determines his worth is equivalent to a few cups of coffee, that's on him," I tell Valencia, smirking at the frown on Parker's face.

"It sounds way less glamorous when you say it. I was thinking of everyone when I asked! I wasn't gonna keep it all to myself."

"*Ugh!* Men," Valencia rubs her forehead a few times before shaking it off and focusing on me. "Let's just get out of here and figure out our plan back home." She doesn't wait for me to respond before grabbing my hand and pulling us from the room.

I follow her lead, nearly floating the entire way out of the palace and into the garden before taking us back to the cave.

She may not realize it, but she called it *home*, and for once, I feel like it might just be.

CHAPTER 24
VALENCIA

THE TRIP BACK TO the cave is uneventful, and for once, that sick feeling is completely nonexistent. Parker gags a few times, but he doesn't get sick like he has in the past.

Van is sitting on Corvus' couch, slowly flipping through a book. The cover is blank, but it looks worn, as if old or well read. The bright gold detailing catches my eye.

"I imagine the meeting went well considering you're all alive and have all of your extremities." He doesn't look up from his book.

"It went well until Parker offered to sell his body to the Devil for some coffee," I blurt, forgetting who I'm talking to. Van shoots Parker a vicious look and opens his mouth but Parker beats him to it.

"Listen, I don't want to hear it, I love coffee and feet pic's didn't seem like that big of a sacrifice." Parker stomps into the living room and slumps down into one of the leather chairs. It's the furthest from Van, but much closer than he's purposefully positioned himself in relation to the large Fae since the incident when they first met.

"There are creatures here who are sold to sex slavery, with no control over their body's use or *who* uses it. Yet you carelessly offer your body for free. You humans truly are despicable," Van storms off into the cave without another word. He didn't try to kill Parker, so I'll take that as a win, but I'm sickened by what he's said. It's not that I didn't think it was happening, I just didn't *think* of it. I purposely put that out of my mind when I learned there are people that are forced to fight in death matches. But just because I tried to not think about it, doesn't make it untrue, and Van makes a great point.

We all have to be careful of what we do and say, because who knows how our actions could affect those who are suffering here in Hell.

"Should I consider adding this to our list of crusades?" Corvus asks from the kitchen, drinking one of his preferred beers from Earth; I recognize the tan can. He looks at me with a serious expression, no sign of sarcasm or teasing in his tone.

"Absolutely," I admit.

"I wasn't trying to piss him off. There's no winning with that guy." Parker gladly takes the beer Corvus hands him.

"There are very few things that would help you win Van over, and coffee isn't one of them. Don't give up trying, though, if anyone could warm him up to humans, it's you."

I join them in the kitchen, a plan brewing in my mind as they chat.

"Where would we go if we wanted to seek this demon out?" I ask Corvus. I'm on the opposite side of the bar with my back to the door.

"Tornil's. It's really the only place in Hell where lots of demons gather," Corvus responds, a sour look on his face. I know he's not happy with the decision, but we don't have much of a choice at this point.

I absently rub at my wrist where I felt the slight burning sensation earlier. It was there and gone in a flash, but intense enough that my mind keeps going back to it.

"In the entire realm, the circus tent is the only place demons gather? How does it hold everyone? There's got to be a larger population here than can fit in the one tent. No cities? No small bumpkin towns with dive bars?" As Parker rambles through his questions, memories of Ole Joes and the fun we had there flash through my mind.

"There are cities—and towns—but they're dangerous places to go. Most of the gangs control them. Tornil's is at least regulated to no killing outside of ring, so you see a lot of demons go there to have some fun. And it's enchanted, so no matter how many show up, they'll fit regardless."

I'm somehow not shocked at the knowledge that there are gangs in Hell, and I never liked cities much anyway.

Tornil's tent, though overwhelming, is at least somewhat familiar.

"Will we have to watch more fights? I don't think I'm up for that just yet," I admit.

"Not likely, there's always a different show going on each night, some more gruesome than others. But it's not announced, so we won't know what's going on until we get there.

"So there could be something worse than the fights," I ask, disgust written all over my face.

"A very good chance," he confirms without hesitation.

I don't want to know what the '*worse*' is, so I don't ask.

"Well, we won't know till we get there, so let's not worry about it. What we do when we get there is more important anyway. I'd suggest splitting up, but I know—"

"Nope," they both say in perfect unison.

"*But* I know you guys will disagree, so we've got to come up with another plan." I finish with an eye roll.

"I may be new here but I'm not blind. I think our presence will kick up enough gossip that whoever is after you will know when we get there. If we just act like we're there for a bit of fun, they might expose themselves," Parker suggests, a plan seeming to form in his mind as well. He always was a good strategist. It helped keep us alive many times in our years spent fighting fires together.

"I agree, judging by the looks we got last time, our being there is sure to draw a crowd." The leering eyes we had pointed our way last time was not something I was hoping to experience again so soon, but this is our best option.

"The best way to do that will be to hang around the bar and dance floor. But we've got to mask Parker's humanity before we go or we'll be in more danger than necessary." Corvus finishes his beer. Pointing to Parker, he explains, "*He* smells like a human. Me and every demon in Hell can sense that his soul is still intact. I'll have to take him to an enchantress who'll put a spell on him to block that so we don't cause a frenzy when we get there."

"How come we didn't have to last time?" I ask.

"Primarily because we didn't have time. There are only a few enchantresses worth trusting in Hell who could do that kind of spell work, and of the few, I only know of one who is currently available. Secondly, last time we were in and out of the crowd and were not forced to mingle. Remember how everyone seemed drawn to him? This time will be much the same. Ten minutes in his presence, and they'll start to sense that there's something different about him. Twenty minutes, and they'll be clawing to get to him. Thirty, and we'll likely all be torn to pieces."

"Okay, point taken. Enchantress, here we come." Parker quickly walks around the bar to head to the door so they can leave. Corvus kisses me on the cheek as he passes. I'm about to ask why he thinks it's okay to leave me behind, but he reads my mind.

"You stay and work with Van. Have him show you some self-defense, or work on drawing more into your powers. Considering his mood, he'll probably be in the training room. Just follow the lights there. I'll take care of Parker with my life,"

"You know the consequences if you die, Corvus," I warn, completely serious about bringing him back to life just to kill him once more. My heart can't take that kind of loss again.

"It'll be quick I promise; a ten minute job and no dying allowed." He grabs my face and kisses me passionately before stepping away and leading Parker from the cave.

I panic for a second, unsure of what to do with the solitude. I used to love my alone time. It was how I would reset my mind after a hard job—or basically anything social—but, lately, I've been so consumed with everything that's going on, the thought of being alone is almost scary.

I take a second to breathe in the peace of the quiet space around me, and contemplate the benefits of just grabbing a book off the shelf and reading until I fall asleep, but I saw the look on Van's face when he stormed off. I almost wonder if Corvus asked me to go to him for a greater purpose than a lesson.

If I actually manage to learn something in the process, that'll just be an added bonus.

I follow the lights like Corvus said but still manage to get lost twice before finally finding Van in the large training room. I'm gonna have to ask Corvus to put up some damn signs or something until I get a better feel for this place.

Van is thumping away at a wooden pole, a long staff in his hands.

Thwack.

Thwack.

Thwack.

The rhythmic sound beats in my ears with every hit. His movements are methodical yet graceful, like those of like a skilled fighter but also beautiful like a dancer's. He's nearly as tall as the wooden post, and the staff is easily the same height as him, but he moves it around like it's an extension of himself. It whirs in the air like the blade of a helicopter, and smacks the post a couple more times before standing, using the weapon as if it were a simple walking stick to hold his balance.

"Corvus sent you," he says. It's clearly a statement.

"He did," I admit.

"He's too soft, I'm fine."

"No one said you weren't," I argue.

"You're thinking it, though. I can see it on your face. Save your pity, I'm not worth it." He walks past as if to leave the training room.

"You say you're fine, but that statement clearly shows you're not. Why fight it?" I turn as he passes me and face him with my hands on my hips. I have no room to talk, really; I'm the same when it comes to facing my traumas.

He freezes, his body stiffening. I tense in return, my senses catching on to the predator-like actions. The staff is still in his hands, so I eyeball the rack of weapons. I don't know how to use most of them but I spy an ax, and I at least know how to swing that. The real question would be if I'd make it there before he got to me.

"I'd kill you before you were able to take a step," Van snaps, now facing me. I jerk my attention to him, not having realized he'd turned around.

"How?" There's no way he could kill me, from ten feet away, before I was able to take a step.

"In Sycoraxia, our abilities are closely related to nature. Some have a closer affiliation to the elements, while others are more closely connected with animals. I possess both affinities."

"How would you kill me with nature powers?" I ask.

He doesn't move, and I think he's just going to leave. I cough lightly, a tickle in my throat. That tickle then turns into a burning sensation, which causes me to cough more. Within seconds, I'm straight-up choking, the air completely gone. As the burning travels to my lungs, my airways open and I'm able to breathe again.

"An air elemental seems whimsical until you realize they can control the one of the only things keeping you alive." Van's voice is matter-of-fact, no malice or hatred directed at me, but I'm pissed enough for the both of us.

"If you're gonna choke me, you might as well fuck me while you're at it," I snap, the air burning my throat and lungs with each large intake.

"Corvus would make me eat my own cock if he even thought I'd attempt it," Van says in response.

I laugh, the word 'cock' sounding almost strange in his accented voice. I've heard him cuss plenty, mostly at Parker, but there's something intimate about that word, and it sounds weird hearing him say it.

"I didn't mean it, anyways." I don't know why I feel the need to ensure he knows that.

"Trust me, you're not my type." Van stalks past, back into the training room instead of away, so I count it as a win.

"What, brats aren't your type?" I chuckle as I follow him.

He just shakes his head and leads us back to the wooden post. "Here," he says as he pushes a new staff in my direction. This one is far shorter than his but is still equal to my entire height.

I grab it but then stand there, simply staring at him.

"Surely you know the basics?" Van's brows tip down, enhancing the angular shape of his eyebrows and cheeks.

I just remain quiet, knowing he probably wants me to hit the post. At this point, I'm enjoying toying with him, so I just shrug.

"You." He points at me. "Big stick." He points at the staff in my hands. "Bad guy." He points at the post. "Chop." He makes a slashing motion with his hand.

It takes a lot to not laugh at him.

I step back and shift the staff lower in my hands before taking a big swing, purposefully swinging it right at his head. He's forced to duck to avoid it and I do accidentally miss the post entirely in my ploy to mess with him, so I embarrassingly swirl around in a circle from the force of the swing.

Thwack.

The sound of Van catching the staff is louder than I'd expected.

"How in stars name he puts up with you, I have no idea," Van mutters under his breath, righting me before pointing to the post again—but, this time he takes a big step back.

"I give a mean blowjob," I say with full seriousness.

Van is silent for a second before asking, "What's a mean blowjob?"

I pause, turning to look at him. "Van, are you a *virgin?*"

"Absolutely not," he says. His face is confused, as if I'm the one asking weird questions.

I lean my weight against the staff, completely distracted from what I'm supposed to be doing.

"Okay, so you *have* had sex, but you haven't had a blowjob. Like ever?"

"I don't know what this word means. I now assume you mean some sort of sexual favor, given the context, but I've never heard this term before."

I contemplate how to best explain before stating, "A blowjob is oral sex, normally when referring to oral performed on a man—but it can be used for women, too, it's just not as often."

"I've never partook in either" he states, having taken a second to think about what I've said.

"*Never?*" I ask, shocked.

"You said you give mean ones. The last thing I want is some vicious demon with their teeth wrapped around my cock. Corvus is into darker stuff than I imagined." Van stares off into space, a slight cringe on his face.

I can't help but laugh. Sometimes, when Van talks, it sounds like he's a thousand years old; and at other times, he sounds so human.

He looks at me. "I don't understand the joke," he complains.

"I didn't mean, *mean*, as in with angry teeth. I meant *mean* as in good." The smile on my face is wide, my cheeks pulling at the edges.

"Well, let's hope your fighting skills are better than your communication skills, because that confusion would have been entirely avoidable if you'd just said what you meant."

"It's called slang, Van; it's just a part of language on Earth," I say, thinking of how many other things he probably wouldn't understand. Urban Dictionary would have a field day with this guy. I start to think of all the things I want to tease him about. Parker would love to do it, too, but I think Van would kill him—so I'll keep the joke to myself for now.

Chapter 25
Valencia

Van and I spend the better part of an hour working on my technique with the staff. He stiffens for a moment and almost doesn't dodge the swing I send his way, but he recovers quickly. It's the first time he's stumbled the entire hour.

"What was that?" I ask, taking a second to catch my breath.

"They're back," he says with a grimace. I wonder if it pains him to not voice whatever insults he's clearly saying in his head.

"Can you hear them?" I have no idea how he knows they're back because I can't hear a thing besides my own heavy breathing.

"I can if I concentrate." His lip curls like he's holding back a growl. "I can smell *him*."

The murderous tone to his voice clearly indicates that the *him* is Parker. I still don't understand why he hates Parker so much, and Corvus said that it wasn't his story to tell, so I guess I'll have to ask Van myself.

I hate to dig up someone's trauma but we have to find some common ground if we're all going to make it through this alive. According to Corvus, Van is extremely powerful, and he's an ally we desperately need.

"Van, why do you hate Parker so much?" I ask softly.

He ignores me, pointing to the staff with a stiff, "Again."

I ignore him in return, not moving.

"Your form is abysmal, your stamina even worse. If you don't want to try, shall I just kill you now? Because you'll be useless otherwise," he snaps.

"Lashing out at me is not going to help. He's my best friend, Van. And you're Corvus'. Neither of you are going anywhere. Are you willing to leave us all behind, simply because you're too stubborn to talk about this? Because, I promise you, if Corvus finds out that you've threatened my life, I think you'd find it's yours that'd actually be in danger."

We enter a staring contest. Arguably, he's far better at it—much more menacing those predatory eyes of his—but I don't give in. When a couple minutes pass in complete silence, I try a different tactic.

"How about this, we'll trade stories. It doesn't have to be your whole life, but you've gotta give me something to help me understand why you act the way that you do," I urge.

He stares at me for a little longer before slightly tipping his head down in agreement, however, I can tell that he isn't happy about it.

"Okay, I'll go first. My family died when I was eleven." Emotion builds in my chest, but I ignore it. Better to rip off the damn band aid than beat around the trauma-bush.

There's no pity or sadness on Van's face when I say it; it's like he simply takes the information in and stores it somewhere. He offers me a nod as his only response.

"I lost my parents when I was very young, as well," he says tentatively. His large body holds so much tension, I think I could use *him* as a weaponry staff if I wanted.

"So we share similar childhood trauma's, we're off to a great start." I readjust my stance into a more stable fighting stance and fix my grip on the staff. Van's body instantly responds, losing tension in his shoulders to adopt his own stance. It's not hard to tell that he's most comfortable when fighting—and I figure we can maybe continue my lesson while also learning a little more about each other.

"When my family died, I was forced into foster care by the state. That's where random adults take in orphaned children," I explain, not sure if he'd understand the phrase on his own. "I was very troubled; I had lots of survivor's guilt, so I was not the best kid to home. Families tried, but always gave me up until I was eventually considered an adult, and able to live on my own."

As I tell more of my history, the familiar bubble of panic grows in my chest—the one that brings flashes of that night to the front of my mind and forces me back to that moment. This time, I focus my attention on the set of movements Van taught me, putting the acidic emotion into use and find that it helps fuel the power behind my hits. The sound of the staff hitting against his own wooden batons as he blocks is now louder than it was earlier.

"The Fae do not believe in 'foster care', as you called it. I was on my own for many years, living off the land until my sister found me, half-starved to death. Though it was against our culture, she took me in." He blocks a few more of my hits before stopping to adjust my stance.

"Is she older than you?" I ask, following his directions. Despite only subtly shifting my hips, my stance tilts the smallest amount, and the staff is flows much more easily.

"She was, by many years. Aging is a human thing—and almost everywhere else, you exist until you don't, and old age isn't usually what kills you in the end."

That's not the first time I've heard that; Corvus told me something very similar once—that when humans figure out how to treat aging like a disease, we'd all live longer. Well, I guess *they'll* live longer, considering I'm not as human as I once thought.

It makes me wonder what my parents were really like. They only ever seemed human to me. I never saw them wield any special powers or showcase supernatural traits. They were just mom and dad, the lovey couple who enjoyed spending time on their farm more than going to town. They loved us kids. My mother was harder on us; she was definitely the disciplinary parent, but my dad was usually the one getting us into trouble, so she always let it go. She loved him like I've never seen someone love before.

I never saw my parents so much as argue but I was so young, maybe they did so behind closed doors. I saw plenty of my foster parents argue and fight. A lot of them seemed to hate one another. It was a weird transition, going from a happy home to one of chaos and strife. I imagine it's why I still hate conflict as an adult.

What would I be like if they'd never died? Would they have told me about my heritage and taught me how to control my powers? Would we have stayed on the farm, in our own happy bubble, or would we be constantly running for our lives? A knot forms in my chest, and this time it takes my breath away, forcing my lungs to squeeze and beg for air.

The panic from thinking about the past too hard is familiar; I'm used to the trauma taking over, yet no matter how easy it is to read the signs that it's coming, I can never seem to stop the panic attack when it starts.

Thwack.

"*Ouch!*" I snap, my wrist burning as the staff drops out of my hand.

"You're not paying attention," Van says, holding a baton against the wrist he just hit.

"What's your sister like?" I ask, ignoring his statement. He's absolutely right, I was spiraling and I don't wish to go back to that place. I reach down and pick up the staff, resuming my stance. Van eyes the staff as if he's about to say something.

"She was a notorious Earth Elemental. It was her only power, but she was extremely strong in it." He mirrors me.

"Were you close?" I swing the staff around, clearly too high because Van doesn't even attempt to block it. Instead, he steps back out of the way before re-entering the fight like nothing even happened. I have more control of my body now, so I at least maintain my stance enough to continue the motions.

"No. She was like a parent, too much older than me to be a friend. But," he pauses, his blocks stuttering enough that I manage to catch him in the upper arm with the staff. My swings must be improving, because he hisses in pain—I can see it in his eyes, but whatever hurt he's feeling, I gather that his arm is the least of it.

I start to pull back and apologize for hitting him too hard, but he charges instead. He smacks the staff out of my hands, drops his batons, and wraps his large hands around my wrists. Pain blooms where his fingers grip too tightly. He yanks me towards him, effectively throwing me off balance.

"Never let your guard down, and don't ever try to apologize for landing a hit. It'll be your death if you do." his voice is full of anger as he effortlessly swings me around and throws me onto the ground.

Air wheezes out of my already-tired lungs as he stands over me with a self-satisfied smirk on his face. But I see through it. He's shown me too much through our brief chat to hide his pain behind that attack. He tries so hard to hide the deeper emotions behind aggression and tactics, but now that I know that's what he's doing, I can recognize them clear as day.

"Who else did you lose, Van?" I ask softly.

Clearly, the trauma he told me about isn't the only thing he deals with. He shared the death of his parents like it was no big deal. He acted like his community leaving him to die didn't create severe abandonment issues. But something about his sister has crushed him enough to finally force a reaction.

I see a lot of myself in him now. Someone just trying to make it through the day after losing an important piece of themselves.

"Her name was Liora," he says with a great heaving breath.

I nod my head, understanding that whoever she was, she's a great piece of his trauma. Whatever he's experiencing in his mind right now is probably similar to the panic attack I nearly had. His eyes are blank, and there's no doubt in my mind that he's not here anymore. He's back wherever he lost her.

No one should have to relive their traumas.

Still on my back, I swing my body around to hit him on the back of the knees with my shin. He topples to the ground like a tree, the most ungraceful move I've seen from him yet. The sound of his knees hitting the hard ground reminds me of each time he blocked my staff.

He doesn't react, just kneels on the ground, his body slumped over.

I pick up one of his dropped batons and scramble to my feet. I probably look like a potato rolling around compared to his skilled moves, but he already chastised me once for pulling back, so even though he's vulnerable, I walk up to him and press the baton lightly to his neck.

"Who was she to you?" I ask. I'm in a position of power, standing over him this way. Yet, despite having a weapon pressed against his throat, he could still probably kill me in a second if he truly wanted to. It's a risk to push him further, to force his trauma out of him, but we're so close to making a breakthrough—and for Parker's sake, I'll do what it'll take to get there.

"My sister's daughter," he chokes on emotion, making his normally even tone rough and gravelly. "But she was my best friend. She was more of a sister to me. Her mother raised us together. Sh—she died."

I don't have to ask how, or what the circumstances were. I understand him fully. This is not a man who lost someone. This is a man who lost *everything*.

I don't apologize or offer my condolences, just like he didn't offer them to me. Our grief started long ago and *sorry* won't do anything for us now.

I step away, walking to his front so I'm no longer standing over him. I hate to see him in this much pain, but there's still one piece of information I need to know.

"Why do you hate Parker?" I need to understand so I don't ever have to make him feel this way again.

The eyes that look up at me are no longer green and full of life; they are emerald flames, the green inside of an inferno. A kaleidoscope of pain, grief, and anger. He unfolds himself to his full height, standing over me and instantly taking all of the power I had a moment ago. Fear claws up my throat and tries to steal my breath, burning me with each inhale.

His vicious eyes lock onto mine, and I swear I see his pupil transform into a slit. I try to take a steadying breath, but the burning intensifies, and I realize I'm not struggling to breathe because I'm scared, but because he's taking my breath away. I press a hand to my chest, reaching the other out towards Van.

I thought we'd moved beyond the choking—from earlier—but it appears I was wrong.

"The humans killed Liora and I'll kill the *Rat* human you brought with you right after I finish you first." It's no longer Van who stands in front of me. This is an animal that's been backed into a corner, snapping and snarling at anything it can.

I attempt a growl, but the choked sound just comes out as a garble. Regardless, he's ignited a different fire inside me. Just the thought of losing someone else, after everything I've been through, awakens the rage.

Red-tinted vision and the familiar fire in my hands consumes me as my claws rip through my fingertips in rush. I focus on that feeling, how the pain in my fingers feels like sticking my hand in hot steam, searing the sensitive skin. It's inescapable, but the more I focus on it, the more I'm able to draw into it. I feel it spread, traveling up my arms. The burning on my skin replaces the burning in my lungs.

My chest stutters, ribs and cartilage shuffling, as if searching for a single space left for air. There's so much heat in my hands, arms, and torso that the lack of air no longer registers.

Van hasn't moved; his eyes are still full of furious intent, but they do narrow the longer I go without air.

It's a slow realization that I am apparently completely fine without breathing. Fire has taken over my body. There is now no part of me that doesn't feel touched by the searing heat.

My fingers almost feel cool compared to the scorching intensity I feel everywhere else. My muscles burn, but they remain still, poised as if ready for attack. My body feels different, as if it's somehow no longer mine. Or no longer *just* mine.

My gaze sharpens, seeing so many more details than I normally would through the tinted haze. It's like I've suddenly become slightly colorblind, but the room now seems larger. I can see parts of the training structure that I couldn't see moments ago, and I'm able to focus on Van more closely than I normally would.

I can see the pulse that beats in his throat, a smooth and rhythmic pulse that slowly ticks faster and faster the longer we face off.

The muscles in my shoulders tense, cords of strength in my legs coiling as if in preparation. For what, I can't name. I'm no longer fully in control.

"Impossible," he hisses, assuming his own fighting stance. He doesn't look nearly as graceful now as he did before, and I notice how he slightly favors his right side, just the barest of weight he shifts each time he moves. His hands clench into fists, and his teeth grit in a growled grimace.

My heart rate spikes at the sign of aggression, and I bare my own teeth.

I hiss in pain as a sting ignites across my lower lip, and swipe my tongue across it, the copper taste of blood filling my mouth. Another sting shoots through the tip of my tongue and I realize the culprit. Large canines, sharp and vicious, hang from my upper jaw. The two canine teeth on my lower are much sharper than usual, but they remain their normal size.

Van charges, tired of waiting for me to take the offensive. I appreciate it, considering I get a brief second of warning before he reaches me, allowing me to counter his swing with my own. I'm still no skilled fighter—whatever magic has taken over me in this new form hasn't magically instilled any grand fighting techniques—but I'm now able to *see* the fight much more clearly.

It's like he's broadcasting each movement he's planning to make a second before he moves. I'm able to dodge, counter, and even strike as we battle around the room. The sounds of our animalistic growls echo, broken only by the grunts of our rushed breaths as they escape us with every forceful hit. It comes as a shock that I have no idea when I started to breathe again.

There is no way I didn't go entirely too long without taking a breath, but for some reason, whatever overcame me overrode Van's power, keeping him from using it against me. It's so easy to ignore now that I have no idea when I am and am not breathing, and don't feel out of breath or strained from having it taken away.

If this is some new power, I can foresee my choking kink steadily increasing.

I rely on my own speed and new agility to counter his attacks. Since I am so much shorter, I'm able to use his large size against him, and circle around to his back and leaping onto him. I dig my claws into the meaty part of his shoulders. Surprisingly, he remains quiet except for a low grunt in pain. He reaches for me, but he's not quick enough.

Van freezes as the sharp points of my new canines dig into the skin of the back of his neck. I can smell the iron tang of his blood in the air, but even that sense is now ten times stronger. His muscles seem bunched and ready for anything, but he remains still. Large huffs of breath escape him, his back heaving as he keeps from moving.

"I understand, my Lady," Van murmurs. He slowly lowers himself down to his knees. I let go of his neck and pull my claws from his skin. He hisses in pain but still doesn't move, allowing me to move around him.

He's back to kneeling, nearly in the same position that we started this conversation in earlier. His head is tilted slightly to the side, as if baring his throat in a sign of defeat, and the predator in me chuffs at the submission, pleased by the outcome. The human in me shakes with confusion at what. *The. Fuck. Just. Happened?*

My eyes bounce back and forth between his neck, where red welts have risen from where my teeth just were, and slow trickles of blood glide down his shirt where several small pools gather at the top of his shoulders.

His blood and deference start to eat through the haze, rage finally taking a back seat to reality once again.

My jaw starts to ache, new teeth feeling too big in my mouth. My cut lip burns anew, as if irritated by the extra stretch and that familiar feeling of panic builds in my chest. I feel as if I'm once again being taken over by something I don't understand. What is happening to me, and how do I get it to freaking stop?

Am I going to be stuck like this forever?

Able to breathe once again, my lungs now heave with anxious movements.

Van doesn't move, but his calm tone reaches my sensitive ears. "It goes away in the same way you called upon it. That feeling you focused on in the beginning? Focus on it now."

I try, searching for the searing heat that consumed me earlier, but everything feels cool now. The heat had been replaced by a warm, comforting blanket that covers my skin. The more I try to force the heat back into my body, the colder I seem to get. My hands start to shake and goosebumps rise along my arms.

"If you don't calm down right now, I'm going to call for Corvus and then both of us are going to have to explain what just happened. And then he will likely kill me, so *please*, calm down," Van begs, a pleading note to his voice. I feel the way he says *please* roll over me, as if there's power behind the word, and I vaguely remember through the panic that things like gratitude and requests have power when regarding the Fae.

It's the thought of causing his death that finally snaps me out of it, though. I never wanted to kill him. Not even when he threatened Parker's life. I just had this insane need to put him in his place and show him that was unacceptable. I forced trauma out of him that he shouldn't have had to live again, but it was necessary for the safety of the group. All of us hinge on our ability to work together as a team. I feel like we have a better chance now that I have an idea of what he's been through.

I focus on the part of me that still feels fueled with rage and mentally envision dousing it with water—*like,* a big fucking bucket of water. A fire truck full of it. That's at least how much it takes to get the rage to settle back down to a simmer before it goes away completely. Red-tinted vision slowly bleeds back to my normal color-filled sight, and the room narrows as if my eyes zoom in but lose focus.

It's strange and disorienting.

Van nods his head, slowly acknowledging that I'm back, and it's just me standing in front of him—no longer me and *whatever else* that just was.

"We don't talk about this to anyone," I mutter, overwhelmed with shock.

"Of course, but you will need to tell him eventually. Until then, we will continue to work on your ability to call on your power and your fighting lessons. Meet me again tomorrow," he nods one final time, his head hanging low before me. He stands and slowly exits the training room. It's hard to tell, but I swear I can now hear almost a limp to his gait. It's as if that small stitch in his movement I noticed before is now showing itself as clear as day.

Or the predator in me never really left—but leaves me with a lot more questions and some unsteady emotions.

And fear. Plenty of fear.

Which is strange, considering I've never truly been scared of myself before. But there is a part of me that seems capable of deadly things, and the more of my buttons that get pushed, the deadlier she becomes.

Chapter 26
Valencia

Time goes by slowly for the next few days—or, what I'm calling days, at least. Shortly after the incident with Van, I found Corvus and dragged him back to his room. It took little provocation before he was ripping our clothes off and claiming me in ways that still make my toes curl to think about. I'd needed it desperately, that reminder that I'm real. That I'm still *me*. I appreciate him more than he knows for recognizing my needs almost before I could recognize them myself.

We settled into a steady rhythm like falling back into old habits. During my firefighting days, routine was instinctual. On non-fire days we had a fire house full of tasks to complete. Fire days were their own kind of routine. Now, in this strange new life, the routine has changed, our habits now focused solely on training, but the structure, itself, feels familiar.

It's been a weeks' worth of the routine, and time is finally starting to make sense.

Parker and Corvus always go off somewhere else—secretly working together or, more accurately, giving Van plenty of space. Van's been quieter than usual, not even looking at Parker when we're all in the same room. I expected some dirty looks, and I even figured the snarky digs wouldn't stop, but it's like Van has become an entirely different person. He hasn't reacted to Parker once. All I cared about was that he'd stopped threatening him. Van's taken it to a whole new level. Now, he simply acts like Parker doesn't exist. Which is making Parker's normally bratty behavior even worse. He knows Van is ignoring him, so he antagonizes the large Fae at every chance he gets.

I thought Van was going to crack a few mornings ago. Parker—in a particularly sour mood, asked Van if the *'roots matched the trunk'*, which caused a twitch in Van's eye—but instead of responding, he told me he'd see me in the training room and left. I'd asked Parker where he gotten the stupid idea to push the buttons of the guy who constantly wants to kill him.

"I'm not scared of the Great Tree," is all he'd said in response. I wasn't fooled, though, considering he'd kept a close eye on the doorway Van had left through for the better part of the next hour.

Since then, training has become a continuous cycle of getting my ass handed to me by Van, and then rinse and repeat. He's calmed down a lot, almost as if he's gained some sense of peace since our fight.

I've been more frustrated than ever. I haven't been able to get that darker, animalistic side out of me again, no matter how hard I try. When I finally had the courage to tell Corvus what happened, his first response had been to hunt Van down. Predictably. So, I'd obviously made sure to tell him when we were naked so he'd had much more of an incentive to stay and hear me out—and then go and hunt his best friend down so he could murder him.

My tactic had worked, but Corvus unfortunately wasn't able to offer any advice on how to pull that side out of me, either.

Since, Van has even gone so far as to threaten not only Parker and me, but also Corvus. Unfortunately, my subconscious must know he doesn't actually mean it this time, because the rage stays oddly quiet.

We also attempted to recreate the ability to bypass Van's elemental power—but again, no such luck. I'd almost passed out before he finally gave up and let me breathe again. I'd cursed at him—for holding the air hostage for so long—but he'd said he'd wanted to see if my almost dying would trigger the powers into action and cause my body to try and save myself.

It appeared my superpowers did not care.

Which doesn't feel very *super* to me now as I'm literally about to keel over. Though, I will admit, the control over my claws has come fairly easily. Now, I can extend and retract them without a second thought; it's much less painful as well. One minute, I have normal, pale nails. The next, familiar curved talons take over.

The time it takes for them to extract is so fast that I can barely catch it with my eyes, but I can still feel it in my hands.

The intense burning I felt before was likely from how my skin tore. Now that I don't have to deal with that anymore, it's just a dull ache. It feels like I've punched something a little too hard whenever it happens. My knuckles grow, and my fingers seem to lengthen slightly. My hands transform into deadly weapons with ease, a simple thought, and there they are.

What hasn't happened instantly is learning everything else. The slow progress is a torture of its own and each day that I fail, the harder it seems to get.

Van continues to remind me that it could just take time. "This isn't something to learn overnight. Many have entire human lifetimes to learn before they're on their own. Don't expect yourself to fully learn something in what is considered a second for most of us."

He also says it's extremely rare for someone to be able to partially shift. When I asked him about what had happened during our fight, he'd said the only thing that had changed were my teeth and eyes. My pupils turned to slits, like how a cat's eyes would look, and my smell changed from a smoky citrus to a darker, burned ash smell.

He said the predator in him had recognized the predator in me.

He also said I'd 'topped him', not in those exact words, but that was the point. It still makes me cringe considering he's Corvus' best friend, so I choose to not think about that part.

Corvus still hasn't agreed to go to Tornil's tent, saying he wants us all to spend some more time training. We got into a particularly heated conversation about it last night. His argument is that we're not ready—mine is that there isn't *ever* going to be a time when we're ready, and we need to take the chance now, before it's too late.

After a few more rounds, we compromised—one more day of training. Tomorrow, we will go to Tornil's and put our plan into action. The air is still charged with tension, but we came to a settled idea because, no matter how much he hates it, he knows I'm right. The longer we wait at a standstill, the longer our enemies have to prepare.

As much as the last week has been comforting, I'm tired of pacing in circles. Settling into our routine in Hell has offered comfort but unless we get real answers, that comfort will always be endangered. The training has helped, though, I can't deny him that. I feel sharpened, like a dull blade forged across stone. Strength I didn't know I possessed has awakened within me; preparing for what's to come instead of just existing in limbo has helped ease my anxieties.

Corvus is anything but eager. He holds onto control with a white-knuckled grip, demanding early starts and long hours. His tense reluctance has added stress to the situation, and every suggestion of more training or more time comes with flickers of unease. He hasn't said the words, but they're there in his every movement, in his desperation to control everything he can about the situation. He's not worried about what will happen, he's worried about what he can't control or prevent from happening.

I wish I could offer him comfort, but the decision had to be made. The path is uncertain, but it's the one we're on and it's time to take the first step.

That's how I ended up flat on my ass in the hot sand outside of the cave.

"You've got to watch your feet! You're acting like a goddess-damned headless chicken," Van snaps, irritation evident in his tone.

"Watch it," Corvus growls from a couple paces over, where he and Parker are working.

"This is why you're banned from being a part of her training. If you treat her like a delicate flower, she'll die like one. Crushed under some demon's shoe. If you want me to train her, cease yapping and focus on your own problem." Van points at Corvus.

Parker and I smirk at each other. The two have been bickering all morning. First it was Van's idea of coming out here to train in the first place. Corvus did not like the idea of us all being exposed. Van made a great argument that if anything tried to hurt us, they could easily handle it. It was a 3-to-1 win for training outside.

Then, once we got out here, they went back and forth on where it would be best to train. Corvus wanted us to stay by the door, but Van won the argument again after he mentioned there was no shade by the door, so we're now about 20 yards away, the oddly-colored sun blocked by a large red rock pillar that juts high into the sky.

The rest of our time has been a never-ending fight of them picking on each other's forms, training techniques, and overall strength. Eventually, I asked if they just wanted to fight it out but all I got was a growled *no* from both before we all went back to normal lessons.

"You can't ban me from her, she's *mine*," Corvus turns his full attention towards Van, a new darkness in his eyes.

Parker's eyes widen at the sound, stepping back a smidge to put more distance between himself and the angry demon.

"You don't scare me King Crow," Van snarls in return.

"Okay, that's it, break time!" I loudly call out. I get up and stalk over to Parker and grab his wrist, pulling him to the side. We both lean against the rock wall and sip the water we brought out with us. The sun is hot, and the hours we've spent training has us sweating even in the shade. The cool spring water feels beyond refreshing as I take a long gulp and watch as Corvus and Van continue to argue.

I'm not thirsty, despite the harsh exercise, but the motion is comforting. It reminds me of hot days in the sun fighting fires. I'd go through gallons in the summer. Sometimes I'd be so dehydrated that drinking directly from the fire hose didn't feel like a bad idea.

I spent four years in Montana. Mild summers and freezing winters made getting used to the humidity of Hell a task. When we decided to work outside, my first request was for a water bottle. We would never leave the station without one, and this felt no different. And, after spending the last few hours working tirelessly, a water break is a much appreciated reprieve.

I pour a bit of the water into my hand and rub it across the back of my neck. My body instantly cools, it's like rubbing ice over my heated back.

"Do you think they're gonna fight?" Parker quietly asks beside me. I notice he doesn't drink much of his water either, just holds the bottle in his hand. Parker used to drink twice as much water as I would, but it now seems that need has lessened considerably.

I look at the two friends who are still staring each other down. "I hope so, if only to get over this shit so we can move on and actually learn something."

When neither of them make so much as a single move, I decide to take matters into my own hands. I pick up the staff I left leaning against the wall and stalk towards them. Van said we wouldn't be using them much, but I've come to love it. My skill with the staff easily outweighs my skill with my hands—and definitely outweighs what I can do with my powers.

Parker stays back, off to the side where he's not likely to accidentally interfere but is able to keep a close eye on us. They don't see me approaching until the last second, too consumed with their argument

I settle into my fighting stance with each of them to my side, until we're all in a triangular standoff. Neither of them have weapons at hand or even close by, but even with the little bit I know about the staff, I'm still at a great disadvantage.

I quickly go through the scenarios in my head, moves on a chess board playing through my mind at hyper speed. If I go for Van first, that will give Corvus time to react. He's most likely to back me up and come on the offensive with me, but the point isn't to attack Van, it's to break them out of whatever this is.

If I go for Corvus first, he'll be shocked, which means I might even get in a hit. Regardless, he's one of the most powerful demons in Hell and would probably react in time, despite said shock.

Van is also most likely to realize what I'm trying to do and jump into fighting as a group instead of individually. Corvus would see an attack against Van as a sign of danger, and who knows what he would do to Van in that instance.

Corvus is unpredictable. I know Van's fighting style, but that means he also knows mine. He knows that I favor my right shoulder when I swing because no matter how many times I tell my brain differently, all I can think about is swinging with the shoulder means more power. Van has shown me time and time again that that's not true, yet it's a mistake I constantly make.

I try to call on the predator, hoping she deigns to make an appearance, but there's no sign of that happening anytime soon.

Deciding on a plan, I grip the staff in my hands, feeling the smooth wood against my palms. Then, I swing. The tip of the staff arcs over Van's head in a direct path for Corvus' face. Van doesn't duck or show any sign of reaction to my ploy. He must've caught on in that freaky way of his as soon as I moved.

Corvus reacts exactly as I'd expected him to. The vicious smile on his face is quickly wiped away, replaced with shock as the tip of the staff sails right past Van's head.

He steps back quickly, avoiding the blow to his face, but gathers himself rapidly. His fighting stance is much less posed than Van's, more of a tensing to his muscles, a readying of his body. His eyes narrow on me, but I actually have learned a thing or two with Van, so I'm already on the attack. The tip of the staff hits the outside of his arm. *Hard.*

He hisses in pain, wrapping a big hand around the end of my staff. Yanking me towards him, he growls, "You're in so much trouble, kitten."

Before he can pull me into him, Van smacks his hand off my staff and takes the offensive as well. We continue in this for a few minutes, not really putting any meaning behind our hits, just practicing the movements. They're so skilled that I can tell they're dancing around to avoid hurting me as much as they dance around each other. Each hit echoes slightly through the wide open space.

My lungs sing with the exertion, begging for more air, and I breathe deeply as Van instructed. There's a slight burning in my nose with each inhale as small pieces of sand score the inside of my nostrils. Corvus and Van aren't even breaking a sweat. Their breathing is even, and neither shows any sign of growing tired anytime soon.

"*Agh!*" Parker's scream drowns out all other noise.

I turn to find him on his back, being dragged along the sand by a round animal. It scurries away, holding Parker by his pant leg. His body leaving a large grove in the sand.

Van is the first to react, pulling a knife from his waist belt and chucking it at the creature. With an oddly loud *thunk*, the blade buries deep into the animal's head, the dark hilt rattling from the force. The creature crumples to the ground, squealing loudly before dying with a few rattled breaths.

I rush over to Parker, who is currently scrambling away from the dead animal in a crab-like shuffle on the sand. "What the fuck is that thing?" he wheezes.

After making sure he isn't hurt, I look at the animal. My stomach turns at the sight of large welts and decomposing skin, that sits beneath an entirely exposed skeletal system. There are no exposed organs, but muscle and bone has been freed from their usual confines. Its bones are a sickly gray color, and the skin appears to be in varying stages of decay.

And the smell. Holy *fuck*, its smells.

Now that I'm close to it, it's so bad I have no idea how we missed it sneaking up on us.

Milky eyes full of green goop are bloodshot and bulged, and the blade of the knife is buried to the hilt in the top of its head. Black ooze spills around the knife, dripping down its body to create a small pool in the sand.

"Bone rat," Van mutters, ripping his knife out of the rat's skull. He wipes his blade across the sand a few times before tucking it back into his waistband.

"We need to get inside," Corvus snaps from behind us, a look of unease in his eyes.

Van nods his head in agreement, the first time they've been on the same page in days.

"Why, what's so bad about this thing?" I help Parker to his feet. Sure, it's way larger than a normal rat would be—likely closer to a capybara—but it's just one rat, and Van killed it easily enough.

"Where there's one, there's more," Corvus grabs my hand and we all round the pillar to head back to the cave.

We freeze at the sight that greets us.

Standing between us and the door is an entire herd of bone rats.

"What the fuck do we do?" Parker whispers with a tremble in his voice.

The sight is sickening. Bone gray faces stare back at us, eyes cloudy and bodies swaying as if they can barely stay standing. They're round as if well fed, but skin and fur flake off of them, and their exposed bones creak with each movement.

My hands start to shake uncontrollably, claws slipping free from my fingertips, but I don't know how useful they'll actually be. I don't want to get close enough to these things to have to use them.

Corvus slowly bends down to grab something out of one of his boots. Light catches the bright red blade, leaving a flash against the ground before disappearing as he stands back up.

"Are we going to have to fight them?" My heart rate spikes at the thought.

"Use your staff just as we've been practicing, but aim for the head. Their bones are weakest there," Van says back as he slowly pulls out his own blades.

"What are we waiting for?" Parker says as he steps just behind me. He's the only one here without a weapon—and the one who's in the most danger.

"Shut up, Rat," Van spits.

"Okay, seriously, I do not resemble those things at all." I want to laugh, because I'm only now realizing just how bad Van's nickname for Parker is, but I'm too scared at the moment.

Sand starts to shift, mini whirlpools popping up as ten more rats crawl out of the sand to join the already large herd. Their heads tilt and twitch, pointy noses tipping in the air before focusing back on us. A shiver runs down my spine at the unusual sight.

"No time like the present," Corvus mutters, and with a flourish of his hands, the ten new rats burst into flames. They immediately start to panic, running around the herd and setting others on fire. Those trapped in Corvus' flames scamper every which way, clearly no longer concerned with us, but there are still so many who that are unaffected by his flames. As if under a collective order, the herd charges us.

More start to catch fire but it's too slow, leaving plenty of them to head our way.

I grip my staff tightly and start to swing it around in the way Van showed me. I track the closet rat, steadying my grip, and when it's in range I swing the staff high before slamming it down on top of the rat's head. The sound of bones crunching is so loud, I swear I hear rocks cracking from the cliff edge. Black blood bursts from underneath my staff, and the rat falls limp to the ground. I have no time to prepare before the next rat is closing in. The staff catches this one on the side of its head, caving it in, and the rat runs a couple of feet more before toppling end over end to land at my feet. I kick it away, expecting it to go a couple of feet, but it sails through the air, far lighter than it appeared.

Another wave rushes us, and I'm forced to flip the staff around, hitting a rat with each rotation to keep them from getting too close. Van runs through the herd, jumping over rats covered in flames, to crush the heads of the others. Corvus flits between setting them on fire and smashing their heads in with the heel of his boot.

"*Agh*, fuck!" I scream, pain searing up my leg from my ankle.

I hear Parker curse before the rat attached to my ankle goes flying through the air. Parker's leg swings back down from his kick, light brown boot now covered in black sludge.

"These things are creepy as fuck to look at, but man, you can really punt them," he mutters with a deep scowl on his face.

I nod, smashing my staff into another rat as it charges us. There aren't as many now—over half have been burnt to a crisp, just piles of ash, and others still run around coated in flames, their movements slowing as the fire consumes them.

Van leaves a trail of dead rats behind him as he finishes off the last few. I turn to Corvus as he twists his heel into the head of a rat that's trapped under his boot. It seizes a few times before going limp.

"What the hell was that about?" I mutter, my chest heaving with exertion. I look around at the ground littered with bodies, the red sand saturated in a deep black sludge of blood.

Corvus looks at the body of the rat by his foot, tapping the scorched creature with his toe. "Bone rats typically travel in packs, like this one did, though they rarely attack such a large group. They're scavengers. They like to prey on those that are already dead or those who are alone. For them to attack all four of us together is out of nature. Not only that, but they were waiting for us."

His voice trails off as her looks around the sandy valley. There's no signs of life besides us. For many more miles than the eye can see, there isn't a structure, town, or monument even resembling another population of demons—begging the question, what led the rats all the way out here?

"They were being controlled by someone." Van stalks towards a carcass and slams his boot through the bony ribcage. He reaches into the hole and pulls out a shriveled muscle. It's black and full of oozing veins. It's in the shape of a heart, but large tumors hang from it, preventing me from telling what the organ really is. He holds the offending object up for Corvus to see.

"Enchantress. Everyone, inside now!" Corvus points to the door, fear evident on his face.

CHAPTER 27

VALENCIA

A LOUD ROAR FILLS the canyon. I cover my ears against the sound; Parker falls to his knees in pain. The sound of dragging nails reverberates around us and there are *clanks* as falling rock bounces off the cliff edge. I try to look up, but the bright gray sky blurs my vision. The sound of an eerie laugh fills the air with an omniscient tone.

I feel like I've heard that laugh from somewhere, but it's so loud and distorted that I can't focus on anything other than the pain in my inner ear.

Corvus and Van frantically search the rocks above us, the various ledges of red rock not giving anything away. I try to follow the direction they're looking but my senses are overwhelmed with the sound of laughter.

"What is it?" I ask, searching the cliff face for more bone rats.

"Fuck," Corvus mutters, his voice breathy. I can't see his face, but his shoulders are tense and his knuckles have turned white, clenched around his red dagger. The door is only ten yards away, but neither of them make a move for it.

They both slowly back up towards Parker and me, standing right in front of us.

I hear a *thump* as a giant creature sores from a hidden hole in the rock wall to land a couple of yards away. I peek around Corvus' shoulder to get a better look at it, and instantly regret the decision.

This thing is a literal living nightmare—pale skin that sticks out against bones, eyes bright red and teeth bared, dripping with blood-red saliva. Its large body resembles that of a bear, but the scaly skin and long tail suggest something closer to a reptile. A giant fucking reptile. The sheer size alone would be enough to induce fear. Its twisted frame of misshapen bone creaks with each movement, and my stomach drops, the sound sending a chill down my spine.

It hunches its deformed shoulders, bones sticking out of thin skin in places. With slow methodical steps, it paces in front of the door—our only means of escape. Muscles bunch under scaly skin. Matted fur tufts up in spots, leaving other parts bare. The fur is dark brown, but covered in soot and the creature drops scales as it walks, littering the sand with its dead skin.

A patch of skin on the center of its chest flutters with every rattling pant. There's a wet and unnatural cadence to its breathing. It looks half dead, emaciated and grotesque, but its eyes are full of life. As it paces, it doesn't look away from us for even a second. Intelligence burns behind its red irises, one slightly sunken into its bony cheek. It has giant tusks with serrated edges in place of canines, and its other teeth are sharp like the blade of a saw. In the back of its cavernous mouth is a second row of knife-like teeth. Jaws unhinge too far with an open-mouthed roar, and the loud ringing in my ears intensifies, the sound piercing. Everyone flinches as if in pain.

Every inch of the creature exudes wrongness, like something took horrors that shouldn't exist and stitched them together. The darkness behind its sunken eyes seems depthless.

I shift my weight, panic mounting, but the movement catches the creature's attention and its red, oozing eyes focus on me.

Eyes brighter than fire, it doesn't look away, and the awareness sends ice through my veins. I'd beg for that rage, but she's currently hiding in a dark corner of my soul, cowering at the predator in front of us.

This isn't an animal acting on instinct. It *knows*. It understands my fear, and relishes it. Large teeth clatter together as it chuffs. Iron permeates the air, and the humidity makes the scent of death overbearing. I want to cover my nose, but I'm afraid to make a single move and entice it to attack.

No one else has moved; we are all frozen. The sand shifts around its large feet, each movement silent. Its tail starts to flicker rapidly, bony scutes like an alligator's reflecting the bright light. A deep groove gouges into the sand and it pauses. It faces our group, nose pointed to the sand, and stares us with terrifying intensity.

"*Knooock Knockkkk,*" a distorted voice calls out. The creature's mouth doesn't move, but I know it's responsible. "*Dedzzz dooorrrr.*"

The voice is so garbled, I can barely make out what it's trying to convey. Corvus jerks, the move so miniscule that I barely catch it. He hunches slightly, leaning the tiniest bit towards me.

Without warning, the creature charges us. Corvus and Van both crouch into a fighting stance, their weapons at the ready. I grab Parker to push him behind me, but I'm too late. The creature steamrolls through us, breaking our group in two. Air whooshes by, leaving behind the stench of death and decay.

Corvus has his arms wrapped around me, his body blocking most of mine, and I watch as Van ducks below the tail, the thick wedge of it nearly missing his torso. He then runs into Parker, knocking him to his knees as the creature turns and looks between us, oversized body sliding through the loose sand. Its deadly eyes zero in on Van, who is helping Parker to his feet. With a flying leap, the creature jumps towards them.

"*No!*" I scream, pushing against Corvus' arms, but he pushes me behind him instead. He charges the creature, red blade in one hand and a ball of flames in the other. Driven to protect my friends, I follow.

We're not fast enough.

The creature descends on Van and Parker with snapping yellow teeth the size of small blades that drip with a pungent acid. Its gums are red with blood, while its skin is a sickly gray, and more scales rip off as its protruding bones burst through the weak layers.

Sensing the danger, Van shifts his body in front of Parker's to protect him from the mouthful of sharp teeth before slamming his dagger down into the creature's bony head—but the blade just bounces off. It snaps its jaw around Van's leg and pulls him backwards across the sand. He screams in pain, blood pooling down his thigh. He tries to scramble away, but his trapped leg dangles awkwardly. The sand is too thin to latch on to. Parker tries to help, lunging for Van's arms, but their hands slip and Van is dragged away.

I reach Parker and pull him to his feet while Corvus rounds the creature on the other side.

The sound of fabric and flesh ripping as the creature releases Vans leg makes my stomach twist. He drops to the ground, the air leaving him in a groan. Delirious with pain, he starts to slump and the creature lunges, snapping at Vans vulnerable head. Corvus sends the ball of flames right at its face.

The creature scrambles back, swiping its large, clawed paws to put out the flames. Van is left behind as the creature battles Corvus' rapid fire. Parker and I simultaneously jump and pull Van further away, but his leg has been torn to pieces. Blood coats the sand as we roughly drag him and he moans in pain before passing out. His large body weighs a ton and I slip, falling on my ass.

Loud groans of pain mix with the haunting laughter from earlier. When the creature finally extinguishes the fire, it looks back up at us. Half of its face has been melted off, one eyeball scorched and hanging alongside its angular cheek by a few tendons.

I think I'm going to be sick with fear.

Fueled with anger, the creature scratches against the sand a few times, shoulders hunched and tail swinging wildly. Parker groans as he tries to pull Van up by himself, but he's seven feet tall and despite Parker's hard-earned muscles, he struggles. I'm trapped under Vans body, and no matter how much force I use to push him up, there's not enough leverage.

Time slows as Corvus looks back at us with unfiltered fear. His jaw is tight, mouth tipped down in a frown. His hair is disheveled from the fight. There's a barely perceptible tremor in his hands as he flexes his free hand open. The red dagger in his other hand shakes. Dark eyes, normally sharp and full of mirth, flicker with sadness. I can read the desperation all over his body—a demon used to being in control whittled down to making an impossible decision.

"Don't you dare Corvus! Portal us away!" I yell at him, despair in my voice. He doesn't listen, gripping the red stone knife tighter in his hands.

He swallows hard, and his lips part as if to say something, but no words come. His eyes don't leave mine, and that's when I understand; he doesn't fear for his own life, he fears for *mine*.

I shake my head, tears starting to trail down my cheeks. I'm still trying to get out from under Van without causing him any more damage.

Something shifts in Corvus. His expression hardens, eyes darkening with anger. His stance widens and he turns his back to me, fingers no longer shaking, the knife steady in his grip. He lowers into his stance.

The creature hunkers down as well, preparing to attack.

"I love you, Val, you've been the best friend," Parker murmurs, terror in his voice, like he thinks we're all going to die. Van lies limp in my lap, his blood covering me as I'm trapped beneath him.

Corvus stands before us, alone, as he faces this deadly creature.

"*Deathhhz atza doorrrr,*" the creature howls before leaping into the air. Its wicked claws aim straight for Corvus, who stands proud.

"No!" I scream, extending my hand out in front of me.

Power bursts through my body, blinding me as it shoots out of my hand. A beam of light slams into the creature, knocking it to the ground, and Corvus ducks out of its way as the creature slides through the sand.

I lose all sense, only able to focus on the creature and the pain. My fear has been washed away—but so has everything else. I can't see beyond the distorted image of the creature I thought was going to be responsible for our deaths. Small beams of light start to pierce its scales, flesh scorching.

Limbs flail, and if I thought the wailing screech from earlier was bad, the sound it makes now is ten times worse. It starts ripping pieces from its own body in an attempt to destroy the light penetrating it, but the struggle is futile. The torn-away sections of scale only provide more space for the burning light.

Pain bursts through my entire body, but my head pounds with a vengeance. The feeling of knives stabbing into my ears nearly topples my concentration, but I scream through the pain. I hold out my hand, blinded but determined not to let it go, no matter how much it burns.

There's a loud ringing in my ears, and the world starts to shift to the side. I can feel warmth track down my cheeks, but I grit through the pain. My body shakes as I try to hold onto the light a little longer. As the creature thrashes in the sand, its howls of pain damaging my ears, the light slowly dims enough to take the shape of chains.

With a life of their own, the chains snake around the creature's body, tightening until its limbs are contorted and its head is bent at an awkward angle. The longer I hold out my hand, the tighter the chains seem to become. Its body is now confined to a ball, limbs broken and compressed, tail completely severed. A chain drapes through its mouth like a horse bit, holding it open, and the soft part of its throat is exposed. There's no more thrashing, all movement withheld by the confining shackles. It whines in pain, those eyes meeting mine with a plea.

I may not be able to see it, but I can feel the warmth of Vans body as it lays against mine. The seeping blood that covers my legs from his damaged one.

I'm reminded of the look on Corvus' face as he came to terms with what he would need to do. My soul hardens with resolve.

I snap my fist closed. The light flares so brightly to the point where it becomes almost blinding. The chains snap closed in a luminescent burst, and all that remains of the creature is ash. It trickles into the sand slowly, like a feather floating on the wind.

My hand drops to rest back on Van's chest and my eyes roll back in my head. The last thing I see before everything goes dark is the fear on Corvus' face. Only, this time, that fear is directed at me.

Chapter 28

Corvus

She's been asleep for three days with no sign of waking. With each day that passes, I lose a little more of my sanity.

Van is mostly healed thanks to a healer we had come in right after the attack. They checked Valencia over, too, but she wasn't able to wake her nor tell us what's wrong with her.

The healer said she's completely healthy—just unconscious. She wouldn't do anything more unless I explained what happened, like I was the one holding back the cure. It's infuriating. Valencia's clearly *not* fine, and the healer just stood there with her hands tied, waiting on me to give her answers. I wasn't willing to tell her the whole story, so I decided to wait it out. However, if Valencia doesn't wake by tomorrow, I may have no other choice.

We have to be careful with who we tell about what Valencia did.

When the mocker showed up, I thought we were all dead. In all my years in Hell, I've never heard of one being defeated. Mockers are demented creatures, born from the waters of the Erebus River. Their ability to mock phrases has been widely used to impart an enemy's final words before they celebrate your death.

I've gone through what the mocker said again and again over the last three days, and I've nearly driven myself mad. It doesn't make sense, but whoever sent the rats must've been hoping they'd throw us off so the mocker could finish the job.

None of us should be alive. Whatever power Valencia used to kill the mocker is not something of Hell. If anyone finds out she has the power to wrap the damned in holy light and decimate them from existence, she will no longer be feared as a powerful entity.

She will be feared as a death-bringer to us all.

If she's able to kill a mocker, the deadliest creature in Hell with that power, there will truly be no reason that she couldn't do the same to powerful demons.

Van was knocked out for the first day, but as soon as he woke I'd told him what happened and had him research that power in his many books. He's been stuck in his room healing, so he's been more snappy than usual. The worst part is that Parker's had to be the one taking care of him. I can't stand to leave Valencia's side in case something happens.

I warned Van he had to let Parker help or he could leave. I didn't really mean it, but he must've heard the desperation in my voice because he'd sullenly agreed. They've argued nonstop over the last few days, but Parker's still alive, so I count it as a win.

Valencia rests peacefully, even rolling around to get comfortable in bed and star fishing at times. It's like she's just in a deep sleep—just one that she hasn't woken up from in days.

The glow stones on the ceiling shine so dimly I can barely see them and thoughts run rampant in my head, painting pictures of doom and devastation.

Valencia shifts in her sleep, rolling closer towards me. I can't resist the urge to pull her in tighter. She hums softly as she settles in with her head now on my chest. The arm that's wrapped around her back presses in tightly and I can feel each time she breathes. The assurance she's alive offers me some comfort; I just need her to wake up.

I need to see her pretty blue eyes and hear her voice. I need reassurance that despite the new powers she's gaining, the woman I love is still in there.

My hand trembles slightly as I brush against her hair. It's long and dark, as usual, but I swear there's an even darker hue to it now that wasn't there before. Like the power of the light she used in those chains sapped the light out of her.

No matter how often I lie with her in my arms, I've barely managed to sleep. I'm exhausted—there's a weariness I can feel in my bones—but each time I close my eyes, I see those chains shooting from her. I see the way her eyes became completely consumed with light. How her hair drifted in the air as if caught in a stiff wind that wasn't there.

I've never felt the urge to get on my knees before someone, but the power she showed made me want to worship at her feet.

It absolutely terrified me, but I also worry it'll change her and that this new version may no longer want me.

I know a major part of being with someone forever is loving them through their changes, but what if this changes her so much that she doesn't love me anymore?

She hasn't said the words, and I guess I technically haven't said them either. I'm afraid that if I do, she'll be forced to say it back—and I never want to pressure her. We've got forever together, and forever is a long time. I can wait as long as she needs. There's no rush for her to come to terms with what she's feeling.

Although, lying in bed beside her, unsure if or when she'll wake, I'm starting to worry that I might've missed my chance.

Driven by the fear of no tomorrow, I close my eyes and envision myself standing in the void. It takes a few deep breaths to calm my racing heart enough to take on the sedated state required for realm travel, but the familiar darkness finally descends like a comforting blanket.

***

There's black all around me, and though I can feel pressure against the bottom of my bare feet, there's no floor beneath me. I'm shirtless and in dark jeans—exactly what I was wearing in bed. A cool breeze blows past, raising the hairs on my arms.

"Nightmare, I need to speak to you," I call into the void. This place of in-between is much like the place I go to when I portal. This chill is familiar, if not a little cooler, but the pitch black nothingness is very similar. I wouldn't be surprised if it's the same place, but they have very different purposes for each of us.

"Lord Crow, it's been a long time since you've visited the dreamscape." Nightmare's voice carries to me steadily from my left. I turn just in time to see him walk out of the shadows.

"Is she here?" I ask, unable to hide the urgency in my voice.

He blinks a few times before shaking his head. "I have not seen her since I visited you on Earth in that dingy cabin."

I cringe internally.

Nightmare, with his sharp, pressed suit and clean look, is known for preferring the cities to small homesteads. He's amassed a lot of wealth and power over the years, enough to convert a penthouse in one of the major cities in Hell to his liking.

I can't imagine what he'd think of my cave.

"She's been asleep for three days with no sign of waking." I'm not outright calling him a liar, but there's almost no way she's been asleep for that long and hasn't dreamed once.

He narrows his eyes at me, adjusting his suit to fit more comfortably. "Just because she's asleep, *and dreaming,* doesn't mean I can reach her. We've already established she's not susceptible to my powers, Lord Crow."

"Right, sorry." I rub the back of my neck, the stress building more tension in my sore muscles.

"This is why I refuse to fall in love. She weakens you." The sneer on his face when he says 'love' would kill Cupid on sight. But he's wrong—so wrong. There's nothing about her that weakens me.

This worry I feel is annoying—and sure, could become a problem if she doesn't wake up. What he and everyone else in Hell doesn't know, is that she's very likely stronger than us all.

"Is it you, Nightmare?" I ask, my eyes tracking his every move. I'm desperate for even the slightest sign. A flicker of a lie in his eyes. Tense shoulders as he tries to deceive me. *Anything*. I've never thought it was him, especially after he came all the way to Earth to warn me. I am just having a hard time ruling anyone out when we have no clue who it might be. Every day that goes by fuels an angry pit in my stomach, and I'm very close to turning my back on every alliance I've made in Hell to simply find the answers.

"If I wanted her—*and* you—dead, I would've done it in the cabin," he states, tucking his hands into his coat pockets. It's a sign of disrespect, but I ignore it. He's calm, collected, and staring me down without a hint of deceit.

"Do you know who it is?" I question, really hoping that he says no. I can't hurt him in the dreamscape, but he can absolutely hurt me, and if he tells me he's known who it is this whole time, I'm not sure how I will handle it.

"I will not say. This is your problem, Lord Crow. Every time one of the Lords has gotten involved in another's business, one of them has died. I covet my position too much to risk it, even for you. I wish you luck, may your pieces on the board of war fall into place."

He disappears with a flourish of shadows, leaving me alone in the dark.

I growl in frustration, irritated I'm no closer to figuring out what's wrong with Valencia or who's after us. I feel it's a reasonable assumption that Nightmare isn't the culprit, but there are still so many more that it could be.

I feel as if this is like that human saying—*like finding a needle in a haystack*—except the needle is drenched in poison, and you're blind as you try to find it.

***

I wake with a start, the sound of running water drawing me from sleep. I have no idea how much time has passed. The dreamscape is like everywhere else—a stealer of time.

At the soft splash of water hitting rock, I jump out of the bed and rush into the bathroom.

I don't give her any warning, just jump into the water and wrap her in my arms. She holds me just as tightly, chest stuttering with uneven breaths.

"Is Van alive?" she asks with a watery voice. I can't see any evidence of tears, but maybe that's why she's in the shower. I wiped her down the first evening, cleaning the dirt and blood from her skin while checking for any injuries. I could've burned it all away, but the motion of doing it by hand was soothing.

"We all are," I respond, pressing my face into her wet hair. My jeans, already completely soaked, feel like they weigh a hundred pounds.

I release her and step back to undress fully. She watches my movements before closing her eyes and tipping her head back under the water.

Once naked, I step into the steam and wrap her in my arms again. There's something in me that claws my insides at the distance, and I agree with it. Not seeing her eyes or hearing her voice for three days was too damn long.

"What happened?"

"What do you remember?" I ask, unsure if I even want to tell her what she's now capable of unless she remembers it by chance.

"I remember everything, yet I understand nothing," she says quietly, so softly I barely hear her over the pattering of the water.

I take a deep breath, trying to wrap my brain around how we go from here. "You... seem to have the ability to kill the damned." I can't think of any other way to say it.

"I thought we already knew that? I killed Davgus," she responds, bewildered. She holds her wrists to her chest, lightly rubbing one as if to ease away an ache. There's not a mark on her but maybe she's still sore from using her new power.

"You killed his host, meaning he's no longer alive, but parasite demons can be called upon and put into new hosts by other demons."

She nods, pieces of the puzzle finally coming together for her. "So if killing his host didn't actually kill him, how do demons *actually* die?"

I push her back a little so she's able to look at my face. "Removing the head of a demon and then setting the body on fire is one way." I pause.

"The other?" she urges.

"The other can only be only done by angels. It comes in various forms, but it is the deadliest ability they have. It's also very rare."

"What is it, Corvus?" she snaps, panic rising in her voice.

"There isn't a specific name for the power, it's always represented differently by each individual who can wield it. In your case, it's chains. You killed the mocker with chains made of holy light. Remember when I said a holy relic would cause extreme damage to any damned? You didn't just cause damage, you eviscerated it from existence."

She shakes her head rapidly, her eyes closed and fingers pressed against her head.

"I don't understand. I remember the chains, but how did I create them?"

I contemplate that for a second. At this point, we know that one of her parents was an angel, and we've concluded that her other parent was most likely a demon. "Your parentage means you had a one in a trillion chance of existing. Any time a mixed heritage like yours has been attempted before, the young has either died before birth or been killed at an early age. On the extremely rare chance the young survived, they always became crazy, with only half of a soul to guide them. It makes sense that you were raised on Earth. Your parents knew you'd be in danger your whole life. We'd need to know more about whichever of your parents was an angel and what their power was to learn more, however. I have Van researching it, but there's not much more we can do."

"I refuse to believe that's all we're left with. There must be more we can do. I can't keep walking around Hell with a power inside of me that could kill everyone; I'll be as good as dead when this gets out." Valencia looks at me like I might have all the answers in the realm, and I truly wish I did because she's not wrong.

"We just have to make sure no one finds out. This is something we keep very close to our chests. You protected us in a time of need—we just have to ensure it doesn't happen again until you're in more control of your powers."

"That's what's frustrating," she replies with a huff. "I don't have any control over it."

She slides her hand across my abs as she walks past me to get out of the water, done with her shower. I was already half hard and the little tease had to go and do that. Now I'm fighting a semi-stiff cock, having to think of infected wounds as I stare pointedly at the shower head to take my mind off the sight of her naked body.

She may not have control over her powers, but she damn sure has control over my cock.

I finish my shower and follow her into the room. She's already mostly dressed, hiding her body from me with a knowing smirk. I know it's not the best time for sex, but since she's come into my life, I've been in a constant state of need. When she isn't driving me crazy with worry, she's making my dick so hard it could fall off.

"What are you getting dressed for? Let's get back into bed." I approach her as she sits on the bed, lacing her boots.

"I just woke up. I'm not getting back in bed anytime soon," she laughs, but the laughter doesn't reach her eyes.

"I think we've established I don't need a bed," I murmur as I slide my fingertips up her neck to her chin. I tilt her head until she's looking up at me. Our height differences positions my cock right at her eye level. She eyes it briefly, her pupils expanding before she looks back up at my face.

"Not now, King Crow, I'm in a vicious mood."

Sadly, this does not help my situation. She smirks at me as my cock gets harder at her words. There's no reason to even try not to be hard at this point, so I might as well just suffer and move on. It will eventually go away. Hopefully.

I tighten my grip on her chin with a smile and lean down, pressing my lips to hers for a brief kiss. She sighs, the sound soft and comforting.

I suck her bottom lip into my mouth, scraping it with my teeth, before swiping my tongue across it to soothe the ache. She hisses, but her lips chase mine as I pull back.

"You're safe from me for now, darling, but your time is running out." I walk away from her, finally convincing myself to put some space between us so I can think a little more clearly. She stays in the room while I get dressed.

We make our way through the cave until we find both Van and Parker sitting in the living room, both them and the couches loaded with books.

"Parker, you're reading?" Valencia asks quizzically as she walks up to them.

"I had to give him fairy porn just to shut him up," Van responds without looking up from his book.

"It's not *porn*, there's a *story*!" Parker snaps at Van. His auburn curls bounce lightly as he shifts his focus back to Valencia. "Thank God you're awake."

He wraps her in a tight hug that she returns just as eagerly. Van eyeballs them with a scowl. I can't help but wonder what's been going on between them since Parker's been taking care of him; Van isn't one to feel comfortable in someone's care, much less a human.

When he shrugs at me, I take that as a sign that everything is okay, at least for now.

"Have you found anything?" I ask Van, noticing the titles of the books surrounding him.

Angel Lore and Histories, Chronicles of the Fallen, and *The Silent Battle, 9th Generation—A History of Deception.*

There are many others, but the titles are all similar enough. I settle into the large leather chair so I have Van and the other two directly in my eye line. Even tucked away in our cave, I'm more paranoid than ever.

"Why read about the history of the 9th Generation? The Silent Battle is common knowledge in Hell," I ask Van. It's the book he has sitting next to him, resting on the arm of the couch. His injured leg is elevated on some pillows, but there's only some scarring left on his bare leg. I'm sure it's still extremely sore, mockers have nasty acid-like saliva that eats away at anything it touches.

"If she is part angel and demon, then her parents most likely met during that time. I was looking to see if there were any angels mentioned to possess the same power."

I nod, thinking back to what I know of the Silent Battle. I was created in the 10th Generation, so it was just before my emergence in Hell. As a legion general, I had to know all about the Silent Battle. Angels infiltrated Hell in droves, killing demons indiscriminately. Not always for righteous reasons, either. Many of the damned were killed, their souls ripped from existence entirely. For the first time, the Devil couldn't bring them back. Thus, Hell entered the 10th Generation—the century of war, booming demonic populations, and a whole bunch of new problems. Eventually, the angels were defeated and run out of Hell, but the losses are still felt to this day. We're now in the 17th Generation, and I personally know some demons who lost so much during that time.

The corruption of the 10th resulted in the conception of the Scales of Balance, a fate-driven entity that demands there be balance between our realms. We can fight all we want, but we must be conscious not to tip too far to one side, or else we'll all pay. It's another reason that Valencia is such an anomaly. Not only were her parents on opposing sides of a very deadly war, but they were both extremely powerful. Normally, the fates refuse such a creation of power, especially when it's intended to side with one realm or the other.

Gaining her soul for Hell was a major win in the war, but it only begs the question—what does Heaven have that meant we needed such an extreme counterbalance in Hell?

Since he doesn't elaborate and instead focuses on the book in front of him, I imagine he's not been able to figure anything out so far.

"See, he gives half answers and then goes back to reading as if you don't exist," Parker complains from his own couch, where there are far fewer books and far more crumbs. Seems Parker has gotten into my snack collection at some point.

"We need to get back out there. We're not going to figure anything out here, and I'm going crazy sitting on my ass, continually waiting for something to happen." Valencia gets to her feet, brushes crumbs off her pants and pulls Parker to stand as well.

"If that attack showed us anything, it's that we're not prepared to face what's after us. We need to stay here and plan and strategize while you learn more control of your powers," I respond, the thought of going outside causes anxiety to build in my chest. We were so close to dying. I was close to losing everything... I'm not eager to get back to that.

"That's all the more reason to take the offensive," she urges, determination heavy in her tone. "If we keep waiting for the perfect time, whatever's out there will sneak behind us and stab us in the back while we're too busy getting ready," Valencia insists, her hands resting by her sides.

"It's not happening Valencia, we're not ready." I implore her to understand, but I can see the resolve already on her face.

"Then we go back to the Devil for help. We make ourselves ready. There's no more time for sitting around."

"No, I don't trust *him* either," I snap, anger towards the situation seeping into my tone. She flinches, though, assuming my harsh tone was meant for her.

Before I can take it back or tell her I'm not mad at her, she responds just as angrily, "I don't need you to babysit me. If I want to go talk to the Devil, I will."

"Yeah? And how do you plan on getting there?" I taunt, knowing she has no idea where we are in Hell, much less where the Devil lives. It's something I need to remedy immediately, in case something happens to me, but right now doesn't seem like the right time.

Knock.

Knock.

Knock.

The sound of someone banging on the door makes us all jump—even Van.

Valencia's head turns sharply at the door, surprise taking over her face.

"Valencia, dear? It's me, Greta," a woman calls through the door. A woman who should definitely not be able to even see the door, much less rap her knuckles against it.

"Valencia, *don't*."

Her eyeballs bounce back and forth between me and the door. I'm on my feet heading for her as soon as I see the decision cross her face, but she beats me there and swings it open with a flourish.

Sure enough, there stands the Devil's butler in her modest black dress and primly put up silver curls.

"Hello, dear, I'm here to bring you to the Devil."

I'm shaking my head, but Valencia is facing away from me so only Greta sees it.

"How did the Devil know I wanted to see... him?" Valencia's asks, an edge in her voice.

"Words have meaning here in Hell, and he just wanted to offer assistance if you needed," the older woman responds, a light note to her voice and a kind smile on her face.

"So he can hear everything we say?" Parker asks, an odd look making its way onto his face. He's standing right next to Valencia, but turned my way enough I can see his expression.

"No, only when he's mentioned directly," Greta answers, eyeing Parker briefly. She thankfully doesn't note the grimace on his face and focuses back on Valencia. "Shall we?"

Valencia looks back at me. I'm too far away to stop her from going—and the last thing I want to do is force her to stay—but my insides curdle with the thought of what could happen if she leaves without me.

"Please don't, we'll figure out what we need together," I say to her, anxiety building in my chest.

"I need answers, Corvus, we all do. I know you don't believe it, but the Devil can be trusted. I'll be fine, we'll talk when I get back."

Before she's even able to say goodbye, she and Parker disappear into thin air as Greta teleports them to the Devil. I stand dumfounded, looking through my open door at the empty space where they just stood. Gone to see the Devil while I'm stuck here in the cave—back to worrying.

"You pushed her to make that decision," Van says, still lounging in his spot on the couch.

I stomp over to the cold storage, grab four beer cans out of the cool water, and find my way back to the leather chair.

I slam three of the four beers back to back before asking, "How do you fucking figure?"

"She needs answers, and she's not the type to sit around and wait for them. This is a person whose entire profession has been to go out and face danger head on. You can't expect that to change about her. Just because the setting has changed, and the danger has become something different, doesn't mean she has; she's still the same person."

I open the fourth can and take a drink. "I hate when you're right," I grumble. "But I hate worrying about her more."

"You should be worried about you, and what she'll do to you if the Devil tells her your secrets." Van eyes me over the top of his book.

"I don't have any secrets?" I mean for it to be a statement, but it sounds like a question even to my ears.

Van's gaze lingers before he offers a humorous laugh and tells me, "We all have secrets, Corvus. The question is not *if* you have them, it's which ones the Devil might tell your mate. Do you even know what secrets of yours the Devil is privy to?"

The silence is thick and uncomfortable as hundreds of years of bad deeds, mistakes, and dark shadows lie waiting to haunt me.

CHAPTER 29

VALENCIA

GRETA TAKES US DIRECTLY to the small library I've been in once before. The deep red walls are covered with depictions of the Devil in various stages of artistic skill. The rest of the space is filled with bookshelves and there's a small seating area in the middle set up with leather couches and a cozy fireplace.

Parker stiffens beside me, his hand still wrapped around my wrist. I'm not sure if that's why he was brought here with me, or if Greta brought him on purpose.

"My dear, you and your friend can take a seat and get comfortable, Devil will be in shortly," Greta tells us before leaving quietly through one of the wooden doors.

There's no windows in here, so we can't see anything outside of this room. It's familiar to me, but last time I was here I didn't have a chance to really take in the details, too worried about Corvus.

Parker follows me as I slowly make my way around the room, checking out the various pieces. My personal favorite is a picture, clearly drawn by a child with crayon; it's so bad. The Devil is depicted as short and overtly rotund, with boxy legs and x's in place of eyes. Standing beside the Devil is Spiderman, holding a giant spear he's used to skewer the Devil. I can't help the laugh that escapes me.

Who knew Spider-Man could defeat the Devil so easily?

We continue through the rest of the room, but all the other paintings are more serious. Beautiful renditions of a fallen angel, a man with the most insane physique, but an evil look on his face in every painting. None of them accurately portrays the woman I know to be the Devil. Part of me wonders if she experiences multiple personality states, constantly being surrounded by evidence of people believing she's something she's not.

How long can you act like someone else before you slowly start to become them?

I eye Parker. Since we've been friends, he's been constantly dragged into my shit. Now I've gotten him into a realm so dangerous, he had to have a spell put upon him to simply prevent the population from ripping him apart. He's taken it in his stride, as always, without complaint or voice of concern. Next to me, he looks at the paintings just as I am, his handsome face tipped in intrigue as he studies the various depictions. If he saw her for who she really is, he'd be smitten in an instant. Though, I'm not sure her male form is any less enticing to him.

The Devil enters the room in a flourish, one of the doors on the far end flying open.

"I don't care, Greta!" a female voice snaps. I see her clearly in her female form. Her long auburn hair swishes around as she whips back forward, facing us. I hear a gasp beside me.

As I expected, the Devil's stunning aesthetics have claimed another victim.

"Sit, sit. Let's chat." The Devil stomps over to the small bar beside the fireplace and pours herself a drink. She's sporting another burgundy suit today, though this one is more purple than red. Her shoes are sleek black pumps with recognizable red bottoms,

Parker and I both settle into one of the couches. His presence offers me enough comfort to feel like I'm not alone. I'm still pissed at Corvus, but I wasn't really prepared for this conversation and the thought of doing it alone makes me sick. I hate that we argued but I'm proud of myself for not giving in. The hardest part is that I understand why he feels the way he does. I just hope that when we get back, he'll understand where I'm coming from too.

Once settled across from us with her drink in hand, the Devil smiles at me. "You don't have to be worried, I won't hurt you or your friend."

Her smirk is more taunting than comforting, and those odd golden eyes seem to track my every move. The front of her suit is wide open, showcasing the black, see-through lace corset underneath. It takes a lot of willpower to not focus on her breasts and check whether her nipples are visible. I'm not romantically interested in women, but I'm also not blind.

"I'm not so worried about that," I admit. I've always had a strange sense of trust in her, even when I had no reason to, and that's no different now. A part of me just *knows* she isn't out to hurt me.

"Then what has your heart racing?" she asks.

"What Corvus will do when we get back." It's not so much a fear that he'll hurt me—I don't think he would *ever* intentionally hurt me. It's more the fear that I've hurt him, and that I may have to face that.

"Oh, don't worry about that old bat, he'll be fine. Us ladies have to stand up for ourselves," she says as she sips her drink. It's so strong I swear I can smell the cinnamon from here.

"Can someone explain what's going on?" Parker asks, his voice taking on a dreamy note as he stares the Devil down.

She laughs at his bewildered look and then stands, walking directly in front of him, knees just barely touching his. He looks up at her, his head tilted back.

"Hello, I'm Lifera. But you can also call me the Devil," she purrs, the words taking on a note she's never used with me. It feels weird to watch, like I'm seeing a coworker hit on my brother right in front of me. Parker, on the other hand, is eating this shit up.

"Lifera," he buzzes as he grabs the hand she has reached out, and places a kiss on the back of it.

"Seriously?" I ask with an arched brow. Parker chuckles and lets her hand go, but my statement was directed at her.

Lifera laughs, pulling away to reclaim her seat on the couch across from us, giving me another flash of red as her soles click against the wooden floor. "So, what brings you here?"

I think about that for a second. Now that I'm here, my mind has become blank, and I can't think of all the reasons I begged Corvus to leave in the first place. There are probably a million things I could ask her, but the truth is, I need to know more about my history than I do anything else.

Van said he suspects one of my parents was a demon, and the chances of Lifera—the creator of demons—knowing who they might be seem pretty high to me.

"I want to know about my parents."

All the humor seeps out of Lifera, her body stiffening. Her eyes glow brightly for a brief second, before cooling back to their unusual gold. "What would you like to know about them?"

"I want to know everything you know."

The room seems to grow colder as she contemplates. "Do you have time to hear about hundreds of years' worth of history?"

"So you knew them well?" The question pains me. To know that she got hundreds, maybe thousands of years with a parent I never truly got to know.

"Well is an understatement. Your mother was my best friend."

The devastation on my face must match what I see on hers, because she looks at me with pity in her eyes. Tears well and my chest starts to ache. I've been waiting my whole life to learn what happened that night, but now that I'm here, all I want to do is run in the other direction.

"Val's mom was a demon, then?" Parker asks, one of his hands lightly rubbing my back. Emotion has a chokehold on me, and no matter how badly I want to get the questions out, fear of what I could learn keeps my lips sealed.

"Yes. A shifter. A very powerful one. Her name was Thara; she was originally a part of the Rabidhides—a pack of feline shifters. When she shifted for the first time, she was a small house cat. In a pack of predator felines, you can imagine how that went down."

I can't imagine, because I have no fucking idea about *shifter pack culture*.

I'm eager for every morsel of information she tells me but silence still has its cold grip on my throat, so I'm saved from being reduced to a begging mess.

Lifera senses my desperation and continues. "When Greta brought her to me, she was a young woman about your age. She had run from an arranged marriage wearing nothing but a nightgown. Her feet were bloody, her skin torn, and hair a mess. I met her and Greta at the door in my glamor but she could see right through it. She was the first to see me—*truly* see me—in over five generations, and instead of commenting on my true form, she told me, '*If you plan on sending me back there, you might as well just kill me now.'* No matter how hard I tried to scare her, she never backed down. She had so much spirit, it was like a fire lived inside of her. An eternal flame that sparked upon her creation. I refused to be the one to put that fire out."

"How did you become friends?" Parker must be able to hear the thoughts screaming in my head.

Lifera smiles, a genuine one. "I knew there was something special about her. So when the pack came looking for her, I told them she was no longer a part of their pack but was indebted to me, and they would not be seeing her again. This made the alpha extremely mad, but what could he do? I'm the Devil." She says it with sass, the kind someone attains from years of leadership with no sign of that changing anytime soon.

"Her family was abusive?" I croak, the words almost impossible to understand. Parker flinches beside me.

"They were, extremely. I can't imagine what she went through while in that pack. The Rabidhides are known to be vicious. I'm sure the abuse became much worse when her shifted form was revealed to be a house cat. A fact that would royally bite them in the ass later on."

"How so?" My brain struggles to wrap itself around the fact that the woman I see in my head, her dark eyes and kind face, is the same woman Lifera speaks about.

"She spent many years with just that form, but she needed a lot of time to heal from the abuse. As we grew closer as friends, I began training her. I had a feeling there was more inside her. She was so full of fire, there was no way that all she could do was turn into a cute little cuddly creature. Her temper alone could bring down demons twice her size." Lifera's eyes become blank, as if caught in a memory. I want to beg for her to explain in great detail, but I don't want to lose track of the story she's telling.

"Anyways, I pissed her off enough one day—and boom—out jumps this giant black panther, ready to bite my head off."

"A panther?" I utter, amazed and eager to learn more.

"Yup. But that wasn't it, not even close." The glee is evident on her face, like the memories of this time she spent with my mother were times she was truly happy.

"When the panther came, we knew her family had been wrong. She wasn't a dud. We kept training, and then eventually came more. Through sheer will, she'd master a new animal—and not all of them felines. She had wolves, bears, snakes—any kind of predator you can think of, your mother could shift into. Only one shifter, in the entire history of Hell, has showcased that level of power since."

"Who?" Parker leans forward, as engrossed in the story as I am.

"Thalor. He is a wolf in the Red Guardian pack."

A memory sparks; the last time we met with the Devil, we discussed who in Hell could be powerful enough to come after us. Thalor was one of the demons mentioned. We didn't go into detail about him, but it seems he's definitely someone of interest if he is the only other shifter that powerful.

"Why's he so special?" Parker asks and leans forward with his arms resting against his knees. He was quiet the last time we spoke with the Devil, but he apparently didn't miss a thing. I eagerly await Lifera's answer.

"Remember I mentioned a shifter who was tortured and experimented on?" We both nod in unison, the conversation easy to recall. "Good. That's Thalor. They tried to steal his wolf. Shifters are unique, as they share a soul with their animal half. They had hoped to rip that animal soul from him, leaving him weak and incomplete, no better than a lesser demon. Instead of successfully separating the two, they only succeeded in making him and his animal stronger. Created something entirely new. Thalor is the only shifter to have the ability to shift into a hellhound."

Corvus described hellhounds as giant wolf-like creatures with red glowing eyes, super speed, and the ability to hunt anything down.

"This Thalor was a powerful shifter. And Val's mom was a powerful shifter. Were they related?" Parker muses.

I turn my head at Parker's question, knowing what he's asking but shocked that it never crossed my mind.

"So you're not just something pretty to look at?" Lifera says with a devilish smile. I turn back to her, waiting for an answer. "They were. Thalor is your uncle."

The shock is all-consuming. I've spent my whole life thinking my entire family died in that fire. To learn I have relatives who are still alive is jarring. Instantly, I long to meet him. To see if his features match hers. I lose a little bit of her memory more and more each day, but could I look at him and be forever reminded of her face?

Something dawns on me. "Wait, you said her family was abusive. Was he a part of that?"

I don't want to meet an uncle who facilitated my mother's abuse, no matter how much it would mean to me. Just because he's family doesn't mean he's earned a spot in my life if he's an abusive peace of shit.

"Not in the slightest. They abused him just as they did their daughter because he stood up for her. Thalor was younger than your mother, but that didn't stop him from trying. I was able to save her, but it was at the cost of him. When he shifted for the first time and his wolf came out—in a pack full of felines—he had no chance. Your mother never found out about what they did to him. She thought that because he was their son, the heir, they would treat him better. I never told her what happened," the Devil admits, and I swear I see regret on her stunning face.

My stomach sours at how many horrible things have happened to my own family—and I never knew. It's like we're all cursed or something.

"Fuck." Parker stands and paces away. From the little I've learned of his past over the years, I can't imagine the pain this conversation causes him.

Lifera and I both let him go, allowing him to settle on his own.

"Could my mother partially shift?" I ask, thinking of the claws, teeth, and predator-like senses that overtook me in my training session with Van.

"No... is that something you can do?" Her voice is quiet, head tilted to the side just so.

Words sit frozen on my tongue. I hesitate, unsure of how much I should share. I know for sure I don't want her to know about the chains, but maybe she can help me understand this side of me that I must've inherited from my mother.

"I can," I say slowly, softly, as if there are ears in the walls listening.

"Very interesting," she nods, contemplating. "That is not an ability I'm familiar with. As far as I know, you can shift, or you can't. Those who have attempted a partial shift are typically stuck that way. No one attempts it anymore. It's actually a known torture method because it traps the animal and causes them immense pain. I could see great benefit in an intentional, partial shift."

I notice how she takes in information and from it forms a strategy. There's a clear reason why she's the leader; intelligence radiates out of her like she's constantly seeing a battlefield laid before her, and with each new piece of information, the pieces shift and the war changes.

"The Fae is training you, I assume?" Her focus zooms back onto me, golden eyes glinting with unseen emotion.

"He is," I confirm.

"Good, he will be the best teacher for it. But don't let him deceive you, he has more tricks up his sleeve than he probably lets on."

I don't really know what else to say about Van, and don't comfortable talking about him when he's not here, so I shift the conversation back to our original topic.

"If my mother was a shifter demon from Hell, and my father was an angel, how did they meet? How did they fall in love?" The question replays over and over in my head.

Lifera's eyes lose all their light, darkening once again. It seems this conversation is as much of an emotional rollercoaster for her as it is for me.

"Many years went by, and over time your mother and I became friends. She was my closest ally. Because I presented as a male all those years, everyone thought we were lovers. They dubbed her the Queen of Hell—something we laughed about many times in secret. She helped me make tough decisions. We were constantly being infiltrated by the angels. They were able to sneak into Hell without issue, and every time they did, they decimated thousands of demons. I wasn't powerful enough to close the borders to Hell myself. One night, however, an enchantress came and told me that she could help to close Hell's border, but that it would take so much of my power, I would need to appoint another to share the load. So many demons were dying, creatures I'd created, that I felt responsible; so I agreed.

"What the enchantress didn't tell me is that in doing this, I would trap myself in this realm, never to leave again. But, if presented with the same options, I would still choose to save the demons. Though not without guilt, they were innocent.

They didn't ask to be made, nor did they ask to be on the wrong side of good versus evil."

Lifera gathers her thoughts and continues. "I asked Thara to take the mantle, join me and hold power over Hell—be a true queen—but she refused. I didn't understand then, but I think I know why now. I think she had already met your father. By taking power, she would be purposefully separating herself from him. But she also understood the importance, so she helped me find another. We decided that it would be impossible to pick a demon ourselves, so we created The Games. A series of tournaments occur each time a new Lord is chosen. That is how the First Lord, and all the other Lords, obtained their titles. It's demon culture to fight and kill for what you want, so it made sense."

"If she was already with my father, why would she need to leave Hell?" I ask, confused.

"Your father would've never survived in Hell. Not even the most powerful enchantress could've masked his angel heritage." She gives a pointed look to Parker. "He could've chosen to fall from grace, but that wasn't his style. He was very loyal, and I'm sure falling in love with your mother was a hard enough trial against his conscience. She loved him fiercely and wouldn't have asked him to do something he wasn't comfortable with. So, no, they couldn't have stayed in Hell."

She taps her toe against the floor with an anxious click. "But I know she didn't want me to be alone. We had been friends—family really—for generations. That amount of time in Hell isn't even comparable with time on Earth. Think of a generation not in a human sense of familial procession, but as entire cycles of creation itself. Whole lifespans of ageless beings, endless and electric. Time enough for entire histories to be written. We are currently in the 17th Generation; your mother and I met in the 4th. That's a long time to know and love someone, only to lose them. Still, I could not hold her back. Your father gave her something I never could've." Her eyes meet mine, a pointed look I don't understand.

She continues without explanation. "Your mother was an amazing strategist. I think she hoped that the Lord who won would be able to help me in the ways she did, but it didn't turn out that way."

I start to ask why not but she gives me a knowing look and continues before I'm able. "The First Lord is known for his battle strategy; in that way, he rivaled Thara.

But none could ever be as good at deception as he is. Not even me. I suspected he was plotting against me behind my back from the beginning. Demons were dying, and angels were still sneaking across the border regardless of everything I had done to prevent the possibility. Stories were circulating throughout Hell that we weren't the only realm suffering these issues. I was stuck here, unable to see what havoc he was inflicting elsewhere, so I sent Thara to Earth to investigate. She returned, with many stories that confirmed the First Lord's betrayal, but also with even more love for your father. He had apparently been badly injured in a battle and was left there to die. She not only wished to stay with him, but most likely saw the benefit of remaining on Earth, away from all the dangers of Heaven and Hell.

"It was then that I knew she'd eventually leave to be with him; it was only a matter of time. She loved him unlike anything I'd ever seen, and I never once saw them together. I was afraid the First would come after your mother, since they assumed she was my lover, so I faked her death. I sent her away to Earth, and in my grief, I had another tournament set up. A second Lord was chosen. He only lasted a few hundred years before he was killed by a pack of hellhounds. Shortly after that, Nightmare won the Games and became the new Second—a title he's held onto ever since. I had hoped that I would come to trust them as I did Thara, but it seems even I am not free from the trauma of her loss, both when I sent her away, and when she died."

"You knew when she died?" I ask, a sick feeling in my chest.

"The entire realm felt your family's death. They also all felt the surge of your power that night. What happened, Valencia?" The way she asks the question makes me feel like a lance has been shoved through my chest.

Pain is familiar, I've been living with it for years. But the darkness that descends across my vision is a new kind of prison. The memory of that night consumes me, trapping me in visions of the past. I'm eleven again, frozen like a statue as I watch my whole life *burn*.

CHAPTER 30
VALENCIA

Eighteen Years Ago

The barn is cold—probably too cold for me to be out here—but I'm wearing my coat, so it's not like they can get mad about it. Except, if Mom knew I snuck out, she'd skin my hide.

Or maybe it's tan. Maybe she'd tan my hide.

I don't remember how she says it, I just know that she hates it when I sneak out here by myself at night.

I've lived on our small farm in Montana my whole life. It's not a lot—some of our neighbors have large ranches—but I love learning how to care for the animals and garden with my parents. Playing tag in the woods with Elijah, my little brother.

I love it *here*. At night, the stars are so pretty that I sneak out just to see the way they shine like little fairies in the sky. I love glitter and shiny things, so it's no surprise I want to be outside at night.

Wind outside rattles the wooden boards of the barn. A creepy squeaking sound that makes me nervous. I ignore it as best I can, enjoying the way the moon shines through the cracks in the walls. There's a dark shadow to the side of me, unpierced by the moonlight. No matter how uncomfortable the dark makes me, I can't go back inside.

Sugar is about to have her baby.

Sugar pushes her large head against my side, nudging me for more pats. I scratch under her large, rounded belly where I know she likes. I always have to do it because Mom can't reach this spot. Mom's not as small as me, and Sugar isn't the biggest horse—not like those giant ones the neighbor had a few years ago.

I rub my hand over warm, red fur, the short bristles rubbing softly against my palm. She's got three white socks and a pretty white blaze down her face. My parents got her as a Christmas present for Eli last year, but they weren't expecting her to have a baby. I don't know how you forget a baby's coming, but every time I ask Dad how babies are made, he gets a weird look on his face. His cheeks turn red, and he starts mumbling about bees and some bird he used to have.

When I asked Mom, she just said, "I'll tell you when you're a little older."

I'm starting to think my parents don't know how babies are made, which is strange since they have both my brother and me.

Sugar groans, her belly muscles twitching under my soft scratches. I sit next to where she lays against the soft straw, cuddled between the hay and her large body. Mom says it's too dangerous to do this, but Sugar would never hurt me.

"I kind of hope I don't figure out how babies are made, this does not seem fun, girl," I tell her. She blinks a big brown eye at me, her tail swishing back and forth. It thumps softly into the straw with a *thud* each time. She's been in pain the last few days, and mom says it's because the baby is almost here. I've been sneaking out of the house every night to be with her.

I didn't want her to be alone; what if she needed help?

Not that I could help her, but I could get Mom if she was in trouble. Mom knows how to do *everything*. Dad is constantly grumbling that she beats him at everything they do, but she just laughs and kisses him.

They always get this weird look on their faces when they look at each other, but when I asked why, they said I was too little to understand. They're always saying I'm too little.

Sugar's head jerks up and her ears point forward. The shadows move, shifting quietly in the night. The corner stays dark, but my eyes search for further movement in the barn.

I can't see anything beyond the stall, the small lantern I brought with me the only source of light I have. Dad wired a whole lighting system throughout the barn, but I don't use it when I sneak out here, afraid it will wake them up and they'll force me back to bed.

The lantern leaves a soft glow but doesn't extend very far. The rest of the barn is still pitch-black, besides the soft glow of the moon that's coming in through the other stall doors. The main door is also open, but it doesn't bring light far enough into the barn to reach Sugar's stall.

I can hear the other animals shuffling. The goats softly bleat a few times, and the pigs snuffle through the straw as if in search of something. Sugar's soft neigh is a rumbling sound I feel through her skin, where my hand lays against her side.

This is the third night this week I've come out here, but this is the first night the animals have acted this way. I'm normally comforted by the sounds and smells in here, especially cuddled with my girl. Her warm body feels tense. I'd thought it was from the pain. Now I'm not sure. Things feel darker tonight. Movement to my side catches my eye, but all I see is the tall shadow that the light refuses penetrate.

My heart rate rises as I look into the darkness. I can't see anything out there, and the animals make too much noise to hear anything else that might be going on outside.

I try to convince myself that it's nothing, but a pit forms in my stomach and a part of my brain starts to demand I go back inside.

"I'm not scared of the dark," I say to Sugar, a shake in my voice. I have to remind myself of this every night when my parents turn off all the lights after putting me to bed. I'm not a baby like Eli; I can't be scared of the dark. When Mom asked if I still wanted my nightlight or whether she could give it to Eli, I'd told her to give it to him, even though I really didn't want her to. I didn't want her to think I was a baby.

"I'm not scared of the dark," I mutter again, quieter this time. I press closer to Sugar's side, drawing in more of her warmth.

Silence greets me. The sounds of my heavy breathing louder than normal. The animals no longer shuffle around, the pigs and goats completely still. Sugar's ears prick back and forth, but she doesn't move. I can't even hear the bugs outside anymore.

I start to panic, remembering when my dad told me that if the forest grows quiet, there's a predator nearby. What if there's a bear or something outside?

I stand slowly, the rustle of my coat far too loud in the silence.

Footsteps sound outside, drawing my attention to the main door, and my heartrate spikes. I press my back hard against the wooden wall of the stable. The shadows seem to shiver in response and my lantern shuffles around in my grip.

"Valencia? You out here?" Dad calls from the main door.

I rush out of the stall, crawling under the rope that keeps Sugar in and run towards him. I wrap him in my arms, pressing my face into his stomach.

"Hi, Princess," he murmurs and pulls me in close. "What are you doing out here?"

"I didn't want Sugar to be alone," I mutter, fear making it hard to get the words out.

"You're too sweet. I'm sure she appreciates your company, but you need to come in for bed," he replies softly, holding me just as tight.

"Okay," I wrap my fingers through his when he grabs my hand.

We start to walk through the barn and back towards the house, passing the stalls full of animals. The shadows seem to move with us, but they don't scare me anymore. Dad's steady presence anchors me, a constant reminder that I'm safe when he's around.

Dad freezes just inside the main door and pulls us to the side, further into the dark.

"Don't make a sound," he snaps in a quiet voice.

I jump at the command. He's never talked to me that way. I try to look outside of the barn but his large arm prevents me from seeing anything past the edge of darkness.

I start to shake, fear creeping back in for reasons I can't explain. That pit in my stomach grows to a stone that weighs me down, holding me hostage.

Dad pushes me a little farther into the barn until I'm hidden by the big wooden door. He pushes me into a seated position in the cold dirt and whispers in my ear. "There's someone out there, I don't know who it is. You stay right here until I come back for you. Do not move until you see your mother or me, okay?"

I nod my head in response, fear robbing me of words.

Dad brushes his hand against my head and presses a kiss to the top of my head with a whispered, "I love you, princess," before sneaking out of the barn.

I shake, the slick material of my coat brushing against the wood beside me. I feel tears falling down my face, but I don't understand their purpose. I don't understand why I'm so scared, or why daddy left me here alone.

I never told him I was scared of the dark. Maybe if I'd told him I was scared, he would've taken me with him.

"I'm not scared of the dark, I'm not scared of the dark, I'm *not* scared of the dark," I chant quietly to myself, the sound barely escaping my lips. The shadow curls in closer, as if to conceal me further.

I start chanting it in my head and try to stay silent like he told me to, but I'm shaking so badly that my slick coat audibly rattles.

Or maybe that's just the chattering of my teeth I hear inside my head.

A flash of light catches my eye, and when I turn my head, I notice there is a small crack in the wood I can see through. The house is just away from the barn, open and nestled in a small clearing of trees. The moon shines down on it, making the normally white walls shine a bright gray.

I can't see him anywhere, just the house and the woods behind it. All the windows are dark, and there's no sound to be heard besides that which I'm making, myself.

I expect to see one of my parents come out of the door any minute, but time goes by and no one does. Longer and longer I sit here, and as badly as I want to go inside, Dad told me not to move.

Eventually, I fall asleep, the stress and cold leeching my energy.

A loud crackling sound wakes me. My eyes instantly sting when I open them and my throat feels tight. When I try to look through the crack in the wood, my eyes burn against a bright orange light. I can't focus enough to see what's going on out there, and the longer I sit here, the harder it gets to breathe.

I rush out of the barn, my arm over my face as I run towards the house. Suddenly, a flash of heat scorches me, and I stumble backwards a couple of steps. I squint through the pain until I can see my house again.

Completely consumed by flames.

It's so bright, my eyes water and there isn't a place that hasn't been taken by the flames. The boards are all black, and the inside is consumed with bright orange.

There's so much smoke, it rolls out from the roof and upstairs windows, reaching so high into the sky that I can't see the stars.

They're in there. I know they are. But that pit in my stomach holds me in place, and I'm forced to watch as my childhood home burns to the ground with my family inside.

Tears stream down my face. I call out for my mommy and daddy, but they never make it out of the house. I'm left alone, lost in the dark that's now a sea of flames.

A dark shape forms in the fire, and I almost wonder if it's them, about to escape, but the roof caves in and a burst of heat shoots through the front door. It's so hot, I fall to my knees and am forced to crawl away, my hands digging painfully into the rocks.

"I'm scared of the dark," I sob, my voice hoarse. "Daddy, I'm scared of the dark, I don't want to be alone."

No one answers. Just the sound of burning wood and roaring flames.

"I'm scared of the dark," I yell, praying my Mom hears me. Praying that she runs out of the flames to save me.

"I'm scared of the dark," I try to yell, but my throat is too sore, and I can't get the words out.

I sit back on my butt, wrap my arms around my knees and set my chin on top of them as I cry. I can feel the heat from the flames, searing my hands and face, but I can't look away. I rock back and forth, and the longer I sit, the hotter I start to feel.

I feel the heat inside of me build, my body burning on the inside as hot as the inferno in before me.

I see the flames, bright orange flashes that dance behind my eyelids. They beg for release, a quiet lullaby of peace if I just let them out.

"I'm scared of the dark," I whisper one last time as I let the fire inside me free, following my family in the flames.

CHAPTER 31
CORVUS

"THEY'RE STILL NOT BACK yet," I mutter to Van for the tenth time. It's not been more than a couple of minutes since the last time I said it. I can already feel an uneasy pit in my stomach starting to form.

"I'm sure they had a lot to talk about. If we're right, and one of her parents was a powerful demon, then it's a very good possibility that the Devil knew them."

"I just don't feel right," I say, a strange sense of doom filling me from head to toe.

"Corvus, give her time. It's clear she can take care of herself, and the Devil has more reason to keep her alive than kill her. You're just paranoid." Van's voice is at least soothing, not containing any of his normal indignation. This recent injury has certainly tamed him a bit.

"Fuck," I mutter as the dread consumes me completely. It's unfamiliar in its heaviness, causing my unease to grow tenfold.

I don't hesitate any longer, and portal straight to the Devil's palace.

I can't land directly inside the palace, so I'm forced to land outside in the garden. His wards are too intense, and I can't get past them no matter how hard I try. I can enter on my feet, though, and do exactly that before storming into the palace, following the sick feeling of dread in my chest that points the way.

I have no idea what's happening or how I know where she is, but there's something about her that calls to me—some immense pain.

I shoulder through the doors of the main room, one of them splintering off its hinges with a loud bang. When I see that the dark room is cold and empty, a loud yell escapes me. I'm about to start tearing through the walls when Greta rushes into the room.

"This way, Lord Crow," she snaps, already turning on her heel and running from the room. I'm forced to follow, and I can't hold in my growl at her slow pace. I can feel Valencia's pain—a deep-seated agony that begs I fall to my knees and crawl into a ball. Despite the crippling emotions, I push through.

Greta unexpectedly halts at a blank spot in the wall and starts to feel around. I'm about to smash her through it in a rage when the soft *snick* of a lock unlatching sounds. A whoosh of air flows past me as the wall moves to reveal a hidden door, and I unceremoniously shove the older woman out of the way and storm into the room beyond. Better that than running her over.

I rush into the room. There's a flash of movement and a spike of pain in my head, but I power through. I race to where Parker and the Devil both stand, leaning over one of the couches. I can hear Parker frantically trying to get Valencia to wake up, but I can't see her from this angle. Barreling through, I barely see what's around me, and when I finally reach her, my heart plummets.

She's sitting as though undisturbed, but her eyes are completely black, and she's as still as death.

"Valencia," I say as I approach, softly laying a hand on her face. Parker and the Devil both step back, giving me space. "Wake up."

It's a demand, a snapped command that flows out of me with little care, but she doesn't respond—clearly trapped by whatever has her lost inside her own head.

"It's a memory; she has to experience it completely before waking," the Devil mutters from behind me. I whip around to snap at him, to demand he tell me what's going on, but the look on his face stops me short. The only way she'd be trapped in a memory is if he forced her to be there.

"What did you do?" I question accusingly.

Parker's eyes flick back and forth between us, his expression momentarily shocked, before he slowly backs away. His reaction sets me on edge, and I unfold to my full height to stare the Devil down. Anger boils in my veins, begging to burst out of my skin in a ball of fire. However, the Devil doesn't back down and holds his shoulders high. The skin around his eyes is pulled so tightly, it looks almost painful, but it's his eyes that worry me the most. I almost recognize the look he's giving me.

I snatch him by his throat without care that he's my maker; he could be God—or some other deity—and I'd still feel the same. He's standing between me and the one thing that means the most to me.

Blunt nails claw at my hands, cutting through the skin, but it fazes me none. I squeeze tighter, relishing how his eyes become bloodshot with every second that passes.

I know it's futile to ask questions, because he clearly can't answer, but I do so anyway. "What did you do?"

"Corvus! See reason," Greta pleads from somewhere behind me. I can tell she wants to reach out, but she wisely stays back.

The Devil simply blinks at me, his body struggling more due to the strangulation. He's done something to Valencia, trapped her in some kind of nightmare, and I'll kill him without a second thought if Valencia doesn't wake soon.

Despite all of the shit the Devil has put me through, I'd never thought of truly ending him—until now. I never thought I'd have the strength, but whatever courses through my veins right now makes me feel more powerful than ever.

A sharp sting of pain flairs through my right ankle as his boot heel jams down, but still I don't let go. The true demon inside me, the part of me that was intended to rule Hell, preens at the surface and savors the pain I'm inflicting like it's a delicate treat. He whispers in my ear how easy it would be to rip his head from his shoulders. The demon is hungry for the Devil's blood. When he looks at the Devil, he doesn't see a threat.

A rush of power flows through me, equally addictive and euphoric as he lends me more of his power. I'm not able to tap into it easily. Normally, the only way to do this is to shift into his form completely, but I'm unwilling to give him that much power.

I trust him with free rein as much as I trust the Devil.

His delicate skin stretches in my fingertips, starting to break under my curled nails, and the demon preens at the smell of iron. I feel so powerful; it would be easy to clamp my fingers together and sever his head completely—a potentially deadly blow that shouldn't be possible.

My hand unclenches slightly—realization a stark reminder. The Devil takes a deep breath in through his nose, bright amber eyes sparking with malice.

"You'd be wise to let me go, and never try this again," he growls menacingly.

My hand slowly drops from his throat. The demon rages inside of me, angry that I'm giving in, but I know something the true demon doesn't. No matter how strong I feel, I'll never beat the Devil himself. Rage and anger for the woman I love are no match for my creator.

The Devil twists his neck, skin patchy with red marks and bloody half-moons, but he doesn't show any sign of pain.

"Val, we need you," Parker pleads, his voice stiff with concern.

"I will allow that to go unpunished because I understand the scene is concerning, but next time you attack me without provocation, there will be consequences." The Devil straightens his suit, eyes malignant and angry.

My blood thickens. Just one more second of allowing the demon control, and I would've made a very grave mistake. "What have you done to her?" I question, accusation heavy in my tone.

"I did nothing," he explains, waving a worried Greta away. "I only saw part of the memory, but she'll need to see it all. If fate trapped her in a vision of the past, the only way out is through."

"You were there with her?" I scoff, never having heard of such a thing.

"For a part of it, till someone distracted me," his eye twitches as he looks at me.

"Corvus?" Valencia croaks from behind me.

I jerk towards her, kneeling on the floor in front of the couch, the Devil forgotten. The ocean blue of her eyes that I love so much stare back at me. Their watery depths call to me, and without a word, I pull her into a hug. I can feel her fists wrap around my shirt, pulling it tightly against the back of my neck. Twin spots on my chest cool as her tears seep through the fabric, but I just hold her tighter, cherishing that she's back from whatever dark place she disappeared to.

"What happened?" I mutter the words against her head, my breath fanning her hair. Small strands waft up to tickle my face and get caught in my stubble.

"I was back there. The night my family died," she cries, soft sobs wracking her body.

I pull her into me, falling back on my ass. She follows, wrapping her arms around my neck and legs around my waist. We sit like that for a while, her head tucked into my throat as she lets the emotional event flow through her.

Sometime later, after her sobs finally quieten to hiccups, I pull her away to look at her face. Dark hair sticks to her sweaty face, tear tracks streak her cheeks and neck, and her skin is scattered with red splotches.

"Do you want to talk about it?" I ask her softly, slowly brushing my hand up and down her back.

She shakes her head, tears already re-forming in her eyes. "Not in the slightest."

I nod my head in understanding, not wanting to force her to experience it again.

"Sorry to interrupt, but I insist we do talk about it."

I growl at the Devil standing over us, albeit far out of arm's reach, and scowl at the pristine look of his face and suit, irritated that he no longer looks like I nearly choked him to death.

Valencia shakes her head, fear evident in her eyes, and I'm about to tell him he can shove his insistence right up his ass when Valencia speaks. "Stop with the damn mind tricks. If you expect me to reveal my sordid past, you better do the same. I'm going to tell him anyway."

My brows dip in confusion. "Tell me what?"

I look at the Devil. He still stands over us, looking down on the scene with unnamed emotion in his eyes. I'd guess fear, but that's impossible.

"Maybe I'm not ready to reveal this secret," he says, slightly shifting his weight. He's uncomfortable, that much is clear—I just don't know why. I look to Valencia for answers, but she's focused on the Devil.

"You better get comfortable fast, then," she snaps. Her anger only puts me more on edge, and I slowly stand, placing myself between them.

He doesn't take his eyes off of mine, but it doesn't matter. In a faster flash than my eyes can track, the place where the Devil once inhabited stands a striking female. Tall, with long red hair, pale skin, and a purple suit that's more than revealing. But the Devil's predatory eyes remain the same.

She smirks at me, shifting her weight to one leg to pop a hip to the side. The truth is like a hot knife between the ribs. Primal instincts in me start blare a warning.

"That's not possible," I mutter, racking my brain for any knowledge that the Devil can shapeshift.

"You mean you don't recognize your maker, Corvus?" she sneers in a sassy tone that is all too familiar—a tone I've heard a thousand times before, but never from a feminine voice. The face was a deception, a mask to hide her true nature. If she's always been powerful enough to voluntarily shapeshift, why hide it?

"Devil?" I ask, hoping I'm wrong. I saw the change with my own eyes, yet it's unbelievable. It feels like a trick. The thought of the King of Hell hiding like a phantom unseen in the shadows is laughable. His entire personality is centered on showy power.

"The one and only, but you can call me Lifera, if you prefer," she purrs, the words rolling off her tongue in a smooth and lightly accented lilt.

"All this time... you let us believe you were someone else?" I know for a fact no one knows about this besides Greta, who still hovers uncomfortably in the corner, and clearly Valencia—which only opens more questions. Why reveal herself to Valencia and not the very demons she created?

The Devil created thousands of demons—filled this entire realm with a population intent in being the Devil's subjects, and not a single one knows the truth?

"Yup," she pops the *'p'* like some petulant pre-teen on Earth.

"Why?" I demand, more confused than ever. All those generations I took orders from the Devil, without realizing that the seductively powerful male persona was an illusion.

"Because it felt safer," she shrugs, crossing her arms over her chest. The sound of her feminine voice sets me on edge, and the rage I felt before comes back.

I shake my head. "I don't believe that for a minute. What's the real reason?"

Her smirk is evil as she steps closer, but I can't back away with Valencia and the couch directly behind me. Her eyes gleam, and my fist ignites in a defensive response.

In a deliberate show of power, she extinguishes my flames with a flick of her wrist. "I never said a word because the demons fear a king. A *queen* is overlooked, and that is where the true power lies."

I shake with anger, ready to ignite my entire body this time and go back on the attack. I never trusted the Devil, and this only proves my assumptions were right. This feels like another harsh betrayal—like the ground beneath me has split and I'm left on trying to balance on a crumbled foundation.

I'll never trust her around Valencia again.

"Valencia, let's go," I urge without turning my back on the Devil. I can't stand to hear any more. If I could portal us out of here right this second, I would.

"Not so fast—we need to talk about the memory." The Devil reclaims her seat on the couch, slouching back in a relaxed position.

"Okay," Valencia tiredly agrees from the ground.

Parker shocks us both. "Val," he murmurs softly, walking towards us and crouching down so he's eye level with her. A growl escapes me, the true demon uneasy with another being so close to her while she's in such a vulnerable state, but Parker ignores me. I can't take my eyes off the Devil, in case she decides to attack, but I hear him. "I know it's painful, but don't run away from the memory. You'll regret it. Take the chance to face it head-on while you can." There's a note of despair in Parker's voice, and I can't help but wonder whether it comes from his worry for Valencia or emotions that have been dragged from his own past.

Her silence finally intercedes with my need to watch the Devil's every move. When I turn, she's still wiping the tears from her eyes, but stops to slowly grab my hand and pull me back down to sit beside her. I do so, but am on edge—unable to fully lean back—but I squeeze her hand in mine in an offer of support.

Valencia tucks into my side while Parker and Lifera take the other couch. Lifera, who still grates on my nerves every time I look at her, ignores me. She doesn't press Valencia, though, and waits patiently for her to start.

"That night," Valencia's voice breaks, and it takes her a second to compose herself enough to continue. Her shoulders are tense, nearly touching her ears, and her hand quivers in mine. "I was told that a wildfire started in the woods, and the house caught fire. They said that they found me sitting in the driveway between the house and barn, surrounded by fire on all sides. They had no idea how I'd survived—nothing on our farm did, and the wildfire continued to burn for another 5000 acres before they managed to contain it."

Her voice is soft, eyes downcast and blank as the memory comes back to her. "I went outside to check on our horse; she was pregnant and about to have her baby. I remember sneaking out every night to be with her. My Dad—" again, I see her struggling to get the words out, as if the pain has a grip on her throat. I gently rub her leg, squeezing her hand in mine. "My Dad found me in the barn. We were on our way out, but he pushed me to the side and told me to be quiet—that he'd heard someone outside. I hid in the dark for so long, I fell asleep. It was cold and I was scared, and I just remember thinking that he'd come back for me. He'd never sounded so serious, and I didn't want to disappoint him by moving. Next thing I know, I'm waking up, and the entire house is on fire. I ran out of the barn, but I could only make it as far as the driveway; it was too smoky to get any closer. My muscles didn't work, and no matter how much I screamed, my family never came out of that house."

Her brows furrow as if she's trying to search her memory for the details she needs. Her head shakes a few times, but no words come for a moment. "The fire department that rescued me said I was sitting in the middle of the fire, rocking and crying, untouched by the flames. No one knows how I survived. The entire farm—the house and the barn—burned down that night; nothing was salvageable when they arrived. What I've struggled with my entire life is how the Hell I didn't die alongside them."

The words sit heavy in the room, a tension that feels tangible against my skin. There's no true reason that explains why she made it that night. Maybe it was her father hiding her before he went to check, maybe it was her falling asleep, maybe it was intentional. How are we ever to know, when the only witness was a terrified child?

"Thara was an extremely gifted shifter, but she couldn't wield fire magic for shit," the Devil ponders, her pale face tipped down into a frown. It's my first clue into the parts of Valencia's history that I didn't know. The dots connect with a blinding light. If Thara—the Devil's rumored lover he's supposedly killed—was Valencia's mother, then her demon side is even more powerful than I expected.

Knowing the Devil is actually a woman... I wonder if the stories of Thara that I've heard are even true.

"Remiel was an archangel, but his powers are unknown to me. He was great in battle, but he was never very vicious, always wanting to do what was right," Lifera continues. Her amber eyes analyze my every reaction.

Valencia's attention zeroes in as Lifera shares more information about her parents—interesting information, considering Lifera doesn't know of Valencia's father's powers, which means there's a chance she doesn't know about Valencia's other power. If anything were to make the Devil want to attack us, it would be knowing that Valencia wields a power that only the highest-ranking archangels are suspected to have. It seems Remiel wasn't *just* an archangel.

"If they were caught by surprise, especially by a skilled fire wielder, there's a great possibility they didn't even have a chance to fight back." Lifera bolts to her feet and slams a hand down onto the coffee table in front of her and Parker, sending shards of wood flying. "Thara, you fool!" she yells, raw emotion in her tone.

Parker leans as far away from Lifera as he can while Valencia and I watch, wide-eyed.

"Forgive me, Valencia," she continues, "but love made your mother dumb. She gave up so much to be with Remiel, even though I begged her not to. My love for her made *me* weak. I could've forced her to stay, but she was my best friend, and I just wanted her to be happy. To know that her death could've been prevented," Lifera's voice breaks in a rare show of emotion.

That rage is visible in her bright golden eyes and the glow shines onto her cheeks. Light red veins begin to pop out along her cheeks, their color a stark contrast against her pale skin.

"Why do you say it was preventable?" Valencia asks, confusion and grief clear in her tone.

"Wards can be put in place to prevent fire magic, or demons in general, from coming onto a property on Earth. Both Thara and Remiel knew this, but they wanted nothing to do with their past lives. They wanted to have peace on Earth, away from the chaos. The *humans* can't even have peace on Earth, I don't know why they thought they were special."

Lifera stands atop the destroyed coffee table, shards littered everywhere. It's the most raw and *real* reaction I've seen from a demon—or anyone, really—in Hell. To express this much pain is dangerous. Just as Lifera said, Thara was clearly a weakness, and even this long after her passing, she still feels the pain.

If she feels this much for Valencia's mother, it's no wonder she wanted her in Hell in the first place. All this time, I thought she was against us, but it seems she just wanted a piece of the woman she loved to be close.

"Whoever is after you killed Thara. You have full rein of Hell, Valencia. Make my realm yours and hunt that motherfucker down." Lifera holds her head high as she stalks out of the room, her deadly black heels clicking as she goes. Her body is rigid, but she moves with the grace of a predator, but we all see the tear that slides down her face.

Parker, Valencia, and I share a tense look. I now know there's no way I can put off hunting this mysterious shadow. Lifera—the Devil—just gave us full rein of Hell.

Shit is about to get messy.

CHAPTER 32
VALENCIA

CORVUS FINALLY AGREES THERE'S no time like the present to go after our enemies, and transports us back to the cave so we can change. Then, we gather outside the cave, ready to head straight to Tornil's tent.

Van refuses to be left behind, despite Corvus' insistence that he stay back. He's still got a limp, though barely noticeable, but I side with Van and Corvus accepts with an exaggerated eye roll.

I pull at the deep V of my black dress, self-conscious of the extra skin it shows. It's made from a comfortable sweater-like material that fits a little too tightly against my chest. The black leather straps, which wrap around my arms and torso, accentuate my figure further. The skirt is long, brushing against the ground in the back, but there's a long slit up the side, allowing my leg to peek through with each step.

It was the only option in the dresser, and I thought about demanding another but decided I'd keep it on when Corvus' eyes darkened, if only to torture him.

He smiled when I put on the jewelry he gave me the first time we visited to the tent, and a warmth filled my chest at the look. There's just something about him that reaches inside me and pulls at the dark pieces I have hidden. All the desires and wishes I'm too scared to voice.

He came up to me before we left with a small strap of leather in hand. I thought he was about to offer me a collar, but before I could rip him a new one for even thinking about it, he sank to his knees before me and wrapped the small strap around my upper thigh, still hidden by the dress but easily accessible thanks to the skirt's slit. In the strap, he tucked his red blade, tightened it enough so it wouldn't fall out, and placed a kiss right beside it.

We didn't say a word, but I could see the hesitation he didn't voice. He gave my leg one last squeeze before rising to his full height and transporting us to the tent.

My black combat boots make a soft scuffing sound as we walk along the dirt path at the main entrance of Tornil's tent. Like last time, there are hundreds of people milling around in some state of intoxication, but we make it inside without issue. Corvus remains tense, however, and doesn't lessen his tight grip on my hand.

"What do we do?" Parker murmurs, looking around the room.

The inside of the tent is packed. Everywhere, bodies dance in various stages of undress, and the thumping music is so loud that I can feel it in my chest. The walkways above are gone, and the ceiling now resembles a starry night's sky. Brightly-colored lights bounce off the walls and bodies to the beat of the music.

"Let's find a place to sit and scope the place out," Corvus responds, disdain in his voice.

He leads us towards a row of booths against the wall next to the bar. They're mostly full of large and small groups alike, chatting animatedly over drinks scattered across the table tops. Each group looks our way as we pass, their eyes wide as they take us in.

To me, we appear no different to anyone else. Most I've seen resemble humans of some form—maybe an unusual eye color here, or a small set of horns like that one bartender had there—but for the most part, there haven't been any monstrous creatures roaming around. When I asked Corvus about it, he'd told me that most demons hide their true form behind a glamor. There are so many intricacies of demonic culture, I fear no amount of time in Hell will allow me to understand them all.

"This will do," Corvus says as he gestures for me to slide into a round booth. The seat is made of comfortable, leather-covered cushions with opulent buttons and polished wooden details. The light that hangs atop of the table is dim and sparkly, shining through a clear crystal shell. The table itself is made from shiny red wood, covered in dark lines, that's been polished to a smooth finish. I haven't seen any trees in Hell, so the extravagant woodwork throws me off.

I rub my hand across its surface, reveling in the fine detailing. It's so hard to see, but small engravings have been etched into the surface. Depictions of battle and love, stories of triumph and defeat. I'm so lost in the artwork, that Van's smooth voice makes me jump.

"Beautiful, is it not?" he says from across the booth. He sits at the very edge, and I can't tell if it's because he wants to be as far away from Parker as he can, or if he prefers the easiest escape route. Parker, who sits close to my side, is as engrossed in the tabletop as I am.

"It's... its—I don't even know how to describe how beautiful it is. I wish I could commission another piece from the artist!" I exclaim.

"I'm sure he would be happy to make you something," Van says with a laugh. I look up, confused by his tone, but he just points at Corvus.

"Are you *blushing*?" I demand, pulling Corvus' face back towards me when he tries to look away. "Did *you* do this?"

He swallows stiffly, the muscles in his jaw flexing under his hand before nodding, a soft smile on his face.

"I didn't know you worked with wood. I didn't know you were an *artist*," I say, smiling at him brightly.

"There's still a lot we don't know about each other," he responds softly, eyes tracking my hand that still rubs across the top of the table.

I tense, not sure if he's upset. It seems like an underlying comment about all the other things we haven't said, but he kisses my temple with a whispered, "We have plenty of time."

I release my breath, appreciating his willingness to give me time to come to terms with everything. I want to tell him how I feel, but something keeps me from saying those words each time I think about it. Thankfully, Parker finds the perfect time to make a joke and bring me out of my confused thoughts.

"I feel overdressed," Parker says with a laugh, finally looking at the crowd. I follow his gaze, watching as bodies grind and flow against each other. They're somehow all in sync, despite being in pairs or large groups. It surprises me that the scene doesn't look all too different to the clubs I've been to on Earth—only, many of the demons are barely dressed and I can spot a few who I think are completely naked. I divert my eyes away from one couple I'm pretty sure is having sex, and instead focus on the people who stand around the bar.

"What do people drink in Hell?" I ask, suddenly curious as to which kinds of alcohol are popular for a crowd that doesn't need liquid courage to do something crazy.

"Lots of the same stuff you see on Earth—it's all made the same, and plenty of demons here have been to Earth, so Tornil finds it easier to have it brought in. There are also some made specifically here in Hell, but they're rare. There's always the chance an enchantress has cursed a batch, or someone has poisoned it." Corvus looks at the bar as well. There are hundreds of bottles sitting against the wall, and a myriad of colorful lights shine through the glass. The blue-haired bartender from before flits around, serving drinks at breakneck speed. I'm not sure how he manages it, being the only one back there.

"Should we get drinks?" Parker asks.

"Best if we all stay sober and focused. They'll know we're here by now and will most likely already be watching." Corvus' dark eyes track the room, but to me, there's nothing to see besides dancing demons.

Then, my eyes widen. Lowly, I whisper, "Shouldn't you be a little quieter about why we're here?"

"The booth is warded; no one can hear what we're saying," he assures, keeping a keen eye on the crowd. Just like the booth on the fight night, they can't hear us, but we're not hidden from view.

"Won't it look suspicious if we aren't drinking or at least doing something?" Parker asks, running a hand across the wooden tabletop.

Van snorts, but doesn't take his eyes off the dance floor. "Rat is right, we need to blend in and not look like we're scouting for the enemy."

I look at Corvus, brows raised, but he doesn't notice. I look at Parker, who smirks at me. I notice he doesn't acknowledge Van like he normally would.

"Nobody leaves the table," Corvus snaps, before getting up and stomping over to the bar. People scramble out of his way, his dark mood causing them to leave a wide ring of open space around him. It seems our last time here left an impression.

We watch as he flags the blue-haired bartender whose name I can't remember. The demon saunters over and leans across the bar and into Corvus' space. I can't see his face very well from here, but I can imagine he's flirting after spotting the demon lord alone. Clearly, he's not worried about Corvus' dark mood.

That familiar warmth sparks in my chest, and a vision flashes through my mind of me slamming that little shit's face against the bar top. It's only a minute or so before Corvus is making his way back with a tray full of glasses and a large glass bottle full of some blue liquid.

Van gives me a knowing smirk as the tray slides across the table.

"Hush," I snap.

"I didn't say anything," Van smirks.

"You were thinking it."

He just laughs, reaching for an empty glass and the bottle.

"What?" Corvus looks at me, but I just shake my head.

"So what's this?" I ask and take a small sip from the glass Van hands me. He serves Corvus and me first, then himself, but sets the bottle down on the table, forcing Parker to fill his own glass.

The flavor is bright, almost like blueberry, and sparkly like soda. There's no sharp tang or bitter aftertaste, so I hope there isn't any alcohol or we're in big trouble.

"It's called Blue Sunrise. A popular drink to be mixed with clear alcohol here in Hell—but I told him we didn't want the alcohol. It looks like we're drinking, but we'll stay sober. Just make sure you don't—"

"This is excellent," Parker exclaims as he slams the glass back in one gulp.

"Slam it," Corvus mutters, giving Parker a look full of exasperation. "If this had alcohol in it, you'd be drunk off your ass. So act the part."

"Easy peasy," Parker says with a fake slur.

He grabs my hand and starts scooting around the bench towards Van, dragging me with him. I grab my own drink and slam it as well, enjoying the crackling flavor that pops along my tongue.

"What are you doing?" Corvus demands, concern in his eyes.

"Back off, Rat," Van snarls as we get closer.

"Then move," Parker snaps, an odd note of ire in his tone. Instead of lashing out like I expect, Van simply scoots out of the booth to get away.

Parker pulls us to our feet and wraps an arm around my shoulders. He smirks at Corvus, who now sits alone with a vicious look on his face. "We're gonna dance; you keep watch."

With a wink, he turns, and we wade to the edge of the dancing crowd. I can still see Corvus, whose face is full of fire, but he remains stiffly seated, eyes on us and the rest of the room like a hawk.

It takes me a second to warm up and match Parker's easy moves. His black shirt lies half open, pale, muscular skin moving fluidly as he dances to the music. I let the music flow through me, feeling each thump of the bass as I dance. I get lost in it, letting the moment still my mind, and enjoy the silence in my head as the loud music drowns out all other thoughts.

Parker smiles at me, his white teeth bright against the flashing lights. I smile back, feeling freer than I have in a while. There are so many burdens weighing us down, but for this one small moment, I let it all go and just live.

The demons around us give us a small amount of space, not much, but more than they offer the others. It takes me a second to realize why, but after a demon catches a glimpse of the red stone earrings that shine brightly in my ears—and jumps as far away as the crowd will allow—I catch on.

They aren't as interested in Parker, either, not like the last time we were here but that doesn't mean he hasn't caught the attention of quite a few of the demons around us, male and female alike. The enchantment Corvus was adamant Parker have placed on him seems to be working.

One brave female, with dark brown hair that reaches low on her back, saunters forward. She smiles seductively at Parker, but focuses her attention on me.

"Is your mistress allowed to play with others?" she purrs, her voice as seductive as her looks. She's wearing a long white dress that easily flows with her movements and allows brief glimpses of skin to be seen underneath. I'm caught off guard by her statement at first, trapped in her milky white eyes.

I know it's impolite to stare at people's features, but her eyes are both ethereal and creepy as hell.

"The mistress does like to play," Parker fake slurs as he pulls her into his body, clearly snapping out of the haze before me.

The three of us dance for a while, Parker and the female curling around each other. I thought it would bother me, how she snuck her way between us, but for some reason, I'm happy. Elation fills me, drowning me in happiness. I love watching Parker enjoy himself, pleased he gets to also take this moment away from everything that's after us and just breathe.

He's so focused on her body pressing against his front, his face buried in her hair, that he misses when she snatches my wrist in a tight grip.

"Keep dancing," she snaps, voice icy and cold, no longer full of heat. I feel a flare of rage rise within me, but it's immediately buried under feelings of joy and comfort.

I smile, dancing to the music despite how the bones in my wrist begin to crush under her tight grip. Even through the pain, I enjoy her touch. Her eyes, once ethereal, now seem cold and bizarre. The warm feeling of goodness starts to fade, and I attempt to pull my wrist away from her grasp, a frown taking over my face.

Then, my eyes nearly roll to the back of my head as a tidal wave of delight fills me from head to toe. It's consuming, like running through a field of wildflowers on a sunny spring day. It's like hiking to the top of my favorite mountain, fishing in my favorite lake, hanging out with my friends at the station. I can see them, clear as day in front of me, smiles on their faces as we all sit around a fire pit, telling funny stories from our years fighting fires together.

She loses interest in Parker, passing him off to another demon who pulls him father into the crowd. That happy feeling grows, happy to see my friend enjoying this moment as much as I am. A scared voice calls my name, but I don't have the capacity to listen. There's no room for fear.

"This way," the woman bites, drawing me back to the present. I smile at how her dark hair flows behind her as we rush through the crowd. She still has a tight grip on my wrist, but it's not needed; I'd follow her anywhere.

We crash through a door, and the cool night air soothes my overheated skin. She drags us through the tents and bodies and fires, all too engrossed in their own world to notice us. That elated feeling brims, so full I feel as though I'm gonna burst with it. We finally round a large tent, off in the darkness, where the lights from Tornil's and the others don't reach. As we rush inside, she drags me behind her like a life-size doll. Jell-O has replaced my bones, which now feel soft and pliable at the slightest urging.

The inside of the tent is mostly bare, besides a large wooden desk and a leather chair that is currently facing away from us. Two large men stand on either side of the chair, their faces covered by their masks. I pinch my brow and take a second to look around. Two more men stand by the tent flap we entered through, faces are also covered by masks.

I smile at them, enjoying their spooky Halloween-like costumes. They all did a great job coordinating their outfits, all dark clothes and black, emotionless masks. Someone out there with a very specific kink would have a heyday with these dudes.

"I brought her, alone, just as you asked. Now release the curse," the woman snaps, her voice sour and filled with spite. It's not an attractive look, but she's still beautiful enough. I guess no one can be perfect.

"Oh, Embaral, you do not make the demands around here; I do." The dark voice comes from behind the desk, but since neither of the guards facing us makes a move, I imagine there's someone in the chair. I smile, the mystery of it all delighting me despite how I don't normally like surprises.

"You promised," she hisses, hand crunching my wrist beneath her grip.

"And you failed. I asked for Corvus first, and you failed to bring him to me. Now I am left to do all the work myself. You'll be fine—the curse isn't even on you, so what's the urgency?" The chair still doesn't turn. I can't understand why, but I'm unable to feel anything other than extremely happy.

"Then I'll take her back to Lord Crow and tell him everything," the woman sputters, yanking me by the wrist once again.

"Cato," the dark voice snaps.

I turn as an ominous shadow saunters forward. He's huge, tall like Corvus and thick with plenty of muscles. His form is stealthy, moving with grace and fluidity despite his size, face hidden behind the blank mask.

There's a smile on my face as he backhands me into the dirt.

CHAPTER 33
VALENCIA

THE FEELING OF ELATION disappears. No sunshine feeling of goodness remains—just pain where that bastard backhanded me. My fingers dig into the dirt, curling as blood drips steadily from a cut on my lip. I shake my head, trying to clear the stars from my eyes. I don't know if he intended to knock me out, but he definitely rattled my brain.

The force of his hit knocked the tight grip the female had on me to release, allowing my natural emotions to flood back in. It's with a heavy sickness filling my stomach that I realize she was manipulating my emotions, controlling me through a simple touch. This constant talk of being all-powerful really went to my head. I didn't think I was invincible, but I didn't think I'd be so easily maneuvered, despite it being against my will. It really proves that power isn't equal; even the strongest have weaknesses.

"No!" she screams, drawing my head in her direction, and the world slowly settles, stars racing away to leave a dull headache behind.

The big one that hit me descends on the female, her white milky eyes scrunched in fear. Her brown hair is now tangled in a meaty fist. He constricts a tight grip around her throat and drags her, kicking and screaming, out of the dark tent. I want to be angry, hate her for the position she put me in, but I feel bad for her. Not *that* bad, because the bitch did manipulate me, but part me worries what's to come for her. It sounded like she had a reason, that whoever she brought me to had promised her something she desperately needed.

A dark laugh echoes from the chair, drawing my attention away from the swaying tent flap that they dragged the female through. My brain pulses painfully with each rhythmic staccato.

The leather is a warm brown with dark black patches, as if time has aged it. It's pristine, though, not a blemish or speck of dirt covering it despite the dusty floor. The tent is canvas, beige, and completely empty besides the desk and chair.

Leather creaks as the chair starts to slowly swivel around. The wooden desk hides most from view, its dark paneling concealing what's beyond. Anticipation causes anxiety to course through my veins. I hate surprises, and I have a feeling that whoever is in that chair is *really* not a friend, which makes them my enemy.

My jaw aches, my head is pounding, and I can feel a slight burn in my knuckles as my fingers elongate. I curl them into dirt to hide my claws from view. It's the first time they've released without my consent since training with Van.

The figure in the chair finally comes into view. He's masculine and handsome, even for an older guy. Dark hair, with flecks of silver edging his temples, and a beard is peppered with gray make him rugged with a striking quality. Worn black leather encases his torso, and a dark red scarf covers his neck. I can't see his lower body behind the desk, but his smile gleams with a maniacal edge.

I slowly start to stand, unsure if they'll knock me down again. I'd rather try to make it to my feet than cower in the dirt on my knees. I curl my fists together, the pain of my claws biting into my palms grounding me, and wince inwardly as I come to my full height, my lip burning intensely. I can feel the trail of blood slipping down my neck, but it's slow and I no longer see stars, which gives me comfort that I most likely didn't suffer any brain damage.

I mean, I'm in deep shit, but that hit doesn't appear to have done a ton of damage.

The male stands, his leather jacket crinkling with the movement as he rounds the desk. He leans back against the front of it, ass resting against the edge as he faces me. There's something strange about his movements. He crosses his jean-covered legs at the ankles and gives me his undivided attention.

"Hello, darling," he sneers, an evil look to his eyes. "You look just like your mother."

I bristle at the compliment, knowing my mother was a beautiful woman. My father never shut up about it. We looked alike, he'd always said that; I got her athletic frame, tan skin, and dark hair. My blue eyes are from my dad, though, which the man now focuses on intensely.

"But your eyes are so much like your father's." There's a sense of familiarity as he looks me over from head to toe.

I try to contemplate how he could know who my parents were, or what they looked like to discern if I look similar. I try to piece together everything the Devil has told me about my parents, but matching the new information with what I already know is like a puzzle made of glass. If not handled carefully, one could break and be lost forever. Each memory I lose of my family is a piece of the puzzle that will remain forever empty. I can forge new pieces to fill the outer edges, but what's lost will never be filled again.

"How do you know that?" I demand, my voice scratchy. The sting in my lip is not as prominent, and the blood is starting to feel dry and itchy.

His head twitches to the side twice before settling. Pops of cracking wood reach my ears, drawing my gaze to where his hands curl around the edge of the desk.

"Your mother is... *burned* into my memory." He laughs hysterically, eyebrows jumping up higher on his face, deep lines jumping around his mouth with each whole body laugh.

If I wasn't already sure, that laugh would be an absolute giveaway. The man before me is responsible for the deaths of my family.

My breathing increases as my chest tightens. Muscles in my arms bunch as my claws dig even deeper into my palms. Darkness attempts to descend on my consciousness, burying me in grief, but I use the pain to maintain focus.

"So much like her," he laughs, watching my reactions like a hawk. "Your mother had a temper, too. I see the fuse has remained short. But I wouldn't give in to it if I were you. Unless you don't care what happens to your friend. Although, I'm curious, is he a lover? Are they all your lovers, or is there a special one?" he rambles, a dark interest in his equally dark eyes. The large mustache on his face jumps with each exaggerated expression.

Confusion wars with the rage. I'm the only one in the tent, having left Parker behind in the club when the woman dragged me away. I can only hope that he made it back to Corvus before anything bad happened to him. His implications bring too much stress; clearly, someone I care about is no longer safe. And—why would he ask if they were my lover? Is he not aware that Corvus and I are together romantically? He questions if I've more than one lover, as if he's truly curious, which means he doesn't know the level of Corvus' care for me. I can't decide if that's a good or bad thing.

But none of those contemplations answer the most important question either: who is in danger right now?

Besides me, of course.

"Who are you?" I ask, ignoring his previous question. If I make it out of this alive, it will be very important information to know.

"Oh, fine, keep your secrets!" he exclaims, like we're two old women gossiping. He says it with a deep southern accent, which he hasn't spoken with till this point. He pats his thigh, as if truly humored, before speaking normally once more. "Don't tell me which one is your lover, it's no matter."

He steps up, off the desk, and into my personal space. There's a glint in his eye as he grabs a long strand of my dark hair and rubs it between his fingers. I want to flinch away from his touch, but I keep a steeled spine, unwilling to show any sign of fear.

"How fascinating it is to be the villain hiding in the shadows, but I think it's time we properly meet." He's quite a few inches taller than me, but not near as tall as the three goons who stoically wait around the perimeter of the tent.

"You still haven't said who you are," I remind him, though it's a risk. He has an oppressive air of authority—the kind that speaks of retribution if he feels disrespected. I'm more afraid of offending him than I am when around the Devil.

"Ah, eager for introductions. Fine, I'll oblige." He steps back, offering me space to breathe before bowing in an overly exaggerated move. "I am the First Lord, but you can call me Death."

It becomes real. All those times I almost died—and now learning it was literally *Death* that's been after me this whole time.

I blink at him—at his vicious smile and normal-looking face. This isn't the face of a man who has wrecked my entire world over and over again. This can't be the face of the man who has committed unspeakable crimes, even by Hell's standards.

This guy is too *normal*. He could be someone's hot, older dad, or the grandpa all the single moms secretly want. Not actual Death.

"Cat got your tongue?" Death teases, eyes bright and head tilted in a way that would indicate he's expecting more of a reaction from me. "You're not laughing, that was a good joke!"

When I remain quiet, he gives me an exasperated look. "You don't get it, do you?" I slowly shake my head. I don't *get* anything. "*Cat* got your tongue? Ya know, the cat thing you and your mother do? Seriously," he says to the goon to his right, "what happened to people's sense of humor?"

The tall figure doesn't move an inch, but Death doesn't seem to be put off by the lack of response.

"You know I can shift?" I ask. Which is a stretch of a question because I can only partially shift, but I also know that the longer I keep him talking, the more likely Corvus is to find us and save me from whatever disaster I've found myself in now.

"I know all about that!" His glee comes across as fake, but I don't call him on it, not sure what's with his constant mood swings. "Your mother had the same power, and it makes sense that you'd have it, too. A shame your father was only a healer. Super healing comes in handy for you, but it doesn't do *me* any good. Truly a waste of Thara's genetics; you could've been so much more, had I been involved."

My brows pinch together. Death's involvement has only brought my family an early end. The only thing he could offer is his namesake—an early grave. Whatever he had to offer my mom, she clearly wasn't interested.

My father passed down a far powerful gift than Death could ever imagine, but if he doesn't know about it, I'm definitely not going to be the one to tell him. Only one demon in Hell knows I can wield holy light, the most dangerous weapon the damned could face, and it will stay that way for as long as I can manage. If word got out, it would shake the foundation of Hell.

Death wants something from me, there's no doubt about that, which offers me a small amount of power. He set the dynamic, but that doesn't mean I can't play by my own rules. I've faced hundreds of unpredictable disasters as a firefighter. It's time I tap into that experience and use the problem-solving skills I learned.

I've spent nearly my entire life surviving unpredictable foes; now it's time to turn that experience into strategy.

I think of the female who brought me here. Death told her she'd failed to bring Corvus, his intended target. I grow angry at *that* all over again—at the thought of her trying to manipulate his emotions like she did mine. To use him against his will. What she could've done to him while she had him under her control. But I guess it's a pointless concern. He was powerful enough not to let her powers manipulate him.

"You're at least much quieter than your mother; couldn't get that girl to shut up," Death says as he rounds the desk and finally sits back in his chair.

Power.

He did everything for more power, and I'd bet he's after more. Greed is sick that way. No matter how much power he obtains, he'll never be happy with what he has. That makes him extremely dangerous.

"Well, I guess the fun is over." He pauses, with the way his eyes track my movements, it must be for dramatic effect. *This hasn't been very fun for me at all.*

When I don't respond, he continues, "I want you to kill the Devil."

I take a slow breath, steadying my racing heart. "Why?"

"Because I hate him," he explains, as if that's answer enough. It doesn't go beyond my notice that he thinks the Devil is a man. Lifera's truth remains a well-kept secret.

I don't miss the look in his eye that proves there's so much more to it. He needs *me* to deliver the kill—I can see it in the way he measures his words, concealing the truth behind simple answers.

"Why not do it yourself; you're clearly powerful enough," I say, tracking his every move. I have no idea whether he's powerful enough to kill the Devil, but I can feel his power leaking from him, filling the air with the dread he must constantly feel inside. Lifera mentioned that the First stole much of his power and was an amazing strategist. It seems odd to me that he went through all of this to get me to do something he could've done himself.

He preens at my compliment, misinterpreting my intention. "Oh, you flatter me. I think I'm starting to like you."

Please, for the love of God, don't.

"Why do you need me to kill the Devil?" I reiterate.

"Because I don't want to," he explains with a flippant flick of his wrist. "But you—he likes you; you can get close to him. It makes you an easy solution."

"The Devil is the most powerful being in Hell; he'll kill me before I can even try." I could technically kill her, but the holy chains are a power beyond my control, and I have no desire to truly harm the Devil.

"Well, I guess that's your problem then," he says with finality. His demeanor takes on a darkened edge, as if he took personal offence to my comment about the power hierarchy.

"I don't believe you," I hum, my blood burning through unspent adrenaline. "If you really had my friend, you'd have flaunted their suffering. I don't think it's because you don't want to kill the Devil yourself; I think it's because you *can't*. Your need to negotiate is telling."

He leans back in his leather chair, face blank of all emotion. One hand drums an erratic beat on the armrest. "You are quite the strategist. I like that in an opponent. I don't like it when it's too easy. But remember your place," he growls, white teeth shining, eyes black voids.

"Touched a nerve, did I?" I smirk, though it's a ploy to conceal my fear at how dangerous this situation is. "You went through all that work to track me down and bring me here. What do I get in return for doing your dirty work?"

"If you don't do this, I will have your friend's head removed from his body. He will not escape Death this time." He steeples his fingers and stares at the tips like he's looking down the barrel of a gun. The mood in the tent instantly grows thick with my fear. The word *friend* is an immediate trigger; I can't comprehend who he might be threatening. Corvus and Van should be able to take care of themselves, and I know for a fact that Corvus would protect Parker. So it begs the question: which friend is he speaking about?

There are too many possibilities, and that's exactly what he wants—my uncertainty. He's expecting this bomb to spearhead my panic and get me to agree to anything he says. The only way out I can see is for me to shift the balance of power; if I chip away at his threat, he'll lose the illusion that he's already won. Taking a hostage is meant to cause desperation, to alter the balance of reality and create an immediate need for reaction.

I roll my shoulders and shift into a more relaxed stance before taking a couple of deep breaths to release the tension in my hands. It takes a second longer than it usually does, but I retract my claws. The sting in my palms helps to fuel my hairpin control on my temper. Anger will only deliver more problems.

"What makes you think you could capture one of them as easily as you did me? They're all stronger than I am." Well, maybe not Parker. He has more emotional strength, but being human has definitely landed him at the bottom of the power totem pole.

He cocks his head to the side and studies me before bursting into laughter. A sickening sound that has haunted my dreams since I was eleven. It's a shocking change from the calculated coldness. "You don't know," he wheezes, hand pressed to his chest. "Oh, that poor boy; you don't even know he needs saving. What a shitty friend you are."

Panic wells in my chest, and my heart begins to race as possibilities flit through my mind. Has he somehow already captured the others while I was trapped in here? The precarious shift in power I thought I had falls back to his side.

The bright smile on his face tells me he knows it, too.

"Go on; ask me. Ask me who's in danger if you don't do this for me." The look on his face is one of pure delight.

"Who?" I whisper, not wanting to hear the words. Not wanting to learn who I've put in danger. There are so many options, but I can't fathom how any could be possible. Corvus? No, he's too aware of the danger and wouldn't be easy prey. Van? His keen ability to think like a predator makes him just as unlikely. Parker? He's under Corvus' protection. Everyone else that I care about is back on Earth.

He doesn't answer. Instead, he rises from his chair and walks around the desk to stand in front of me once more. His steps are soft against the sand, but I can feel them like resounding thunder in my chest. My advantage has slipped through my fingers like ash.

"Before I tell you, let me reiterate what will happen if you fail. I will not only kill your friend; I will kill Corvus and Van, I will kill that redhead you call a best friend, and I will hunt down every human you've met on Earth and kill them, too. So, for everyone you care about, I'd suggest you start planning." He condescendingly pats my head and steps around me, heading out of the tent.

"Who else is there?" I demand, voice trembling in a way that makes my fear evident. He just named everyone I was worried about, as if he read my mind. He knows far too much. I swallow hard, confidence unraveling.

Death turns back to me, a vicious look on his face. "I'll be sure to tell Tucker you send your regards."

The name is like an iron brand being shoved through my chest. Bright with joy but burning so hot, it sears my insides. The tent tunnels in darkness for a second, and flashes of the mountain where Tucker died flicker across my vision.

A stitch in my lungs forces me to hold my breath, the pain too unbearable. The weight of what that sentence implies makes me feel like I've been buried beneath a tidal wave; a tsunami of grief rolls over me with each second that passes.

The tent comes back into view, the beige walls and tall goons exactly the same as they were before. But everything's changed. The world has ground to a halt, and the only thing left is the distant roar of my failures screaming back at me.

My knees weaken. My hands shake, and I know I'm seconds from collapsing.

Death's laugh snaps me out of the fractured daze. "I'll see you in Velruin Canyon. You have three days."

"I can't kill the Devil!" I snap, tears welling in my eyes as the words are ripped directly from my aching chest.

"It's either the Devil's head, or Tucker's." He smirks before disappearing from the tent. The goons follow silently. They don't acknowledge how I crumple in the center of the tent.

CHAPTER 34
VALENCIA

I STUMBLE THROUGH THE bodies that litter the ground, trying to avoid them as best as I can. I ran out of Death's tent as soon as I could convince my legs to start moving and have been making my way towards the large circus tent for a while, struggling to traverse the large population that's drunkenly scattered around it.

I sigh in relief as I finally near the main tent, when a roar echoes through the entire camp. A few stir at the noise, most remain slumped over, but I perk up at the sound and move quicker.

I'm not sure how I know, but my body urges me towards that roar, and I run on instinct alone. The shock of finding out that Tucker is still alive—and has been this whole time—overrides the shock that I finally know who's been after me for the last eighteen years.

I can't imagine the horrors Tucker has faced since that night on the mountain. I need Corvus' presence to ground me. I need him to tell me to stop thinking, that I didn't fail Tucker. But I didn't just fail him on the mountain in Montana, I've failed him every day since then, too.

A loud scream pierces the air before a body flies past me, straight out of the tent and through the canvas wall. They roll a short distance before stopping in a heap. When I hear the telltale groan that he's still alive, I peek into the tent through the now-gaping hole.

The middle of the dance floor is empty besides a small group of people I instantly recognize. They stand around one another, listening as Corvus and Tornil argue. They're the same height, so they see eye to eye, but Corvus has a considerable amount of muscular bulk to his body that Tornil doesn't.

Others cower around the edge of the tent, clearly unwilling to step into the fray. The room has been torn into pieces. The beautiful wooden tables at which I marveled are now scattered, in pieces, around the room. There's another large hole towards the other side of the tent, and the edges have been scorched by fire.

Behind the bar, where hundreds of glass bottles once sat, is nothing but darkness. Liquid seeps on the floor beneath the edge of the wooden bar, and shards of glass reflect what little light there is.

The tent now resembles something normal; whatever spell that was once cast that allowed it endless space has been broken.

I step through the giant hole and walk around the crouched bodies, heading for my group. Broken glass and splinters of furniture crunch under foot.

Engrossed in their argument, they don't hear my approach.

"It's our many years of *friendship* that is keeping me from banning you forever, Corvus. You wrecked my fucking bar! Don't push it," Tornil snarls from the middle of the group. His dark tattoos stand out against the now-pale light that shines from above. Dark eyes, almost black as night, zero in on Corvus.

"It was supposed to be safe here, Tornil. You have guards around the entire perimeter. You can't expect me not to react when Valencia just disappears into the crowd and not a single guard knows a *damn thing*!" Corvus' voice has taken on a high-pitched edge. I'm sure he's one small inconvenience away from burning this place to the ground. A ball of flames writhes against his lower arms, scorching his shirt sleeves and exposing tattooed muscle.

"Hey, guys," Parker says, catching my eye, but they ignore him. There's relief on his face as he spots me.

I search for Van, but don't see him with the group or amongst the crowd. I'm not sure where he's gone, but it would've been helpful to have him here to diffuse Corvus.

"You didn't have to throw Hammal out like that!" Tornil points to the hole I witnessed a body fly through.

"Yeah? Well, Hammal didn't have to tell me that he saw her being torn apart by ten shifters in rut, now did he?" Corvus growls the words, his muscles so tense that I think I can see a tendon in his neck. The flames burn brighter.

Parker slowly backs away from the two, eyes bouncing between me and the tense pair still engrossed in their argument.

Tornil pauses, a frown taking over his angular face. "Okay, so Hammal deserved that, but who's going to fucking pay for the enchantment? I had to break the spell to stop you from ruining the entire thing!"

"You have all the money in Hell, Tornil, don't give me that bullshit." Corvus steps closer, his voice low and dangerous. The flames on his arms extinguish, but not for comforting reasons. Blackness slowly seeps, coating his arms from fingertip to shoulder, until it covers every inch of exposed skin. "If you do not tell me who took her, I will make sure there is *nothing* left of this tent." The *or you* feels implied.

Tornil's head starts to tip back as Corvus slowly grows larger. When the black has reached his neck, Tornil steps away, raising his arms in a surrendering gesture. "Corvus, calm down."

Corvus growls in response. "*Where is she?*" It's no longer his voice that comes out of him, and the bodies who are crouched around cower even lower, while a few whimper in fear.

Before Corvus can do something he'll regret, I step between them. "Corvus, I'm right here."

Corvus jerks, and all the darkness leaves him in flash as he hears my voice. He grabs me, hauling me closer. "Where the fuck have you been?"

"Not here," I whisper with a subtle shake of my head.

He silently buries a hand in my hair while the other wraps around my back. His entire body shakes as he holds me closer. He smells like burnt fabric. "We're leaving," he snarls to no one in particular.

Parker rejoins us and tentatively places a hand on Corvus' shoulder, ensuring he's able to portal with us. We blip out of the tent and land back in the cave. Corvus stalks past me, an irritated gate to his posture as he faces away from us. His head is bowed as he leans heavily against one of the bookcases, and I see that his entire body lightly shakes, black clothes pulled tight against quivering muscles. The room is full of that oppressive darkness he exudes when he's really angry.

I swallow around a knot in my throat, not sure where to even start. With Corvus' sour mood, I decide to start with Parker. He's still standing in the middle of the room where we landed. He's not taken his eyes off me, as if afraid I might disappear again. That smile he wore while we danced is gone, replaced with a look of uncertainty. The past hour flits through my brain in rapid succession, and before I know it, I'm so overwhelmed with details that I blurt out the first thing I can think of.

"Tucker is alive," I breathe, tears welling in my eyes. I haven't moved either, stuck standing in the middle of the room as I feel my world crumbling around me.

"What?" Parker looks down at me, stumbling a step away. The backs of his knees bump into the edge of the couch, causing him to fall back onto it.

"What did you say?"

I look to Corvus, who has stood from where he leaned against the shelves. His dark eyes are now pointed in my direction, driving that dreadful feeling further into me.

"He's alive. He's been in Hell this whole time." The words rush out in a heap, and my chest stutters with the weight of withheld tears.

"How do you know that?" Corvus vents, a harsh dip in his brows. It's a rare look on him—at least one I'm not used to being directed at me—and one that makes me uncomfortable. I've spent a long time being independent, only having myself to rely on. It's why I've fought so hard against my feelings for him. For this very reason. Because he has the power to break me. Truly break me.

I go to answer, but pause. It's not an easy question. I can't tell him how I know without telling them everything. I don't want to mess up any of the details, but I'm consumed with volatile emotions, and Corvus' apparent anger isn't helping.

"Corvus, I understand you're pissed, but can you come over here?" I soften my voice, hoping the calm eases some of his tension. It's not even close to how I'm truly feeling, but I hope he doesn't notice.

"I'm not just pissed, Valencia. I was *terrified*." He rubs a hand across his forehead, but finally joins us. We settle onto the couch beside Parker, with more space between us than I'd like, but I don't want to push him too hard before he's ready.

The words try to become caught in my throat again, but I force them all out and tell them everything that happened from the moment the female showed up to when I found them. Despite the voice in my head telling me not to get them involved, I know I can't do this alone. Death *technically* never said I couldn't tell them, so I'm hoping this doesn't get me killed.

Corvus somehow doesn't descend into a rage when I tell him the First, Death, is the one who has been after us this entire time. But, when I describe the female to him, a sour look crosses his face.

"You know her?" I ask, his expression confusing me.

"Yes. She was a past lover, but she normally has red hair. You were too far away for me to see her eyes, or else I would've recognized her immediately. When I saw you all dancing, I thought she was just some random demon focused on Parker—that is, until you were suddenly being dragged through the crowd, and no matter how much I called your name, you appeared to let it happen. Parker was shoved into the nearest demon, which just so happen to be another freaking incubus. If Van hadn't gotten to him in time, he'd be caught in a sex den somewhere."

I look to Parker, whose face is flushed. He won't meet my eyes, so whatever happened must've been bad. Not only that, but the fact that Van had to be the one to save him could be a part of the reason he's not here now.

I think about how Parker's eyes rolled in pleasure whenever they touched. So she manipulated him just like she did me. I hadn't realized it was happening, already caught in the thrall, but now the signs are clear.

"You said Parker was pushed into another Incubus?" I ask, trying to piece together what little knowledge I have if the damned species so far.

"Succubus. They're both sex demons, those who get their power from sexual energy. Incubi are the male, succubi are the females." Corvus growls. The fact that his past lover is a sex demon sets me on edge.

Something inside me wants to maim someone at the thought of him with another, but I forcefully tamp it down. I can't hold his past against him, and I had plenty of lovers before him, but at least none of mine have tried to kill us.

"Something was off about her," I contemplate, thinking of her milk-white eyes and beautiful face that was nearly constantly warped into an expression of desperation.

"Succubi are able to manipulate the emotions of anyone they touch—and she's pretty powerful. I should've known she'd be there," Corvus says, guilt heavy in his tone.

"I know she altered my emotions, made me feel really happy, but there was something else. The way she talked to Death was like he had something over her. She was desperate to have him cure some curse." I try to think of every detail, but as more time passes, more of the memory blurs away. Especially considering the goon, Cato, knocked me on my ass with a heavy backhand. I lightly touch the spot where my lip split, but the skin has already closed and is healing.

"Manipulation is one of his games. It's not too far-fetched to think he did something to force her to do it," Corvus contemplates, a look of deep thought on his face.

"Well, she's definitely in trouble now," I mention, remembering the way Cato dragged her out of the tent kicking and screaming.

Corvus rubs his brow before meeting my gaze. "So, he wants you to kill Lifera, and he's using Tucker as collateral?"

I nod, unable to force out words past the Tucker-sized knot in my throat.

"How do we know he's telling the truth?" Parker asks, slightly pacing back and forth behind the couch. "He could be lying. Tucker's dead."

"*You're* the one who said he could've survived the stab wound," I remind him.

"I was trying to calm you down, I didn't actually believe it!" Parker's voice heightens in pitch; he's as overcome with emotion as I am.

"His body disappearing was suspicious, though." I disappeared, too, but Parker said Tucker's body was never found. Dead men don't walk around and pick their own grave site.

Parker looks at me, but he's elsewhere. His eyes seem to stare off into the darkness behind me. "Who knows what he's suffered since."

"You don't want to know," Corvus mutters to me, finally standing. "And it's extremely likely that Death is lying, but we don't want to take the chance that he's telling the truth."

He's right, if there's even a chance he's alive, we can't take the risk and not at least try.

"You guys aren't actually thinking about killing Lifera, right?" Parker's eyes are wide with fear. Or maybe exasperation. The emotions look the same right now.

"No, of course not, but we've got to at least make it seem like we did." My mind rattles with the impossibility of this situation.

"Well, that's good, because she definitely knows we're talking about her, so it would be pretty useless to even try." Parker re-enters the living space, having gone to the kitchen for drinks. He hands me a large glass of cool water that I gratefully drink.

"What do you mean?" Corvus asks, taking a sip from his own glass.

"Last time, she said that she can overhear conversations if she's directly being spoken about. We've mentioned her name multiple times now, so I'd imagine she's heard this entire conversation. And probably the one you had with Death."

My mouth hangs open, as if waiting for a bird to make its nest in it. How did I forget that? It seems Death definitely doesn't know that little fact, either, or else he wouldn't have blabbed his entire plan to overthrow the Devil.

"Death wouldn't know that. It seems you two have collected more of Lifera's secrets than every demon in Hell has ever managed, at this point." Corvus looks as if that fact irritates him.

"Let's use it to our advantage," I encourage with a smile. "But I don't think you're going to like my suggested plan."

"It can't be much worse than what I've dealt with up to this point." His shoulders rise and fall with a large sigh.

"We get the Devil to fake her death. No one has seen her without her glamour, so she'd be able to easily pull it off. And, ultimately, he just asked for her head, it's not like I have to present him an entire body. Then, she would have to stay hidden here until we dealt with Death."

"There are multiple holes in your plan." The look on Corvus' face confirms he is *not* a fan of it.

"Where?" Parker and I ask in unison. It's nice to have at least one person on my side.

"Seriously?" He asks us both. When neither of us respond, he continues, "One, good luck getting the Devil to actually agree to faking their death." I notice he doesn't say 'her' often, as if he's still unsure of who the Devil really is. "Two," he ticks off another finger, "where do you plan to get a head? Because it's going to have to be a real one to make the plan work. You can't fool Death with a fake head."

Okay… he's got me on that one, but again, this is Hell. There has to be bodies lying around somewhere that no longer need their heads. I just think I'll leave the harvesting of said head to someone else.

"Three, you're not going to meet Death by yourself, ever again. And four, *no*."

"That's only three actual arguments, and those can all easily be solved. So, unless you have a better plan, this is the one we're going with," I argue. *Easily* may be a stretch, but no other ideas are coming to mind.

"Just give me more time to think of something," he growls.

"Death said we had *three days*," I mutter, the words getting lost in the dark spaces of the room.

Corvus' head drops into his hands.

None of us wants to voice the inevitable truth; but the reality is, we might not have that much time.

Tucker might not have that much time.

***

We go through the plan, noting every scenario we can think of. There are tons of problems that arise and few have a clear solution. Thankfully, Corvus solves our 'head' problem, so that's blessedly out of my hands.

We all startle as Van rushes through the front door. I know Corvus mentioned he has access to the cave, but I'm still caught off guard by his sudden arrival.

"Where've you been?" Corvus asks. To my surprise, instead of biting his head off, Van simply stomps into the kitchen and fumbles through a few cabinets before joining us in the couch area with a bowl full of some dry snack that he immediately starts to eat.

"Where have you been?" Corvus repeats, giving Van a dirty look.

"Purging my darker emotions," Van responds, tossing some nut-like snacks into his mouth. His eye flicks to Parker before focusing back on Corvus.

Parker ignores him, face blank as he stares into the fireplace.

Corvus and I stare at Van a little longer, but he seems content to sit in the silence, not offering any more details as to where he's been. I hadn't had a chance to ask Corvus when we left the tent, and he didn't seem too interested in offering up details at the time. Thankfully, while still angry, his heated emotions have settled into a calmer level of irritation now that we're safe in the cave.

"The Devil is here," Van finally says, continuing to munch on his snack.

"How do you know that?" Corvus' dark brows dip low as his friend makes himself at home.

"Because I slammed your door in his face." The smirk on Van's face is absolutely wolfish.

I jump up and head straight for the door, but don't make it very far before a large arm wraps itself around my torso, and I'm dragged back into the warmth of a body that's pressed tightly against me.

"Not so fast; you're not pulling that on me again, *brat*," Corvus murmurs in my ear. "And don't think I'm not going to punish you for the shit you pulled at the tent earlier."

"The shit *I* pulled? That was out of my control," I argue.

"*Mhmm*, sure." He lets me go but walks around me and opens the door himself.

"Lord Crow," a smooth, masculine voice purrs from just outside. I can't see them from behind the wall of Corvus' back, but there is no mistaking that voice. "Do you plan on letting me in?"

Corvus grunts but doesn't move, so I pull him back by his shirt. He hisses as the fabric pulls tightly against his throat. "Come in," I say, my eyes pointed at the Devil's chest. I still can't stand to look at her face when she's like this. Something about the constant shift between forms gives me an intense headache, but I've found that if I don't look directly at her face, it's not as bad.

Corvus growls as both the Devil and Greta enter the cave. We all ignore him, which earns us another low growl, but he doesn't stop them. Lifera saunters towards our group while Greta takes a seat in a chair in the kitchen.

"Why are you a man?" Parker asks, which prompts Van to volley his head between them.

"You know he can't lie; it would be ill-advised for him to know this secret in the event that he were to be captured," Lifera tells Corvus, instead of responding to Parker directly.

"Who can't lie?" Parker asks again, but he's now also volleying looks around the entire group.

"We will include him regardless," Corvus snaps, tension heavy in his tone.

"I disagree, it's not—"

"He deserves to know," I tell the Devil, and mere seconds pass before she changes back to the woman I've come to know as Lifera, wasting no more time on arguing. I have no idea why she listens to me. She was close to my mother, which earns me little right to command her, but she does, for whatever reason.

Van sucks in a shocked gasp, rising to his feet. "*You*," he snarls, a sound more suited to an animal than a man. He stalks towards Lifera, deadly intent in his movements but Corvus jumps in his way and places a hand on his chest to prevent him from getting any closer.

"Finally he hates someone as much as he hates me," Parker mumbles, but I'm too distracted by the giant intent on killing the woman next to me.

"Does it hurt, Wolf? Knowing the many times you begged to be between my legs, you were talking to the person you hate most?" Lifera's smooth voice is filled with sex, but an emotion I can't place tinges the end; it would be barely noticeable if you weren't paying close attention.

"You two know each other?" Corvus questions as he holds Van back, but looks over his shoulder as Lifera stands beside me. They ignore him as if he really were just a wall between them.

"I would *never* beg," he snarls over Corvus' shoulder.

"Okay, maybe you didn't *beg*, but your eyes did," she smirks, those golden eyes shining, canines sharp.

"If you continue to antagonize him, I will take his side in whatever he wants to do to you," I say to her, arms crossed over my chest.

I'm in such a weird place, stuck between them. I care for Van. He's Corvus' best friend, but we've also carved out our own friendship. On the other hand, there's a deep connection I feel to Lifera. And though I disagree with most everything she does, there's a part of me that wants to be close to her, if only to feel closer to my mother.

"Fair enough, darling, fair enough." Lifera turns from Van and takes a seat on the couch beside Parker who beams at her, cheeks bright pink with a blush. "So, how do you plan to fake my death?"

Everyone takes a second to settle and Van paces angrily in the kitchen—but at least he doesn't leave.

"So you *can* hear everything that's said about you?" I confirm, figuring that's why she's here.

"Yes. There are limitations, of course, but for the most part, I can. It's a big reason why I'm able to keep tabs on everything that goes on throughout the realm. There are a few who take precautions, though they're successful for reasons they don't understand." Lifera shrugs, back pressed against the couch and one long leg crossed over the other at the knee. She doesn't elaborate on the reason why she can't eavesdrop on those conversations, which I imagine is an intentional tactic.

"Did you hear Death?" I ask, unsure if she was witness to that conversation, too. I didn't notice anything out of the ordinary when I was dragged into the tent... although I haven't noticed anything any of the times before that, either, so maybe that's the point.

She slowly nods her head. "It's how I know he's been after me for so long. He's too self-important to ever consider the possibility that I could have more power than he's aware of. Death likes to forget that I am the original demon and that I created him, even if indirectly. I would be stupid if I didn't have some safeguards."

"Then how come you didn't tell us he was after us?" Corvus snaps. He's leaning over the chair I'm sitting in, hands curling into the leather at the top. It crinkles under his tight grip.

"Because I didn't know he was after you. Just me. I can only hear conversations that are specifically about *me*. Anything else is blank. It's like a teleprompter coming in with half of the information redacted." She explains this as if its common sense, yet *nothing* is common anymore.

"You know what a teleprompter is?" Parker asks from his spot beside her.

"Oh, dear boy, how I could corrupt you," she says condescendingly with a pat to his thigh. He blushes again.

"So you know we have to fake your death?" I prompt, getting us back on track before Parker can combust into sexual embarrassment.

"Yes, I caught most of that conversation. Sad what he's done to the poor succubus, but she got herself into trouble, she'll have to find her own way out of it." Lifera shoots a glance up at Corvus, but he doesn't say a word.

I don't hold onto the rage that starts to grow in my chest, and start to go over the plan with Lifera to make sure it's something we'll actually be able to pull off. We iron out a few more details and then decide to rest, since everyone has had a long day. Van storms off when he realizes Lifera will have to stay in the cave, muttering about how we've let the wolf in to kill us all. I think he's being a little dramatic, but if our previous conversation was anything to go by, his reaction to her is probably justified.

Parker heads off on his own, saying he knows where to go, but I notice he snags Van's abandoned bowl of snacks on his way out.

It takes Corvus a while to get a room set up for our two guests. I remember he mentioned before that there are plenty of rooms, but not many are furnished. If we keep collecting strays, I fear our home decor budget will need to go way up.

I try to ask Lifera more about my parents, but she's unable to offer much about my father, having not known him well, and she seems oddly tight-lipped about my mother. But, the pain in her eyes makes me realize that my parents' passing is as fresh and raw for her as it is for me, so I don't press. Instead, we get onto the topic of Van, and she happily dives into the drama of it.

"Van is known to frequent Tornil's tent on a very specific night. We've met there a few times, though he was unaware of who I was due to my going in my true form and not the normal illusion I show as the Devil."

"Why risk people recognizing you?"

"There's not much of a risk. Everyone is forced to wear masks that mostly conceal who we are. We got carried away one night, and he revealed my face." She stares off to the side, a slight smile on her face as if the thought of that moment brings her joy.

"You two have hooked up?" My brows raise in surprise.

"*Hooked up?* Not in the slightest. He doesn't have the knot that shifters do." She shakes her head, another smile on her face.

My eyes widen. "*Knot*?"

"Oh, honey, the shifters are truly one of my favorite creations," she purrs, and the sound clearly gives away why she likes the shifters.

"Wait, isn't that kind of like incest?" My face scrunches in disgust.

"They're not my children!" She also grimaces as if *I'm* the crazy one.

"You said you created them!"

"Well, you misheard me; I didn't create them *all*. Most were born to parents, just like your mother was."

"You're still related in a sense, though," I argue, a laugh trying to escape at the look on her face.

"Well, humans still marry their cousins, so don't come at me for enjoying the creatures *far* removed from my family tree."

I can't help but burst out laughing. "Okay, you win."

For once, that soft smile that looks so strange on her face is directed at me. It's unnerving. I've spent so long missing that kind of look on my mother's face, that it feels like a slight betrayal to enjoy receiving it from another.

"You're so much like her, it makes me want to cry," she whispers.

"I wish I knew her more," I quietly murmur, the somber mood darkening my tone.

"Here, my dears," Greta says, sneaking up beside me. I jump at her sudden appearance, but take the steaming cup from her hands. I forgot she'd sneaked in when the Devil got here and parked herself in a kitchen chair. She's so quiet, I didn't even notice her. She stands in front of me with a small smile on her face as I check out the drink she handed me.

The citrus flair of lemon wafts up with the steam that drifts from the cup, and a soft sip confirms it's one of my favorite drinks. Lifera sips her own, matching cup, a smile on her face as Greta settles next to her.

"A Hot Toddy. One of my favorites," I murmur savoring another sip. I have no idea how she found the ingredients for it in Corvus' kitchen, but I appreciate it, nonetheless.

"I know," she says with a smile that quickly shifts to apprehension as she looks at Lifera, avoiding my questioning eyes.

"We might as well tell her," Lifera says with a slight shrug. "She knows every-thing else."

"Tell me what?"

Without a word, Lifera lightly taps Greta's shoulder, and with a blur of motion that's too fast for my eyes to track, Greta disappears and a face I thought I'd never see again takes her place.

"*Irma?*" The words rush out of me in a harsh exhale.

"*Ja*," she confirms in an all-too familiar German accent. "Good to see you, *Mien Flamme*."

I choke on the Hot Toddy in what's more of an inhale than anything else. The hot water burns my throat like liquid fire, and I choke on staggered inhales.

"W-what? How?" The words stutter out of me in fast succession.

She's much older than Greta; deep grooves line her face from age and those bright blue eyes shine back at me. Greta's are normally brown, but she's changed completely.

"Please explain," I manage to get out.

Greta... Irma?

The older female and Lifera share a look before Irma turns to me. She stands, the movements more fluid than I've ever seen, as if she's lost 20 years despite still looking to be in her late seventies. She comes to sit on the arm of my chair and places a familiar cold hand on my shoulder. The similarity is stark and shocking, and goosebumps erupt over my arms.

"Lifera never wanted you to be alone, so I was there to watch out for you." No German accent whatsoever. It sounds like Greta is talking to me through Irma's body.

I look at Lifera, my eyes wide with shock.

"I wasn't willing to lose you, too," she says, emotion heavy in her eyes.

Chapter 35
Valencia

Emotions well inside me, and I know if I don't get away from her, they'll burst.

It's harder to have this in common than I'd expected. Sharing grief with someone feels like it should make it easier, but I feel like all we do is bounce emotions off each other. Neither of us has come to terms with my parents' deaths, for different reasons.

"I... I'm," I pause, unable to get the words out without letting the flood of despair that brews just below the surface out.

Lifera doesn't look away, as if she'd rather face the pain head-on than run from it—and maybe I'll get there one day, but today is not that day.

Thankfully, Greta notices my distraught face and jumps into action. "I will handle our sleeping arrangements. You go get some rest."

I just nod, looking into the familiar blue eyes that have offered me comfort over the years. I want to be angry at her for deceiving me, but I can't find it in me to be so. And, though she wears Irma's face right now, Greta has been kind to me from the first moment we met.

I feel bad for leaving them in the living room to fend for themselves, but my will to do anything other than fall face-first into Corvus' large bed and cry myself to sleep is very low.

I'm stumbling through the cave hallway, a lantern swinging wildly in my hand, when he finds me.

"The rooms are done, if you—what's wrong?" His voice wraps around me as his hands settle me. His touch on my arms is gentle as large fingers encircle my upper arms. I try to focus on his face, but the familiar lines grow blurry behind the tears in my eyes.

I try to tell him that I'm just being emotional, but I can't seem to get the words out. A choked, "I can't", escapes me, but the rest is muffled as he pulls me into his chest.

Corvus sweeps me into his arms, and I consider protesting but I'm too tired to care, so I curl into his warmth. He heads back in the direction he came from, further into the cave.

"Lifera, your rooms are ready. Follow the lights in the hallway to the training room, then take a right. There are two rooms in that direction that have been set up. Do *not* go left."

His deep voice rumbles through his chest with every word. I wonder if she can hear him, or if it's her creepy conversation eavesdropping that allows her to hear where their rooms are located. I almost ask why he tells her not to go left, but then remember that's where Parker and Van's rooms are. I appreciate him separating her from Parker, but imagine it's more for Van's sake.

When we reach the room, Corvus sets me on the edge of the bed and turns to ensure that the leather hide door is securely in place. He remains faced away for a beat, taking a few deep breaths before turning and stalking over to me.

"Are you mad at me?" I ask quietly, tears slowly tracking down my cheeks.

Dark eyes penetrate mine with an emotion I can't name before he slowly crouches in front of me. Wordlessly, he begins to take off my shoes, tossing them to the side before methodically undressing me, hands steady and sure as he removes each article of clothing until I'm left in nothing but a bra and underwear. I shiver as a chill slides across my skin. The separation between us feels cold, but I can't get a read on his emotions.

Unexpectedly, he leans forward and places his forehead against my shoulder, wrapping long arms around my torso, and it's then that I realize he's trembling.

"Corvus, what's wrong?" I ask quietly. My voice is steadier than I expected, but it seems focusing on his turmoil helps me to forget about my own.

"The fear of losing you terrifies me," he mutters, voice muffled by my shoulder.

"I'm right here," I say soothingly as I run circles on his back.

He leans back on his heels and finally looks me in the eye, tracking my features with his own before lightly resting his hand on my cheek.

"You don't understand Valencia, the things I was willing to do tonight when I couldn't find you." He shakes his head, as if ashamed of the thoughts. "If I were to be sent to the bottom of the Erebus River to return as evil reincarnate, I would still not be as dangerous as I would've been if you did not return when you did."

The confession is deep and terrifying. To know that he feels so profoundly. It's the kind of declaration of love I would expect from a demon lord of Hell, and I almost feel bad that, if he had to, he'd tear this realm apart for me.

"I'm right here," I reassure, not entirely sure what he needs in this moment.

"I'm not angry with you," he says with a deep exhale, as if knowing I'm here is enough to calm him. But as his breathing settles, mine increases. Without needing to offer comfort, my own issues come slithering back.

Corvus leans back on his knees, taking in my face. Something he sees must set him on edge, because he grabs my shoulders, more alert.

"What's wrong?" he asks, worry evident in his tone.

I shake my head, trying to force out the words that keep getting stuck. How do I explain that what I need is *him*? His body, his touch, his *everything* to remind me I'm alive.

But I'm so full of guilt, I feel like I don't deserve the reminder.

"I *need* you," I finally manage.

"I'm right here," he repeats my own words back to me. Unfortunately, they're not enough to penetrate the self-loathing.

"I don't deserve you; I don't." It's painful to hold in the sob that wants to escape. What I deserve is to feel every failure like a knife flaying me to the bone. A distraction isn't going to be enough to relieve me of the weight of what I've done...or what I failed to do.

"What do you need?" Corvus asks softly, his voice steady in the darkness I'm drowning in.

"I need...to pay for what I've done. Make me feel it until it doesn't own me anymore." I whisper softly.

He stares at me for a long time. Long enough that I start to become uncomfortable. I'm just about to pull away when he starts to slowly unfold to his full height.

He towers so high that the back of my neck strains to maintain eye contact. "I promised you a punishment; would you like that?" His voice is soft, the question leaving room for me to approve or deny without fear of retribution. "Be absolutely sure this is what you want," he urges, eyes tracking my face for any sign of doubt. "I refuse to use you when you're feeling strong emotions. I never want it to feel like I would take advantage of you but I've also learned my lesson—I won't deny you if it's something you really want."

"I need it," I confirm, my eyes taking in his glorious body.

"I love when you need me," he smiles, and there's a dark edge to his tone I haven't heard directed at me before. I think I secretly like it when his darkness comes out to play. A vacant spot in my soul awakens when his baser instincts emerge.

Deep down, I know that he would never hurt me—not intentionally. I also know that if I were truly overwhelmed and just needed some company, I could tell him. He would wrap me up in his strong arms and hold me until I was okay.

And, as tempting as that sounds, it's not what either of us needs. I need a distraction from my grief, and he needs a reminder that I'm here—that I'm safe. Ultimately, this little punishment is exactly what the doctor ordered, and I know how to tell him that.

He doesn't move a muscle, giving me all the time I need to make my decision, but I can see the tension in his body. He expertly holds himself back, but the strain is evident in the stiffness of his shoulders and the black voids of his eyes.

I slowly start to slide off the bed and come to a kneeling position before him. He's so tall, my head barely reaches his waist. The view of the dark-denim-covered legs in front of me causes heat to build in my core; I know the power they hide. I reach out to start unbuckling his jeans, but—lightning fast—he grabs my hand and stops me.

"I need to hear you say it," he demands, his voice as dark as his eyes.

"You can do it," I say with a slight nod, anticipation bubbling in my chest and heat building in my core.

"Not good enough." The sound puts me on edge.

"You... can punish me?" I mean for it to come out as a statement, but I can tell it sounds like a question.

"Try again."

My brows furrow in confusion. I'm not really sure what he wants from me. This is a different side of him that I'm unused to, and to be honest, I'm out of my depth when it comes to this kind of submission with a partner. Normally, submitting to someone isn't even a concern, as we're only there for the quick reprieve of fast release, and the men I've hooked up with in the past never seemed worthy of me actually relinquishing control in the moment.

As if he can somehow hear the turn my thoughts take, Corvus growls—a low and dangerous sound that causes the hair on the back of my neck to stand straight.

"You're *mine*," he snaps, pulling my hand up high, so my body is forced to stretch. The light kiss he places on my palm contradicts everything else about him right now. "You once said you'd kill me if I tried to die again. I will kill *everyone* if anything happens to you."

I suck in a breath at the extreme declaration, unsurprised by the statement itself, but shocked nonetheless by the knowledge that he would and probably *could*, if he were ever in a position to follow through on the threat.

"I'm yours," I repeat, trying to appease the side of him that seems to teeter on a deadly edge. Judging by the vicious glint in his eyes, it's still not good enough.

Corvus releases his grip on my wrists with a light squeeze and reaches down to unbuckle his pants, dark eyes never once looking away from me.

"Put your hands behind your back and then *don't move*." His command is absolute, and I follow it without complaint. Lacing my fingers together, I already know I'll struggle to follow his orders.

"Look at you," he says to himself, words so soft I can barely hear them. "On your knees, begging for your punishment."

I want to give him attitude, reiterate that I'm giving us an outlet, but I'm *not* begging. I barely manage to hold the sassy words in. He must notice a twitch in my lip because he smirks, though it looks more like a snarl.

Two large hands rest on either side of my head, and his thumbs start to slowly rub my cheeks. "Oh, you're begging, baby," he says, and drags a thumb across my bottom lip. "That sweet little pussy is begging for me to fuck her, but I'd rather fuck this bratty mouth of yours right now, so she'll have to wait."

Damn him, but he's right. So unbelievably right. Arousal pours from me in a flood of need, and I can already feel it spreading to my thighs with each little shift. His nostrils practically flare, and there's no doubt he can smell it on me.

I want to say something—anything—to bolster the wall I keep around myself, but he sees me too well and shoves a thumb in my mouth before the words can escape. The pad of his thumb presses down on my tongue, halting my ability to talk. Wetness instantly pools, and a small trail slides out from the corner of my lips where his thumb rests.

His dark eyes track its trail, and he smiles slowly before grabbing the thick shaft of his cock with his free hand. My eyes flick down to where he squeezes it tightly, forcing a small bead of white to pearl at the tip. I breathe through my nose, mouthwatering even more at the thought of his taste on my tongue.

Corvus holds me steady, thumb still shoved in my mouth, as he slowly tracks the tip of his cock across my lips. Precum smears, leaving a trail on my bottom lip, so I can just barely taste the salt with the tip of my tongue.

I think he's going to keep teasing me, and clamp my legs together in frustration, but my mouth is suddenly stretched full as he pushed the tip past my lips. His flavor bursts on my tongue, the salty mix of precum and his natural scent intoxicating to the point my eyes nearly roll back into my head. He still hasn't removed his thumb, so I'm forced to allow my lips to stretch to their max. It's a tight fit.

Like, *really tight.*

He can barely fit in more than the tip; his large thumb takes up too much room. My throat constricts, gag reflex trying to trigger against the onslaught of stimuli, but I squeeze down on my fingers, using the pain to force the sensation away.

His eyes flare, and he slides himself in a little further. "You'd let me do whatever I want to this slutty little mouth, wouldn't you." It's not a question. We both know there will always be lines, no matter how close we are. Love doesn't negate boundaries.

But arousal sure does blur them. And right now, I'm pretty sure I'd be willing to ignore a few of my previous hesitations so this magnificent demon could destroy me in the most delicious of ways.

My hesitations for things the society on Earth told me were wrong are quickly burning away in a fire fueled by pure need.

I need *him*, or I swear I will combust on my own. And if that looks like him taking his anger over our situation out on me by fucking my face till he comes down my throat, I'll sit here like the little, slutty good girl he claims I am, and let him do *exactly* that.

We both know that my desires for him to own me do not make me a slut in the way most use the word as an insult. Would I ever want him to call me that in a moment of true anger? No. Hell no—but there is something about when used in the heat of a consensual moment that just seems to light the fire higher, not put it out.

I swallow as saliva pools, causing my tongue to glide along his smooth skin. He jerks in response, his large body curling slightly at the shoulders. He pulls out slightly, only to thrust straight back in. His hard cock glides in and out easily, and the obscene amount of spit that now covers his hand, cock, and my face makes the motion smooth.

He pushes in a little further, thumb slightly slipping out so his cock can take the opened space. I swallow, which causes him to shudder above me. I'd bet that if I touched him right now, he'd be shaking.

I may very well be a slut at this moment—on my knees—but I hold all the power.

"You're dangerous," he compliments, a dark fire in his eyes that's meant only for me. He finally pulls his thumb all the way out while simultaneously shoving his cock in as far as it will go. I'm unable to breathe for a brief second before he's pulling back out to just the tip. Both of his hands return to the sides of my head, thumbs resting on my cheeks. The one that was in my mouth spreads spit across my skin as he holds me steady.

"Open your mouth and stick out your tongue," he murmurs in awe, strain now evident in his voice.

I manage to open my mouth wider, but my tongue only reaches so far, and the tip of his cock blocs the way. His fingertips bury themselves into the sides of my head, pulling my hair slightly as they curl in pleasure.

He starts thrusting, driving in as far as he can go before pulling out. He goes so far that I'm robbed of air with each thrust, forced to press down on my own thumb to keep myself from gagging as he hits the back of my throat.

I thought I was a champ at giving head, but it appears my skills are better suited for cocks that are below average. His eyes sparkle with each shuttered breath, that menacing aura of his begging to consume me as well.

My knees start to ache, the hard floor offering no reprieve, and since I'm forced to keep my hands behind my back, I'm unable to counter my weight elsewhere—although, the ache just adds to the anticipation.

Heat gathers inside me like a flame being brought to life as he continues to use me, to take his pleasure in whatever way he needs. I want to touch myself, and I start to war between getting myself off or continuing to listen to his demand. My arms shake with anxious energy. I need to get off soon or I'm going to be kneeling in a puddle of my own arousal, but no matter how sultry of a look I give him, he doesn't relent.

He fucks my face with a focus only a demon set on destroying you has. I'm borderline ready to beg, but he's stuffed my mouth so full, I can't even do that.

"You get it yet?" he asks, husky voice rough and gravely.

He must not actually want an answer, because he shoves his cock further in my mouth instead of pulling out to let me speak. It wouldn't matter either way; I don't get whatever *it* is.

"I could never hurt you." He groans when I hum around his shaft. "But I can keep you from coming for *hours*."

This bastard. Had I known that was his plan all along, I wouldn't have gotten down on my knees so eagerly. The whole point of putting myself in this position was to do just that. Come. For hours, preferably, just as he suggested. Though I like my version far better.

My hands itch to reach forward and grab at him or push him away, but I remain strong, not wanting him to trick me into more punishment.

Though... is it really punishment if I like it so much I'm currently flooding the floor?

"I know you want to get off, baby. Have you earned it yet?"

I hum around his cock, but the words *'obviously dumbass'* remain trapped in my throat. He purrs in response, clearly having no idea how badly I'm insulting him in my head.

He starts to fuck my mouth harder, clearly making me *earn it*. Wetness drips past my lips to cover nearly the entire lower half of my face. The sounds of him sliding in and out of my mouth are obscene as they echo off the rock walls and high ceiling,

My eyes catch flashes of the glow stones on the ceiling above Corvus' head, and even they seem to blink in humor at the position I'm in.

Well, it's all fun and games until it's my turn to bring the demon Lord of Hell to his knees.

"*Agh, fuck,*" he groans, body giving into the sensations as he draws closer and closer to his release. "Yes, yes, *yes,*" he mutters with each thrust.

His moans spur me on, and I tighten my lips around him and hum deep in my throat. Power surges through me at the prospect of getting him to finish with just my mouth.

A shudder rolls through his entire body, his thrusts uneven and shallow, and I think I've finally won. I've managed to top him, even from my knees, with nothing but the bratty mouth he loves to hate.

I close my eyes, anticipating the hot spurts of salty come to fill my mouth. When nothing happens, my eyes snap open. They meet dark pools of desire and a vicious grin.

"We're not even close to being done."

Chapter 36

Corvus

My knees shake, and I think I'm going to collapse if I don't come in the next five minutes... but I can't let her know that. I can't give away how close she brought me to the edge with nothing but that sexy fucking mouth of hers.

Her lips are bright red from the misuse, and her face gleams with the wetness I forced out of her mouth with each thrust. I can smell the arousal that drips between her legs, and it's like a beacon of blood to a hellhound. I'm in sex infested territory, and if I don't get inside her soon, my dick might actually fall off.

I slip out of her mouth, my cock standing tall as it bobs in her face. The room is slightly cool, but nothing could touch the inferno she builds inside of me. I swoop down and lift her into my arms before carrying her from the room and through the cave.

"Where are we going?" she squeals as we breach the privacy of our room. She squirms in my arms, her small body twisting and curling to escape me.

That's what she doesn't understand. There will be *no* escaping me.

The true demon fuels me, guiding me through the cave as he demands more from her. He scratches at my skin with vicious talons that burn me from within as he attempts to make his escape. He wishes to be closer to her. He'd probably be weird and ask to crawl inside her skin or something equally fucking creepy, so I'm glad to be the one in control.

"Corvus, seriously. Where are we going?" She stops struggling and homes in on me, her arms wrapped tightly around my neck. I bury my face in her chest, lips brushing along the tops of her breasts as I draw in her scent and allow it to settle me. Calm the parts that beg to ravage and rage. I was so close to committing mass murder tonight. The true demon was seconds from clawing its way out of my skin by force and decimating every single being in Hell until I found her. No friend nor foe would've been safe from my wrath. I feel bad for wrecking Tornil's tent, but I was already past reason at that point. Had she not shown up, the demon would've been released, and who knows what he would've done once he gained full control.

I slowly guide my nose across her soft skin, letting my harsh edges smooth to something more manageable. I don't bother to look where I'm going. I could track this cave in my sleep if I needed.

I feel the heat of the river room before we reach it, and the bitter smell of the minerals are a drastic change to the earthiness that fills the rest of the cave. It's not a bad smell—just different. It doesn't matter, though; nothing could compete with the smoky citrus scent of my woman in my arms.

"What are we doing in here?" she asks, voice showing her apprehension.

I don't answer—not because I'm ignoring her, but because I fear that opening my mouth will allow something crazy to come out.

Desire still rides me heavily, and my cock still bounces, hard as a brick.

I set Valencia at the edge of the warm pool and let her watch as I slowly undress. My boots go flying, which causes a smile to beam across her face. I almost rush after the one that lands in the pool, but ultimately ignore it; I can just get the dresser to get me another pair.

She stands, her body slightly stiff as she shifts her focus between me and the door we came through.

"No one is going to interrupt us," I assure, my boxers sliding down my thick legs.

Her eyes get lost in their perusal of my body for a second before she meets my eyes again. I can't help but notice, and enjoy, how heated they become when she catches a glimpse of my stiff cock. "How do you know that?" she asks, hands rising to her hips with that attitude I've grown so fond of.

"Because they know I would rip them to pieces if they so much as glimpsed an inch of your naked skin," I respond, slowly stalking forward.

She paces back, the water quietly lapping at her calves as she backs deeper into the water. It's a crystal blue, the minerals keeping it clear of all bacteria that would dirty it. The rock bottom of the pool is smooth against our bare feet.

"What about Parker? He's very curious and he's—"

"Don't," I snap, not wanting to know where she's going with that statement. "Van will stop him if he heads this way."

She halts, no longer concerned about my advance. "Is that safe for Parker?"

"Let's hope he doesn't find out," I growl before surging forward and wrapping her in my arms. She squeals as she holds her body close, and I drag us both into the deeper end.

The lights here are dim, and lanterns scatter the room, giving it a moody vibe. I take us to a darker section that's surrounded by rocks on almost three sides, and set her on a smooth ledge before stepping into the space between her warm thighs.

I can see everything through the clear water, and so can she; her ocean blue eyes track my cock as I grip it and slide the tip along her thigh. She sucks in a gasp when I get close to her opening, but I don't move any farther. The slight tension in her thighs gives me pause.

"What's wrong?" I ask, my eyes boring into hers. It was a tiny movement, possibly something she didn't even intend to do, but I'm so attuned to her that I think I feel each time her heart beats within her chest.

"It's just—" she pauses and looks over my shoulders, a light blush tinting her cheeks. I don't respond and simply wait her out. When she sees I'm not going to push, she continues. "You're more likely to get pregnant in a hot tub, and we don't use protection."

"You have the IUD?" I ask, remembering that she brought it up the first time we were together. I'm not even sure what it means, or what an *"IUD"* entails, but she believes it keeps her from getting pregnant.

"Yeah, but why should that still work? Human inventions—like a tiny plastic thing that affects hormones—doesn't really seem like something that would work on a mythical hybrid." Her eyes widen, and before she can voice the thought, I say exactly what she's thinking.

"You're thinking of all the times I've filled this little cunt, aren't you?" I push my cock forward so the tip presses hard against her clit and she gasps, her body involuntarily rolling against the sensation.

I continue to tease her with my tip until the backs of my knees are shaking and she's rolling her body to meet every thrust. She looks down where our bodies meet, and I can see the apprehension in her face. The water is so clear, you can see every detail, and the distortion of the water's surface can't take away from the image of her pretty lips and dusting of dark hair. My cock is so hard, I have to force it to remain under the water with a stiff fist, or else it would be bouncing against my belly button.

The smell of the room around us dampens her natural scent, which drives me crazy, considering I want to bathe in it.

On my next shallow thrust, I tip my cock down so it brushes against her opening again. She gasps, legs jerking as if to close before they're stopped by my hips. My eyes meet hers, and I'm met with equal parts desire and worry. We can't have that.

"Conception is different here than on Earth. Not all demons can conceive. Sex may be an open source in Hell, but offspring are not. Having children requires not only consent for sex, but consent for the child. If you don't *want* to get pregnant, you won't." I say, teasing her clit with my tip. It's an angry red color from my tight grip.

It's a wild oversimplification of why she wouldn't get pregnant, but I don't have the patience or attention span to go over the details with her right now.

"And if I *do* want to get pregnant?"

The question throws me so off guard, I freeze as my eyes snap back to hers. My nostrils flare, and I can practically feel my pupils dilate until my entire eye is black. I search her features to see if I can catch a hint of her feelings on the matter, but she's as stoic as the stone I've become. The demon rattles the cage my body has him trapped in, and he's never been more eager to break free. If he had his way, he'd have already put a baby in her the first time I came inside of her.

Damn breeding kink.

I growl, and it's a dark and dangerous sound—a mixture of his and my emotions combining. I truly couldn't care less about a child. The idea is only appealing if it's something she wants. It's the thought of filling her up so much that she's dripping from every hole with my cum that fires my blood up to boiling.

Just in case. Every hole, *just in case.*

I'm not a total Neanderthal, I know how babies are made, but tell that to the part of me that wants to claim *every* part of her.

Just as the tip finally slips in, I get my answer.

"I don't want kids," she stammers, eyes watching as I slowly drive the tip in and out. She huffs a moan and leans further back to give me more room. If it were just her and I for the rest of eternity, that would be okay.

"Not yet, at least," her voice comes out husky, eyes rolling slightly when my hips stutter at her confession, forcing my cock in another couple inches.

Oh. Well, okay then. I can work with *not yet.* That leaves me plenty of time to practice till she's ready.

I reach down and grab her hips with two hands before pulling her closer to the edge. My cock drives inside of her and I nearly collapse as her inner muscles clamp down on me. Her arms shoot out behind her to catch her from falling back.

Hooded eyes meet mine, and with a dark look, she rolls her hips slowly. She does this a few times, getting herself used to my size while also driving me to madness. My hands shake against her, fingers digging into the soft flesh. Each movement causes one more brain cell to burst into nothing but raw need.

"You gonna fill me up?" she purrs, her voice persuasive as the seductive rasp crawls over my body.

"You little succubus," I growl in response, absolutely falling victim to her charms. And though she controls me completely, I have to regain the upper hand somehow. This is meant to be *her* punishment, not mine.

I take another step back, bringing her hips off the rock entirely and forcing her upper body to relax back onto her forearms until most of her body now lies beneath the water. The crystal-like flow glides up and down her soft skin and encircles her breasts, and they become beacons that call me.

I start to thrust, languid movements that focus more on pressure than movement. She softly moans my name, arching her back even higher. Her long, dark hair floats in the water, creating a dark and sinuous crown.

I bend down and suck a nipple into my mouth, lathing it with my tongue before nipping it into a tight little ball with my teeth. She's so responsive, her body reacting to the simplest touch from me.

"Yes, *right there*," she moans as I drag in and out of her. I start to fuck her harder, forgetting the sacred rule of *'don't change what you're doing when she tells you you're doing it right'*. I can't help it, she drives me crazy, and though she now moans louder at this new rough treatment of her sweet little pussy, I don't miss the side eye she sends me.

I would smack her clit at the look, but the water protects her from that, so I slip a hand around her hips and start to rub circles around the tight ring of her ass. She tenses, her body going taut in my arms before she moans loudly, relaxing into it.

"That's it, baby. Let me in," I groan out, my mind buzzing with thoughts of release as her body greedily sucks me in. I can't get my fingers in her ass, she's not near prepped enough for that. I'm not an animal, I wouldn't hurt her for my own enjoyment—and I'm not an idiot, I know water doesn't work as a lube. I'm content to just tease her with my fingers as I fuck her slowly.

She allows me to continue teasing us both for a second before her strong legs wrap around my waist and she curls her body up. Her abs flex with the movement, and I feel her muscles tense.

We both groan as she settles into the position, her arms around my neck for more stability as she sits deeper. My hands rest on her ass cheeks and hold her up as I try to get my brain back into working order.

I intended to fuck her long and hard to put her in her place, but after the intense blowjob, all I care to do now is bask in the feeling of her.

That *clearly* is not going to happen.

"Are you going to fuck me, or do I need to—"

I don't even let her finish the statement before I rip her away from me. My movements are forceful as I turn her around, shifting both of our bodies forward and forcing her body flush against the rocks. My cock slips between her thighs, and the sensitive tip brushes the rough rock. I growl low in my throat and force her upper body forward with one hand, leaning her over the edge. She folds, but puts out her hands to keep her head above water. I wrap the wet strands of her hair around my fist and wrench her head back.

"I know exactly what you were gonna say," I growl, leaning in so my breath bushes her bare neck. "And I should follow through on that threat to not let you come for thinking you could get away with it."

Her laugh is evil and just as dark as mine.

I don't wait a second longer, I lean back, and with a sense of control I didn't know I possessed, I enter her again in one long thrust that makes her groan. The strands of her hair must be pulling tight against her scalp, but she doesn't complain and just uses what little leverage she has to push back against me.

I lose the last thread of control I was holding onto and I fuck her just like she asked for. My thrusts are hard and fast, and there's no slowing down. The crescendo builds within us both, and my balls tighten in preparation for an orgasm that's sure to fry my brain. I don't slow down.

Her moans echo off the walls. I don't even think *she* knows what she's saying anymore. No longer is my name leaving those delicious lips—no words are at all. Just sounds of a woman getting exactly what she asked for: a good fuck.

And fuck her, I do. And *fuck me*—my thighs burn, the water is lapping salaciously around her body, her hips have to be sore from the rock—but I can't stop. No matter how hard my legs shake, or how many times she comes—has it been two or three now—I keep going.

Fire builds in my groin, my cock gets harder, and I feel the teeth of release nipping at my resolve. I don't know when I let go of her hair, but her head has tipped to the side as she looks back at me, dark hair splayed across her muscular back. My grip tightens on her luscious hips.

"Fuck, I'm gonna come," I curse, anger bleeding into the words. I'm not angry at her, I'm angry I can't go for longer. I'm angry I can't just stay here forever and fuck us both into eternal oblivion. Seems like a lot less drama.

Cum shoots out my cock in bursts and my back bows over hers as it's forced from my body. Her little pussy tightens and flutters around my aching cock. She moans my name and I think I see stars, but she doesn't come. She's come plenty tonight—but I'm not satisfied with *plenty*, I want them all.

"Corvus, you came," she murmurs, as if she can still feel the force of it.

"So," I state, thrusting my hips in the same punishing rhythm. It takes a couple of stuttered movements before I get my rhythm back. With each thrust, more cum is forced from her, and the once clear water becomes murky with our combined arousal.

"But, I can't," she moans, her head tipping down. "I can't come again."

"You can," I answer, knowing I plan to rip at least one more out of her. I lose track of her eyes, and my grip on her hips is all that keeps us both steady, so I can't grab her hair. "Look at me."

Her head snaps up, eyes bright with desire and flashing at the tone of my voice.

"Watch me fucking wreck you." The words are dark and full of promise. Bright blue eyes roll back in her head, and for a second, she squeezes them as tightly together as her pussy squeezes my cock.

I can't contain the moan that rips from my throat. She's shaking, her body trembling under my hands, and those beautiful eyes watch as I destroy us both with this urge to ensure she knows she's mine.

Her bottom lip is red and swollen from the number of times she's bitten down on it, and I can't imagine we'll be able to go much longer before one of us passes out from exhaustion.

Water and fire don't mix, so I can't use my flames to tease her clit and instead dance my fingers across her ass once again.

Three thrusts and a bit of harsh pressure down on the tight ring of muscles she hates to love being played with, and she's going off around my cock like a nuke. Despite having just come, she rips another one out of me just as savagely as I did her.

We both tremble now, our bodies beyond spent. I gather her in my arms, cuddling her to my chest, and manage to get us back to my bed before I collapse. The walk through the cave is brutal, but my strength at least lasts that long.

We get the sheets wet, but neither of us seems to care as we settle into the comfort of one another. I can smell our combined arousal wafting off us both and want to look, see the evidence of my claim leaking out of her, but I have no energy left.

As we lie together, both easily drifting off to sleep, I wonder if I'm really ready to destroy the entirety of Hell to keep her. Because I just might have to.

It's with a smile on my face and the knowledge that I *will* do whatever it takes, sleep finally takes me.

CHAPTER 37

VALENCIA

THE FAMILIAR HEAT I'VE grown accustomed to isn't there.

I've almost started to associate the start of each new day with being surrounded by an oven of heat. No longer did the glorious yellow sun wake me with each rise. No—now it was the sinful inferno of being wrapped in a demon's arms that helped me greet the new day.

Today, it seems, is a cold wake-up.

I hate it.

With a pained groan, I stretch, and the soft sheets slide down my body, baring my entire torso to the cave. I'm still entirely naked, having not felt the urge to put on clothes after the events in the pool room.

My cheeks heat from the thought of us having sex in there. Anyone could've walked in. Corvus was nearly feral in his lovemaking, truly giving in to his darker side. I loved every second of it, and I absolutely plan to entice that side out of him at my earliest convenience.

But damn am I sore.

My hip muscles pull as they strain against the sensitive skin that had been pressed against the rocks. It was smooth, for the most part, but the pressure alone left some tenderness. My lady bits are also begging for some relief. He didn't hold anything back—that's for sure.

I stumble to the bathroom and crank the shower to as hot as I can stand, then luxuriate under its warm spray, allowing my muscles time to relax. I'm dying for another trip to the river room—though, maybe this time I'll hold off on the public sex. I just hope Parker and Van weren't able to hear us, or if they did, they'd better not bring it up. I'm not mentally prepared for that kind of embarrassment.

"*Ugh,*" I groan, pressing the heel of my palm to my forehead.

I laugh softly to myself, imagining if Parker or Van had accidentally walked in to a full view of Corvus' naked ass. Not to mention Greta—or the Devil, herself. I wouldn't be able to look at them the same if they'd seen that.

Unintentional voyeurism is always oddly embarrassing. Parker and I still laugh about the day I walked in on him with one of his flings in the back of a firetruck. He was so embarrassed, he hadn't been able to look at me for a week, but now all we do is start rolling with laughter each time it gets brought up.

I rush to finish cleaning off, wanting to run from the thoughts and get started on whatever shit show today is sure to bring; there is no possible chance that we aren't getting into something absolutely bonkers.

By the time I finally make it to the kitchen, everyone else is already here. Surprisingly, Van is seated alongside Parker at the kitchen table—closer than I've ever seen them intentionally position themselves, and though Van is silent, he isn't glaring.

Greta is flitting around the kitchen, her body reclaimed, wearing a modest black gown. She's a couple of inches shorter than my 5'5, with light brown hair that's wrapped in a neat bun at the back of her head, showcasing her slender neck and smooth pale skin. Her bare feet fly across the floor in a silent hurry as she hustles to prepare a meal for everyone. Lifera sits on a couch in a mint green nightgown. She mindlessly flips through a book, seemingly not paying too much attention to the words.

"Morning, my—"

I walk right past Corvus, cutting him off, as he leaning down to kiss me on the head. My feet make loud stomping noises as I hustle to where Lifera sits. I stop in front of her and snatch the steaming mug off the side table. She looks up at me curiously but doesn't comment as I rudely take a sip straight from her cup.

"*Mmm,*" I groan, the burst of flavor dancing on my tongue.

Coffeeeeee, I moan in my head.

"I expected this reaction from the redheaded foot-heathen, not you," she chuckles, her face devoid of its normal tension.

I take a second to let the warm liquid glide down my throat, humming in delight with each second.

Parker walks up beside me, a beautiful red rock mug full of the steaming black gold in his outstretched hand. I take that one from him and try a sip. It's a little more bitter than how Lifera made hers. She must be an extra sugar gal. I prefer mine with a little more bite, which Parker knows. The smile on his face confirms it.

"Heaven, right?" Parker smirks from behind his own mug, this one a more green-hued rock.

"Odd place to be in to be praising the Almighty," Lifera unfolds herself from the couch, her long green dress flowing prettily with every move. It hides her form completely, too large to distinguish the body beneath, and not nearly as revealing as her normal suits are. But her wolfish eyes match the color, and her auburn hair seems to shine as it rests against the soft fabric in gentle waves. She plucks her mug out of my hand, a genuine smile on her face with that same spark of mischief in her eyes.

She turns those bright eyes on Parker, who stiffens with the attention. He's normally extremely charming and a downright flirt, but around Lifera, he stumbles through his words at every turn. Right now, he's not even talking and just stares back at her over the rim of his mug, as if he can hide behind the small piece of ceramic.

Warm lips press against the side of my head, startling me slightly.

"Come eat," Corvus murmurs, his breath fanning across my face as he presses another kiss to my head. Must be making up for the one I skirted earlier in my attempts to reach the coffee.

I take Parker's place at the table, and Greta promptly places a plate full of food in front of me. It's covered in foods that I recognize and some I don't, but it smells so good so I set my mug down and instantly dig in. Van smirks as he watches me scarf the plate down, his sharp canines peeking through.

"What?" I snap, though there's zero malice behind the word.

"I thought I heard an animal sneak into the cave last night, but now I'm wondering if that was just you," he says mockingly.

My face instantly flames and I hide my eyes behind a hand. Assuming they heard us and *knowing* they heard us are two different things, and I would've preferred it be the former.

Van chuckles, his smile lifting his copper cheekbones into a soft expression, but I can't help noticing the ice remains in his eyes. We never got around to talking about what his issues with Lifera were, but I can imagine it's not easy to have her here in his space.

Once again, I've brought someone he hates into a space he thought was safe. How many hits can this poor guy take? I open my mouth to apologize, but I close it, not wanting to insult him by alerting the others to his unease.

He must have a good understanding of my body language, because he gives me small nod, and a little bit of the ice in his dark green eyes melts.

"So team, how are we killing me today?" Lifera asks from the edge of the kitchen.

Van's face instantly transforms into a snarl, but he doesn't say anything.

Parker is still struck dumb, standing behind Lifera just to the side as if he were a loyal guard dog. More like a lap dog, but I don't mention that, and stuff down the laugh that threatens to break out. Greta is still rummaging in the kitchen, her back is to me so I can't see what she's doing. And Corvus, my dark Lord of Hell who fucked me three ways to Sunday last night while saying every dirty word in the book, just stands to the side, arms relaxed at his side while he watches us all in turn.

Where is that bossy attitude now, I wonder? And—more importantly—what do I need to do to draw it out of him again?

Corvus' dark eyes flash to mine as if he can hear my thoughts. He squints at my suspicious smirk in his direction.

My dreams were plagued with nightmarish possibilities all through the night, but one idea kept coming back to me. "We'll glamor a head to look like yours, and I will take it to him. You will all be there, just out of sight. He never said he wanted me to come alone, but I imagine it was implied. We'll wait until he brings out Tucker, then I'll make the trade. If he attacks, then all of you will be there to ensure he's never able to do this again."

Everyone is silent, eyes darting around, except for Lifera. *She* beams at me as if I just offered her a million souls.

"I knew you'd be perfect," she exclaims, a vicious, joyful gleam shining in her eyes. The possibilities she could be cooking up in that mind of hers make me uneasy.

I ignore her delight and look between Corvus and Van. They're the ones who will know how to take my idea and turn it into a worthy battle strategy. I'm no strategist, no matter what Death said. I'm the type of person who faces an emergency and flies by instinct alone. My days of firefighting may be long gone, but the muscle memory of facing a threat far greater than I could ever match is nothing new. We just needed to go in with the right plan and execute it.

Simple as that.

***

It was *not* that simple.

We've been going round in circles for hours. Which is possibly an exaggeration, as I have no real way to tell time, but that's how it feels.

Lifera is firmly on my side, and agrees with the plan, but Corvus is against it. That one didn't surprise me so much; he has an inherent need to protect me.

Parker seems neutral, another reaction I'd fully expected. He doesn't know this new world we call home, so he wouldn't want to decide.

What I didn't expect was the vehemence with which Van disagreed. But, I suppose he wasn't outright upset with the plan itself, but with the fact that Lifera would be involved. He doesn't trust her, and I'd guess his reasons are most likely valid, but I'm not sure we can afford to *not* trust her.

"Van," I start, but he cuts me off.

"She has already proven to be a liar. How can you trust her?" he snaps.

"Because it is easier to trust her than Death," I respond, facing him fully, though it makes my heart race like it would if I were facing down a bear. I don't mention that she's earned my trust, and that it'll stay that way until she proves otherwise. He's already volatile, I don't want to make it worse.

He growls like a grizzly, deep and dangerous, "I will deal with Death myself if it keeps you away from this snake."

"Now that's a little insulting, I was never the snake in *that* story," Lifera mocks, her body appearing completely at ease as she leans against the back of the couch.

I ignore her. In my very limited knowledge of religion, I know she's referring to the story of Adam and Eve in the Garden of Eden and how the serpent convinced Eve to eat the apple despite it being forbidden. Many interpret the Devil as the serpent, the creator of temptation, but I avoided religion at all costs growing up. I harbored too much resentment in my heart to get anything beneficial out of it. Part of me wonders if that's why this whole situation has been so easy to fall into. I don't have some preconceived belief about Hell or demons, so I don't judge them based on what little humans think they know—which apparently is wrong, anyway.

"Van, even you can't deny the strategy of her coming along. No one but us has seen her face, and Death will never see her coming," I argue, trying to bring the conversation back into focus.

"She is just as likely to stab you in the back as she is to end Death," Van argues, unwilling to give up, even though I know I saw that shine in his eye. I know he's blood thirsty for a good battle plan, and this is the best plan we have, no matter how hard he wants to fight it.

The most uncomfortable part is that Van can't lie, so he truly believes what he says.

Van looks between us before focusing his attention on Corvus. "You're going to let your mate waltz into the fire without protection? Is that what you're allowing?"

"Careful," Corvus snaps, his relaxed frame becoming taunt in an instant. "You know I'm against the plan. I will not allow Valencia to go in without backup, and I do not trust Lifera to go with her alone."

I want to argue—interject and demand that they believe in me—but I can't get the words out. I barely believe in myself, and had Death not brought up Tucker, I'm sure I'd be choosing to pretend this was all just a bad dream for a little while longer.

"But," I perk up at the sound of Corvus' soft reply. "We don't have any other choice. We all know it's the only way this is going to work. Neither you nor I can go alongside her outright, we are too recognizable. Parker is human, and Greta is also too recognizable. If Death is to be deceived, that means we need to put more trust in Lifera than we'd like."

Corvus turns his dark glare to Lifera, who brings her arms up in a surrendering gesture without a word. She may try to appear innocent, but all it takes is one close look for you to see the predator she truly is.

Van acts like he still wants to argue, so Corvus continues, "You would not leave a warrior behind, Van, no matter the circumstances. Don't start now."

"This is not a warrior, this is a *rat*." The words ooze out of Van's sharp mouth like knives. "I would not risk someone I love for a *human*."

Anger sores in my blood like an alarm clock for my rage, but I force it down. Van is lashing out from pain, and his harsh words towards humans, though extremely irritating, don't affect me as much. It's hard to be mad when I see each insult he throws as another traumatic wound he's exposing.

"Van," I placate, a soft note to my voice. There's no sense in riling him further, but we must move on, and if Corvus is okay with it, then it's time to go. "You don't have to participate. You can stay back. I know this is asking a lot of you, and I won't force you to do something you're not comfortable with."

"You insult me," he snaps, green eyes flashing with derision.

Woah. Definitely *not* my intention. Before I'm able to backtrack, he continues, "I will not skirt the battle like some weakened human." *Clearly a dig at Parker.* "I will be by your side the whole time, waiting in the shadows to tear her limb from limb as soon as she betrays us." His look is directed at Lifera, who smirks at his ire. I can tell she's not a fan of the continual insults. If we don't get this show on the road, the battle might be far closer to home than any of us intend. I also don't miss that he says it as if her treachery is a sure thing.

It seems I'm the only one who has faith in Lifera. I realize how crazy I am for gambling my life with the Devil. "If she betrays us, I give you full permission to rip her arms off and beat her with them," I tell van seriously.

Lifera gasps from her spot beside me, but I can hear the undertone of a laugh, so I release the tension in my spine.

Van, on the other hand, gives me a look of pure joy, relishing the vicious statement.

"My pleasure," he growls. "Though, it would be better if I use her legs, they're sturdier."

I choke out a laugh, not able to get words out.

"Valencia once threatened to rip my dick off and beat me with it." Corvus pipes in, the tension gone from him as well. Or at least as much of it as he can spare despite the stressful situation.

I smirk at the memory.

"That wouldn't work," Van states, his brows tipped low in concentration.

"What?" Corvus and I ask at the same time.

"That wouldn't work," Van repeats. We both look at him incredulously. With a sigh, as if we're the crazy ones, he explains, "A severed penis would be too floppy to properly cause any damage. Better off just using severed limbs or your fists."

Corvus and I stare at him in horror. The fact that he's thought this through is scary in itself. What really gets me, however, is that I wouldn't be surprised if the only reason he knows it wouldn't work is because he's tried it.

Chapter 38

Valencia

In no time, our three days are up. We managed to find the head needed to convince Death that I killed the Devil. We had some time to get a couple more hours of training in as well. I'm still rusty with bladed weapons, but my claws haven't failed me yet. I've also become really skilled with the staff, but I'm not nearly as deadly with it as Van is. It's a great tool for defense, but that's about it.

We didn't even attempt to practice with the holy light I can wield. It felt too dangerous to try with Greta and Lifera in the cave.

Now, the journey has started, and the wait is over.

The trip to where we're supposed to see Death doesn't take long thanks to Corvus' and Lifera's abilities to teleport the entire group.

Though I hate the feeling of shifting between worlds, and how cold the nothingness between them is, I'd rather go back there and sit for hours alone, than try and calm myself enough so I can go and face my family's killer.

My teeth smash together at the reminder this isn't just some random advisory pissed off that I'm powerful or that I joined Hell. This is a male who's been after me for nearly my entire life. Someone who set his sights on my mother at some point and was angry he didn't get her. He took everything from me, and if given the chance, I truly hope to return the favor.

I purposefully ignore the black bag Van's carrying. I refuse to ask how they got a head, and despite knowing exactly what's in it, it sickens me still. My stomach rolls a few more times, so I force myself to take a few deep breaths. I need to do this, and no matter how much I hate the thought of carelessly treating some poor person's severed head, it has to be done.

He didn't need the head anymore, anyway. Or she. What if it was a female they stole the head from and then made the glamour look like Lifera in her male form? Is that worse? For some reason, my brain wants to say *yes*, but in a place like Hell, there isn't really a gender issue. There are too many different types of demons, and everyone seems to be interested in everyone, so things like gender roles don't seem to exist.

Still, logically, it would make more sense that we'd gotten a man's head, and slightly shifted the features to match what we needed than have to use a female's head we would've had to change entirely. Why work harder than we must?

"Val, you're spiraling," Parker murmurs, a few steps away. "You've not stopped looking at the bag for five minutes straight."

His calm call draws me out of a dazed stupor that I had no idea I had fallen into, and I drag my eyes away from the black bag to focus on our surroundings.

It doesn't matter whose head it is, so long as Death believes it's the Devil.

We stand at the top of a large, red rock canyon, not too different from the Grand Canyon in Arizona. Sparse plants of varying colors smatter the rock faces. None are green. Plants in Hell are weird; they're always a strange color. Purple was pretty popular, but I'd seen pops of blue, hot pink, and even a strange, golden color that could've fooled even the smartest gold miner.

"She's doing it again," Parker mumbles, though I'm still able to hear him.

I draw my eyes to the group, but Corvus walk up and steals all of my attention.

"If this is too much, tell me now and I will have us back at the cave so fast that the image of this place won't have time to imprint on your memory," he exclaims and lightly traces my wrist. I try not to frown as his fingers lightly brush over the sensitive skin. It's been hurting for a while, some weird nerve pain that just won't seem to go away.

He's so poetic, my demon.

"I wish," I start, and judging by the gleam in his eyes, if I don't hurry up I'll find myself whisked away whether I ask for it or not. "But Tucker could be out there. I just gotta get my shit together." I take a deep breath, but it's not nearly as fortifying as I need.

"Have no fear, you will not be alone in this," Lifera coos as she saunters up to us. We've all changed into the same black tactical work gear, but her lethal body makes it look like it belongs on a runway, not out here in the desert.

Van starts muttering under his breath, but Corvus' rough growl cuts him off.

"You remember the plan?" Corvus asks, patting my body down to double-check all the weapons he stored on me before we left are still there. It seemed kind of pointless at the time—I have no idea how to use any of them, but I guess something is better than nothing.

We have to split into two groups to be able to accomplish everything we need to do while maximizing not only our safety, but Tucker's. Lifera and I will walk up through the main entrance, hopefully drawing Death's attention there while Van will follow close behind, hidden, to protect us from any foe we may face before we get there.

Corvus and Parker will be taking out the guards in Death's castle, as well as checking the dungeons for Tucker in case Death tries to double-cross us.

The goal is to contain Death until we can get away and let the Devil deal with him, but my goal is slightly different. I haven't said it out loud, but I plan to use my holy chains on Death. We can't risk him escaping. I can't risk him regrouping and coming back for revenge. It ends today, no matter what. I just have to wait until Tucker is safe; then, Death is mine.

Knowing Tucker could be out there right now, within reach, makes me jitter with anticipation. It doesn't seem real. It seems like the perfect lie to tell, but on the off chance it's the truth, I've got to try.

When I was getting loaded down with more blades than I knew what to do with, all I could think was that I wished I had my staff—and that this was all just some hyped-up version of Van and me training—and that there wasn't someone's life on the line.

I couldn't bear to lose Tucker a second time.

I nod my head, unease stealing my ability to talk through the plan anymore.

This feels like when you're waiting to play a board game, but you haven't even started because everyone is arguing about the rules, and you know that if you just started playing, it'd be easier to figure out than going over it a thousand times.

Corvus grips my arms tight as he finishes his last checks. His dark eyes bore into mine, every emotion he's feeling flashing across his face.

"I'm finding it hard to let you go," he murmurs, thick lips tipped down in a frown. His dark facial hair masks a lot of his features, but I can see the same unease mirrored back at me.

I want to reassure him, give him something to help him get through this next part with less stress, but the words won't come.

Neither will the other ones I so desperately want to say. For some damn reason, they remain trapped in my throat.

I'm so afraid that if I tell him I love him, he'll be ripped away like everyone else has. So trapped they stay, locked behind a vault of past trauma and survivor's guilt.

He nods in the knowing way of his, drawing me in for a tight hug. He starts to lean back and step away, but I reach up and grasp his neck, pulling him down to me. He comes eagerly, body folding till our mouths meet in a heated kiss.

It's passionate and far too explicit considering we're in public, but it expresses all the things I can't say.

When we break, he leaves his forehead against mine and we take a couple moments to breathe in each other's existence. If I were brave enough, this is when I would say it. But I'm not, so I remain silent, and so does he.

With a knowing nod and one last peck, he turns and leaves, signaling for Parker to follow. Parker pauses, looking at me with a quick nod before turning to follow Corvus. He knows he's the most at risk, and so he's stuck following Corvus around. Van was originally meant to go with them, but he wasn't comfortable leaving me unprotected. Corvus swears he can handle the task, even with Parker in tow, and I have no choice but to believe him.

Lifera, thankfully having not interrupted my very public, private moment, waits until I'm able to muster the determination to head the opposite direction.

Van stands off to the side, staring Lifera down like an angry statue.

She ignores him as she comes up to me. Her pats to check me aren't as obvious as Corvus, but it's clear she's checking that everything is in place.

"This will not be easy," she warns, a serious look on her face. She's taller than me, her long legs and combat boots putting her a couple of inches over my head, but it doesn't bother me. She should be a hundred feet tall with the personality she has.

"I know," I mumble, a knot in my throat.

"I don't think you do," she tightens a small strap on my chest that holds Corvus' cherished blade. Van growls low in his chest but doesn't move, and my brows pinch at the reaction. I look to Lifera to see if her features give anything away.

My stomach plummets out of my ass at the look of doubt on her face. "You don't think we can do this. You don't think *I* can do this, do you?" I sputter, fear leaking from my pores.

"It's not that," she insists hurriedly. "It's not about your ability at all. You are extraordinary. Just as your mother was. Just as Remiel was, though it pains me to compliment an angel." I can't help but laugh a little. "Death is far greater an adversary than you should have to face at this age. I am remiss that I allowed him to remain alive for so long. I may not have known that he was after you specifically, but I've always known he was a despicable male, and I could've had him killed many times, but I was lazy. I will forever curse myself if you must pay the price of my inaction."

Her sincerity must've surprised Van, because his angry growl abruptly cut off; but it didn't surprise me. This isn't the first time she's talked to me this way, just the first time we've had an audience outside of Greta.

"Why not kill him yourself?" I ask, the itching need to know why she hasn't taken the chance to clear this up herself too great to ignore.

She snorts, the most obnoxious sound she could've made. "I've told you Death is very strategic. He was always clever in the ways of battle, but his true skill has always been survival. No one in Hell has been in more danger of dying than Death himself. He is vile and thus has made many enemies over the generations. Those who follow him do so simply from fear or subjugation. But, alas, he avoids his namesake because he is wily, and those who come after him are never strong enough to defeat his schemes. The only person who could easily defeat him," she waves her hand, indicating herself, "has been cursed from ever doing so."

"What does that mean? Like, you're not strong enough or you're truly cursed from being able?"

"Ha," she scoffs. "Not strong enough? Not likely. I could kill him with a thought if I so pleased, but I cannot. I literally *cannot*. I always thought it weird that he fought so hard to become the First Lord, when the consequence meant he would gain such responsibility. What I failed to realize is that it was also his greatest protection."

"Does this story have a meaning, or..." I watch as she talks to a blank space over my shoulder, but there's only the red canyon beyond me. I don't want to be rude and tell her to land the plane, but I'm afraid she won't understand the metaphor, so it isn't worth the wasted air.

"Right," she places her hands on my shoulders and lightly squeezes. Van shifts closer, his large form moving in the corner of my vision, but I don't take my focus off the woman in front of me. "I cannot kill Death, because I cannot kill any of the Lords. It was agreed by many, myself included, that I would not be able to kill those who also hold such powerful titles. This was, in truth, a way to ensure that I didn't needlessly kill the Lords. The Games are meant to be as fair as can be in Hell, and if I were able to kill them, I would be taking away that impartiality. It goes both ways. I cannot kill them, and they cannot kill me—a safeguard put in by the enchantresses who helped create the seals around Hell."

"But they can kill each other?" Van asks from my side. I turn to him, surprised he's come so close. There's still a sharp edge of scorn on his face directed at Lifera, but his curiosity has overrun his anger for the moment.

"Yes. This is Hell, and the strongest should prevail. It's our way. If a leader can be challenged and lose, then they shouldn't be a leader anymore," Lifera responds.

It's not the power structure I'm used to, but I can't begrudge it for a culture built of battle-hungry species, and she makes a great point.

"That's a very animalistic outlook," Van responds dryly.

"Well, the shifters are my favorites. Don't tell the others," she jokes, winking at me.

I want to blush, but not even the overly sexualized dick-knots she so callously complimented can lighten the mood. I appreciate the effort, though.

I want to blurt that I can't do this. That it's too much to expect of me when it was not so long ago that I didn't even know this all existed—but resisting change will only get me swept away, and I'd rather be up shit creek without a paddle than drowning in shit creek without a clue.

I take a deep, fortifying breath, step away from Lifera, and steal my spine.

"Now there's the girl I know." Lifera smiles, white teeth gleaming.

I turn and look to the canyon. Red rocks surround us, and the oddly gray sky is bright as day, but there's no sun in sight to help with direction or timing. This is truthfully the definition of winging it.

Death said I was to meet him in the Velruin Canyon. Which is where we are now, but the only reason I've even made it this far is because everyone else knew what and where it was. How the fuck I would've accomplished this alone, I have no idea. It's not like there's a MapQuest for Hell that I could've gotten.

Velruin Canyon is a sight to behold, with glimmering red rocks in the light of a false sun and plants sprinkled throughout. Judging by the structure of the rocks, there may even be a winding river somewhere.

All I can think about is dark eyes with a kind, boyish face. The thought that Tucker may have survived that night on the mountain brings me both elation and consternation.

I'm under no illusion that Death is anything other than horrible; a despicable male who Tucker has apparently been held hostage by for weeks in Hell's standard of time.

Terrifying things can happen in a single moment, and much time has passed. I have no idea if Tucker is even going to be whole anymore. It isn't unlikely that he'd now be a shell of his former self. Torture is known to rip away a person's personality. If he found peace in the darkness inside of himself, a way to escape his torment, then I couldn't blame him.

I could only blame myself.

But catastrophizing won't accomplish anything more than me doubting myself. This is the kind of battle I need to face with as much confidence as I can muster. I need to believe that I can do this, or else Death will see it on my face, and he'll surely use that doubt against me.

I take another breath and close my eyes.

I imagine this beautiful red canyon covered in flames, every plant and rock somehow touched by the fire. Whatever animals may call it home scramble in terror as the heat licks at their heels. They run as fast as they can to escape, but not all are fast enough. The plants go up in an instant, and the pretty garnet color of the rocks is forever changed, scorched black by the heat.

In my mind's eye, I see the destruction of a wildfire that is far greater than any I've ever faced. My lungs expand, another breath filling my lungs as I add the scent of smoke to the otherwise pleasant aroma of rocky nature. It's burning. I can hear the crackle of dried leaves and pounding of escaping feet. The smell of burning ash and the roaring of flames. It's familiar. It's peaceful. I know how to fight this foe. I know how to face it, running headfirst into the danger.

Even as I open my eyes, I hold onto the thought of an imaginary wildfire. An enemy I've faced many times before. An enemy with no plan, no strategy—just destruction. This battle requires spontaneity, courage, and skill—just as any fire I would've fought on Earth.

This may be an entirely different realm, and it may not be a fire I'm facing, but the stakes are just as high, and I've spent a long time hunting this enemy down. Now it's my turn to take control.

Chapter 39
Valencia

Lifera and I make our way through the canyon. Its high walls offer few paths, and the one we've chosen is quick but steep. I thank my many years spent training, traveling in the mountains, because this is grueling. My legs burn, and I'm grateful we didn't have to pack anything to carry with us.

When I asked Lifera why we couldn't portal to Death, she said that she'd never seen his castle with her own eyes. We would need to hike till it was in sight, then she could quickly take us the rest of the way—but traveling on foot also allows us more stealth and time to prepare.

Van follows close to my back on silent feet as I track Lifera. The only reason I know he's there is his quick and gentle touches as he helps me along the path whenever I slip. He also carries the bag. I know at some point I'll need to take it from him so he can hide, but I can't help holding off as long as I can.

We walk for what feels like another hour before Lifera finally motions for all of us to crouch along a rock ledge.

"Just as I expected," she whispers, her voice so low I can barely hear it.

I follow her gaze and marvel at the view before us.

The canyon, which has been narrow and winding up to this point, opens, and the rock walls create a near-perfect circle. The canyon opening is large enough that there is a small lake to its side and a small forest behind it that leads back into the winding narrows on the other side.

In the center is a large castle, built of deep red rock, climbing as high in the sky as the canyon does.

"What did you expect?" I ask just as quietly.

"His castle is bigger than mine. But don't let it fool you, castle size does *not* equate to cock size at all," Lifera doesn't look at me, and I swear she doesn't even smile.

I choke back a laugh. "You don't even have a cock."

"Exactly," she mutters.

The red castle is *definitely* bigger than Lifera's, towers and offshoots far larger than the palace I've visited, even from far away. I can't imagine how it will feel to stand on the doorstep.

"I will get us into the forest, where we will walk to the front along the path, just as any other visiting demon would. Van will watch from the shadows, and I imagine the crow has eyes on us even now," Lifera states. It's the only part of the plan we've been actively able to prepare, but it's nice to hear it again, anyway.

Van is to stay hidden in the woods and only come out when needed.

If.

If *we need him*, I remind myself.

I force myself to release all worries for Corvus and Parker. They'll be fine. Corvus is confident in his abilities, so I need to be as well.

I'm going into this with the hope I'll be able to toss the nasty head to Death's feet, claim Tucker, then—when everyone is in a safe spot—I'll blast Death into tiny pieces of ash. Judging by the knot in my stomach, I know that's wishful thinking, but it's one I'm desperately holding onto.

"Are you ready?" Lifera asks, hand already lightly resting on my shoulder.

I nod. I'm not ready in the slightest, but I don't want to wait a second longer. It takes only a moment for me to blink my eyes before the view changes. When I open them again, tall trees stand before me, black from trunk to leaves. Gray light slips through the cracks, but the dark forest offers zero reflection, leaving us in darkened shadows. We're just off the path. I can see the red dirt winding just barely through the trees.

Fingers wrap around my wrist before a heavy rope is placed into my hand. The weight pulls against my shoulder, and I grimace but tighten my grip.

"I will be watching the entire time," Van says softly, bending down closer so his voice doesn't have to carry so far. Lifera is already stepping away, but before I follow, I turn to Van.

"If Tucker's is really there—if his trauma has been too much and he asks for death, what do we even do?" My chest squeezes at the thought, but I know there's a very unlikely chance that Tucker hasn't suffered immense trauma if he's truly been Death's hostage.

They both freeze. Van's dark green eyes search my face while Lifera hovers over my shoulder. "What are you asking me?" he asks softly.

"I won't be able to kill him; I love him too much," I state, my brain filling with poisonous thoughts.

"Valencia, it will not come to that," Lifera urges.

"None of us know that—know what he's been through."

Van stares at me in quiet contemplation. I wait for him to eagerly agree, but it never comes. A look of anger crosses his face, but he schools it immediately. "I may despise these humans to my very soul, but have faith in him. We can endure far more than we expect." He doesn't explain further, and I can tell he's as confused as I feel.

I drop the subject. He's right. There's no sense in worrying about *what-if* scenarios.

The thick rope is a heavy burden as I turn and head towards the red path. Lifera follows on my heels, quickly catching up and walking silently by my side so our shoulders are not close enough to touch, but close enough that she could grab me in an instant. Van is already a silent shadow, traveling with such grace, he is lost on the wind.

We make our way along the path, red dust covering the toes of our black boots. I have to readjust the bag a couple of times to keep it from dragging on the ground before making the mistake of looking at it, and the sight of dark black blood dripping from the bottom sickens me. I hadn't noticed that before.

"Had to be real," Lifera mutters under her breath.

"Still fucking hate it," I snap back, my words a whisper.

Her shoulders bounce with a silent laugh.

It's not long before we see the first sign of life. A pair of demons stand to the side of the path, sitting at a wooden table where they appear to be playing some game. Above, the sky still shines bright, but poles holding large lanterns line the path since it's so dark in here. Looking beyond the demons, I see that they continue the rest of the way like little lights leading us to our deaths.

Their boisterous laughter echoes through the dark forest. One is very human-looking, his features similar to anyone on Earth, but my brain struggles to comprehend the other's features.

Lifera powers on, walking straight past the pair as if she can't even see them. I follow her lead, averting my eyes so as not to draw unnecessary attention to us.

Just when I think they've ignored us entirely, my hopes are shattered.

"He! Wure do ya think yer goin'?'" one calls, his voice rough and broken. He's not ugly, but he's not handsome, either. He looks like a normal man, but instead of teeth, he has a black void for a mouth. I can see his lips moving, but there's nothing to watch beyond.

Lifera stops, so I do as well.

"We're to see Death," she replies, her voice strong and sure. It sounds completely different to what I'm used to. The power's there, but the tone is completely different.

"O'ya? Says who?" The demon saunters over to us, his long legs eating up the space between. The second demon, who remains quiet but watches with a careful eye, joins his buddy.

This is what I'd expected in Hell; he's shaped like a human, but there are plenty of features that scream *he's something more.*

He's tall—taller than first—and thick. His large body, though covered in a dark material, is clearly stacked with muscle. Wide shoulders lead to a trim waist, and I'm sure his dark clothing hides an abundance of rippling muscle. What skin I can see matches the color of the gray sky, but it's covered in ridges and marks that are far lighter, nearly white. I can't tell if it's a skin pattern or scarring, but I'm rudely staring, and he notices.

"See something you like, female?" he purrs, deep and inviting. It takes me a second to realize he's talking to me. I look up at his face, and am once again struck by his odd features.

Now this demon *is* handsome.

His angular face is far less human, but similar features are there. His lips are a darker shade of gray than his skin, and instead of eyebrows, he has two dark ridges that match the tone of his lips. His ears point high in the sky, and each tip is adorned in silver jewelry that appears to be as sharp as a knife.

He quirks a ridged brow at me, a deadly smirk showing off a full mouth of sharp teeth. I notice movement behind him, and my eyes dart in that direction. I fully expect to see Van running full steam towards us, but it's just dark. He turns slightly, as if to look back there as well, and my gasp escapes me in a rush.

He turns back, his smile now brighter as the cause of the movement I'd notices rustles behind him.

Wings. He has fucking *wings*! Bat-like things with thin membranes and deadly claws.

I think I might faint.

"We would like to see Death," Lifera says, her voice dripping in sex appeal. Both the demons turn their attention to her, and it's like I can suddenly breathe again. I knew I'd see some truly astounding things in Hell, but truthfully, demons who looked more like gargoyles weren't on my bingo list. *Sexy* gargoyles were definitely not on there.

Both demons look at us as if weighing their options, before the gray one pulls a slip of something from a pouch he has hidden on his hip. With a quick flick of a claw, he hands it to me. The weight surprises me, and I realize it's not a slip of paper as I expected, but a thin pane of rock.

"Take this with you and show the others, they'll let you pass," he says, black eyes focused on me. There's no white to them, just a boundless depth that seems to see more than he lets on.

I nod in thanks and start walking down the path without another word. Lifera silently follows. It's a while before the next light, and I imagine the next set of guards. I expect to make the trip in silence, but when we're about halfway there, Lifera's smooth voice jerks me out of my thoughts.

"Let me see the back of the rock."

I pull it out of my pocket and hand it over, and she laughs.

"What?" Her reaction is making me uneasy.

"He put his name on it," she says, like that's supposed to tell me something. When I don't respond, she continues, "It's the equivalent of a man giving you his number. The gargen—the type of demon he is—can find you anywhere if you say their name out loud. He is hoping you'll call on him."

The thought makes me shudder, but I laugh lightly at the crazy situation. "You keep the rock, I already have a sexy demon," I tell her. And who knows, maybe she likes gargens as much as she likes the shifters.

"You know, I think I will," she responds with a knowing smirk.

"Why didn't that other demon have a mouth? He was talking, but there was nothing there, just a void." I ask, the thought of the demon's cavernous mouth making me shiver.

"He was a chipher. They are able to draw in a being's life force through their mouths, but they need contact to do so. If you ever see one try to kiss you, don't do it."

I just nod, because there's no reason I would ever want to kiss one anyway.

Sure enough, the guards we pass along the way take one glance at our rock note, and let us by without a word. They're all in pairs of two, and many are either playing games, taking turns sleeping, or working on some weapon or another. There are a few other species of demons I don't recognize, but I don't have time to focus long enough to distinguish their unique features.

When we're almost to the castle, having passed the last guard station, I mutter under my breath, "Will we have to worry about all the guards we passed coming to Death's rescue?"

"Not likely. Wolf is dispatching them as we pass."

I tense, gearing to turn around, but her snapped halt stops me, and I continue facing forward. Looks like Lifera won't be needing that gargoyle's name after all. I want to ask her why she keeps calling Van 'wolf,' but we're too close to the castle to risk being overheard.

The castle before us is equally as beautiful as it is deadly. The bright red rocks seem to shine in places, as if full of random spots of gemstones. Shiny silver spikes cover the edges of each ledge and structure, so it all looks as sharp as a blade.

It's everything I expected it to be and somehow so much worse.

I pause in the middle of the dirt path at the foot of a large staircase. I knew it was too much to hope we could handle this outside, but the thought of going in there is too much. The edge of the woods is behind us by about twenty feet, and

I take comfort in the knowledge that Van is there watching. If we go inside, he won't be able to help as quickly.

"Death! Get your ass out here!" I yell at the top of my lungs. Beside me, though it's subtle, Lifera startles.

"Thara would've loved to see you thrive," Lifera says, regaining her composure. I don't let her words distract me, or the brief pain from grief control me.

A few minutes go by, tense and silent. I mentally prepare for the sound of pounding boots, but it never comes. No guards surround us, no creatures come to kill us. We just stand in the red dirt drive before a red rock castle, and wait.

Waiting is torture, and I imagine it's why he took his sweet ass time.

With a flourish, the two large doors at the top of the stairs fly open, and Death saunters out. He takes the stairs smoothly, his body moving with grace, as he comes to meet us at the bottom of the stairs. He's wearing a pair of low-waisted, brown pants, and his cream top hangs loosely from his body. It doesn't hide his muscular frame or detract from his looks, but it softens his appearance. Death can be as fashionable as he wants, but he'll still be rotten from the core out.

"What have you brought me?" he asks eagerly as he sits and lounges back on the stairs, contorting his body in a way that is meant to be sexual. He's attractive for an older man, sure, but the action still comes off as extremely strange. Lifera doesn't react, and stands calmly by my side. His focus bounces between us, but I can tell he's more interested in her.

"She's just my taxi. How else was I supposed to get here?" I respond with a shrug, not wanting to give him a reason to question her presence.

I'm the one who's supposed to kill Death, not her. She's my backup. My safety plan.

"A taxi? How human!" he exclaims, clapping his hands together. The whites of his eyes are showing, and his teeth gleam behind a manic smile. He looks at Lifera a little longer, but seemingly dismisses her easily.

"Where's Tucker?" I snarl.

"Your friend? He's on his way! I've taken very good care of him while he's been here." Death's eyes track to the black bag in my hand, but I grip it tighter.

"Where is he?" I ask again, my voice turning into a growl. I can't handle the wait any longer; I can feel the rage clawing its way to the surface. Angry thoughts flood my mind, and though I try to stay calm, it's a losing battle.

Death was right when he said my fuse was short. He must also realize this, because he jumps up from his relaxed spot on the stairs to come closer. Lifera and I both tense, but don't move away.

Death moves with a restless energy, as if something wild has been trapped in his skin. "You're feisty, just like your mother!" His head twitches to one side a few times. "I convinced her family to force her to join me but she thought I was, in her own words, *a worthless ballsack who she'd rather die before marrying.*'" He mocks my mother's voice in a high-pitched cadence, sounding nothing like the woman I knew. His tongue darts out, wetting already-reddened lips. "A shame," he sighs with false nostalgia. "I would've *loved* to ruin her."

Within me, anger spikes as he speaks about my mother so callously. He seems to feed off my reactions, the emotional response only fueling his crazed delight.

"Speaking of lovers, where is your Crow?" Death paces and searches our surroundings. The question comes across as casual, but I understand it for what it is. A threat.

My original thoughts, that he knows exactly who my lover is, are proven—and the asinine question he asked in the tent if I had more than one lover was nothing more than a hidden tactic.

He enjoys the game—enjoys playing with his food. And right now, he thinks I'm the piece he's toying with. That he can dangle my relationship over my head, as if he knows something I don't.

Now it makes sense why my mother wanted to escape her family so badly. It's no wonder, if they were trying to sell her off to *him*.

Chapter 40
Valencia

"Where is Tucker?" I snap, not wanting to hear any more of his unhinged stories. I'm here to save my family; I can't do anything for the ones already gone.

"Where is Corvus?" Death repeats in a mock girly voice. He laughs, low and satisfied.

"Corvus is not my keeper. I don't need him to handle my problems." A lie, I absolutely need him, and have since the moment he came into my life—but I'm not about to admit that.

"No, but he is your fuck toy," Death chortles. "Have you tamed the Third Lord, or is he still a philanderer? Ya know, I get why Embaral loved fucking him so much, I hear he's a *very* giving lover."

My eyes pinch at the corners, realizing he's talking about the redheaded succubus who led me from Tornil's tent. I don't let my reaction out, no matter how much jealousy eats away at me. I know what he's doing, but he's misplaced his tactic.

It would've been a good strategy used on anyone else, but I have eyes and a brain. Corvus is a very attractive male in a position of power. There would've been no reason for him to be chaste with his affections, especially not before me.

"Where. Is. Tucker?" He's wasting time and we all know it—we just don't know *why*.

Death pauses dramatically. "Now, now. That was quite demanding, young lady." Again, he takes on that strange, feminine southern accent. I sneak a glance at Lifera, but she looks back at me with equal confusion.

Great, even she wasn't aware of his bat shit crazy personality.

"No more games, Death. If you want the Devil's head, you'll get Tucker right now." I hold up the black bag, not even cringing as blood drips from its base. It's heavy in my hand, the rope pulling tightly against my palm. I'm barely grasping what little sanity I have left, my patience ground to nothing.

His eyes latch onto the bag like a laser, finally drawing a true reaction out of him. His smirk fades, desperation evident. "Here I thought you'd like a bit of foreplay before the main event, but I guess given the stakes, you have reason to be persistent."

The air is thick and humid. We both need something, yet are willing to give in.

"Cato!" Death shouts, his voice borderline erratic.

The sound of rustling rocks reaches my ears, and by the time I turn, Lifera is already looking that way, having heard it before I did. I want to keep my eyes on Death, but the sight before me nearly brings me to my knees.

Tucker.

Kicking as two large guards drag him towards us. I want to rejoice in his fighting spirit, but the damage done to his body sickens me. He's clearly been badly beaten, and the signs of old and new wounds prove that he's been susceptible to torture for a long time. A huge scar rests over his heart, and the memory of the angel feather protruding from his chest flashes through my mind.

His skin, normally a dark tan from a lot of time in the sun, is covered in dirt and dried blood—but I would recognize his face anywhere. He's naked, nothing on his body besides the chains that bind his wrists and ankles. I nearly throw up, bile burning my throat that I have to force down, when I note the large group of cuts, bruises, and bites around his groin.

Every mark is a reminder of my failure.

The same masked guards from the tent drag Tucker to Death and throw him down into the rocks. Tucker jerks in pain, but then grunts before attempting to get up and flee. The chains are short and snap taut before he's able to get away, and Death shoots his arm out, gripping Tucker by the back of his neck.

I step forward, nearly lost to the rage, but Lifera holds me back with a firm grip on my arm. A rumbling sound rips from my chest.

Death smirks as he forces Tucker to look at me and Lifera, yanking his head back by his dirt-covered hair. Dark brown eyes briefly widen with recognition, and as soon as he realizes it's me, he fights harder to get away.

"No, no, no," he whimpers wildly.

"Be still, or I'll fuck you right here in front of her and show her what a little cock slut you've become. Then, I'll kill her and make you watch me fuck her corpse," Death snaps with a harsh yank on Tucker's hair.

A shiver runs through Tucker, and he stills instantly as tears track his dirty face. I can see the stark lines as if they were written in blood.

Or maybe that's because the haze has lowered over my eyes, the familiar red fog that signals the rage is here. I have more control over myself, so I keep my claws retracted. He smirks as though nothing has happened, but he has signed his demise ten times over.

I'm shaking, my entire body wracked with it, but my voice comes out surprisingly calm. "Release Tucker. I killed the Devil, just like you asked."

"Show me," he begs, his eyes full of mirth.

Without hesitation, I open the black bag. My fingers curl in the dark hair at the top of the head, and with more resolve than I knew I had, I tear if from the shadows inside.

I grit my teeth to keep from throwing up. The sight of the gouged-out eyes and dangling flesh of severed skin around the neck makes my head spin. I revolt internally, but manage to keep my reaction in. I'm supposed to be the one who severed this head from its body. I can't make it believable if I vomit at the sight of it.

No matter how horrendous the sight is, nothing is worse than seeing Tucker with clear signs of torture and abuse covering his entire body.

I toss the offensive sight away, the squelching sound sending another shiver through me as the head lands at Death's feet.

He leans forward, a speculative look on his face, but doesn't let go of Tucker. With slow deliberation, he lifts the toe of his black dress shoe and gives the head a light, playful tap. His brows furrow with unsettling seriousness, as if he's trying to find a single hint of a lie. It looks exactly like the Devil when she's in her male form, yet he studies it as if unsure, in deep thought, while he pokes and prods the head, smearing blood all over his boot and pants. The head starts to gather sand, the eye holes filling with it.

He attempts to lean closer, but his hold on Tucker prevents the movement, and his fingers around Tucker's neck flex, making him wince in pain. Tucker's blood-matted hair shakes as he renews his struggle to get away. Just as I'm about to scream, Death drops Tucker like a forgotten toy and grabs the head. He clutches it reverently and hugs it to his chest, getting blood everywhere.

"Thank you!" he exclaims, a giddy edge to his voice. He twists the head to face him and giggles like they're sharing an inside joke.

Tucker wastes no time and scrambles across the dirt towards us. The guards standing nearby don't move to catch him, still stoically watching.

I jump forward and out of Lifera's grasp to grab Tucker, my arms wrapping around his too-lean body. He shakes violently, sobs escaping him. A hand pulls me back by my shoulder, but I wrap my arms tighter, not wanting to let him go for a second.

"I know, honey, I know. But you must let me take him, or do you wish his abuser to go free?"

The question snaps the taut cord of pure fury inside of me, and I'm finally able to let go of Tucker so I can face Death. Tucker whimpers as Lifera pulls him toward her, and the sound rips through me, but I don't turn to look even as I hear rustling as Lifera takes him.

Death continues to embrace the severed head, but his brows are tipped down in a look of agitation. Growing angry, he pulls at the severed head, ripping out chunks of hair and skin.

"You lied!" he screeches and points at me. His eyes widen in shock as he realizes Tucker is no longer by his side. "This is not the Devil, you bitch! *You tricked me.*"

His snarl is vicious and deadly, and the guttural sound raises the hair on my arms. Something *wrong* descends him.

Red consumes where his eyes were once white until no trace of the former color is left. Blood drips from his tear ducts, thick and dark, and trails down his cheek like tears.

The air around him bends with force as he bursts out of his clothes. His muscles contort, and bones shift underneath skin, distorting his body into something unrecognizable. Large bones pop out of his upper back until fabric seams pop under the force, the sound loud as a gunshot.

His face elongates into a reptilian snout filled with razor-sharp teeth and bulging eyes. His hair all falls out, and his ears fall unceremoniously, forgotten in the sand.

A deformed monster stands before us.

I stumble back a step, my breath catching in my throat. My mind screams at me to run. But the soft sound of crying behind me helps to steel my spine against the horrific sight.

It doesn't matter what form Death takes. He'll always be Tucker's abuser.

The guards remain stoic, as if this is nothing new to them.

"Oh, Death, I warned you that taking too much power from others would change you. I just didn't expect *this* to be the outcome." Lifera seems calm and almost aloof as she addresses the monster Death has become. She never mentioned this was possible, but her calm demeanor tells me she at least guessed it would be. I try to channel her calm, drawing some into myself, but I still have a hard time looking at the offensive monster in front of me.

It seems his greed truly did have a nasty outcome.

"*You*," it snarls in a distorted and choppy voice. Death points a clawed hand, with seven finger-like appendages tipped with sickly white talons, at Lifera.

"Ah, yes, did I forget to tell you?" Lifera says with a curl of her lip. "You always thought you were the best trickster, but it seems you are still beneath me."

With an enraged roar, the monster charges.

"Whatever you do, don't let him touch you!" Lifera screams as she charges as well, leaving Tucker behind her in a heap on the ground. A long, thin blade appears out of nowhere as she jumps into the air with a battle cry, flying towards the monster. Death swipes at her, but he's now so large that he's slow enough for her to easily get by, cutting across both of his thighs in the process. He roars in pain and turns to follow her, a large fist slamming to the ground right next to where she lands.

I stumble back, pulling Tucker out of the fray as I do. I'm eager to jump in, but protecting him is my first priority. The two guards are finally released from their frozen prison, and robotically turn towards Tucker and me.

I breathe in fire and let it consume me as my claws easily extend from my fingertips and fangs descend from my gums. I haven't fully mastered shifting like everyone expects, but knowing what my mom was capable of gives me hope that I one day will. I shift my weight, positioning Tucker behind me so I stand between him and the guards. He's in no condition to fight, and I've got built-in weapons.

I lean further into the haze; the predator in me sees so much better, and *she's* able to track the two guards easily. They both jerk to a stop, eying me before simultaneously shifting into giant tigers. The transition is flawless—there's not a single hitch in their movement, not a wince on their face. It's seamless. I've seen wardrobe changes in the theater that are more chaotic.

Each time I've shifted in some sense, there's always been a delay—a paused moment in time where my cells change into something else and the being that seemingly lives quietly inside of me wakes. For these creatures, who now prowl around me as any predator would, the difference is startling.

Fire burns bright in their eyes, and they start to circle. I shift my body with their movements, covering Tucker as he's crouched near my feet, and draw deep breaths to ground myself. That surge of power I felt after using the chains was abrupt and limitless, but I don't feel a speck of it now. No matter how much I try to charge up the power to use later, it sits too far out of reach. I'm left with defensive options, and seeing how lethally the shifters move, I'm at an extreme disadvantage.

I back up a step, my calf pressing against a body—Tucker. He leans into the touch, shaking heavily.

The tigers continue to circle, and I know it's only a matter of seconds before one of them pounces, but the sound of pounding steps distracts us all. The tigers jerk their large heads towards the woods, bodies tense with anticipation.

Light briefly glints before a long spear flashes and stabs the tiger on the left through its chest. The spear rams through the tiger's body so hard that the spear and tiger become stuck in the ground. It wails in pain, thrashing wildly, but remains rooted to the red ground.

Out of the darkness leaps a large figure, his long black hair tied in a tight braid and his sharp cheekbones covered in streaks of red, as if he dipped his hand in paint and dragged his fingertips down his face. A gray feather has been added to his braid, the soft tip sticking high into the air.

My shoulders slump as relief floods me.

The other tiger attacks Van, swiping a large paw full of claws. The tall Fae jumps to the side, thankfully away from Tucker and me, drawing the danger further away. Without his spear, he seems to mainly be working on defense right now.

A roar draws my attention back to Lifera, who still dances around Death. His monstrous form now has many slices that range from minor cuts to a few fatal-looking gashes. She flits around him, a professional in the art of evasion, as the monster continues to lumber around her.

I'm momentarily frozen as I watch them fight. They both seem to be handling their foes equally well, but I know Lifera can't kill Death, so it'll be up to one of us to finish him off. If it's not me, with the power of my holy chains, then we run the risk of him coming back—but no matter how deep I dig for that power, it sits too far from my consciousness to reach.

An arm wraps around my leg, thin and weak. I can feel the cool touch of his cold skin through my clothes. I'm too afraid to take my eyes off the fight, so I lean further into him. "It's going to be okay."

I hope it's not false assurance.

Blood spurts out of the remaining tiger's throat, covering Van, but he turns to me. "Corvus must still be dealing with the guards in the castle. I will help with Death."

"Don't let him touch you!" I snap across the courtyard. Van nods briefly before jumping into the fray, and unease unfurls in my chest. Van says that like he'd expected Corvus and Parker to be here by now, but I don't see anyone else approaching. They've been in the castle this whole time, checking the dungeons in case Death was keeping Tucker there despite the deal, and eliminating any extra guards who may try to defend Death.

I stand still, watching as Lifera continues to toy with Death. He's so blinded by rage he doesn't realize he's alone now. Van killed his two shifter guards and has joined Lifera. They keep Death spinning in circles, darting out of his reach at the last second while continuing to cause more and more damage to his deformed body.

Footsteps pound behind me, and I jerk around. Tucker's got such a tight grip on my leg I almost fall, but I manage to regain my balance thanks to the quick reflexes my predator side allows.

"Fuck, Tucker!" Parker slams to his knees beside us, wrapping his arms around our friend's beaten body. He's no longer sobbing, but his body hasn't quit shaking since he was brought out here. Plenty of tears still run down his cheeks.

My attention is split between the fighting and Parker as he cares for Tucker, the fight so loud I can barely focus on anything else.

"Corvus is going to take us to the cave, buddy. We're going to get you out of here," Parker explains as he holds Tucker close. My hand rests lightly on the top of Tucker's head—the only place I can see that isn't caked in blood. I don't want to cause him more pain, but something urges me to reach out to him, if only for a second. My heart contracts painfully, making it hard to breathe. My claws look vicious against his dirty hair, but they rest far away from his delicate skin.

"*Agh!*" The loud, gurgling groan fills the air, and Tucker to flinches as if in pain. He buries himself deeper into Parker's arms.

"We're out of time," Corvus says lowly as he rushes to our side, having materialized from somewhere in the castle.

Lifera and Van trade sharp slashes at Death, his monstrous form now covered in blood and cuts, but he doesn't stop fighting.

I crouch down next to Tucker and lightly place a hand on his face. He looks at me, but his eyes are vacant. He shakes profusely, his skin cold to the touch. Still, he leans softly into my palm.

"I'll make this right," I promise him. "Go now."

Parker doesn't respond, just nods as he stands and rips off his shirt. With a harsh yank, he easily tears the fabric in half. Black tactical pants sit low on his hips, showcasing the pale muscles of his torso. With Corvus' help, they get Tucker to his feet. He doesn't collapse, but I can tell by the way he squints that it causes him pain. Parker then takes his torn shirt and wraps it around Tucker's waist, giving him as much privacy as he can.

"Hey man," Parker says softly to Tucker, his lean body supporting most of the weight. "Corvus is going to take us to his home. He's a good one—you're safe now. I've got you."

Tucker lays his head against Parker's shoulder and cries.

Corvus' eyes briefly flash across my body before he places a hand on Parker's back and lightly wraps his other arm around Tucker's body. Tucker doesn't comment, but he jerks at the touch.

One second they're standing there, and the next they're gone. I know Corvus will be back as soon as he can. Minutes maximum. He won't want to stay gone very long, but he's got to get into the cave before he can come back.

Considering how heavily Tucker leaned on Parker, I know it was a good idea that he came along. I just hate wondering what he might've seen while he and Corvus were clearing out the guards in the castle.

Not a single one of us will leave here without some form of trauma after all of this is said and done.

I turn back to the fighting, stepping around the dead tiger shifters as I draw closer to where Van and Lifera have cornered Death. His monstrous form has been backed into the corner where the castle wall and stone steps meet. Each time he tries to advance, one of them lashes out, forcing him back. A few clawed fingers lay lifelessly upon the ground, and more than a few large chunks have been cut out of his thick hide. There are deep grooves in the gravel where Death's clubbed feet have dragged through it.

I want to finish this for good. No coming back, no starting over, just death. Real death. The First Lord will be no more when I'm done with him.

My blood boils, the rage making my body feel like it's on fire. The sharp tips of my canines poke against my bottom lip. I've partially shifted once again, not a master over my body or my mind.

Just stuck, precisely as I was the night my family died.

No matter how badly I want to join the fight, I can't convince my muscles to move. Now that Tucker is safe, and Parker is as well, I'm frozen, spending too much time trying to figure out how to end Death instead of doing it.

How the fuck do I do this?

CHAPTER 41
CORVUS

Landing in the living room of my cave is mediocre at best.

Tucker has lost all the strength he had remaining, and there's barely a second of time to catch him as he falls. He grunts and yanks out of my arms, slamming into Parker, who stumbles back before regaining his posture and wrapping Tucker in his arms.

"I'm good here," he says. "I'll take care of him, you go back."

"Just don't let him wander," I say, softening my tone so as not to frighten the poor human further.

His body, though probably once muscular, is severely emaciated. Too many bones are visible through his dirty skin, and there isn't a spot on him that's not covered in dirt or blood. He's also got torture marks all over him. Slashes, punctures, bites, and bruises show a map of what this poor kid has been put through over the last couple of weeks.

When Parker turns them both, Tucker's feet practically dragging across the floor, I barely contain my roar of anger. My fingers curl into tight fists. I want to slam it down onto the coffee table and destroy it, but I've worked this hard not to frighten Tucker and won't start now. Destroying Tornil's tent felt nice—it was a great release for my anger, directed towards someone who could handle it. Losing control of my outburst now would only serve to terrify the poor kid; I don't think I can stand to see him flinch at the sight of me again.

They disappear into the hallway, Parker heading deeper in the cave to start caring for his friend. I don't wait any longer and fly through the in between back to Death's castle.

It doesn't matter that the trip is only seconds—I spend an eternity in the nothingness with visions of Tucker's shredded back being the only thing I see. Fury builds to a crescendo as the marks of torture refuse to go away.

It's one thing to torture a demon or a human that's been sent to Hell for truly heinous crimes, but I cannot stand for torturing humans who have done nothing wrong. Who have committed no sins, made no grave mistakes. Who are simply in the wrong place. Death has taken being damned too far.

I pop back to the same place I left, joining the scene as if no time has passed.

"You *whore!*" Death yells, his voice hoarse as he uses deformed vocal cords. He's swinging for Lifera's auburn head but is too slow, and she's gone before his fist can connect. As Lifera darts away, Van takes her place and swings his deadly dagger, clipping Death on the shoulder. Blood instantly pours down his elongated arm.

Valencia's eyes briefly meet mine before looking back at the fight. She stands beside me, having not moved from her spot, but she stares Death down like she's ready to rip his heart out.

"You can end this," I tell her. My own rage boils beneath my skin, begging that I jump in and inflict my own pain on the vile creature Death has become.

Valencia doesn't respond, and her silence worries me. Feline line eyes track the monster's every moment with calculated precision, her clawed hands twitching with each swing, as if she's mentally become a part of the fight. She watches with deadly focus, but this is not the power we need from her. We need her to release that holy light and eviscerate Death from existence entirely.

It was a nice idea, containing Death so he could be sent to the prison in this realm to pay for his crimes, but Hell will never be safe so long as he's around. There's no way I'm willing to risk him ever coming back, and I didn't kill every guard for Lifera and Van to dance around Death all night.

Valencia is stuck. Simmering in her own anger, from what I can tell; I recognize the struggle from her stillness. She's trying to calculate the best possible course of action, but when it comes to fighting demons, spontaneity is best.

Unfortunately, we've not had any time to practice wielding her holy light, and I'd guess she's struggling to reach it. From what little Van has told me, her powers are heavily tied to her emotions... so perhaps I need to work harder to encourage her to release that beautiful power.

"They tortured him," I say, anger deepening my voice. "His back is flayed to the bone in spots."

Valencia doesn't respond, but I see her body tense. Her eyes track Death, and I can tell that whatever her shifted animal is, it's begging to be completely released so it can join the fray. She's clearly a fighter, but for whatever reason, Valencia doesn't set her free.

Maybe she doesn't know how, but anger has always been her outlet.

Van's battle cry draws my attention back to the fight. Death has regained some footing, leaving the tight corner they had forced him into, and Lifera has to dance even faster now that the monster's range has lengthened. Van runs behind Death, a blur of movement, but the tang of blood that fills the air says he hit something important.

Regardless, Death keeps fighting. They'll never win. Lifera can't kill him—she can't kill any of the Lords—and Van won't be able to, even with my help. We could incapacitate him, but it would only leave room for more problems later on.

We've got to get rid of him for good. I hate to throw Tucker's torture at her, but I know it will fuel the flames inside her as much as it does me. She's the only one who can end this *and* ensure he never returns.

"They raped him," I spit the words out, their toxic burn unpleasant on my tongue. "He clearly fought. He's incredible for surviving as long as he has, but that means he's been beaten, starved, and raped for weeks. How does that make you feel?"

Those feline eyes shift to me. "Destructive."

Silent like a true predator, Valencia finally charges. She ducks under Death's arm and swipes her claws across his abdomen. Blood instantly wells, four long claw marks appearing on his shirt before blending into a large batch of dark black.

I join the fight, using my fire to clamp down on Death's ankles and hold him in place as the flames sear through his clothes and skin.

He roars in pain, arms flailing haphazardly.

Lifera and Van both take a step back to catch their breath. The blood-stained tip of Lifera's sword rests in the red dirt.

Valencia takes the lead, inflicting damage on the already wrecked monster. She doesn't pause for a breath or to strategize; she takes advantage of every opening and moves with grace, her body more controlled than ever before. I narrow my gaze at her technique, watching as she uses her claws to flit around and slashes with the daggers I secured to her body. She must've been paying more attention in training than I'd thought.

Death grows frantic, and I almost see an internal buildup of her power. It slowly fills the air, its tiny fingers pulling at my skin, drawing power from everything they touch. I brace myself, hoping she will release her chains and end this for us all. We didn't discuss this part out loud, but it's what needs to be done. We'll deal with the aftermath of the Devil finding out later.

Death screeches, folding forwards and pounding his large, blistered fists against the ground. The screech shatters the hold of power in the air, causing it to disperse back through the atmosphere.

We all freeze, eying him suspiciously as his back heaves in great jerks. He's doubled over, cracked knuckles trembling against the ground. A shiver races down my spine. I feel like I should know what this means—what he's doing—but it's lost on me.

No one moves an inch, waiting to see what happens next. The low sound of a droning starts in the distance.

"Corvus, did you kill the guards, or did you knock them out?" Lifera snaps, her golden eyes glowing as she looks at me.

Fuck. *Fuck, fuck, fuck.*

It was a mistake to rush and kill them all.

"Corvus, tell me you did not kill them," Van pleads, his features matching the worry on Lifera's.

"What's wrong?" Valencia asks, looking around the group. She's safely out of Death's reach, but that puts her further away from me.

A scratching sound emanates from behind us. I slowly turn, keeping an eye on Death as much as I watch the two large tigers that lie twenty feet away. One is on its side, blood-covered body still as a statue. The other, still stuck to the ground with a spear shoved through its chest, begins to twitch, large claws scratching into the dirt.

Low rumbling growls start to grow louder and louder as the tiger starts to reanimate. It swiftly becomes crazed, so focused on escaping—scratching the ground so hard—it spins around the handle of the spear.

I turn to Death, who slowly starts to stand.

"Time's up," he laughs, the sound haunting and full of malice.

The roaring I heard breaks into a crescendo.

Van steps a few feet closer to me, putting our shoulders side by side. Tension radiates. We've faced this number of demons before, but we had advantages on our side. My focus splits between the oncoming horde and keeping hold of Death.

Seconds later, a flood of dead demons rush from the front of Death's castle. They stumble down the stairs, many falling, but they quickly jump back up.

Lifera curses, lifting her blade back into a fighting stance as she faces the deadly crowd I just eliminated, as Parker and I tore through the castle searching for Tucker.

They're all barely humanoid now—lesser demons when they were alive, but after coming back from death, they have reverted to their demonic forms. So lost in their creature-like nature, they're not smart enough to tell friend from foe. Despite having been ripped from the peace of death, they're still no brighter than when they were alive.

Three of the lesser demons—boar-looking creatures—turn on the other demons, ripping through flesh with vicious tusks and chomping through bones. The demons that are unlucky enough to get caught in their path succumb to a gruesome second death.

I send a blast of flames to the two tiger shifters, not wanting to worry about them reanimating. Van storms past me, taking the crowd of risen dead head-on. He manages to rip his spear out of the burning tiger and uses it to decapitate three demons in one swipe.

Death begins to pull at the fiery prison, despite the damage it's doing to his legs. Skin and muscle burn so hot that they bubble into large blisters before slowly melting down his legs. One shin bone is already exposed, the milky white stark against the dark blood that sears away as soon as it touches flame.

Lifera and Valencia jump back to attacking Death, one with a sword and the other with claws—though they now have to dodge outside of his reach, unwilling to run through the flames at his feet.

"You're dead, Death!" Lifera screams, keeping Death from harming Valencia as much as she tries to ensure he does not harm her. If he manages to get hold of Valencia, she'll be dead in a second. Death wields mortality with a single touch.

Valencia, crouched like a panther, races around both Death and Lifera, striking where she can and leaving long slashes across his body.

Flames die where the tigers once were, now only a pile of ash, but it opens room for a few lesser demons to sneak past Van and charge me. I set fire to two on the right and they start to flail, bodies scorched in an instant. The third, a tall and lanky gargen, rushes forward, his stone-like skin making it impossible to penetrate him with fire. His ears become limp in death, and there's a sickly parlor to his stone. Cracks form, as if he's one hit from crumbling to dust.

A spiked club drags on a chain behind him, plinking against the rocks. One of his wings hangs limp, broken at the base, tendons cut clean through. The other curls forward, sharp knife-like claw ready to slice through muscle and bone.

He was one of Tucker's guards; I can smell the human on him. His death was too easy the first time. Black blood covers his chest, the long slit in his throat making his head awkwardly lull to one side so he runs at an angle. He's faster than the others, though, and manages to skirt the flames that consume their bodies. He swings the club high and throws the spiked ball at my head. I duck, letting it fly past my face before reaching out and grabbing the chain it's attached to.

Yanking him to me, his grip tight on the weapon's other end, he stumbles, balance thrown from the nearly severed head. He falls straight to the ground, and I bring up a booted foot and smash it into his face.

I stumble as his head flies clean from his body, the last of the tendons holding it together finally ripping free. His body slams to the ground chest-first, fingers and legs twitching. His head bounces a few times before rolling around to face me. Lifeless eyes watch as he chomps a mouthful of teeth in my direction.

I kick his head into the flames and turn to watch as Van battles three shifters hand-to-hand. They don't swing with any kind of skill as they throw their bodies around, lethal claws ready to rip into Van's skin. I can tell they're shifters as they've been trapped in a gruesome mix between their two halves. Disjointed bones stick out in the wrong directions. Fur and skin mesh into something not quite recognizable. It's a reason why Valencia's ability to partially shift is so rare—this is usually the result of such an action.

Van's spear lies 10 feet away, holding two more demons to the ground as they thrash against each other. They still move despite how the wooden shaft and blade having ripped through their bodies.

Van finishes the three shifters off, using two of them to kill the other before he severs their heads with his dagger. There are still a few left, but they've reverted to their creature forms and have either scattered or started fighting amongst themselves.

I look to Valencia, who still fights Death alongside Lifera, though she seems to be toying with him more than anything. A small yet murderous smile lights her face each time she escapes Death's fists. One flies over her head—dangerously close—and my heart rate spikes, fear and exhaustion getting the better of me.

"Finish it!" I beg, resolve shaking as I continue to hold the First Lord of Hell hostage. She freezes, just out of Death's reach, body now facing me.

He laughs, realizing sooner than I do that my power to hold him is waning. Fire was never my strongest trait—traveling in and out of Hell was what made me famous. Made me a good lord. No other being in Hell can physically leave without the Devil's permission.

Death may have stolen most of his power, but he's still been alive for far longer than I have, and he's been the First since before I was even created. He's stolen a generation's worth of power, and despite being given an extremely powerful gift by Hell's standard, I'm no match for him.

With an evil grin on his baleful face, he rips one leg out of the flames and steps toward Valencia. Bone slams against the sand, sinking in a few inches. He laughs manically.

She doesn't react and watches me as I start to shake with the struggle of holding him down. Her bright blue eyes glow from within as she studies me intensely, not worried in the slightest about what Death is doing.

He reaches out to grab her, and she dodges him easily despite how her attention trains on me.

"Finish it," I growl.

Chapter 42

Valencia

There are bodies everywhere.

Littered across the ground, limbs in odd angles, or reduced to nothing but dark gray ash. The contrast of the burned bodies against the red sand is vibrant. A few creatures run around, all some form of four-legged animal, but they've mostly scattered now.

Death has gotten angrier with each loss, making his movements wild and unpredictable. His large body broadcasts each swing, like a slow-motion slideshow that gives a sneak peek at his every move a second before he makes it.

The rage hasn't lifted; if anything, a part of me begs for just an ounce of more anger. I'm not sure what will happen if I get it. I've been toying with Death to this point—it didn't feel right for his end to be quick—and, even now, I have no idea how to draw out the chains that will finish him. The beast inside me claws to be released, but I have no idea how to let her out. She has a tight grip on my power, the holy light still out of reach.

As soon as I saw Tucker and felt his tormented body press against mine, I had this immediate sense of *pack* wash over me. I'd never thought of it in that way, of considering everyone I hold dear as a part of a pack, but now I know a predator lives inside me, I realize the feelings are hers. But *she's* still me. And now I'm her.

My brain struggles to fluidly combine the new feelings, so I continually feel like I'm having an identity crisis.

All I feel right now is the burning need to prolong Death's struggle for as long as I can. I would torture him for years if I could. I'm struggling to produce the power to truly finish it for good, making it feel a win-win situation. Maybe once he's in a melted pile of skin and bones, I'll lay the holy light over him like a blanket and suffocate him in its goodness.

I can see the strain it's taken for Corvus to hold him this long. There's no doubt that he's extremely powerful, but Corvus has met his match in Death. Having the ability to portal through different realms is an impressive power, but it doesn't help us much now. I'm grateful he was able to get Parker and Tucker to safety, but his fire isn't meant to be a prison, only a trap. A trap Death is making his way out of.

Lifera has gone back to fighting him, her long sword swiping his damaged leg. Death roars in pain with each slash, but doesn't give up. He doesn't shrink away from her oncoming attacks, but watches and waits, striking when she's within range. Little good it does him, his body is deformed and his movements are always off kilter by just enough that evading his strikes is almost easy. No matter how hard Lifera hits him, the wounds heal seconds later. The only thing she's able to do is distract him with pain. She can't kill him outright.

I know I shouldn't get cocky, that I really should finish it for all our sakes. How can I, when he hasn't suffered nearly enough? His suffering should be eternal. A lifetime of pain that not even Hell could offer him.

"You think you are making him suffer by allowing him to live longer, but you're only hurting us in the process." Van's deep voice sounds from over my shoulder. He stands just to the side of me as we both watch Lifera dip and dodge.

I want to argue that he's fine—none of us are hurt, and seeing each new injury on Death isn't a bad thing. But as the argument sits on my tongue, Lifera cries out in pain. She scrambles back on her hands and feet, dragging her body away from Death. He manages to reach her with a well-placed stomp, crushing her knee under his giant foot.

Large sausage-sized fingers grab Lifera by her leg, dragging her towards him and hanging her body high in the air. Her thrashing body proves she's still alive, but Death has a gleam in his eye.

"I can't kill you with touch thanks to that fucking enchantress, but I can rip you to pieces. I'd like to see you recover from *that*," Death snarls, and her body swings as she dangles in front of him.

She fights harder, kicking at his fingers, but he doesn't let go. I take a step forward, intending to get Lifera out of his grasp, but Van holds me back.

"He can't kill her with touch," Van reminds me.

"Doesn't matter," I snarl, tracking all of Death's weaknesses so I can determine the best one to attack. He might not be able to kill her, but he can cause serious harm, and I'm tired of seeing the people I care about get hurt. Especially at *this* monster's hands.

"Valencia," Corvus warns, his voice shaky from exhaustion. The sound of his turmoil only sparks my fury.

"I quite like you like this, though," Death coos to Lifera, her body dangling before his face. "Maybe I'll keep you. Maybe, instead of tearing you apart, I'll fuck you to death. There's no way this tight body wouldn't rip in half when I do." Death's nasty face leans closer to Lifera's body as he takes a big sniff. His yellow teeth gleam behind cracked lips as he opens his mouth to take a bite of her leg.

It's the shudder and quiet whimper that snaps the barrier inside of me that holds the chains in. With a bright flash of light, a chain shoots out and snaps around the wrist that holds Lifera. I clasp onto the end, wrapping my fingers around it in a tight grasp.

Instantly, Death loses his grip. The fingers that curl Lifera's leg spasm in pain and open, and she drops to the ground like a sack, wheezing as she tries to regain her breath. Van leaves my side to pull her further away from Death.

The fire holding Death down by one leg is dim, now only a single strap around his ankle. Corvus grunts as Death steps back, pulling harshly against the flame.

He hisses in pain as the chain tightens around his wrist. I can maintain more control of it this time and keep my grip on my own end.

Death looks to me with mania in his gaze. "You think you can end *me*? I'm Death," he roars, pain and indignation breaking the sound in spots.

His other hand wraps around the chain and yanks, pulling me closer to him. I dig my heels into the ground, but the red sand does little to keep me steady, and I slowly start to slide closer.

"Your father was a fucking kiss ass, but he was powerful. It's too bad he died trying to protect your mother. What a pussy she must've had for him to give his life for her," he taunts. Steam wafts from his skin where the chains burn his flesh.

It's evident by the wrath on his face that he feels the pain of the holy light, but it hasn't killed him yet.

When I used the chains for the first time on the mocker outside of the cave, it combusted in nearly an instant. The chains wrapped around its body, like they had a mind of their own, and within a blink, it was over. Death, however, fights against the power, funneling more from me with each yank. My life force pumps more power into the chain, the light latching onto my very being like it's a conduit. My breath stutters as air gets harder to draw each second we remain in this standoff.

Death begins to take advantage of this power exchange, siphoning my very life straight into himself. He preens, the added power making his fucked up face distort in pleasure.

The holy light was supposed to save us.

"Valencia, let the chain go!" Corvus yells, his voice shaking. "It's not worth it!"

That's where he's wrong. It *is* worth it. My death would be a blessing, so long as I take this vile creature with me when I go.

"Please!" Corvus screams, his voice breaking.

"Please, *oh please*!" Death mocks, scratchy voice dripping with malice. His dark eyes never leave mine, but I can tell he gets some sick sort of enjoyment out of Corvus' pain.

It serves him right, watching me face death. I had to watch him *die*.

Now, I'm not trying to be petty, I would kill this fucker if I could. I want to scream out, *'Here he is. Now what?'* but my focus is taken up by Death.

How the fuck am I supposed to kill him if the chains won't?

"You know, the other little brat had the same power, though his were more like little whips than a chain," Death muses, his meaty hand yanking me a foot closer. Muscles in my back burn from the pain of holding my body as far away as I can, but I'm afraid of what will happen if I let go of my end. "He wasn't strong enough to kill me then; a *child* kill *me*? Impossible. But I expected a little more fight out of you."

I'm using too much of my brain trying to fight while slowly being deprived of oxygen, so his words float around me, taking far longer to catch hold of than normal. My thighs burn with the strain of holding my body back, but I'm almost within reach. I see movement out of the corner of my eye, but I can't focus on anything else.

"*Run, baby! Run!*" Death mocks with a sneer, a high-pitch tone to his voice. "Your mother couldn't save him, it was a worthless effort, but I did love the look in your parents' eyes as I killed their son first. Making them watch was a true treat."

I start to shake as blood drips from my hands. The chains don't burn me like I see them burn Death, his skin melting around the edges, but they're solid in my grip and with each yank, my skin starts to tear. I direct the pain into the chain, giving everything I've got. Death seems unaffected, but his pupils dilate, and sweat gathers at his brow. One of us has to give in first, and if I can hold on for just a little longer, it'll be him.

"Valencia! It's not worth it!" Someone yells from behind me. I can't tell who it is. Death's rattling breaths distort the voice.

I could let go, try another day. Get more comfortable with the powers I've been given. Grow into someone who's easily able to defeat Death—someone my parents could've been proud of. A protector for my little brother.

Elijah. The horrible realization washes over me. He's talking about my little Eli. His curly hair and bright blue eyes flash before my face, a giant smile covered in blue Popsicle. He's sticking his tongue out at me for having called him a Smurf. I teased him a lot, but I loved him so much.

"It's a shame your father hid you, I would've loved to see their faces as they lost you both." Death yanks the chain, his large hand curling it around his fist. His laugh echoes and bounces across the canyon, filling my head with vicious memories of fire and laughter.

Laughter I recognize.

I was so consumed with pain that night, I didn't hear it. But in every dream I've had since, I've heard laughter coming from inside my burning house. Laughter I now know to be Death's, monstrous and rattling.

I keep my grip on the chain, but let my body flies towards him, releasing all the tension in my muscles.

"*No!*" voices scream, the clamor echoing from my side in a pain-filled chorus as Death's grip wraps around my neck. His fingers are so large that my head is forced back, neck straining at the angle. Heat sears my legs as the fire that holds Death to the ground licks my shins. There's a pounding in my ears, and black spots start to dot my vision.

Death smirks, bringing me closer to his face so we're eye to eye. "You've made it too easy, but I guess your whole family was weak; there's no reason you should be any different. You're done cheating Death his due."

Spit hits my face as he basks in his victory, and I feel threads of his power racing through my body, stealing life force through his touch alone. My heart stutters and my lungs contract, trying to hold on.

The chain around his fist presses harshly into my throat, cutting off my air. My body jerks, but I ignore it. I ignore the sound of screams and pounding feet. I ignore the look of triumph on Death's face as he continues to force those dark threads through me.

Just when the shadows in my vision have almost completely taken over, I grab on to them—*all* the threads. Every bit of his power he's forced into my body, I seize.

His eyes widen, and he leans back as if that can prevent me from taking more. His grip loosens, and I can tell he plans on dropping me, but I'm not done taking.

My free hand whips up, and in a flash of light, a second chain flies through the air, wrapping tightly around Death's thick neck. With a jerk, I bring his face back down to my level.

The hand around my throat releases as he rears back. Dust puffs around my feet as I land in the red sand. The flames have dissipated; there's nothing holding Death down, but his legs have been melted to the bone, and his body convulses as power flushes through him and into me. I've taken so much, he's barely able to stand.

His once-imposing form, reduced to something weak and frail.

Power still floods my veins, dark tendrils of his death gift meeting the holy light and bursting into gold inside me. Something ancient swirls in my blood, making me feel limitless. It's impossibly overwhelming, like I'm a second away from disintegrating, but the golden rays of power wrap me in gentle arms and hold me tight. A warm embrace, like remembering a forgotten lullaby, a night light that chases away the dark. All things I feel in this moment.

Death is faltering, powerless for a change, as he crumples to the sand. I stand over him, watching his body fail from the inside out, and I—wreathed in the power I stole—am stronger than ever.

His body finally collapses, withering before my eyes as bones crack and muscle deteriorates. He lies on his back, no longer a monster—just a male on the brink of true death.

His chest sputters, fingers clawing at the chain around his neck. It pulses with light, matching my heartbeat, as more and more is pulled from him. Generations of power siphon through the chains as if they were a hose. I can barely contain it all. My skin feels stretched too thin, and my heart is beating so hard I think it'll burst. But I won't stop until he's nothing but a shell.

Skin sunken, and bones showing, Death shakes his head back and forth.

Footsteps sound, but I don't turn to look. I don't acknowledge anything other than Death's demise.

As the last drops leave him, he laughs. It's threadbare and breathless, but it's as sickening as it's always been.

"You t-think you've accomplished something b-by killing me?" he asks, body curling in on itself as the chains take the last of what's left. Already, his skin starts turning to ash around them. "You've ac-accomplished nothing. You've only allowed a worse enemy in."

I pause, leaving just enough life in him for the chains to stop pulling and his heart to keep beating. If he knows something—knows someone else is out there—is it worth letting him live and getting information out of him? The predator begs for his heart; she wants to hold the bloody organ in her fingers and rip it to shreds with her claws. The human side of me begs for a life full of torment and despair as he continues to waste away for eternity.

"It's time, my love," a soft, deep voice whispers in my ears. "For your family and all the others, he's destroyed; he needs to die."

I turn to look at Corvus, and his deep, dark eyes settle something in me I didn't realize needed settling.

I hate killing. I hate how it makes me feel hungry for power, and I hate that all of Death's power—now inside me—makes me enjoy the idea of his death. I don't want to be a murderer, but Corvus is right. Death can't be allowed to live. No amount of information will ever be worth keeping him alive.

I look back at Death, more strength in my spine than I've had the entire fight. "You celebrated too early. The fight is never over when even a single spark can reignite."

It's a lesson I learned fighting wildfires in the mountains of Montana in what feels like a lifetime ago. Racing through the trees of Beaverhead National Forest, a team of my closest friends by my side as we put one fire out after another.

I fuel the inferno of all those fires flow through my body and into the chains. They flare a bright white, washing out everything around us. Death's body seems to fill with it, his skin bloating as its pierced, bursting into tiny rays before suddenly, in a spray of sparks, he combusts.

All that remains of the First Lord of Hell is the ash that softly wafts to the ground.

CHAPTER 43

CORVUS

I catch Valencia before she can collapse to the coarse sand as the light disperses. My arms wrap tightly around her, and I squeeze hard, burying my face in her hair. Though she smells like sweat and blood, I can't keep myself from drawing deep breaths.

I almost lost her.

Frustration builds, but it's calmed with each inhale of her scent. Blood, sweat, and tears couldn't take away her natural essence. It's amazing how she settles me. Fated soul bonds aren't common in Hell. The only demon species that have them are the shifters, and even then, it's so rare they mostly believe it to be a myth. No matter that no one believes it to be true—I get a feeling every time she's in my arms that makes me want to believe the unbelievable.

I've done nothing in my life to deserve her, but I'm unwilling to ever let her go. She's stuck with me, and the thought of almost losing her nearly makes me rage. I was stuck in place, trying my hardest to keep Death from advancing, my prison of fire waning with each second. When he had her in his hand, I thought she was surely dead, and I was ready to give up everything. What would life be like without her in it?

But with each second that passed, she didn't die. Her chains, though dimmer than when I first saw them, lightly pulsed until eventually, Death was nothing but a husk on the ground. I squeeze her a little tighter, ash floating in the air at our feet.

"I'm okay," she mutters, but as her arms squeeze me back, I hear the sadness in her voice.

Lifera, Van, and I had all heard Death's confession. I could feel Lifera's pain as Death spoke so heartlessly about killing Valencia's family. Van remains silent, but none of us will walk away from this unaffected. I'm sure, knowing his history, that seeing Tucker was a severe hit to his psyche.

"The guards I knocked out should soon wake. Do we want to kill them now, or imprison them?" Van asks, diverting his attention onto something that will take his mind away from what just happened.

When I raise my head from Valencia's shoulders, I see that he stands just to my right. However, he doesn't turn from where he looks out at the forest behind us. He was following the girls, dispatching any guards they met as they went. Arguably the more well thought-out tactic, as it meant we didn't have to fight them a second time. A fact I'm extremely grateful for.

One of the first things we will be doing, after a much-needed rest, is training. Van and I will both work on getting Valencia to a point where she can use her powers at will, where her hand-to-hand skills will match even mine. I will never allow her to be this vulnerable again.

"No more death today," Valencia mutters, her voice muffled against my chest.

"Wise choice," Lifera states. She no longer sounds strained from the fight, but there's an edge to her voice. "But some of them have earned death. We will imprison them and question them all. There is no reason to allow any of Death's minions to poison more of Hell."

Valencia takes a deep breath but nods her head in agreement. It's important that we weed out all of his supporters; there would be nothing stopping them from rising in power and becoming just as much of an issue to us as he was. And I'm really looking forward to not having to look over my shoulder for a knife for a while.

"What did he mean? There's someone else out there?" Valencia asks, looking around the group as she pulls away. I don't let go of her hand, unwilling to have complete separation. I have this driving urge to ensure she's okay.

Van and I share a look, unsure, but Lifera speaks up. "I always assumed someone was helping Death, I just figured it was his underlings. He was able to convince many of them to siphon their power to him. But something about his statement puts me on edge. I'm no longer sure he was the one in charge; maybe he was doing someone else's dirty work."

"I'm not surprised you're as lost as always. You have the canny ability to stick your head in the sand and let others do your work for you," Van sneers, his apparent camaraderie gone.

"Wolf, don't start, I'm too tired and we've too much work to discuss petty grievances." Lifera shoots him a glare but looks at me.

"It's not *petty*, and you know it." Van's body starts to shake, and tension builds in his muscles. He protected her while we all had a common enemy; Van is a hard-ened warrior—he knows the battlefield isn't the place for personal grievances. An ally is an ally. However, it seems that feeling is now gone. Lifera is unfortunately right: there is a lot that needs to be done, and I can't have Van going off her Lifera when we need the Devil to continue running Hell.

"Nightmare will need to be notified. He's now First," I say to Lifera, hoping it gives her a reason to leave and not ignite more of Van's anger, but she stays.

"That means you're Second," she responds with a knowing look I can't deci-pher.

"So, who will be Third?" Valencia asks. She looks to Van, who's still seething, but he offers nothing as he watches the conversation play out.

"*Agh!*"

Valencia hunches, her body curling inward as she draws her arms tight to her chest.

I jump, my hand curling around her back. "What's wrong?" I snap, fear filling me. She whimpers once, and a shudder runs through her back.

Slowly, she stands, a hand wrapped around one of her wrists.

"Let me see," I say gently, pulling her fingers away from her wrist.

Three audible gasps pierce the air as her now-charred wrist comes into view. Dark black lines of seared flesh wrap around her lower arm in a bracelet of fine detailing. It almost looks like lace has been laid around her wrist in a delicate cuff, but the skin towards the edges of the design is bright red. She flinches when I lightly touch her, too close to the damaged skin.

Despite the damage it's caused, it's beautiful, but all I feel is despair.

"What have you done?" I whisper, my eyes never leaving her wrist.

I've seen this kind of mark before. I've felt the same pain as its seared into my skin. Even now, the black lines subtly fade to a light gray, scaring almost instantly as if it burned her. The evidence will remain in a stark white mark against her tan skin.

"What the fuck did you do?" I snarl at Lifera. This is one of her marks of a bargain. I know it like it's been burned into my own skin.

"There's need for a Third Lord of Hell," she says, tone giving little away as she looks at Valencia. Bright, glowing eyes focus intently on the woman standing beside me, who rubs absentmindedly at her healed wrist.

"Why are you looking at me? What does this mean?" Valencia's voice breaks. All confidence is leached from her body as confusion barrels through the group. Her eyes are back to ocean blue, but they fill with unshed tears.

Van and I both start to growl, the sounds deep and dangerous, and the sand starts to shift under his feet as he prepares to launch at Lifera. My muscles tense as I pull Valencia behind me.

"You can't protect her from this, Lord Crow. The bargain has already been made." Lifera adjusts her long ponytail, tightening it severely. Her sharp features pull with the tension, and those golden eyes meet mine.

"What bargain?" I demand, body shaking.

"I told Valencia she'd make a great leader one day. She said, *'Yeah, sign me up.'* Thus, the bargain was stuck."

"I didn't know I was agreeing to anything!" Valencia cries, her eyes shedding angry tears as she shoots Lifera a confused look. The Devil doesn't respond, and remains stoic as she faces us all without remorse.

"You used me." Valencia's arms drop to her sides with the realization. Her voice is low and broken as she continues, "You said you cared, but you just wanted to use me. They all told me not to trust you; I didn't want to believe them."

I close my eyes. Witness the amount of hurt she feels from the betrayal physically pains me.

I turn to Lifera. Van's ready to pounce but waits for my signal. However, Lifera ignores us both.

Sadness flashes across her face before it's wiped away. A calm, neutral emotion is all that's left as her body begins to fade, and I can tell she'll be gone before we'd be able to touch her.

As she vanishes, her words echo through the empty space she occupied moments before. "You'll understand one day. Welcome to the Games."

THE END

SEE YOU AT THE GAMES

Afterword

Wow, finishing this book was a dream come true. I mean, I have truly wanted to be an author since the third grade. Who knew that only two months after releasing my first book, I'd get to once again write "The End". I said to my editor, book one made me feel like an author, someone who successfully wrote and published a book. This book made me feel like a writer, someone who puts their soul into something, and a beautiful result comes out.

These characters really took me for a wild ride while writing book two, but I cannot express enough how much I have enjoyed bringing this group of misfits to you. I feel there is at least someone in these books that we can all relate to. There are more characters to come, and even some old ones we'll meet again, so be prepared for a grand final showdown coming in book three! But that's not the end. When I started writing this series, I always knew that I would want to write stories for the side characters too, so as long as I am able to write, I will be bringing more and more of this universe to you! Book three is the final book for Valencia and Corvus as our main characters, but they will absolutely be seen in later books. It's nearly time for their happy ever after, and I am so excited for us all to experience that with them.

If you're dying to ask questions, talk about the books, and discuss your thoughts for the future books, please join the Emerald Readers Society Facebook page! Don't forget to join my newsletter for sneak peeks, exclusive giveaways and more. And as always, you can catch me on social media anytime!

As a thank you for your continued support, and my extreme gratitude, continue reading for an UNEXPECTED sneak peek at book three!

Prologue

Dumah

On and on and on it goes.

No one talks about HR meetings for angels, but that's essentially what we've been subjected to for the last several hours. However, time in this realm passes differently than it does anywhere else. It's endless, open, free, and uncontained.

But I'm beholden to time, and seven hours for a meeting about fraternization is pointless. Impatience is a sin—one of many I regularly commit —so I try to focus and listen to what Uriel is saying.

He's making a good point; in any profession, sleeping with those in opposite hierarchical settings is usually unwise. His point flies right over our heads, though, and it's more of a blanket warning to us all, as those who are guilty of the sin aren't here to be punished for the crime.

"And therefore..." he continues, but I hear none of it. This isn't a warning I need to listen to anyway; I would not sleep with any angel in this room. My eyes drift to the open window beside me. Bright blue sky and soft clouds drift by. Angels, free from this meeting, fly through the air in flashes of color, their large feathered wings cutting through the air with ease, shining in the sun like a rainbow of silk. Each angel's wings are different in color, a color no other species can see. Our feathers shine with such brilliance that they appear white to anyone else.

Two teenage angels flit around each other, wrestling despite being hundreds of wingspans high. It's a typical training tactic. Judging by the time of day, where the sun sits high in the sky, they're probably getting ready for combat class.

More angels zoom past my window in a hurry. A whole courtyard of angels, going about their days.

The brick buildings that surround the courtyard shine in the midday sun. Tall trees give pops of green, and the many flowers brighten the communal space. It's a beautiful view, and I wish I were out there instead of staring at it through glass.

The large temple where we meet daily for prayer is especially charming, with its intricately designed steeples that point high in the air. A large group of young angels gather just outside, all in uniform lines, while an older angel gives them orders. They're listening, but I can tell by the flutter of their wings that they're eager to get into whatever task they must be preparing for.

Unlike most demons, angels are born . We have parents who birth us, but we are not raised by them. Upon birth, we are all put into Viritrium, the Academy of Light.

There's no doubt that this young group of angels are an academy class, learning the history of the temple. I remember my own days in the academy, before I was a mature angel ready for my selected purpose. That's what we're all doing here in Viritra, the home of angels. We're all just preparing for our next destination. Not many opt to stay here permanently unless they're chosen to teach at the academy or raise the young. It's not often that it happens, but a realm has to be run somehow.

We're born here, raised and trained here, but for many angels, our calling comes from elsewhere.

Some angels are called to be guardians, some to become scholars. Some are caregivers, and others are meant to be warriors.

"You're Archangels—leaders of all angels—it's important to treat that title with respect. Furthermore," Uriel continues, but my attention remains on the courtyard. I've almost entirely lost my faith in angel leadership. In Viritra's hierarchy, Archangels sit at the top—but there's a power structure within this, too. You can work through the ladder to a higher position, but it isn't without hardship. Leadership positions can be stolen, as is often the case with angels of higher status—but I've never understood this method. It feels so... demonic.

Demons debase themselves with violence and murder. They kill because they can, and they don't particularly care what's right or wrong. They care about what makes them happy. What gets them off. What drives them. They're not stuck following protocol or worrying about how their actions may affect others.

Sin shames me like fire. I'm in the most beautiful realm in the universe, yet all I can do is envy the demons. They are free to choose, while I am beholden to my duties.

My attention darts to an angel settling onto a bench, back to me. Her light pink wings flutter to rest over the back, feathers dusting the paved ground. She's got something in her hand, perhaps a book. I can't see her face, but her long, golden-yellow hair draws all my focus. And it's as I stare through the window, watching this angel take a moment of rest, that I'm reminded of those I once protected—and one in particular.

Long ago, my purpose was guardianship. I protected many humans over the years, and I came to love them all. They were like my own children, and I watched each to grow, achieve, fail, and become old, all while surrounded by love. Along the way, I protected them from evil—demons who wished to take advantage of them, or unfortunate circumstances that weren't meant for their fate.

I protected them faithfully and embraced each with open arms when they passed. I still visit each of their souls to this day.

Every soul except hers.

It was ripped from me. Tatters of it spread across the in between. So many, I would never be able to piece them back together.

All because I committed the most nefarious sin a guardian can. I fell in love.

A love that I kept hidden, even from her, as I watched from the shadows. When the fateful accident that was meant to take her life occurred, I pulled her from the wreck on instinct alone, unwilling to see the light of her soul leave her eyes. Her golden hair was covered in glass and blood, her body bruised from the vehicle she'd rolled several times. As I'd held her close to my chest, she'd looked upon my face and smiled as if she knew me.

It was glorious, and for the briefest moment in time, I was given a new purpose. I would've given everything to be with her.

But fate is cruel, and pulling her from the wreck only earned me the chance to watch as her soul was ripped from her body by Death, the First Lord of Hell, who stood over me. Her body, limp in my arms, became a heavy weight I've carried since.

That was so many years ago, and the memory of her face has grown blurry, but her weight in my arms has seared itself into my brain. I searched for her in the in-between, but I saw her soul as it was ripped apart in Death's grip. I saw it and knew in my heart what it meant, yet I couldn't give up.

I'm not sure how long I spent in the in-between, but when Uriel found me, I was a ghost of myself. It took twice as long to get to where I am now—an archangel in my own right—but I still receive dirty looks from the other guardians whenever I pass them.

They don't call me on my shame, angels are supposed to be all forgiving, just as our Father is. But the judgment in their eyes is sign enough that they view me as below them. I find it hilarious that they look down on me. It's not unknown for a guardian or any angel, to seek pleasures from humans, they are an inherently sexual species. They only look down on me because they all know had I been given the chance, I would've renounced my angel heritage to be with her. I would've forsaken the Father in the name of love, and that makes me the worst angel there is. No better than a Fallen and barely better than a demon, one who forsakes good for the sake of himself.

When Uriel sent me for the human female, I was eager to get out of Viritra and remove myself from its drama. But as I watched Corvus, the Third Lord of Hell, seduce her into joining the demons in this never-ending war, I could only feel angry that despite what he is, he's still free to love her, and receive her love in return.

"There's a sickness in the angels, and it is leading us astray. We must be diligent in our purpose and continue to follow the light," Uriel concludes with a flourish, finally ending the meeting with a soft prayer for forgiveness of our sins.

I pray along, the words warming me from the inside as lights dance behind my closed eyelids.

There is a sickness in the angels. It's taken me this long to realize that maybe Corvus wasn't wrong on the mountain.

Something is happening in Heaven, and I'm determined to find out what.

Acknowledgements

Dear reader, I can't thank you enough. It is from the bottom of my little writer heart that I thank you. Without you, I would've never made this dream a reality.

Granny, you have always been my guiding star in this storm of possibilities. After every DWTS episode, I wanted to be a dancer, and you watched me dance despite the fact that I was not at all a dancer. After every episode of American Idol, you listened to me sing and encouraged me when I said *'one day I am going to be a singer'*. And after that poem you helped me published in the third grade, you told me in our kitchen, the biggest smile on your face, that if I wanted to be an author one day, I could. Because you believed that I could do anything, I believed it too.

To my husband, your continual support is what makes writing about love so easy. You show me so many ways I can be loved, that I am able to write love stories for others. These characters thank you for your inventive ways of showing how love can come across fun or silly or meaningful or passionate. Also, thank you xamillion for putting aside your dreams at times, for working with a broken leg, for taking off work, for everything in between to help me make my dreams come true. Loving you is the real dream come true.

Leslie and Lenora, I can't thank you enough for being the best readers an author and a friend could ask for. Continually, your feedback and support has helped carry me through the tough times, and without you, these characters would be far less cool (and way less naughty lol). I love you both dearly and I can't wait to share many more books with you!

To my family and friends who supported me along the way, who purchased a book, who read and reviewed, who listened to me talk about the book, thank you!

To my editor, thank you for messaging me early and showing that no matter that we never met, and no matter that we live on two different sides of the world, you believe in my dream. Working with you has been the best experience I could've asked for. Your willingness to take my ideas and help them flourish into something amazing truly brings joy to me each time we speak. Now on to book 3!!

Finally, again to my readers, because I can't thank you enough for taking a chance on a debut author. Your enthusiasm and support mean the world to me. I hope this story has brought you as much joy and excitement as it brought me while writing it!

Hey There, Awesome Reader!

If you enjoyed diving into this wild ride of a book, I'd love to hear your thoughts! Think of it as leaving a tip, but instead of cash, it's all about those sweet, sweet words. Your reviews keep the magic alive.

If you fancy leaving a review, may your coffee always be the perfect temperature!

About the Author

Hello and welcome! Meet Samantha, a devoted enthusiast of all things Romantic Literature.

Samantha Treat is a debut author who writes stories that are witty, romantic, and steamy. A life long dreamer of writing, she is conquering her goals by sharing the many stories in her head with the world.

Born in central Missouri, she grew up in various places, even changing schools 13 times. As a hopeless romantic, Leo, and all around introverted-extrovert, she enjoys writing characters we can all relate to. She can found reading in her library, traveling with her husband, playing with her dogs, or partaking in some crazy adventure.

Samantha still resides in Missouri, though she's settled in the northwest corner of the state with her two doggos and husband. Finding her very own Happy Ever After, made it all the more easy to write.